The Dreamer and the Marked

Book one of The Arai Chronicles

AIRIC FENN

This is a work of fiction. All characters and events portrayed in this novel are products of the author's imagination.

For a .txt file of this book, contact the author at
airic@airicfenn.com

Cover and maps by Airic Fenn

Edited by Tycho Dwelis

ISBN 978-0-578-31412-9 (hardcover)
ISBN 978-0-578-38842-7 (paperback)
ISBN 978-0-578-31413-6 (ebook)

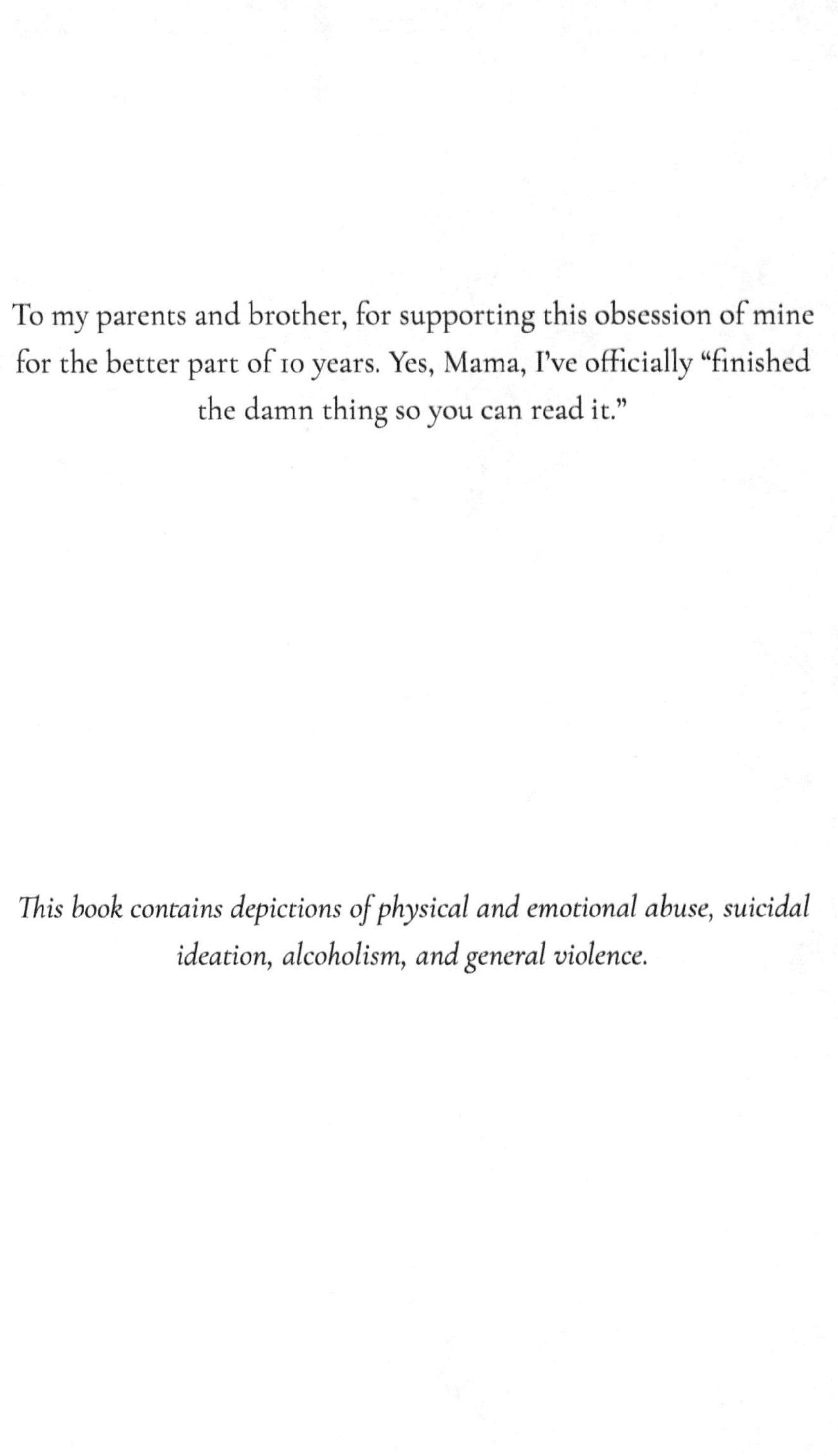

To my parents and brother, for supporting this obsession of mine for the better part of 10 years. Yes, Mama, I've officially "finished the damn thing so you can read it."

This book contains depictions of physical and emotional abuse, suicidal ideation, alcoholism, and general violence.

The Realm of Arai

the wastes

Dalmos

Adonis

Talme

Erothel

Erothel

Adonis

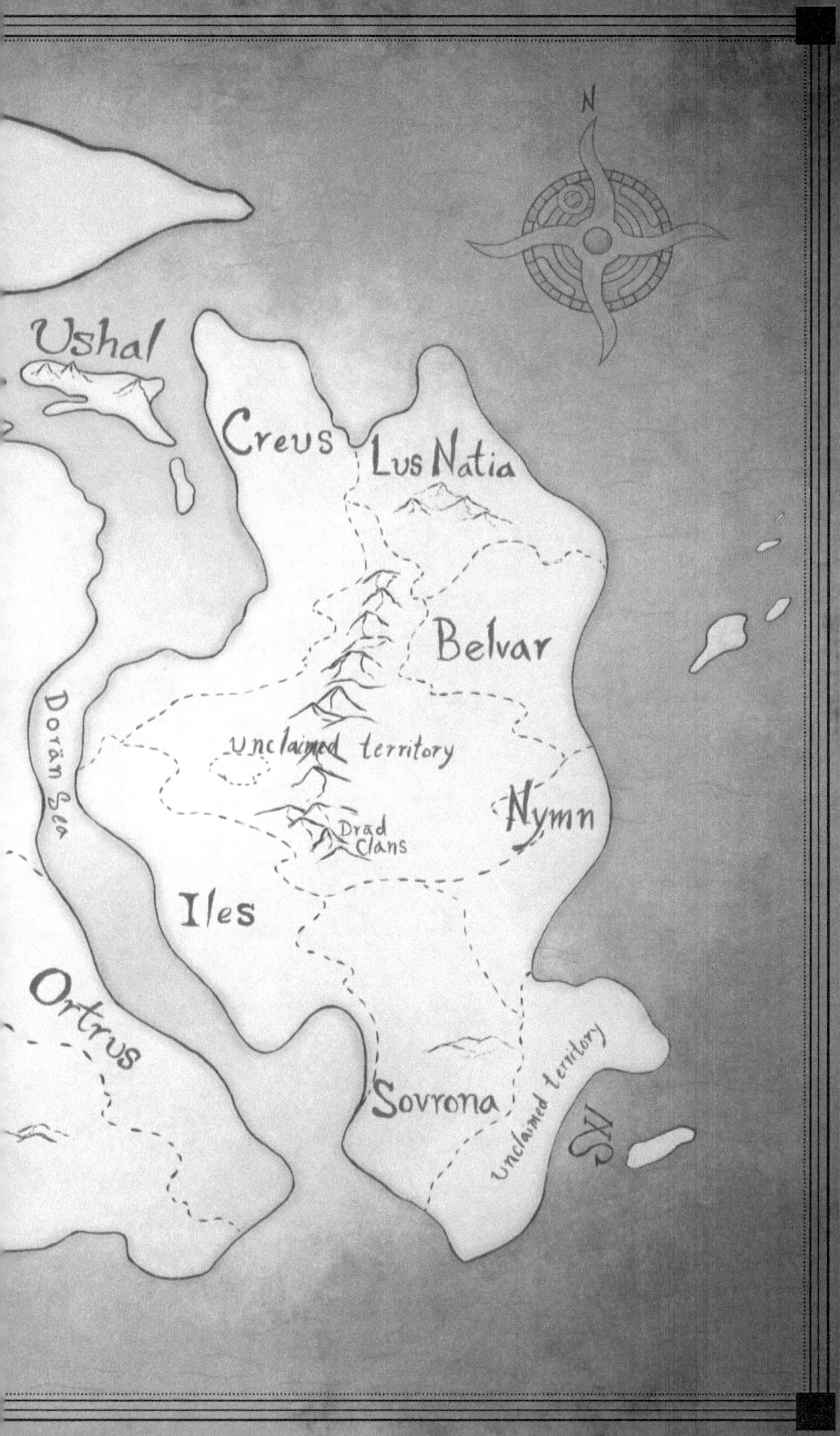

N

Ushal

Creus

Lus Natia

Belvar

Doran Sea

unclaimed territory

Nymn

Drad Clans

Iles

Ortrus

Sovrona

unclaimed territory

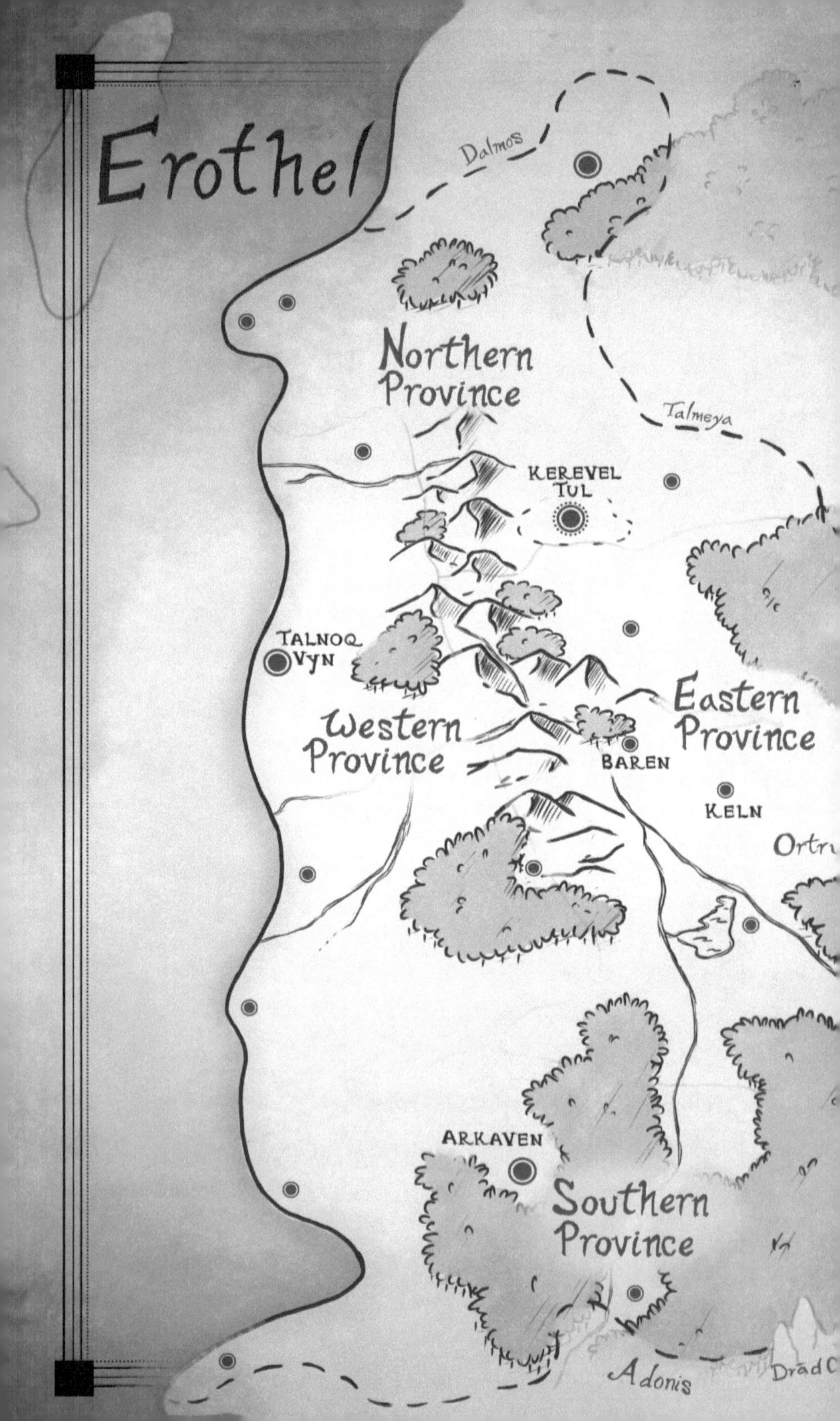

Erothel
Dalmos
Northern Province
Talmeya
KEREVEL TUL
TALNOQ VYN
Western Province
Eastern Province
BAREN
KELN
Ortr
ARKAVEN
Southern Province
Adonis
Drad C

1

THIS WASN'T THE FIRST NIGHT Krystal found herself wandering through the tenebrous halls of the manor that so frequently plagued her dreams. At least, she assumed she was dreaming as she could never remember how she got there.

The first time she woke up in the manor, she had been terrified. The only thing that kept her from completely panicking was the idea of alerting someone to her presence. Something about the manor felt very wrong to her, a heaviness in the air that seeped into her core. Anyone who lived in such a foreboding place could only mean bad news. Krystal had decided it would be best to try to find her way out on her own, rather than attempt to explain to the owner how she got inside. Besides, who would have believed the absurd story that she just woke up in the middle of his home?

It took her an hour to find the entrance that first night, but when she tried to open the grand doors, she fell right through their hard wood and into a night so dark that the sky blazed with a galaxy of stars. She rose back to her feet, her breath caught in her throat. The land stretched out into the darkness, flat and seemingly infinite. A breeze brushed past Krystal's cheeks, carrying with it the smell of salt and humidity, but it didn't affect her ginger hair, as though she wasn't there at all. As she gazed upon her surroundings, her fear melted into wonder. She could just make out the faint outline of a cobbled road that led from the manor to a single glistening light far in the distance. But when she stepped to follow it, she awoke, back in her bedroom in her small apartment.

She was never one to keep a dream journal, but the vividness of the dream had compelled her to rush its details onto a scrap of notebook paper before they could fade away. She certainly didn't expect to find herself in the same dream a second night, and then a third. Unlike in her first dream, she'd retained her lucidity, but they weren't like any lucid dreams she'd ever heard of before. She was aware she was dreaming, yes, only she couldn't control what happened as she expected from lucid dreams. With every step she took across the dark granite floors of the manor, she anticipated an echoing *tap, tap, tap*. Instead, her footsteps were ghostly silent no matter how she moved.

Despite the eeriness of her own silence, she quickly discovered she wasn't alone in these recurring dreams. Humanoid but alien people roamed the manor's halls. Her first encounter had come as a shock when a short, bearded man with bat-like ears wearing a wide-brimmed hat on the back of his head appeared from the shadows at the entrance to greet an equally odd guest—a dragonfly-winged man covered from head to toe in mottled gray feathers.

Krystal had ducked to hide around the corner, but the bat-eared man paid her no mind and escorted his strange visitor away. The feathery man wasn't the only arrival, either. Over the following nights, others would occasionally come and go, each as fantastical as the last. A woman whose torso grew from the lower body of a horse. A man with webbed fingers and fleshy tendrils in place of hair. Another feathered man.

Krystal didn't dare to approach any, instead opting to trail behind them out of sight, still nervous to be caught in a place she didn't belong. That is until one night when she followed the bat-eared man—whom she decided must have been a butler—to the kitchens. He joined in hushed conversation with a young woman with curled horns and the lower half of a deer, or maybe a goat, while she kneaded some dough. Their words were always foreign-sounding, but somehow Krystal could still understand their meanings; she attributed this as a quality of the dream and nothing more. The bat-eared man and the deer woman spoke of a man who must have been the lord of the manor, and who sounded to be upset. Why, Krystal couldn't tell, but when she peeked her head from the hall to the kitchen to hear better, the door creaked open. The pair in the kitchen turned her way and she froze, her heart picking up wildly in her chest. The bat-eared man grumbled as he approached the door. Krystal scrambled back. The man stared directly at her. And then he simply shut the door and returned to his conversation with the deer woman.

After her shock subsided, Krystal nervously phased her head through the door, curious about why he'd ignored her. Neither he nor the woman acknowledged her, not even when she stepped all the way into the room and announced herself with an awkward, "hello." They remained steadfast in their gossip, not like they couldn't see her, but as though they were doing their best to pretend she wasn't there. She didn't bother to sneak around after that, quickly discovering that everyone ignored her, no matter how much she tried to talk to them. Some even seemed to purposely walk right through her.

This made eavesdropping quite easy. Over the two months now that she'd been dreaming of this place, she learned that the people she encountered were either servants in the manor or people of importance, like councilmen and governors. The lord of the manor, too, was a governor of a place called Erothel, although Krystal hadn't met him yet. She wasn't sure she wanted to. The servants rarely had good things to say about their master.

Although she retained a level of caution, Krystal took advantage of her free reign of the manor. Most nights, like tonight, she took to exploring until she woke up. No one ever stopped her, not even when she went into rooms that appeared to be off-limits, as she could just phase through their locked doors.

She made her way to the courtyard. It was surrounded on three sides by arch-lined hallways and a shallow pond with steppingstones partly frozen in the middle. In the weeks previous before the weather cooled, she'd been able to see a perfectly crisp reflection of her freckled face and hazel eyes wavering between the lily pads floating on the surface.

She laid on one of the benches organized around the courtyard and looked up. She liked to stargaze there often despite the dream's stars and constellations being foreign to her. Tonight, though, gray clouds swirled across the sky. Krystal sat up, about to go off to find some other spot to spend her time, when an angry voice boomed, ringing through the corridors and across the courtyard.

"*How dare you let him go?!*"

The shouting came from behind an ornate wooden door. The library. Krystal approached quietly, forgetting in the moment that her feet could make no sound anyway. The next thing she heard was a grunt of pain. She hovered her ear near the door, not daring to peek inside.

Someone, a man it sounded like, was breathing heavily.

"*I didn't. . . he escaped—*" He cut himself off, his pain sounding much more agonized this time around.

"*Do not lie to me. I saw you. You know exactly what you did.*" This must have been the master. After a pause, he said, "*I would like to remind you that disloyalty can and will lead to dire consequences.*"

The momentary silence was broken by the shuffling of feet.

"*I understand. It won't happen again.*"

"*It had better not. Get out.*"

At the sound of footsteps coming nearer to the door, Krystal backed away. The door opened before she could make her escape and the man who exited walked right through her. His shoulders jumped and he stopped in his tracks. He looked around, turning to face Krystal. The man must have been new to the manor because she didn't recognize him. He looked like he might have been quite a few years older than Krystal, and a large mark spread across his face, but the dark made it too difficult to decipher.

The man stared at Krystal. His brow creased, and he turned away, muttering, "*. . . didn't know there were ghosts here, now.*"

Krystal raised an eyebrow. Did he mean her? No one in this place even went so far as to acknowledge Krystal with a nod. She followed after the man as he stiffly limped away. He collapsed on a bench in front of the pond and groaned, swearing under his breath.

Krystal leaned over the back of the bench to look at him. When he noticed her, he started and shot to his feet. Krystal smirked.

"So you *can* see me!"

"*What do you want?*" the man asked.

"Every time I try to talk to anyone here I just get ignored," Krystal said, then paused as she took in the defensive way the man held himself. He favored his right side. Krystal frowned and nodded back towards the library. "Are you okay?"

The man's eyes slowly went wide. He looked around. "*You. . . speak English,*" he said, stepping around the bench. To Krystal's surprise, he started speaking it, too. "Where did you learn that?" His accent was beautiful; light, and he trilled his r's.

"I've always known it," Krystal said.

The man's shoulders remained tense, and he tiptoed closer, regarding her in the way a cat would with something new and potentially dangerous.

"Then you're. . . from Taevalear?"

Krystal cocked her head. "What's Taevalear?"

The man's brow raised. "It's—well—it's the Other Realm. You know, where the humans are from?" The man frowned. "Are you human?"

"Of course I am," Krystal said as the man leaned in close to her head.

His lips twitched up into a faint smile. "No. . . you're not.

You're part fae," he said.

Krystal laughed a bit and couldn't help but crack a smile, too. This was new. The man stepped back, his tension falling away. He leaned against the bench and his face twisted briefly.

"How did you get here?" he asked.

Krystal shrugged and hopped up to sit on the back of the bench beside him.

"You don't know?" he prodded.

"Whenever I go to bed, I find myself here. Where is here, anyway?"

The man stared at her with calculating eyes. After a moment, he said, "You're in the home of Governor Sius Mavell Evi. In Arai."

Krystal echoed him under her breath. Arai. This was certainly no place she had ever heard of before.

"Was Sius who you were talking with?" she asked, eyeing the man's leg.

"Not Sius. Sius Mavell Evi," the man corrected. He paused. "And yes. I work for him."

Krystal glanced at the library door and stood. The last thing she wanted was to be the next object of the Governor's anger. "Why don't we get out of here before he comes out and finds us?"

She instinctively reached for the man's hand to pull him along, but she only phased through him. Still, he followed her from the courtyard then took the lead and brought her to a bedroom upstairs. He locked the door. Krystal knew the people here had their own form of electricity, so she wasn't surprised when the man flicked on the lamps by the bed. His unshaven face now illuminated, his light brown skin shimmered like it had been dusted with flecks of bronze glitter. His eyes were an unnaturally vivid, electrifying blue.

Krystal's breath of awe turned into a quiet gasp as he turned to face her fully. The left side of his face was marred, the tight, sinewy skin scarred almost beyond recognition. His ear was deformed, and half his eyebrow missing, along with most of the hair on that side of his head. It was a miracle his eye was even intact. The scar extended down his neck, disappearing beneath his black turtleneck sweater.

The man pursed his lips, and Krystal realized she was staring. She immediately turned to explore the room. It seemed she'd missed this one in previous dreams.

"This is the first time I've talked to a ghost before. Most of you are incoherent," he said.

"Oh, but I'm not a ghost," Krystal said. Although perhaps being a ghost would explain quite a bit of what she'd experienced so far.

She made her way to the dresser and put her hand on a drawer to open it. The man cleared his throat. She smiled sheepishly and leaned against it instead.

"I mean, I think I'd remember dying if I was a ghost. Are you human?" she asked.

The man shook his head. "Half. You said you've come here before?"

"Yeah, almost every night for the past two months now, I think."

The man silently observed Krystal once again. His brow furrowed. "It sounds like you're soul-traveling," he said.

"Like I'm what?"

The man paused thoughtfully. "You know, soul-travel. It's. . .I don't know how to describe it. Your soul isn't in your body, and you're using it to be someplace else. But I didn't know it was possible to travel between our realms." He frowned suddenly and shifted his gaze to the door.

"What's wrong?" Krystal asked.

"Nothing is wrong, but soul-travel can be very dangerous if you don't know what you're doing. If something happened to your body while you were away from it. . ."

Krystal pinched her eyebrows. "Oh. . ."

The man's concern melted back into the serious lines of his face. "You'll probably be fine though if nothing has happened so far."

He gingerly lowered himself to the bed and groaned. He kicked off his boots, then threw off his black coat. His thick socks and gloves stayed on. Krystal noticed that the first two fingers of his left glove were cut away. The man pressed a hand to his back and grimaced again. He eyed Krystal uncomfortably.

"I take it you don't know how to wake on your own."

Krystal shook her head.

The man closed his eyes. "You can stay here until then I guess."

Krystal hesitantly sat at the corner of the bed and smiled at him.

"I'm Krystal," she said. She almost offered her hand again before remembering that she couldn't touch him. The man considered her, and she gasped, "Wait—that was bad, wasn't it? I wasn't supposed to tell you my name."

The man's lips quirked up into a little smile. "That's not quite how it works. I'm Draqa."

The name sent a shiver down Krystal's spine. "Oh. It's nice to meet you. I don't think I've ever seen you before," she said.

"I'm out most days," Draqa replied.

"But you're a servant here?"

"Something like that."

Krystal leaned to see Draqa's back. "Are you sure you're okay? That seems painful."

Draqa shrugged. "It was my own fault. I went against orders." He moved on before Krystal could persist. "Do you know when you started soul-traveling like this?"

"When I started coming here," Krystal said. Of course, she wasn't dreaming of the place every night. Many nights, her dreams were normal, or they started off that way.

"Were you taught?" Draqa asked.

"No. I don't think anyone I know knows how to do this. Hey, how do you know English so well? None of the others here seem like they know it."

Draqa stood. "They don't," he said. He limped to the curtains and peeked out of them. "The sun doesn't rise for many hours."

"Oh, did you want to sleep? I can leave. It's not like I don't know this place."

Draqa sat back down. "Stay. Tell me about Taevalear."

Krystal was surprised. She wasn't sure there was anything interesting to tell. "It's a lot different than it is here. We don't have any fae or—"

"No, I already know all about that," Draqa interrupted. "Tell me about your history. Or. . . tell me about the imp who could create gold, or one of the trickster gods."

Fairytales, Krystal realized. Luckily, she knew plenty of those. She had grown up on them, after all. So, she told some. Draqa leaned back against the headboard with his hands clasped around his upright knee. He watched her with keen interest. Occasionally, he would scoff at Krystal's words, like he didn't quite believe them. But Krystal continued to tell the tales well into the night, and Draqa barely seemed to tire at all.

Krystal was just getting into her favorite story—one by the Grimm Brothers—when Draqa sat up.

Krystal paused. "What?"

"You're fading," he said.

He was right. Krystal hadn't noticed until now. Her hands were fully translucent, a sign she was waking up. She sighed dejectedly. Just when she was finally enjoying herself.

"Maybe I can see you again," she said.

Draqa shook his head. "You should try not to. Luck doesn't last forever." He hesitated. "But maybe I could visit *you*."

Krystal's eyes widened. "You can do that?"

"There's no guarantee, but I could try if I'm ever in Taevalear. Where do you live?"

A sound grew loud in Krystal's ears. She could feel herself slipping away now, the world around her becoming intangible, overlapping with the back of her eyelids.

"I live in—"

She opened her eyes. Her alarm was blaring its little chime next to her head. She grumbled. Already the dream began to blur around its edges. She tried to remember the man's name, but in the seconds that it took to snooze her alarm and sit up, it was gone. But his face was still there; for a moment she saw a shadow of him sitting next to her on the bed. She turned on the light to make sure. No one.

She got out of bed. With work at Dahlia's today, she didn't have much time, but she quickly took out her journal and jotted down what she could remember from the dream. Writing in the journal had become a part of her daily routine since she began dreaming of the manor, the pages now fat from use. It had only a few blank ones left—she'd have to buy another while at the shop. Dahlia's always had something nice, as they often stocked handcrafted leather notebooks from local artists.

Yawning, Krystal stretched and made her way to the kitchen. She helped herself to a bowl of oatmeal and moved on with her day, but for some reason, she couldn't shake the feeling in the back of her mind that her dream last night was somehow different from the others.

2

Draqa brought his arm back, hurling a knife at the human-like target set up in front of the pond in the courtyard. It skimmed the shoulder and splashed into the water. He cursed. He'd become increasingly distracted since last night. He couldn't stop thinking about the ginger-haired woman with her stories. Krystal. She wouldn't have been of any particular interest to Draqa if it weren't for her unique tale of how she ended up in Arai. From what Draqa knew, to soul-travel across the realms was nearly an impossible feat, even for the most gifted of mages.

There had been something about Krystal, too, that had been familiar to Draqa, but he couldn't quite place why. He had wanted to learn more. He would have asked more, too, but he had been so caught up in Krystal's storytelling that he lost track of time. If only he'd noticed she was waking sooner, then he might not have lost his chance to learn where to find her.

He missed the target again and growled in frustration. He

took his last projectile in hand and sent it carelessly forward. He missed. Only then did he see Governor Sius Mavell Evi walking down the hallway across from him. His heart froze. Sius Mavell Evi stepped back, the knife narrowly missing him. He scowled.

"I see your aim is getting worse," he said, stooping to pick up the knife with one of his four arms. His words ended on a sour note.

Draqa dropped to a knee and bowed. "Sir! My apologies!"

Sius Mavell Evi approached him, and Draqa tensed in preparation to face the Governor's backlash. Sius Mavell Evi simply dropped the knife at his feet. Draqa looked up at him.

Sius Mavell Evi put weight on his upper-right arm as he leaned on his staff, crossing his lower two arms. He scratched his white-flecked red beard. "What has your mind so preoccupied?" he asked.

Draqa carefully stood. He formulated an answer, unsure the Governor would want to know that someone had effectively been sneaking into his home for the past two months.

"An encounter I had in the Vyn the other day," he replied.

"An encounter with whom?"

Draqa thought of how concerned for him Krystal had been. A complete stranger, worried about *him*. "Some woman. She was oddly kind."

"She must have wanted something from you," Sius Mavell Evi said. "No one in Talnoq-Vyn does anything out of kindness."

"Right," Draqa said, holding back the words he wanted to say.

Perhaps the people in the Vyn would have been more willing to be kind if Sius Mavell Evi hadn't allowed parts of the city to fall into the hands of pirates and poverty during his governance of

Erothel's Western province.

It was almost a wonder why anyone still supported the man. There were plenty of rumors about him, from whispers pinning him as a traitor to the country, to word that he had been trying to become Minister of Erothel ever since Minister Monarain's assassination. Draqa didn't think either was true, but Sius Mavell Evi was a highly secretive man. Even after so many years working for him, he rarely confided in Draqa.

Draqa was frankly unable to describe the pure enmity he held for the Governor. Yet despite his efforts, he could not leave his service. He came at a time in Draqa's life when he was almost beyond hope. He had saved Draqa's life. Sius Mavell Evi took him in, giving him what felt like at the time to be a sanctuary.

One thing Draqa learned then was that nothing kind was done without an ulterior motive. This was no different with Sius Mavell Evi; Draqa had never been the same after what Sius Mavell Evi did and had owed service to him ever since. He was forced to do any job the old governor required of him, no questions asked.

Sius Mavell Evi nodded. "Now, for the reason I came out here."

He stepped to Draqa's side, and Draqa had to hold his breath as the pungent smell of perfume wafted under his nose. All four of Sius Mavell Evi's spider-like eyes trained on Draqa's two.

"I'm sure you remember your failure from yesterday," Sius Mavell Evi said.

How could Draqa not? The bruises on his back *still* ached. He nodded.

"Good. Now, a source of mine tells me that the pest is currently hiding out at Arkelo's Huum."

"I'm assuming you want me to take care of him?"

Sius Mavell Evi hummed. "Not anymore. I want you to deliver a message for me. Have him tell that group of *vigilantes* he works for, or whomever it is, that if they ever send someone to come meddle in my affairs again—well—they know who they'll have to deal with."

Draqa gave Sius Mavell Evi a bitter smile. What the Governor really meant was "fuck up the bastard so badly that he'll wish he was dead." It was standard procedure. Draqa gathered and sheathed his knives strewn around the target.

"I'll go right away. Is there a carriage ready?"

"It's waiting for you out front," Sius Mavell Evi said.

Draqa hurried to his room. He tucked two of his pistols into the holsters under his arms. He always kept a spare on him; there wasn't always time to reload the bullets in more intense situations, and he could never be sure what situation he was going to find himself in. At the last minute, he swapped the throwing knives for a dagger and a knife with a short, thin blade, before he rushed outside where a floating carriage waited for him. He got inside, and the driver took him to Talnoq-Vyn.

The Vyn was a large oceanside city and Erothel's greatest center of trade. Traders and merchants with their caravans scattered the cobble streets. Inlets cut through the western side of the Vyn, buildings springing up on either side, with bridges and beam overhangs to connect them. Fishing vessels of varying sizes floated at the edges of docks. Men moved to and from, bringing their catches to shore. Bordering the ocean were out-letting docks. Ships with wing-like sails stretched skyward. At the edge of the

South side stood a station where travelers of all kind boarded streamlined locomotives that hovered above their tracks. Nearby, airships waited in a clearing, ready for take-off with their loaded cargo.

The architecture of the Vyn was something to marvel at. Stained glass, curved archways, and ornately designed facades were a common theme. Each building had a unique personality. Many of the newer ones had *sonnes*—glittering sheets of glass-like material that absorbed sunlight—built into their roofs and windows. They were the main energy source throughout the majority of Arai and helped to power everything from electricity to transportation. The sylfans were the geniuses behind it all. Rumor had it that the humans of Taevalear had recently achieved a similar technology, but it was nowhere near as effective or as widespread.

Draqa's favorite part of this city, however, was that it was always busy. By midday, the entire city bustled with faerish people going about their daily lives. It was an easy place to hide if someone wanted to disappear, unless, of course, that someone needed to hide from Sius Mavell Evi, in which case Talnoq-Vyn was an easy place to be found. Sius Mavell Evi had eyes everywhere in the city.

The carriage let Draqa off in the city square. A few people scrambled to give him a wide berth as he went across the cobble street to Arkelo's Huum. It was a dingy little building rather unfortunately tucked between two larger, much cleaner ones. Draqa entered. The chatter inside quieted as he crossed the room to the man he knew as the manager—not Arkelo but one of his sons. The graying satyr gawked at him from behind his counter.

Draqa leaned against it and tapped his fingers. "I'm looking for a man—an elf to be specific. Blonde ponytail, a forked tongue, and missing half an ear. Have you seen anyone like that?" Draqa asked.

The manager glanced to the side. "A—a lot of people come into this place. You can't expect me to remember all of them—"

"He checked in two days ago, sometime late at night. Now, tell me again. Have you seen anyone like that?" Draqa's voice ended on a threatening note.

Once again, the manager glanced to the side. He swallowed and his eyes trailed back to Draqa. The bell above the door jingled. Draqa turned in time to see his man hurrying from the inn. Draqa took off after him.

The elf ran up the street, hurdling over a food cart that was crossing in front of him. He slipped between the crowds of people with ease. Draqa followed, opting to shove his way through. The elf took a sharp left turn. Draqa slowed and peered down the alley; the elf had disappeared. Draqa swore. The elf was faster than he thought. He drew a knife and cautiously entered the alley, quieting his footsteps.

There were few places to hide; a crate, a trash bin, a door. The end of the alley abruptly stopped, and the ocean took its place. Draqa crept to the trash bin and looked around it, then inside. No one. The crate, too, was empty. Draqa hurried and tried the door. Locked. He kneeled at the edge of the alley and squinted into waters splashing below. Seeing nothing there either, he sighed.

Standing, he drew a symbol in the air. "*Suum hulr,*" he muttered.

A wisp of black matter materialized in his hand. He shook it away and it flowed to the ground like ink in water. It settled and took the partial form of a wolf.

"*Find*," Draqa said.

The spell-wolf circled him, snuffling the ground. It walked to the wall, then to the opposite wall. It circled Draqa again, then sat down and looked up. Draqa looked up as well.

There, hurtling from the roof with blades in each hand, was the elf. Draqa scrambled to the side, the blades narrowly missing him only because he slipped on a slick spot of stone. He turned back to the elf and was met with a sharp pain across his front. He stumbled back, gripping his chest.

"*Attack*," Draqa gritted through his teeth. The spell-wolf jumped at his command and ran at the elf, giving Draqa time to recover.

The elf slashed at the spell-wolf, causing it to evaporate into nothing. The elf came for Draqa next. Draqa brought up his dagger to meet the elf's, deflecting it as the elf brought it down for another slash. He jumped back before any of the other three daggers could make their mark. Elves were always a pain to fight. They were quick, and their four independently moving arms made them almost untouchable. But if Draqa could land a single hit. . .

He continued to block, being steered towards the cold waters at the end of the alley. He tracked the arms' movements. One of them was slower than the others. Draqa took one more step back and felt air beneath his heel. He braced himself. The elf slashed again, but this time with the slower arm. Draqa cut low, slicing the elf's fingers. The elf let out a cry and his blade dropped, along with two of his digits. That was all the time Draqa needed. He licked the elf's blue-hued blood off the blade of his dagger. The instant the warm taste of copper met his tongue, he took control.

The elf dropped the rest of his weapons. He looked about in panic as his body disobeyed him.

"What the hell is this?" he spat, his own body forcing him to his knees.

Draqa shoved the elf onto his back, making him cough.

"I thought I told you to get out of here," Draqa said, kneeling next to him. He pressed his dagger against the elf's throat.

The elf grimaced. Draqa could feel him trying to regain control. "I don't answer to you or your governor. I still had business in the city."

"Killing the Governor, you mean," Draqa said. He dragged the dagger up to the elf's face. "You've made a very big mistake then."

"What? I wasn't here to kill anyone," the elf said through gritted teeth.

"No? Then why?"

"Just some job to watch him."

Draqa wasn't surprised. It wasn't the first time someone thought they could get away with spying on Sius Mavell Evi. They all met Draqa before they could learn anything significant.

"Who sent you?" he asked.

The elf spit in his face. Draqa curled his lip. He wiped the saliva away and pressed the dagger into the elf's cheek. The elf hissed.

"Let me ask you again. Who sent you?" Draqa demanded, putting pressure on the knife.

The elf cried out, "I don't know! I don't know, all right? I never met him. He didn't give me his name. He made a deposit directly over his aspectacaster. He said the rest would be in coin. It was a lot of money!"

The average person didn't have the money or power to hire mercenaries to spy on someone like the Governor. "So he was rich," Draqa concluded. He kept the dagger in place. "Was he government?"

The elf squeezed his eyes shut. "Yes. Yes. But I didn't recognize him as anyone important. Please don't kill me. I don't know anything else."

"Kill you? I'm not going to kill you." Draqa raised his dagger to the elf's lower right eye. "The Governor has a message for you to take back to your client."

The elf's screams would have been music to Sius Mavell Evi's ears.

Draqa watched a crowd gather around the alleyway as his carriage took him from the city. The elf would likely be taken to a healer soon. Draqa turned over a sack in his hands, the wet and sticky contents already soaking through to the outside. He felt he went easy on the elf, despite what Sius Mavell Evi wanted. If only the elf went easy on *him*. He leaned his head back, running a hand over the hurried bandages he wrapped around his chest. He would need to be helped soon as well.

Arriving back at the manor, Draqa found Sius Mavell Evi in his study. He was bent over his desk, simultaneously writing on two separate documents. Draqa tossed the bloody sack onto the desk, and it rolled into Sius Mavell Evi's vision, just short of the papers. Sius Mavell Evi looked at it, then Draqa with a raised eyebrow.

"It's done. He had nothing to say," Draqa said.

Sius Mavell Evi straightened, sliding the papers out of the way.

He picked up the sack, clearly not bothered by the blue trail it left, and peeked inside. His lips twisted upwards.

"You've redeemed yourself," he said. He looked up at Draqa and immediately frowned. "What happened there?"

Draqa felt his bandages. They were completely soaked through with his own red blood. Sius Mavell Evi walked around to him and pulled them down. Irritation crossed his features.

"You were careless, weren't you?" he huffed, "Come with me before you bleed to death on my carpet." He ushered Draqa from his study and led him to the dedicated medical ward across the manor. It was astonishingly complex, full of equipment Draqa didn't understand. Sius Mavell Evi had treated Draqa there many times in the past. Draqa suspected that Sius Mavell Evi was a doctor before he became a governor because he always knew exactly what to do.

Sius Mavell Evi had Draqa remove his coat and lay on the metallic table in the center of the room. He obeyed. Sius Mavell Evi took off his vibrant green waistcoat and draped it over a chair. Rolling up his sleeves, he rummaged through some drawers and brought over a needle and thread and a damp cloth. He removed Draqa's bandages and cleaned his chest with the cloth. After he was thoroughly wiped down, Sius Mavell Evi threaded the needle and started stitching the wound. Draqa looked at the ceiling, wishing the Governor would give him something to numb the pain; just because he couldn't feel much on the surface of his skin, didn't mean he couldn't feel the needle piercing through it.

"So," Sius Mavell Evi said without looking up, "Care to explain why this happened?"

Draqa chose his words carefully. "He caught me off guard."

"You were distracted," Sius Mavell Evi grumbled.

Draqa didn't bother denying it. Sius Mavell Evi would think whatever he wanted regardless.

"If it is the same distraction as this morning, I want you to put it out of your mind. Understand?" Sius Mavell Evi looked him directly in the eyes.

"Of course. . . sir," Draqa said. His thoughts from that morning faded away.

"Good." Sius Mavell Evi's tone lightened with amusement. "Honestly, I'm surprised by you. Who knew Draqa could be so easily distracted by a woman?"

Draqa looked at him. "What woman?"

Sius Mavell Evi smirked. He finished off the stitches and let Draqa sit up. "Either way, you were still hurt because of this. I want you to rest for a week or two, and while you're at it, clear your head. I don't have time for more of your mistakes."

Draqa tried not to nod too eagerly. It was rare for Sius Mavell Evi to give him a break like this. Even when he didn't have something to do, he always had to make himself available in case Sius Mavell Evi needed him.

"You won't need me for anything?" he asked.

"It is a bit late for you to be asking that. I'll call for you," Sius Mavell Evi said.

Draqa was sent away, feeling a great deal happier. No Sius Mavell Evi for at least a week. It was enough to make his day.

A rumble in his stomach led him to the kitchen where Minnos, Sius Mavell Evi's cook, was preparing dinner. Draqa walked behind her and peered over her shoulder. She added chopped vegetables to a simmering pot.

"Stew?"

The poor faun startled at Draqa's voice, letting out a yelp.

"Draqa!" Her huge brown eyes stared up at him nervously. "When did you get here?"

"Just now. Is that stew?"

Minnos rubbed her arm and picked up a few potatoes that had fallen onto the floor. "It is. . . but it's not done yet," she paused, "oh, but if you're hungry please help yourself to anything else here."

Draqa eagerly grabbed a biscuit from a bowl sitting across the counter. It was still warm. He bit into it and sighed.

"You seem like you're in a much better mood than usual," Minnos whispered. "Did something happen?"

Draqa looked back at her, still chewing. "Nothing that important." He gestured to the stitches across his chest, "Sius Mavell Evi wants me to rest."

Minnos stared at his chest. "Does it hurt?" she asked.

What a stupid question, of course it hurt. But Draqa shrugged. "I've been through much, much worse."

"You mean your scars?"

"Mm." Draqa finished off the biscuit and grabbed another.

Minnos continued to watch him. She shifted from hoof to hoof and played with the hem of her apron. Draqa let out a sigh.

"Do you need something?" he asked.

"Well, um. . . Master Governor will be gone tomorrow, so I won't have anything to do, and um, I was thinking it would be a nice day for an outing," Minnos said.

"I'm sure," Draqa replied, uninterested. There was talk among Sius Mavell Evi's staff that she was infatuated with him. He didn't quite understand why, but he supposed it was better than her being afraid of him, as he'd assumed when she first started working there.

Minnos nodded. "I'm a bit nervous to go by myself, though. The Vyn is so big, and I might get lost—"

"Then don't go. Or get one of the others to go with you," Draqa interrupted.

Minnos started, "Oh, but wouldn't you—"

"No." Draqa popped the rest of the biscuit in his mouth and wiped his hands on his pants. Minnos looked down. He patted her on the back and went to his room.

Kicking off his shoes and tossing his ruined shirt to the side, he collapsed on his bed, the down blankets engulfing him. Sleep came to him easily. When he awoke, however, it was only a few hours later in the middle of the night. He opened his eyes and stared at the black ceiling. As easily as it came, sleep and all of his exhaustion had left him. He suddenly couldn't bear the thought of staying in bed any longer and sat up.

There was something he was forgetting. Something prodding at the back of his mind. It had bothered him that morning. What was it? He wracked his brain, trying to remember. He grew anxious when he came up with nothing. The dark around him suddenly became suffocating and he felt around for his table lamp. Feeling nothing, he took a sharp breath. Imaginary hands pulled at him. His finger grazed the switch, and he hurriedly flicked the light on.

Nothing. Nothing was there. He frowned, sure there had been something. He closed his eyes. The face of a freckled woman with hazel eyes and chin-length ginger hair swam in his vision. Of course, that was it. Draqa breathed a sigh of relief as his memory of the ghostly woman from Taevalear returned. All except for her name. Anger replaced his relief. Anger directed toward Sius Mavell Evi and his tricks.

Draqa got up and grabbed a tattered bag from the corner of his room. He had to get away, at least until the week was up. He packed some of his clothes into the bag until it bulged a little.

It didn't take him long to decide where he wanted to go, given that he'd been to the Other Realm many times before despite the illegality of it. Arai and Taevalear were meant to remain apart from each other, the few allowed to cross between them being the High Council's Gatekeepers. The Council claimed it was safer that way. They had been afraid ever since the humans of Taevalear grew fearful themselves of the magic the fae possessed. Perhaps the Council was right, but it had been hundreds of years since then—Draqa found that Taevalear didn't remember Arai, and what stories they did have were just that. Stories.

Regardless, Draqa didn't care much for those laws. What the Council didn't know wouldn't hurt them. Most often, Draqa visited to escape, like he was doing now. He unconsciously fingered the spot between his shoulder blades where sharp black lines that crisscrossed to form an intricate triangle had been magically branded. If only he could leave for good.

It wasn't that he liked Taevalear, no, it was too polluted and the people there were often angry or too absorbed in themselves. But it was a place Draqa could disappear, if only for a little while. No one would know to look for him either, except for maybe Sius

Mavell Evi. To those in Arai, he was only Draqa, the strange man who did the Governor's bidding.

He didn't know when he'd taken the name Draqa, but it had seemed fitting when people began to refer to him as such, so he kept it. Who he was before was a person who no longer existed, and Draqa couldn't be trusted. But people in the Other Realm didn't know who Draqa was. It was a small freedom, but it was freedom, nonetheless.

Once he was ready, he left the manor right away. Checking to make sure he wasn't followed, he made his way to the ruins that sat on the coast some miles to the West. He took his time, arriving at the ruins just before dawn. At the edge of the ruins, near the cliff, towered the Gate. It was old, many of its stones crumbling, and was no longer in use. Draqa approached and stared up at it, marveling again at how it could take him almost anywhere. He took a breath, traced symbols in the empty space under the archway, and muttered the words he knew would take him to Taevalear and the sister Gate that lay hidden within a place humans called, "Colorado." It was a Gate he had crossed through many times in the past; Colorado was a place he liked very much.

As he spoke the incantation, he watched the inside of the archway grow opaque. It began to emit a pulsing hum, and he stepped back. He waited for the Gate to glow and then stepped through. The world around him spun, and he felt his body soar through space. It was exhilarating. Then, everything slowed, and he easily stepped into the world of the Other Realm. This particular Gate had been hidden inside of an abandoned mine somewhere in a forest. Draqa straightened himself up and walked out into the trees. Frost clung to the needles of the pines around him. The cool morning air touched his cheeks. He was grateful that he had dressed warmly, even though the air was much drier than in Western Erothel.

Draqa looked ahead and started down the path he had taken many times before—the path that led him to the city.

3

AN ANNOUNCEMENT ON the overhead speakers roused Ambassador Javis Zevos from his nap. He sat up in his plush seat and stretched, and rubbed his eyes beneath his small, rounded glasses. He peered out the window to his right at the forested city far below. The massive trees made the city appear deceivingly close as the airship prepared to land. Javis sat back, pulled his bag onto the little table in front of him, and checked over the paperwork he needed to give to the Board one more time.

He had just flown out of the mountains outside of Erothel's southern border a couple of hours before, where he had spent the last several months negotiating with the neighboring drād clans. Life was usually peaceful there, despite the dragons' reputation as a tricky and often reclusive people. There were rarely any problems with the drād, so Javis' job mainly consisted of learning their various cultures and the seven local dialects of the drenen language. And of course, keeping the clans satisfied.

The latter task was easier said than done as of late. For the last eight hundred or so years—which for a drād was just over one lifetime—the clans had been relegated to two locations: a mountain range to the South, and a range across the sea to the West. They had lost their lands during the wars against the humans of Taevalear when many countries throughout Arai sought to take advantage of the genocide the humans had committed against the drād. The drād wanted their lands back.

But Javis was only one man, and the Board was difficult to convince on even minor issues. Today, Javis had to report a less-than-minor and rather worrying issue. In the last two months, someone had noticed the discontent simmering within the clans and was trying to use that to turn them against Erothel. There was always a different person sent to stir up trouble, always appearing in a clan where Javis wasn't, leaving him to sniff around at nothing but rumors. But rumors were enough for concern.

Javis had hired a man to look into the matter, and what he found was alarming. Someone in Erothel's government appeared to be the suspect. Javis checked his aspectacaster. He was waiting now for word from his contractor, hopefully with evidence from a meeting that would give the Board a reason to act on his findings. As the airship came to a stop, however, it seemed Javis would have to attempt to convince the Board without it.

He was escorted off the airship into a carriage that drove him from the outskirts into the heart of Arkaven. From ground level, the city was a forest. Most of the buildings were built into or built to blend in with the surrounding trees all nestled close together. The forest proved too dense around the buildings in most areas for any *sonnes* to get proper light, so the roads and pathways glittered with them instead, curving and twisting wherever the sunlight and space dictated.

The only exception to either was the capitol building in Arkaven's center. A lone, round structure built atop pillars that stretched for the sun with its conical roof stood above the woodland.

A guard escorted Javis inside. He looked up with a sigh at the rows and rows of balconies that circled the inner circumference of the capitol building. The only way to reach them and the rooms on each level was the large spiral staircase in the center of the building that stood from ceiling to floor and the hanging bridges connecting to the stairs like the branches of a tree. With another sigh, Javis began his trek up the winding stairs. A sylfan fluttered past him, knocking one of the many floating bulbs of light into his path. He groaned in envy. He reached the top level, then gave himself a minute to catch his breath before he pulled himself together and entered the Board's meeting room.

He turned his head to look around. He was the only one who had yet arrived, so he sat to wait on the side of the ovular table where no one would be able to come in and sneak up on his right.

Bright and warm sunlight filtered into the room through the South-facing windows despite the late-autumn chill that hung in the air. Javis yawned. He bounced his knee and rested his chin in his palm. He scratched at a knot in the table with his thumb. He yawned again. Finally, the door opened, and the others began to arrive. Any longer and Javis might have fallen asleep. He stood.

The elven ambassador to the drād clans in the West took

her place next to Javis. She acknowledged him with a nod but kept her four violet eyes trained ahead. The next to arrive were the ambassadors to Ortrus and Iles, another elf and a sylfan respectively. They greeted the Western ambassador and took their seats. Among the rest to trickle inside were the ambassadors to Lus Natia, Nymn, Belvar, and Ushal, and then Dalmos, Talmeya, Creus, Sovrona, and finally, Adonis. They were friendly with each other and bowed or shook one another's hands.

Javis stood out from them like a plague victim. All of the other ambassadors were some manner of fae—elves mostly, a couple naols, a dwerin. One was half caelkin and faun. But Javis was the only one who was nalingur; part human.

It didn't matter to the others that he spoke Yrlun with the accent of a naolen language, or that his light brown skin glittered just like a naol's. Javis was sure he could have looked fully naolen and that still wouldn't have mattered to the others. His father had been a human, and because Javis had the red blood of the Betrayers to prove it, his presence among his fellow ambassadors was only just tolerated. He ignored it like he always did and greeted them kindly. One of the ambassadors returned the gesture with a thin smile.

The door opened again, and the members of the Board entered. All sylfans, Erothel's leaders took their seats. The ambassadors followed suit. Minister Lhorsan Phar removed his red cloak and stretched out his glass-like wings, twisted and flightless. The sunset feathers on his face were slightly ruffled, and he took a moment to smooth them out. Then, he stood to address everyone.

"My friends, it's good to see all of you. We're eager to hear what you have to share with us today. It seems you're all in attendance, so I would like to get started."

The Minister returned to his seat and gestured to the dwerin on his left.

"How are our neighbors to the North?" he asked.

"Things are going quite well in Dalmos. The King agreed to your terms for expanding trade. He wants to start right away," the ambassador said.

Javis waited in silence while the others updated the Board on their respective countries' situations. He didn't expect to have a chance to speak anytime soon. The Board was more interested in the nations they saw as their equals, the ones they could benefit from; the dragons had no influence or power anymore. Javis met eyes with the Western ambassador. She gave him a tired look in agreement. The two of them always went last.

After an hour, Phar finally addressed them. "I expect the clans are faring well?"

The Western ambassador nodded. "There haven't been many changes in the last six months. They've been relatively content since the Council agreed to let them move freely through the territories surrounding the Algaern mountains."

"Good, very good," said Phar.

When the Western ambassador concluded her report, his gaze passed over Javis and he started to turn his attention to the rest of the Board.

Javis cleared his throat. "The Southern clans are still discontent."

Phar looked at him, the corners of his mouth tugging down. "Ah, of course. We are getting around to that," he said dismissively.

Javis pulled out the paperwork he'd prepared and slid it in front of Phar. "Then you'll want to get around to it soon. People are beginning to notice, and someone is trying to get them to direct their anger towards Erothel," he said.

Phar looked over the papers. "And these are?"

"Flight records. Every airship that's arrived at and departed from the foot of the mountains in the last two months. Most track back to the capital of Adonis and Talnoq-Vyn," Javis said.

Beside the Minister, board member Tavyn Marvec narrowed his pink eyes.

"I'm not sure what you expect us to do with these," he said.

"There's more," Javis said. "I decided to look into the rumors surrounding Governor Sius Mavell Evi, and I think you should do the same. If you keep looking, you'll also see that within hours of flights to the mountains, carriages have arrived at the airstop from Sius Mavell Evi's home. I have good reason to suspect he's sending people there in his place."

The Board muttered amongst themselves and the dark gray feathers on Marvec's head stood on end.

"Know when to hold your tongue, *nal.* Sius Mavell Evi is as loyal as any."

Javis' face flushed. "I—I don't mean any disrespect. But you're all aware of the rumors—" he started.

"We don't have time to do as we please based on mere rumors," Marvec retorted.

Two other board members nodded in agreement. Phar waved Marvec to be silent.

"What you have to say is indeed concerning, Zevos. I will have someone look into it." Phar slid the papers to the side. "However, Marvec is right. We can't afford to waste our resources on rumors, especially not on such bold accusations as the ones you make against the Governor. Now, if you had actual proof. . ."

Javis felt for his aspectacaster. "I'll have your proof. Any day now," he said.

"Then I would be happy to listen. But until you do. . ."

Phar moved on to discuss more important business. Javis sank in his chair. Whatever came next in the meeting, he only half listened. Marvec's pale eyes remained trained on him the whole time.

The ambassadors were released after another couple of hours, and Javis got back on the airship and left Arkaven. He ordered a bottle of spirits for the flight home and poured what he could of it into his flask. He sat back with the remainder in hand and heaved a sigh. Removing his glasses, he rested his face in his hand.

He didn't know why he expected things to go any differently today. Phar may have said he would look into the situation in the clans, but Javis knew he wouldn't. He never did. Maybe, if someone else had reported in place of Javis, Phar would have been more inclined to care. Javis couldn't blame him, though. The Minister had as much reason as the drād to hate humanity.

The only hope Javis had was that his contractor would get back to him. Even then, there was no guarantee the evidence would be what the Board wanted. Then again, knowing Javis' luck, his contractor probably took the money and ran.

He knocked back the rest of the bottle and ordered another.

It was late in the evening when he entered the small house tucked deep within the birch forest on the outskirts of Kerevel Tul. He sighed in relief. Home at last.

Javis fell into an armchair next to a wood stove and melted into its soft cushions. He closed his eyes. He never minded being away, but there was something comforting about having a place to return to when he wasn't in the clans.

Of course, it wasn't really his house. When he first moved in, he thought it had been abandoned, only to find it was already inhabited by a large family of brownies. They let him stay on the condition that he left one of the rooms upstairs for them and that he bought them food when he was around. He would need to go to the city to take care of that in the morning, needing to resupply food for himself as well since he wouldn't be returning to the clans for a month or two. But for now, he was going to let himself have a much-needed rest.

He didn't know what time during the night he brought himself up to bed, but when he awoke early the next morning, he fell right back into his routine. He stumbled blindly down the dark stairwell and made his way to the kitchen. He lit a dim lantern and heated a pot of tea, which he drank seated at his messy desk upstairs in his study. He was in no hurry, so he sketched in his leather journal until his tea grew cold.

He dressed, then stopped in front of the bathroom mirror to try to tame his curly, chin-length hair. He started at the sight of the deformed and sightless atrocity that was his right eye. Usually, he had it disguised with a glamor, but he must have accidentally let the magic fall while he slept.

He hated the sight of the old injury. It was a reminder of his mistakes from his youth. He cast a glamor again so that the eye matched the beautiful electric blue of his left one.

The sky began to lighten as he left for Kerevel Tul. He walked there, as he always did; the forest too dense for vehicles to get through. Javis didn't mind the long walk though. The forest put him at ease.

By the time he reached the city, street vendors were setting up for the day market. He took advantage of the hour and had all of his shopping done by the time the streets woke up. He stopped at a deli for breakfast.

Kerevel Tul was a peaceful city. It was technically not a part of Erothel, but neutral territory. This lent itself well to the attitudes of people around. For the most part, its inhabitants welcomed all who lived there, even nalingur to some extent. The culture was one of the main reasons why Javis moved back there. The other reason was for the Citadel.

One part observatory and one part meeting hall for the members of the High Council—Arai's collective leaders—the Citadel was a grand, stone building that stood watch over the city on a hill. Scholars, students of astronomy, philosophers, and others frequently gathered there to study and speak their theories. Its size was only rivaled by the Kerevel in the center of the city. Javis visited the Citadel every chance he could, as it was also home to Kerevel Tul's library.

He visited again after leaving the deli. He meandered up to the Citadel's entrance and stepped inside. The old building's cool, earthy air washed over him. His footsteps echoed over the polished floors as he made his way into the library's unnatural quiet.

The library was bigger than all of the rooms in Javis' home combined and doubled. Placing his groceries at a table near the front, Javis wandered into the crowded maze of shelves. He had a specific book in mind, but he took his time and stopped occasionally to take in the scent of old parchment while he browsed.

As he went deeper into the maze, a sweet sound drifting from over the shelves caught his ear. He surprisingly knew the song: a drenen folk melody about two lovers who were turned to stone after their failed efforts to be together. Javis didn't know anyone who knew it outside the clans.

He followed the tune to the back of the library and peeked around a shelf. A drenen woman balanced a stack of books and returned each one to its proper location, humming as she did so. A signature characteristic of the drād, her skin was gray, although hers was lighter than most. The scales dotting her high cheekbones sparkled silvery-blue in the light that shone through the skylights high above them. Her glossy, obsidian hair spilled in a waterfall down her back and in two braids down her front, framing her face.

Javis grinned. "Why, is that Talara I hear?"

Talara startled, her cheeks darkening in color. "Javis! I didn't know there was anyone else here," she whispered. Her voice pitched higher than Javis last remembered; her practice proved effective.

Javis approached and beamed up at her. Although several inches shorter than most drenen women, she still stood taller than Javis by a foot, and at a height just shy of six feet, he was by no means a short man. And this was discounting the pair of curved horns that added three more inches to the top of her head.

"You sound lovely, my dear. I almost didn't recognize you," he said.

Talara rubbed the back of her neck. "You don't mean that."

"Of course I do. *Eslu'lir isel'ahn giwen ther*," Javis said in the drenen language of Qo'yul. *Your voice makes my heart sing.*

Talara's face flushed an even darker gray. Javis took her hand to kiss it, but she slid it away and occupied it with the last book in her arms. Javis drew back his own to flounder for his pocket.

"You're always so poetic," she said, averting her amber eyes. They stood out against her black sclerae, and Javis could have stared at them for hours.

"What are you doing here?" he asked. "I thought you were back in Talnoq-Vyn."

"I remembered you were coming back this week, so I came to visit. But I didn't think I would see you so soon," Talara said. She turned to put away her last book. "How were the mountains?"

"Beautiful as always. Your mother sends her well-wishes."

Talara's shoulders drooped. "I am sure she does. I'm sure she wants me to go back, too. I won't."

Javis shifted his weight uncomfortably. It seemed Talara's relationship with her mother remained rocky. "I would never ask you to," Javis said, ". . .but I hope you don't mind if I *do* ask you to lunch this afternoon? We could walk around the city after."

"I have had enough of exploring the city for one trip, and knowing you, you will try to buy me another piece of jewelry I don't need," Talara said. Despite her words, humor played in her voice.

Javis chuckled half-heartedly. It was true, he did still try to buy her gifts whenever they met, but he didn't see anything wrong with that.

"Can I not do things to show you how much I care?" he asked.

Talara gave him a warm smile. She stepped closer and straightened out the folds of his jacket.

"We both know that's not why you do it. If you truly care, start by helping yourself," she said.

Javis looked into her eyes. They only held kindness. "How do you know I'm not?"

"Because I know you. You are stubborn and prideful," Talara said, "and neither of us can change so much in such a short time."

At Javis' raised brow she grinned, adding, "Well, maybe one of us can. I am serious, though. Let go of the past and forgive yourself. You will be a better and happier person for it." She pulled away from Javis, and he longed to follow, but he remained where he was.

"I am trying, Ara. I really am," he said.

But what Talara was asking was much easier said than done. He rubbed his right eye. He had no right to forgive himself, and the only one who could have had been dead for sixteen years.

"Now about that lunch? I just bought groceries, I could fix you something at home," he suggested, ready to move on.

"That would be lovely," Talara agreed.

He held out his arm for her, and she moved to take it when he heard a soft chiming in his pocket. He rummaged for his aspectacaster and held it up. He gasped.

Talara creased her brow. "Who is it?"

Javis held up a hand. He let out a breath of relief. *Finally.* He looked around and pressed a finger to his lips before answering the chiming device.

Normally, a projection of one's face would appear above the screen, but his contractor liked his anonymity, and Javis liked his own.

He whispered, "There you are. I was beginning to think I would never hear from you again. Do you have it?"

A gruff voice replied, "I have it. Do you have the rest of the money?"

"Of course I do. We made a deal." Javis glanced at Talara. She gave him an inquiring look. *Later,* he mouthed.

"Good. Where do you want to meet?" the voice asked.

Javis looked around again and lowered his voice further. "Kerevel Tul. There's a pub with a rooster painted on the side in the Lower District. We'll meet there."

The voice grunted in reply.

"You know, this would have been much more beneficial had you contacted me when we agreed," Javis couldn't help but add.

The voice grumbled, "Oh fuck off. I would have if I was able. You're lucky I even have anything for you."

Javis frowned. "What happened?"

"He heard me trying to leave, sent his guard dog after me," the voice said. "And he has a message for you."

4

"The Storm Catcher, huh?" Krystal asked a child as she scanned a book for him. The boy nodded, a grin plastered to his small face. "Did you like the other two books in the series?" Krystal handed the book with its receipt tucked inside back over the counter.

"They were great! My favorite part was when—"

"Hey, no spoilers! I never had a chance to finish it!"

"Oops. Sorry!" the boy giggled.

Behind him, his mother gave a wry smile, motioning that they needed to leave. The boy waved goodbye and the two of them left the store. Krystal let out a bored sigh and rested against the counter with her chin on her palm. The hours had dragged by since that morning and, she itched to get out into the crisp autumn air, maybe take some photos of the people hanging around downtown, if only she hadn't forgotten her camera. But really, anything would have been better than sitting around waiting for the rare customer to come in during the middle of the day. Not that she could complain about working at Dahlia's Tea and Book Shoppe. With three floors, they had books on almost every topic Krystal could imagine: fiction, poetry, history and politics, cooking, and culture. They had books by local authors, and an entire section dedicated to texts written in other languages.

Then there was the café inside Dahlia's. Originally, it had just been a small section of the store that people could order a tea or coffee to drink while they browsed the books, but then it grew popular enough that Dahlia's opened into the empty storefront next door. Now jars of loose-leaf tea lined the walls, and round tables were placed around for people to sit and enjoy themselves. For a bookworm like Krystal, it should have been a dream. The thought made her groan. She'd rather be out in the world with her photography, collecting stories rather than selling them.

The sound of a coffee grinder whirred over the lo-fi that played quietly over the speakers as Rowen, the owner, prepared coffee for a lone patron sitting with her nose in a book. He brought the drink to her with a charming smile and a wink. Even from across the store, Krystal could see the elderly woman's face flush a bashful pink as she accepted it. Krystal chuckled and looked back down at the register. Rowen was one of the only reasons Krystal stayed at the shop. The other was her Mam. Before Rowen took over two years ago, Dahlia's had been her Mam's shop. Her Mam, not the eponymous Dahlia, but Elowen, was Rowen's great-aunt and had adopted Krystal when she was a kid. Krystal and Rowen practically grew up in the shop together. Memories from Krystal's childhood hid between every shelf, in the cushions of the green armchair upstairs where Mam would read her the Grimm

Brother's fairytales, and behind the pastry display where she and Rowen would get themselves into more than enough trouble. Even the clicking of the cash register had a nostalgic ring when Krystal worked it. Without Mam, though, the shop just wasn't the same.

Someone cleared their throat, pulling Krystal's attention back to the register. A middle-aged woman tapped her foot in front of her, a thin book between her folded arms. Krystal apologized and started to ring her up.

"You're on the job, you know," the woman commented, disdain in her voice.

Krystal drew her gaze up to the woman's hot pink head and blinked. Krystal might have been distracted, but the woman clearly hadn't been waiting long. "Sorry," she apologized again, handing the book back. The woman snatched it up.

"It's no wonder you don't have any business here."

Krystal bit her tongue before she could reply with something sarcastic. Instead, she gave the woman a warm smile. "Well thank you for being a willing customer, then. I hope you have a good afternoon."

The woman cocked her head, but her sneer melted from her face. "You too. . ." she muttered, turning to leave.

When she was gone, Rowen sidled up beside Krystal. "Smooth. That was a lot nicer than I would have been."

Krystal stepped out from behind the counter to stretch. "It was that or probably get held up here through lunch time," she said.

"I'm just saying, you have a lot more patience than I do." Rowen ran a hand through his long, honeycomb hair. "Speaking of which, if you're willing to be a little more patient, whaddaya say we ditch for a bit and get something to eat?" he suggested.

Krystal grinned in agreement. Once the old lady across the shop finished her drink as well, Rowen wrote up a note that read, "Out for lunch," and taped it to the door. Then, the two of them stepped out into the chilly autumn breeze. Rowen chatted as they walked; a cousin had just had a baby. He wanted to get a cat for the shop. He'd met someone. Krystal nodded along, content to listen. She didn't have anything to contribute.

"You know, Krys, we hardly talk outside work anymore," Rowen said. "What have you been up to?"

Krystal redirected her gaze across the street. "Oh, uh, you know. Nothing new." She supposed she could bring up the dreams she'd been having. She'd considered it countless times before, but every time she did, the idea died in her throat. It felt childish to admit how important they had become to her. How *obsessed* she had been.

Rowen hummed. "Nothing? What about your photography? Didn't you say you wanted to enter something into a contest?" he asked.

"Right, yeah, I did. I didn't win though," Krystal said, shrugging.

"Oh, I'm sorry. What was the prize if you won?"

Krystal let out a dejected sigh. After she lost the contest, she had tried to forget about it. "A trip to Poland," she said.

"Damn, Poland's a cool place. And your photos are way more unique than half the people out there. You're bound to win one of these times. You know I'm rooting for you."

Krystal stopped listening.

The pair ate at a sandwich shop located a few blocks down before returning to Dahlia's. The rest of the afternoon crawled by. Before Krystal left, she remembered to get herself another journal from the display near the register. She meandered her way home, driving past her old neighborhood. She was tempted to stop at the old, baby blue house on the corner, the house that she'd spent her childhood in. Mam's old house. She drove past it and went home.

Pine scent greeted Krystal when she walked in the door. She let out a deep exhale, dropping her backpack to the carpet. Kicking her shoes off, she flopped onto the couch with her new journal in hand and flipped through it. Its pages had that new paper smell, prime to be filled with untold stories. Krystal's stomach fluttered in anticipation. Maybe she would dream again tonight. She still couldn't remember the man's name from the night before, but she hoped she might get to see him again. Their night of storytelling had stuck with her. In the moment, it was as if she'd been whisked back to childhood and Mam was telling the magical stories in her place. Krystal closed her eyes as she remembered. Mam's voice came to her as clear as day, telling her one she had once asked for every night before bed.

". . .But you see, the little girl wasn't so easily tricked by the changeling, for she grew up with fairies, and she knew what they looked like," Mam would say, smiling as though she knew a secret. After so many times asking, six-year-old Krystal knew what the secret was, but she would always ask again.

"What do fairies look like?"

"Well," said Mam, "They have wings, of *course*, ones that glisten in the sun like morning dew. They have the most petite upturned noses, and beady little eyes and sharp teeth made for biting the toes of naughty children!" She would pause then, and tickle at Krystal's feet. Krystal would shriek in delight.

When Krystal's laughter subsided, Mam would continue, "But most importantly is how to recognize a fairy when she's in disguise. The little girl knew that all she had to do was look at her ears; a fairy's ears will always be slightly pointed, no matter how well she can hide everything else."

"Like my ears?" Krystal would ask.

Mam would give her that knowing smile again. "Just like them."

Krystal's breath hitched now as she traced her fingers over the points of her ears. Her Mam had made up that story to make her feel better after she came home from being bullied for them one too many times. She'd wanted a doctor to chop them off. Mam told her that her ears made her special, that they were natural because that's how her mother's ears were. The sentiment didn't stick with her as she grew older, and she started hiding her ears behind her hair. But now, a part of her wished it was true: that her mother really was a fairy, if only for the reason that it would mean all of her Mam's other stories had been real, too.

Dahlia's droned with sleepy patrons the following morning. Unlike the restlessness that followed the quiet, dead afternoons, Krystal felt her spirit rejuvenate on mornings like this. The bustle of people distracted her from the heaviness that liked to creep inside her chest while she worked. Of course, the customers didn't always have cheery grins on their faces when they came in, but they weren't unkind, either. Just tired and in need of a coffee and a good book.

Most of the shop's regulars came during the mornings, too. Krystal loved the uniqueness of them all. Today, an older English gentleman wearing his brown jacket and red suspenders sat in the cushioned chair in the corner. He only ever bought black coffee, and he read from the same book every time until he finished his drink and left. Standing in another secluded corner of the shop, a college kid with wide-rimmed glasses and a denim jacket decorated in flag pins flipped through a romance novel. Occasionally they looked up and glanced around, cheeks burning red. And then in line for coffee waited a woman made of spikes—spiked purple hair, spiked black jacket, spiked boots. Her personality was the opposite, though, and she struck up friendly conversation with Rowen or Krystal every time.

Krystal's fingers itched toward her camera bag hiding under the counter. How she'd love to stop working right then and take photos of them all. Sometimes, on slow days she had the time for a break and would ask a particularly interesting customer for their photo, but not mornings. Besides, photos never had the same charm to them when people were aware of it, something unavoidable inside Dahlia's. People tended to become tense or overplay their smiles and actions. They made their lives look scripted. After work, however, Krystal would have her choice of all the life in the world.

An hour from closing, a girl came in. She looked around the shop before she spotted Krystal and made a beeline for her. Krystal looked up from the register with a smile. "Hey, Ema. How was your day?"

"It—It was okay. . ." Ema whispered, rubbing at her red eyes.

Krystal furrowed her brow. "Did something happen at school again?"

Ema shook her head, but as she did, tears formed in her eyes. She quickly wiped them away. Krystal had a feeling she knew what had Ema upset. She was good friends with Ema's older sister, Lillian, and it was no secret between the two of them that Ema was often picked on. The counselors at her school had been informed, but so far, the bullying had yet to cease. Because Ema usually came to the shop after school to wait for a ride from either Lillie or her parents, Krystal always tried her best to make her feel better.

"Can I get a hot chocolate?" Ema asked.

"With whipped cream and chocolate chips, right?"

Ema nodded and paid for the drink. Krystal crossed over to the machines and Rowen stepped back to let her take over. No matter what, Krystal made Ema's hot chocolate. She brought it out to the table where the girl now sat.

"Here you go. Exactly the way you like it."

"Thanks," Ema said, taking a sip. Her expression brightened.

Krystal crouched down by her. "Remember, I'm here to talk if you need to," she said.

Ema only nodded. Krystal waited with her for a couple of minutes, then squeezed her shoulder and returned to the register. She kept an eye on Ema until her stepmom picked her up a half-hour later. The woman fussed over Ema. Ema mumbled and tried to fight her concern, even as it clearly worked to put a smile on her face. Ema took her stepmom's hand and they left together. Krystal watched them go. A twinge of envy curled in her chest before it settled into longing for her own mother figure. Or any family, really.

Rowen hung up his apron and came over to her.

"Hey, Krys, do you think you could handle closing by yourself today? I have to pick up Dad from the airport," he asked.

Krystal hesitated. She had planned on heading out to take photos before it was too dark outside, and if she had to close up on her own, she might run out of time. But Rowen had this planned for weeks and she should have remembered.

"Go ahead," she sighed.

"Oh, thank you so much. I can always count on you. See you at the market this weekend?" Rowen asked.

Right, there was a market on Saturday. "Of course," Krystal assured. "Do I need to bring anything?"

"No, it's supposed to be cold though, so remember to dress warm this time," Rowen said on his way out the door.

Krystal rummaged for her old film camera after closing up at Dahlia's. She let it hang around her neck as she walked downtown. Despite rushing, she had still taken too long to clean up and the light wasn't quite right anymore. She pushed back her annoyance and tried to take a few anyway.

Whenever Krystal went out with her camera visible, she often received mixed reactions from the people around her even when she wasn't doing her usual street photography. Most didn't seem to care, but some would cast distrustful glances her way or politely ask her not to take their pictures. She usually respected that, although, the one man who'd once sought her out from across the street just to tell her he'd sue her if he caught her taking his picture, she had photographed out of spite.

She had since learned a few tricks to help her avoid confrontations. She stopped at the edge of the sidewalk as she spotted a woman in a long, peacock-blue coat crossing further up the street. She raised her camera and peered out the lens at the woman. The woman's red hair reminded Krystal of a character from a board game. Krystal played with adjusting the aperture, taking photos of the woman at a few different levels, then pretended she was still taking photos of the same spot after the woman had passed.

Krystal moved on after. She caught a photo of a bearded man on a bike, and another of an older couple holding hands as they left a restaurant. She was selective though—film was expensive, and she didn't want to waste it when the pictures were unlikely to turn out how she wanted. Not everyone was quite interesting enough to tell a story through their appearances, anyway.

Krystal meandered her way to the park as the light outside grew dimmer and the people on the streets began to thin. The grass in the park grew dry and yellow, and the thick trunked trees around the park had lost their leaves. In just a few days, the entire space for the park would be filled with tents for the fall market that happened every November. Rowen usually tried to get a spot there. It was a good way to bring business to the shop.

Krystal stopped at the edge of the park. A man in a black and red trench coat had just stepped onto the playground, right into Krystal's path. A tattered bag hung over his shoulder. It didn't match his coat. He didn't seem terribly threatening but now wasn't the time to go over and find out. Krystal ducked behind a tree to watch him.

The man adjusted his bag. He put a hand on the merry-go-round and gave it a good, hearty spin. Krystal quietly chuckled and raised her camera. He interested her enough that it didn't hurt to try.

He looked to his right and then his left, briefly giving Krystal a full view of his face. She did a double-take. For a split second, she viewed the scarred left side of his face through her lens. It couldn't be. . .

The man hopped onto the merry-go-round and spun. The film advance lever halted in Krystal's grip. She was out of film. She hurried to grab a new roll from her bag. She rewound the old roll and swapped it out. When she raised her camera again, the man was gone.

She looked around. The playground toy slowed to a stop, the only sign that he'd been there at all. Krystal squinted to see if he had gone around to the other side of the playground equipment. No one. There weren't many places in the park that someone could hide, and she should have at least heard him leave. Then again, she *had* been focused on her camera. Still, a shiver ran down her spine.

She quickly got up and hurried from the park.

5

THE PARK BUSTLED WITH PEOPLE as Draqa walked through the fall market. It was rare that he made it to Taevalear in time for any kind of celebration or festivities. He kept track of many of the realm's holidays, but he often didn't have the chance to visit during those times. Today was a special treat indeed.

When Draqa arrived in Taevalear four nights before, he'd tricked the manager of a motel he was a regular at into letting him stay in one of the rooms again. All he had to do was apply a simple glamour to a handful of leaves, and the manager had thought Draqa paid in green paper money. The leaves always changed back after Draqa went home, but so far it seemed no one had been smart enough to connect their strange appearance to him.

Draqa had spent the two days after that simply resting. Had he been uninjured, he might have spent his time hitchhiking to neighboring towns and cities as he so often did when he visited. But he was content to spend his time bumming around during this visit, especially now that he saw that he would have missed out on the festivities otherwise.

Booths sold an assortment of fine crafts, vendors sold fried food, and music blared. Live music. This pleasantly surprised Draqa. Ever since the humans had developed their technology to play any kind of music with just a few taps on a screen, it seemed that real instruments had largely been pushed to the side. Draqa was glad to see he was wrong.

He listened to the couple on stage play a pair of string instruments as he followed the looping sidewalk through the crowded market. The fiddle, he knew, and the other was a round-bodied thing with a flat face that played an upbeat twang. The jig played over the bustle, giving Draqa an uncharacteristic urge to tap along with the beat when he stopped at a vendor to buy some food.

He paid for his caramel corn—again with the leaves—and stood out of the way to eat it. He watched as children shrieked and chased each other around the playground across the grass. He briefly screwed his face in disgust. He had curiously stopped at the playground the night he arrived and found the idea of it much more appealing when the little creatures weren't screaming and running around it.

"Hey there, are you interested in buying some books?" someone asked. Draqa looked around. Behind him, a blond man at a booth stacked with books watched him expectantly. Draqa turned to face him. The man's eyes landed on the left side of Draqa's face.

"What was that?" Draqa asked, ignoring the man's stare.

The man's eyes snapped to Draqa's. "Do you have a favorite

novel?"

Draqa looked over the books on the table. Certainly none of those ones. "No, I don't have time to read," he said. He went to turn back around when a freckled woman holding two foam cups came up to the blond man.

"Sorry I'm late. I brought some hot chocolate," she said, handing him a cup.

Draqa's mouth fell open. He knew that face. It was the half-fae—the ginger-haired woman from the other night. She started to smile at him, then her eyes widened. They stared at each other.

"Hello. . ." Draqa said slowly. He wasn't sure what to do. He hadn't expected to see her again. He didn't have a chance to plan out how their meeting might go.

". . .Hi," the woman said. She looked just as at a loss for what to do as Draqa was. When the blond man looked at her curiously, she finally asked, "Do I know you?"

Draqa nodded. "We've met. I didn't know you worked at. . ." he slowly read the label on the booth, "Dahlia's Tea and Book Shoppe?"

The woman nodded. How much did she remember? Draqa couldn't just ask her, not with so many humans around.

The blond man nodded as well. "That's right. It's the store I own downtown here. We sell tea and coffee," he gestured to his table, "and of course, books."

Draqa thought about this, and his lips slightly upturned into a tiny smile. "Do you have any books on dreams?"

The woman tilted her head and looked him up and down. "What kind of dream books are you looking for?"

"True—er, nonfiction, if that's what you call it? I had a dream recently where I was staying in a. . . a manor, I think it's called, and a woman arrived uninvited. We hid together, and she told me stories. I'm curious to know if it means anything."

Draqa waited for the woman to show any sign of familiarity. Somewhere, a dog started barking and Draqa realized the couple on stage had finished their playing and were switching places with a band. It made the air feel startlingly silent. A wide grin spread across the woman's face, and she let out a disbelieving laugh.

"That's kinda weird. I had a similar dream the other day," she said.

For just a moment, a real smile snuck its way onto Draqa's lips. The woman's companion spoke up as the band started playing.

"For something like that, you probably want a book by someone like Freud. We have him, but we also have some spiritual books about dreams, too. Here's our address if you ever feel like stopping by." He held out a card to Draqa. Draqa plucked it from his fingers and read it over.

"Rowen Andrew?"

"Mhmm," the blond said, "And it looks like you and Krystal have already met."

That's right. Her name was Krystal. It was a plain, human name, as Draqa had expected. It was the kind that was unfortunately easy to forget.

"Do you have a last name?" he asked her, pocketing the business card.

"Oh, um, Monarain," Krystal said.

Draqa froze, the name hitting him like a ton of bricks. He

stared at Krystal. "I'm sorry, did you say *Monarain*?" he asked.

Krystal nodded slowly. "I did."

"Is it. . .a family name?" Draqa asked. A nalingur with the name Monarain. Could it be Krystal was—

"I think it is. I've never actually met them, though. I was adopted."

That was enough to convince Draqa. No wonder she had looked so familiar to him. There was no doubt, Krystal was part of the same Monarain family that had ruled Erothel twenty-four years ago. But how? Minister Monarain had only had one child. Everyone said his other never had the chance to be born, being killed along with his wife. Unless. . . she'd survived long enough to have Krystal after all. Someone must have sent Krystal here sometime after.

"I see. Well, that's a special name you have there," Draqa said.

Every part of him wanted to drag the woman off somewhere they wouldn't be heard, to continue where they had left off, to tell her what he knew. But he had to wait. If he got too excited, he might end up saying something he would later regret. He needed to decide how to deal with this safely.

"I think I'll stop by your store," he said, his eyes only on Krystal. "For the book, that is. If you'll be around, I would be curious to hear what *your* dream was like."

"I'm there all next week, eight to four," Krystal said.

"Perfect."

Draqa gave Krystal and Rowen a parting nod and went off on his own to think.

6

"MAYBE IT'S A SIGN." Lillie leaned forward in her chair, her eyes eager. "He could be your soulmate."

Krystal laughed. "Soulmate? What's in your tea?"

She was currently on break, sharing with her friend what had happened at the market the day before. When she went to Rowen's booth and met that man there, she had recognized him immediately. She nearly wrote it off as a coincidence. After all, people apparently only dream of faces they've seen before. But then the man had described having a dream like hers. Krystal had texted Lillie about the encounter as soon as she was able.

Lillie was skeptical at first, suggesting that Krystal misremembered her dream, or that it was, again, a coincidence, but she gave in after Krystal persistently swore up and down that it truly happened.

"Well, you never know. If you really did dream about him," Lillie suggested. "You have to tell me, what was he like?"

Krystal scrunched her nose. "It's not like I got to know him."

"Was he at least cute?"

Krystal smiled begrudgingly and thought of the man and his rugged appearance. She couldn't bring herself to think of him as "cute," and he honestly didn't seem like her type. But what he was. . . was interesting.

"I dunno," she said, "he was strange."

Lillie pried further, "Strange how though?"

Krystal sighed and decided to give Lillian a bit of what she wanted. "His face kind of reminded me of the Phantom of the Opera. From the musical version. And his eyes were really unnatural. They were this vivid blue that. . . that were just like those lobsters!"

Lillie raised an eyebrow. "His eyes were like *lobsters*?"

"The blue ones. He also had an accent I've never heard before. I thought it was German at first, but it barely sounded a thing like your granddad's."

Lillie sat back and stirred her coffee. A smile stretched across her face. She was a hopeless romantic. "Sounds mysterious to me. Do you think he'll actually come here?"

Krystal shrugged. "I hope so, I forgot to ask his name. He didn't say when he was coming, though."

"You need to let me know if he does," Lillie said. "But please be careful. I would hate for him to turn out to be some creep. Do you want me to stay with you?"

"I will. And I'll be fine, Lil. You worry too much," Krystal said.

She waited, but the man didn't show up that afternoon, or the morning after. The thought crossed her mind that maybe the man wouldn't show up at all, that he had simply forgotten about the bookstore entirely. Krystal jumped to conclusions too soon. At the end of that day, the man finally appeared.

It had been a slow morning, with only a few people being in the store at a time, if any at all. The situation was no different that afternoon and the last customer had left the store almost fifteen minutes ago. With nothing else to do, Krystal went to put away a book that someone had left at the counter. She set it on its proper shelf and was about to walk away when she heard the distinct flutter of a turning page. She frowned slightly, sure that no one else had entered the store. She peered around the other side of the shelf and took a startled step back. There he was, sitting in the middle of the aisle and hunched over a book. He looked up at Krystal. His mouth moved, but Krystal didn't hear his words. When did he come in?

The man returned the book and pushed himself up. He wore the same outfit as before—a long, black and red trench coat and a fitted black turtleneck—and his dark brown hair remained just as unkempt. He looked at Krystal expectantly.

Krystal felt stupid. All she could think to say was, "You came."

The man nodded. He looked around and casually placed his gloved hands in his coat pockets. "This is a quaint little place your friend has here. I like it. It's quiet."

Krystal cracked a smile. "You wouldn't want to come here on most days, then. We're always packed in the morning and around lunch."

"So, you're popular. What drink would you recommend here?"

"Probably the orange mocha or the chai. Those two are some

customer favorites," Krystal said. "Though my favorite is the black tea with vanilla and cream on top."

The man hummed in acknowledgment. "I think I'll try the orange mocha then. If it's sweet, that is."

"Oh, of course. I'll ring you up," Krystal said. She led him up to the counter and gave him his total. The other employee working that day started making the drink. The man, however, remained to wait by Krystal, even after he paid. He said nothing.

Krystal took him in as she thought back to her dream of him. The man hadn't been quite human in it, but the vividness of his eyes could be explained away by contacts. The shimmer of his light brown skin could have been makeup. His eyes didn't have that fake look that vibrant contacts had, though, and he didn't appear to be wearing any other makeup.

"What are you?" Krystal asked, then clapped a hand over her mouth at how rude her question sounded. "I'm sorry, no, that's not what I—"

"Not here," the man whispered, looking unbothered.

Krystal then remembered how cryptic he'd been at the booth. Her fingers tingled with nervous excitement.

"Did you ever find a good book on dreams?" she asked instead.

The man responded with a dry laugh. "No, I don't believe I need one anymore. I understand well enough what my dream meant. But do you yours?"

The question gave her pause. It wasn't just the man she'd thought was a dream, but all of her nights spent in the manor. If the man was real, did that mean everything else was, too? Krystal shook her head.

"Do you have time for me to explain?" the man asked, gesturing to the tables.

Krystal glanced over to her co-worker, who watched the exchange.

"Can you wait until after we close?" she asked.

The man nodded. "Take all the time you need."

Krystal smiled and turned to go back to work. The man sat down at a table with his drink. Krystal could feel his gaze on her the rest of the time until closing. She closed by herself again, assuring her co-worker that he could go home early. Krystal joined the man at his table the moment she flipped the "open" sign to "closed."

The man nursed his coffee, still watching her intently. It was probably cold by now.

"Where should I start?" he mused.

Krystal turned over all of the possibilities in her head. The man may have been real, but the manor had to be something conjured by their subconsciouses, right? How else could they both have interacted with the same landscape so well?

"Was any of it real?" she suggested, then added sheepishly as she remembered she'd forgotten, "Actually, can you start with your name?"

The man held out his hand. "I couldn't remember yours until yesterday. I'm Draqa."

Draqa. The familiar name made Krystal shiver. She shook his hand. "Nice to meet you again."

"Right." Draqa sat forward in his chair. "Now you ask if it was real. I assume you mean everything that happened when we met?"

Krystal nodded.

"It was," Draqa said, as though his simple answer should have been proof enough. Maybe it was, but the skeptical side of Krystal that listened to Lillie needed physical proof. She leaned over the side of the table to see Draqa's leg.

"You had a limp, before, because you were hurt. Can I see it?"

Draqa's posture shifted, becoming tense in his seat. But then he gave another dead chuckle and turned just enough as he lifted his shirt to show a fading bruise on his back. There it was.

"Is that proof enough for you?" he asked.

Krystal's doubts washed away, and excitement again replaced them. She nodded, eager to understand. "How did you get here?"

"I used a Gate. A Gate is. . .essentially a magical doorway that people can use to travel between our two realms," Draqa paused, "That isn't how you ended up in my realm, though. You somehow soul-traveled there."

"I think you mentioned that before. What was it again?" Krystal asked.

Draqa hesitated, glancing to the side, as though he feared that someone was listening. "You projected your soul outside of your body."

"So. . . I used magic," Krystal said.

Draqa nodded. Krystal could hardly believe it. Here she was with a man, a stranger, who was telling her that not only did other realms exist, but so did magic. And she actually *used* it.

Draqa seemed to know what she was thinking, because he said, "I don't know how you were able to soul-travel, let alone on accident. I mean, you didn't even know that you were part fae."

"What do you mean when you say I'm part fae?" Krystal asked. Draqa took another drink and observed her. She tried to keep herself from fidgeting.

"You're *nalingur*. Mixed human and fae. In your case the fae side being elf and sylfan," Draqa said.

"*Nalingur*? But how can you tell for sure?" Krystal pressed.

Draqa pointed to his ear. "Your ears. They're shaped mostly like a human's, but the inner cartilage is shaped like an elf's, and they're slightly pointed."

Krystal ran her fingers over her own ears. Her chest tightened as she recalled Mam's story. All the times she'd thought she was weird. . .

"So, this is actually normal?" she whispered. She looked at Draqa's ears. They were human-shaped, too, and the tips ended in a point. The cartilage though, while also strange, formed differently than hers.

"It's normal if you're nalingur. If you're mostly human, it's usually just the ears that are affected, but sometimes we'll get other attributes from our faerish parent," Draqa said. He gave Krystal a lop-sided smile, showing off four abnormally pointed canines.

"Who did you get your eyes from?" Krystal asked, still taken by their unique vibrance.

"I got them from my mother as well, although mine are nowhere near what hers were," Draqa said.

"They're beautiful."

Draqa raised a brow and paused as though to consider this. He didn't say thank you, merely uttered a short chuckle.

"So, um, you're human and. . .?" Krystal asked.

"Human and naol," Draqa replied simply. "To what I was saying before, soul-travel is incredibly hard for even powerful faerish mages to learn. You seem to have a lot of potential for magic, so whoever left you here did you a disservice."

Krystal's lips tugged up into a smile. Maybe she could learn some of this magic.

"Are you able to soul-travel? Do you think you could show me how to do it again? So I could control it?"

Draqa shook his head. "Definitely not. My skillset is nowhere near that type of magic."

"Oh," Krystal acknowledged, "What *can* you do then?"

Once again, Draqa took a moment to drink his coffee. The paper cup made a hollow tap when he set it down.

"It isn't important. I only know a few random and mostly useless spells."

"Could you show me?" Krystal pressed.

Draqa declined. Krystal tried not to be too disappointed. After all, this situation was too fantastic to be upset about something as little as that.

Krystal and Draqa talked for a while longer, mostly a little about the different kinds of magic that existed, and then eventually about Draqa's realm, which he called "Arai." He described it as a parallel plane to humanity's realm, which he called Taevalear. The Other Realm. He explained that, back in humanity's medieval times and before, Arai and Taevalear were in constant contact, and humans and the fae traveled between the two realms frequently. Unfortunately, humanity grew fearful of the fae, and started to kill them. In order to protect themselves, the fae sealed Arai off from Taevalear. The only people allowed to continue crossing into Taevalear were the Gatekeepers.

"Which is why, despite being apart, Arai has developed along a similar path as this realm with only minor differences," Draqa concluded, "Part of a Gatekeeper's job is to track this realm's development, and to make sure humans don't rediscover Arai."

"So, you're a Gatekeeper?" Krystal asked. What she would have given to have a job like that, to be able to hop through realms to different parts of the world. . .

Draqa didn't respond to her question. Instead, he gazed out the window. "It's getting late. I shouldn't keep you any longer."

Krystal glanced outside, too. The sky had turned to dusk. "You're right."

Draqa nodded and stood. "It was a pleasure to talk to you, *vara* Monarain."

Krystal smiled and stood as well. "Vara?"

"Think of it like Mr. or miss," Draqa explained.

"Well all right, *vara* Draqa. Could we talk again? Tomorrow maybe?"

Draqa chuckled. "All right. We can talk again tomorrow."

He left the shop, and Krystal followed. She went home, her mind spinning from how carried away she'd gotten. Part of her felt sure this must have been an elaborate trick. Her? Part fae? It should have been nonsense. Any other person in Krystal's position would have probably agreed; Draqa was either delusional himself, or a criminal, trying to gain Krystal's trust so he could do whatever nefarious acts he had in mind. But Krystal felt inclined to believe him. Everything Draqa said about other realms and elves and naols—whatever those were—yes, it was fantastical and there was no solid proof to his words, but if he was real, why couldn't the rest of it be true?

Krystal paced her kitchen after she got home and set pasta to cook on the stove. She could remember all the times she had asked her Mam who her real parents were, or where she came from. Mam always gave her the same answer, once she was old enough to hear it.

Mam had come across Krystal's mother, bleeding and in labor, while she was on her way home from work one afternoon. The woman didn't seem to speak any English, but it was clear she was asking for help, so Mam drove her to the emergency room. The woman gave birth to Krystal and was able to name her, but she died from her injuries a few hours later. No one could figure out where or why she had sustained the injuries. Whoever Krystal's father was, he could never be located. Mam ended up adopting Krystal after she had already spent five birthdays in the foster system.

Mam never learned the woman's name, but whenever Krystal asked about her, Mam always came up with something to tell her.

"I could tell she was special," she loved to say with exaggerated gestures, "Where she was from or why she was here, I don't know, but I can still remember what she looked like, even now. She had long, long black hair, with colorful strings and ribbons braided in. Her eyes were *huge*, and the most vivid green eyes I ever did see, like whole peridot gems set inside her head." She would then have to remind a young Krystal what peridot was.

"Her skin glowed, kissed by the sun, and she didn't have a

single blemish in sight."

At this point, Krystal would always wonder if she looked anything like her mother at all, being pale, heavily freckled, with hazel eyes and ginger hair instead of green and black. Mam would always reassure her otherwise.

"I still remember the most amazing thing about her, too. She had the limbs of a ballet dancer. She must have moved so nimbly, with arms like a spider."

"Like a spider?" Krystal would ask.

"Of course. Four of them. Her dress was even crafted from spider's silk."

"Is that where my scars are from?"

"Maybe."

Krystal had always assumed that Mam's embellishments were more stories to make her feel special, but after meeting Draqa, she now had to wonder.

She brushed her fingertips over the faint, matching scars just between her shoulder blades. Her medical report stated that she had growths that needed to be removed, but what if they weren't growths at all? Maybe her mother really *did* have four arms. Maybe she did, too. And maybe. . .just maybe, Draqa told the truth.

7

A YOUTH SAT CROSS-LEGGED ON HIS BED, *once again reading from the journal he found a few weeks before. He still couldn't believe what was inside it. Old runes and spells, some he was certain that no one knew how to use anymore. The faded words inside were a mix of Yrlun and Qo'yul, and for the first time the young man felt grateful that he had been forced to learn some of the Drenen dialects when he was younger.*

When he read through the book for the first time, he didn't have much desire to try out the spells that he read about. But the more he read, the more he realized that many of the spells were actually very useful. For example, the journal contained one spell that claimed to reduce the time needed for vegetables to grow, and on another page a healing spell had been scrawled. There was even a spell that allowed the caster to control people like puppets. Naturally, the young man had to try out these spells.

His current favorite was a teleportation spell—an enticing offer of escape—so he practiced every chance he could. In previous attempts, he could only manage to teleport a foot or so, but now he had the confidence to try to go farther.

He took a breath and focused on a spot near the paint-chipped wall across the room. He took another breath and muttered the spell. Nothing. He frowned and focused harder, muttering the spell again. His skin prickled, but still nothing.

"Come on," he huffed. He took a deeper breath, focusing even harder. He said the spell louder. He felt a tug, but still he remained in the same spot on his bed. He tried and tried, to the point he gave himself a headache, but he still wouldn't move an inch.

"Come on! Work damn it!" He clenched his fists in concentration, his nails digging into his palms, and growled out the spell.

His body jerked through the air as he disappeared from his spot and reappeared on the other side of the room. He slammed into the wall and fell backwards to the floor.

He groaned, "Damn. . ."

At least it finally worked this time. The young man rubbed his aching nose and couldn't help but smile. He would prove them wrong. Everyone who said he was weak or said he would always live in his brother's shadow because he could barely use magic. He would finally prove them wrong.

Footsteps pulled him from his momentary joy as they thudded up the stairs.

"Boy! What are you doing up there?"

Draqa's smile vanished. He forced himself up and back to his bed. He managed to hide the journal under his pillow just as his father entered the room. The scent of alcohol wafted in with him.

"What are you doing?" his father demanded.

"Nothing, Father. . . I fell out of bed," Draqa said.

His father looked him over with his tired, bloodshot eyes and frowned. "Go clean up. Your nose is bleeding."

Draqa wiped the blood away, smearing red across his hand and face. "Right."

His father grunted disapprovingly and turned back down the stairs, stumbling along the way. Draqa let out a sigh and went to wash himself off. He knew not to expect any care from his old man. At least, not anymore.

There was a time, when Draqa was younger, that his father might have been kind, when he was attentive and drank alcohol sparingly, if at all. Back then, there was no person Draqa would rather be like. After all, he was strong, for a human, and was even able to secure himself a position as the governor of the southernmost region of Erothel. But that was before their life went to shit. At least, in Draqa's opinion it had.

Now, Draqa's father almost never left the house. He didn't pay attention to his sons and didn't care that he moved them to a town full of people who were leery of and even hated humans. Least of all, he didn't seem to care that, with Draqa's brother away at his special little school, his remaining son had no one. That was the worst crime of all.

Draqa stared at himself in the mirror for a moment after washing his face. A bruise already started to form on the bridge of his nose, but it didn't appear to be broken. He let out a sigh of relief. He had gotten his nose out of so many scrapes almost unscathed, he would have been disappointed if it broke because of his carelessness. He glanced at the yellowing bruise under his eye from the other day. Then again, it was only a matter of time before it was broken either way. His father probably wouldn't even notice.

***

Walking into the bookstore café the following afternoon, Draqa had to conclude that Taevalear did it better. Or at least, this little place did. There weren't many places in Arai where one could sit down with a nice cup of coffee and just relax. The overall atmosphere of the "cafés" in Arai were more like that of bars, and it was nearly impossible to find a coffee that wasn't poisoned with the taste of alcohol. Draqa appreciated that the bookstore café was a place he could be without having to be around drunken lunatics.

Catching Krystal Monarain's attention, he walked into line behind her counter. He had to admit; he was a little excited to speak with her again. She interested him, a bit of a mystery to solve and not to mention surprisingly easy for him to talk to. She gave him a wide smile when he came to the front of the line.

"Hey," she greeted.

"Afternoon, *vara* Monarain."

"What language is that?" Krystal asked.

"Yrlun. It's the common language throughout most of where I'm from."

"That's really cool. But you know, you don't have to be so formal with me."

"Now, that wouldn't be appropriate," Draqa said as he scanned the menu. "We hardly know each other."

Krystal raised an eyebrow. "Is that so?"

"It is in my culture. Referring to you by your first name so soon might suggest something was going on between us. I'll have the same thing as last night."

"Well all right," Krystal laughed, giving him a playful wink.

Draqa rolled his eyes. He watched her ring him up. She really did look like her family—her mother and grandfather especially. He wondered not for the first time since finding out what he should do with that information. He almost wanted to take Krystal to Arai, but he couldn't, no matter how much she might have belonged there. It would raise too many issues, especially because it was still very illegal for Draqa to be here. Not to mention, Krystal's accent would give her away the moment she opened her mouth in Arai. At that point, it wouldn't matter if she were faerish.

Draqa pushed the idea to the side. The woman was a death sentence, and he was too busy with Sius Mavell Evi to try to keep her hidden. He could simply do nothing about Krystal's situation, other than keep the knowledge to himself.

Once he received his drink, Draqa went to scan the bookshelves while he waited for Krystal to get off work. He found the book he'd started the day before and once again sat down in the aisle to read it. Krystal finally joined him some time later. He looked up.

"Done already?" he asked.

"Yup! I wanted to get off early today so we could have more time to talk, but oh well," Krystal babbled. She practically bounced with excitement. Draqa cracked a smile. She was strange. Her having grown up with humans, he would have expected her to be much more skeptical of him.

"All right. Where did we leave off yesterday?" he asked, returning the book to its place.

"You were still telling me about Arai. Do you want to walk around while we talk? Or maybe go get some dinner? There's a nice little restaurant just a few doors down," Krystal suggested.

Draqa hesitated. It wasn't often that he went out for food, even in Arai. He felt people's stares much more while sitting down in a crowded place with no way to escape them and he wasn't feeling particularly in the mood for that tonight.

"I don't know about that," he said.

"Well, we gotta leave either way since the café's closing. If you want, I'll pay." Krystal gave him a doe-eyed look. He sighed and agreed, but only because he felt the growl of hunger growing.

Krystal led him down the street to a small restaurant. It wasn't terribly busy, which Draqa was thankful for, and the hostess seated them at a table for two in the corner. Draqa sat with his left side facing the wall. A waitress came over and handed them a couple of menus.

"Have you both been here before?" she asked.

"I have," Krystal said.

Draqa shook his head. He didn't look at the waitress.

"All right. I'll give you time to look. Here's our drink menu as well. We have sodas, and we have wines, draft beers, and some really good IPAs."

"I'll just have water." Draqa said, pushing the drink menu over to Krystal, who handed it back to the waitress.

"I'll have a lemonade, please."

The waitress smiled. "I'll get those right out."

Draqa sighed in relief when she left and read over the menu. The lists of choices for such a small place made him feel a tad overwhelmed. Maybe he would settle on a small salad.

"So, you don't drink either, huh?" Krystal was using her arms to sit up across the table. She watched him intently.

"No, I don't," Draqa said, paying more attention to the menu. An intriguing hamburger made from plant-based meat had caught his eye.

"Was your dad an alcoholic?"

Draqa's menu fell closed. What? He looked back up at Krystal, his eyebrows knitting together.

"How. . . do you know that?" No one knew about his family. Except for Sius Mavell Evi. A horrible thought crossed Draqa's mind that Krystal was a trap set by the Governor.

Krystal blinked. "Um—" but she didn't respond fast enough.

"How do you know that?" Draqa abruptly stood, nearly knocking the drinks from the returning waitress' hand. "Who told you that?"

"Woah! Careful!" The waitress caught her balance and set the drinks on the table. "Is everything all right over here?" she asked.

Draqa looked at her, and then at Krystal, then sat down.

"Yes." He sent her away before she could interrupt any further. He took a breath.

"Who told you about that?" he asked quietly. His heart thundered in his chest. If Sius Mavell Evi knew that he had been visiting Taevalear. . .

Krystal glanced away, her eyes wide. ". . .You did."

"No. I would never tell you that."

"But you *did*. . ." Krystal furrowed her brow and bit her lip. "Wait, no. You were in your room and your dad came upstairs. He smelled like he had been drinking and after he left, you commented how you hated that. You weren't talking to me," she said.

Draqa stared at her, his mouth struggling to find words. "I don't understand."

"It was last night," Krystal paused, "You looked like you were maybe sixteen or seventeen. You were trying to teleport or something and you almost broke your nose—"

"—because I ran into the wall," Draqa whispered. He had dreamed about it last night. But how could Krystal have seen as well?

Krystal nodded. "Is it possible to soul-travel into the past?"

Draqa swallowed the lump forming in his throat.

"No."

8

DRAQA STOOD AGAIN, BRISTLING, his eyes dark. Krystal watched him, shocked, but mostly confused. She didn't think bringing up her most recent "dream" would be a problem. She really thought she soul-traveled again. Then again, now that she considered it, it did feel like she'd heard Draqa's thoughts. Felt his emotions. Draqa seemed to realize that, too.

"Coming here was a mistake. I shouldn't have approached you," he muttered.

Krystal frowned. "You aren't leaving, are you?"

"Yes. This was a *mistake.*" Draqa started to step away from their table.

"Hey—wait a sec! Why would you leave because of this? It was just a dream—"

"A memory. You. Were in. My *memories,*" Draqa accused, voice wavering.

"I—I didn't know. . . I thought it was just like before. I wasn't trying to. . ." Krystal trailed off, thinking of her journal. She'd written about this, too. "I won't do it again."

"Except you don't have control over it, do you? I don't need another person in my head!"

Krystal floundered, trying to sound out another desperate plea. "Then, it's only fair I let you in my head too, right? Like. . . a story for a story," she offered.

Draqa repeated her under his breath, then folded his arms. "That wouldn't be fair at all," he spat.

"Why not?" Krystal challenged, "It was an accident, all right? Don't leave over this." She reached for Draqa's sleeve to pull him back into his seat. To her surprise, he let her.

His eyes searched her face, although for what she couldn't decipher. A lie, maybe. He sighed and adjusted the laces on the back of his gloves. After a moment, he looked at Krystal expectantly. "Well?"

The waitress finally came back and took their orders, but Krystal felt unsure what to say after. Draqa's judgmental stare made her feel like she had entered a contest. Who had the worst past? Because it seemed only a story of equal value could match the sin of stumbling into someone's memories—his most private ones, no less. Krystal couldn't help but wonder what else had happened to Draqa. Regardless, she had no doubt she would lose such a contest. She only hoped that Draqa would give her a chance.

"Well. . . I never met my family," she started, "you probably already guessed that, but yeah. I've tried to find them, but no one's ever come up, so I assume they're dead. I mean, I know for a fact that my mom's dead. She died in the hospital when I was born.

That's a really lonely feeling, though, not even being able to find out if your parents would have wanted you. And yeah. . . I was in the system for a while before I was adopted, and I got bullied a lot in school. I didn't really have friends."

She scanned Draqa for a sign, *any* sign of his thoughts. For him to combat her words with a bristling remark that her experiences weren't the same as his, that this could never be the same because he'd given up his story unwillingly, or perhaps for him to reassure her that he changed his mind about leaving. He said nothing. His scrutinizing gaze betrayed nothing. Krystal grew antsy and turned her attention to her lemonade. What was he thinking?

Krystal tried again to garner a response. "What about you? Do you have a family waiting for you to get back home?"

"What, like a wife? A husband?" he scoffed.

"Yeah, or kids, or even just your parents. Anyone."

Draqa shook his head. "No one." And then, after a pause and a crooked smile, he added, "I mean, do you see this face?"

Krystal frowned more. "You don't look *that* bad."

Draqa raised an eyebrow. "But I remind you of the Phantom?"

Krystal's face flushed to match her hair. *She* said that. She covered her face. "You were *there*? I didn't even see you! Oh God, I'm so sorry!"

"Of course I was! I had to make sure you were safe to speak to." Draqa let out a quiet laugh, making Krystal feel even more embarrassed.

"I swear I wasn't making fun of you. And you really don't look bad at all—definitely not as bad as the Phantom. The other half of your face looks good. I mean—your scars are easy to look past."

She cringed, realizing her words could only be making it worse. But Draqa continued laughing at her. She wanted to curl up under the table in humiliation. She dropped her head and hid behind her arms.

Draqa cleared his throat. "I've heard worse comparisons to what I look like. Though I appreciate your, uh," he chuckled again, "concern for my feelings. And I actually liked that book."

Krystal peeked through her arms at him. "You have a very twisted sense of humor," she muttered.

"So I've heard," Draqa said. Finally, he leaned back in his chair, though his shoulders remained stiff. He tapped his fingers on the table as his eyes wandered the restaurant. An awkward silence fell between the two of them. When the waitress brought out their food, Draqa only stared seriously at his plate, as though gazing through it.

Uncomfortable, Krystal picked at her own food. She itched to escape now; she was stupid to think the situation could be resolved so easily. A heavy sigh from Draqa startled her, and she looked back up at him. He glanced around the restaurant for what must have been the tenth time.

"Can we take this to go?" he asked.

"Oh, sure. . ." Krystal hesitated.

They asked for a pair of boxes and Krystal followed Draqa outside after paying. The moment they stepped into the cool night air, Draqa let out a breath. Krystal didn't dare say anything else though, focused more on whether she might suddenly need to run away from him, until Draqa surprisingly led them to the park.

"What's wrong?" she asked when Draqa sat heavily at a picnic table.

Draqa fell silent for a couple minutes, his brow tight, then he replied, slowly, "I was thinking about your family. . ."

Krystal joined him at the table. "Yeah?"

"Your brother's alive," Draqa stated.

Krystal stumbled over her words. "What was that?" she asked.

"Your brother. He's the only one in your family who is alive. I know him—knew him."

Krystal leaned forward. She had a *brother*? "What's his name?"

"Averil. He's several years older than I am," Draqa replied.

"And you know him?"

"I used to. That's part of why I wanted to see you again after I realized who you were. I didn't plan to tell you but. . . you changed my mind."

That took Krystal aback. She didn't expect her words in the restaurant to have any effect on Draqa, let alone about something like this. She slid closer to him the bench, hoping he would elaborate. Again, his eyes searched her, and he took his time answering.

"I knew your whole family. The Monarains. My family was close with them, especially my father. He and your father, Sal, were both in positions of power in my country's—in Erothel's government."

"What was his position?" Krystal asked.

"Sal was the Minister of Erothel. He was human and sylfan, the first nalingur to ever achieve that in all of Erothel's history. He was. . . a good man. Other people didn't see that, and he was assassinated twenty-four years ago. I had just turned nine, but I remember hearing the news so clearly." Draqa gazed off somewhere past Krystal as he spoke.

Krystal lingered on his words, and her heart ached a little for the father she could never meet. Mam never told her any stories about him like she did about her mom, so Krystal always assumed he was the kind of dad who was never around to begin with.

"Do. . . you remember what he was like?" Krystal hesitantly asked, unsure if the topic of fathers in general was something that bothered Draqa, of if his earlier outburst had solely to do with her invading his memories.

Draqa returned his gaze to her and started to speak, then stopped mid-breath. He looked at the table. "I didn't know him well. To me he was just another one of my father's political allies. Your brother, though, was someone I looked up to when we were children. He stood up for people, even if he could be a—sorry, I don't remember how you call it. . . A pushover, I think?" At his small fumble, Draqa offered an apologetic smile.

Krystal had to smile, too. Finally Draqa seemed at ease, his face relaxing more the longer he spoke. Krystal would need to remember to tread carefully if she didn't want to upset him again. She leaned on the table with her chin in her palm.

"What about my mom? Did you know her well?" she asked, thinking about her Mam's stories.

Draqa shook his head. "Not so much, though more than your father. She was a sweet woman, I remember. She visited once or twice to see my own mother. Her name was Avira Varinin Liir." Draqa said her name with particular emphasis on the "i's" and with his accent he sounded like he could only have been saying a spell.

"That's beautiful," Krystal whispered.

"Elven names often are," Draqa agreed. He mirrored Krystal, leaning against the table, too.

Only one thing bothered her. Draqa appeared so confident about who she was, but how did he know for sure that he even had the right Monarain? She expressed as much. Draqa frowned slightly.

"You're twenty-four, aren't you?" he asked.

"I am."

"Well. . . When Sal died, Avira Varinin Liir was pregnant. She and Averil were sent away to be safe, but along the way, she disappeared, as though she never existed. It only makes sense that she came here, doesn't it?" Draqa suggested. A smile tugged at his lips despite his eyes reflecting a distant sadness. "And you are almost a spitting image of her. Your nose upturns the same way, and your eyebrows have the same soft shape. You have your family's freckles as well."

Krystal ran her fingers over her cheek, pleased by the revelation. If only she could have met them. And to think, in the two years she'd spent looking for answers about who her family was, always coming up with nothing, she'd simply been searching in the wrong place. In the wrong *realm*. "Thank you for telling me this," she said.

Draqa shrugged. "I felt your story needed an answer."

"Does that mean you'll come back?" Krystal asked.

Draqa dipped his head in response and Krystal sighed, relieved. She wanted to pry about why he became so upset earlier. Of course, she would have been disturbed, too, had she been told that someone looked into her own memories, but he'd almost seemed fearful. More so than that, though, she wanted to know what he meant when he said he didn't need *another* person in his head. Another magical occurrence related to dreaming, maybe? Krystal almost asked but refrained when she noticed how Draqa's eyes drooped.

"Why don't we meet up again later?" Krystal suggested instead. It was Draqa's turn to look relieved, and he agreed.

Stretching, he stood and offered to walk her back to the café. "We can meet again tomorrow," he said.

"Tomorrow? Are you sure?" Surely he must have had something else to do? Krystal brushed off her pants and followed him. He stuffed his hands in his coat pockets and meandered back the way they came.

"I'm sure," he affirmed as they reached the edge of the park. "I won't be here for much longer. I want to see you while I can."

When they reached the café, he wished Krystal a goodnight, and they parted ways. As hopeful as she was, Krystal didn't actually expect him to visit her again the following day. But he did, slipping inside an hour before closing. He ordered the same orange spice mocha as before, specifying for Krystal to add extra syrup this time—as though it wasn't sickeningly sweet to begin with—and then he sat patiently between the bookshelves to read. Krystal observed him, wondering how he'd gone unnoticed to her the other day. He wasn't exactly a small man, his crossed legs taking up over half the space in the narrow isle. He must have used magic to hide himself from her.

After her shift ended, she joined him to walk downtown. She pressed him to learn how he was able to hide, and then again on the kinds of magic he knew. Luckily, this only seemed to amuse him, and he answered with a slight laugh in his voice, "Alright, not *every* spell I know is useless. I used a glamor so you wouldn't recognize me." He turned his gaze to Krystal. "That's enough about me, though. I'd rather know about you. Or you can finally finish your story. The one by the Grimm Brothers?"

Pleasantly surprised, Krystal did. But that was the frustrating thing about Draqa, she found. Over the course of the week, they continued to meet at the same time each afternoon, and Krystal would question him. About Arai, about himself, it didn't matter. If Krystal asked one question too far, he cleverly danced around the subject, twisting the conversation back to her. Still, what Krystal could pry out of him made her fascination grow. She began to imagine what it would be like to visit Arai herself. And why not, if she had a brother there? She considered asking Draqa to bring her back with him many times, only to hesitate as she remembered that he'd said a Gatekeeper's job was to keep humans from learning about Arai. He had to be breaking at least a couple rules by talking to her, but she didn't know how far his willingness to break them went, considering he refused to tell her much beyond what he did that first night. On the other hand, Draqa had said himself that Krystal wasn't fully human—maybe she didn't count?

In the café, Draqa became a recognizable presence. More than once, Krystal noticed Rowen approach him in the aisle to check if he needed anything. Rowen pulled Krystal aside during her lunch after the third day of this.

"Hey, who is that guy? Wasn't he at the market?" he asked, gesturing in the general direction of the isle Draqa often read in.

Krystal glanced over as well. "Oh, yeah, that's Draqa."

"Interesting name. You know him?"

"Sort of. We've started hanging out." Krystal debated telling Rowen all that she'd learned recently. She definitely couldn't tell him about Arai—not that he'd believe her. But about Averil, she was tempted.

As a kid, she used to make-believe having siblings. In her mind, they always looked how Mam had described her mother—black haired, green-eyed, and of course, they had many arms. Those make-believe siblings were her only friends before she and Rowen learned to get along and she'd met Lillie. She could even remember a point in her life when she told all her teachers and classmates they existed—at least, she had until she realized her tales of strange sisters and brothers made the bullying worse. Still, it hadn't stopped her from hoping for a sibling while she searched for her family the last two years.

"Really?" Rowen craned his neck as though he might spy Draqa in the isle just then. "Are you dating? You should introduce me."

Krystal planted her palm to her forehead. "What? No, I don't know him *that* well. No. . . He knew my mom's family," she explained.

Rowen raised his brow. "You mean your birth mom?"

"Crazy right? It turns out I have a brother. His name's Averil." A smile grew on Krystal's face as she thought about him again.

"Wow, that's great, Krys. Do you know where he lives? Do you think you'll contact him?" Rowen asked.

The shop bell jingled, and they both paused to see who entered. The patron wandered over to the café counter and Rowen rushed over to attend them, saving Krystal from having to scramble for an explanation. He returned a few minutes later.

"So? Will you?"

Krystal shrugged, ducking under the counter to grab her lunch. "I do, but I dunno if I can. He lives in Europe, and it doesn't sound like Draqa's been in touch with him." And that was indeed a problem. Even if she could go to Arai, she still wouldn't have a clue how to find Averil, not without Draqa's help.

"Just look him up. Maybe do one of those ancestor DNA tests or whatever," Rowen suggested.

Krystal smiled. If only. "Yeah, maybe I will."

She and Draqa walked together to the park that evening. They sat on a swing set at the playground this time, Krystal swinging high while she talked.

"At least tell me one thing," she said, "My Mam always described my mom as spiderlike. Is that true?"

Draqa smirked in response from the other, motionless, swing. "It is. Elves are impressive that way. Your stories here don't do them justice."

The elves were the only people Draqa had given a name to, despite Krystal asking about almost everyone she'd seen pass through the manor. She assumed though that if anything else from folklore and mythology existed in Arai, they too were different than described.

"Does Averil look like that, too?" she asked.

"Not quite. Remember, I said you both are nalingur," Draqa said.

Krystal hummed, biting the corner of her mouth. She slowed

her swing to a stop.

"Yes?"

"Nothing really. I was just thinking how it would be nice to actually meet him," Krystal said. Draqa's look became pensive as she continued. "Can you help me?"

"No."

Draqa's immediate response made Krystal flinch. "Why not? Don't say because it's illegal. You already told me *all* of this," she reasoned.

Draqa didn't answer for a moment, his wary eyes flitting over her person. Then he slowly muttered, "I'm not strong enough to hold a Gate open for two people."

It felt like a lie.

"Okay, but what if you got a stronger Gatekeeper to come back and get me?" Krystal suggested.

Draqa shook his head, standing from his swing. "Right. . . That's a *great* idea, really. If only I thought of that. *Vara* Monarain, realize the number of obstacles I would have to hop in order to get that approved would be unholy."

Krystal frowned. "If I'm originally from Arai, there shouldn't be a problem."

"No one from Arai knows that. There are laws in place meant to keep this realm and Arai separate from contact. I told you this. So, I'll say again, you aren't going." Draqa's voice turned hard with finality.

Krystal kicked some rocks and watched them clang against the metal playground equipment. Why tell her about Arai at all if he wouldn't even try to help her get there? Anger twisted in her chest.

She wanted to point out the hypocrisy of it. A cold wind swept between them, tickling the hairs on her neck. She pulled her jacket closer, her expression souring. She would not give up her chance to see Averil so easily, but for the moment she conceded. ". . . All right. You win."

Draqa stuffed his hands in his coat pockets. "I am sorry. . . our laws can be unfair. But my horse has no bridle. It might be a long time before we can see each other again, but I'll come back when I can. I find I like talking with you."

Panic seized Krystal by the shoulders. "Wait, you're leaving already?"

"Tomorrow. Sius Mavell Evi gets nervous when I'm away for too long," Draqa said.

Krystal's mind raced. She'd known he wouldn't be staying long, but she didn't realize he was leaving so soon. "Wait, wait. Can't you stay a little longer?"

"No, I really—"

"Two more days," she pleaded, jumping from her swing to stand in front of him. "Please just stay two more days. I like talking with you, too. I love sharing stories with you." She didn't think she could actually convince him. But his expression softened after a moment. He gave her the closest thing to a genuine smile she'd ever seen from him.

"I suppose I could try to stay two more days," he said.

Krystal smiled in relief. "Thank you."

After Draqa left that night, Krystal formed a plan. Yes, it was a stupid, impulsive plan, but she had to do it. She deliberated before calling Rowen the following morning. One day wasn't exactly ample notice that she would be gone, not as a friend or an employee, but he would understand. He knew how much she wanted to find her family.

When she told him, he expressed his concerns.

"You already found him?" he asked, his tone full of disbelief.

"Draqa knew where he was after all. We got in contact, and we talked all of last night. Since Draqa's flying home the day after tomorrow, we talked it over and I decided to get a ticket to go with him. There was just enough room on the plane," Krystal said. She knew she sounded believable—it wasn't the first time she'd lied to Rowen.

Rowen, however, was silent. So Krystal kept talking. "I know this is last minute. But the opportunity came up and I didn't want to miss out. Cause I figured it would be a lot easier if I went with someone who actually knows Averil, you know?"

Rowen let out a long sigh. "But do *you* know Draqa well enough? I'm sorry, this is just so sudden. Like, this is how people get kidnapped, Krystal. Do you even have a place to stay when you get there? Who's paying for it? I should go with you."

His words did make her hesitate. She didn't have a plan for any of those things when she got to Arai. She couldn't let that stop her, though. She would just have to figure something out. If there was anything she was good at, it was improvising.

"Sorry, I was going to ask you, but the seats are full now. You don't need to worry about it, though. I got myself a room at a hostel near where Averil lives. He's in Edinburgh." She took a breath. "Look, I'll try to keep you updated. I don't know if my phone carrier will update in time, but I'll be fine. I have everything planned out."

Rowen groaned in the way he always did when Krystal had worn him down. "How long will you be gone?"

"Only a couple weeks."

"Only a couple—*Fine.* But know I'm going to worry about you the whole time. And you'd better at least let me know when you get there. Do you need a ride to the airport?"

Krystal hesitated again. "I'll be fine. I promise."

She called Lillie next, giving her an abbreviated version of what she told Rowen to avoid the same reaction. Lillie expressed much more excitement for her than Rowen had. Everyone would of course worry if she was gone for too long, but she would deal with that problem if the situation came to it. At work that day and the day after, she continued to reassure Rowen, and made sure he didn't have a chance to confront Draqa and spoil her whole plan. The evening before he left, Krystal asked if they could meet early to say goodbye. She wanted to take his picture, too, but conveniently left her camera at home. Draqa did take some convincing.

"I just want something to remember you by. I get photos of everyone I know," Krystal said. Which, to be fair, was true.

In the morning, Krystal met with Draqa at the park like they agreed. As it turned out, he'd never seen a camera like hers before, and he watched, engrossed with it the whole time she got her photos of him. He didn't seem to suspect a thing. The frosty morning sunlight and background of fallen leaves softened his features, and for a moment Krystal felt disappointed that she wouldn't be able to develop the photos until she returned. She pushed the thought aside as she put her camera back in its bag.

"Well, that's that I guess," she said.

Draqa nodded. "We'll see each other again. Either here or if you soul-travel." He started to leave, then paused and turned back to her with a two-fingered wave. "*Nod deg, vara* Monarain."

Krystal watched him walk nearly out of sight and relying on the fact that he didn't know what she drove, she returned to her car. Then, she tailed him. Just outside the park, Draqa flagged down a truck. He spoke with the driver briefly, then got in. The car drove him out of town, and Krystal followed all the way to an infrequently used hiking trail.

The car dropped Draqa off and drove away. Krystal waited until he was well onto the trail before she parked and got out to follow. At the last minute, she brought along her camera bag and tucked her phone inside. She hesitated before the trees, her nerves finally getting to her. But she couldn't turn back now. Gathering herself together, she followed Draqa onto the trail. She crept carefully to not alert him to her presence, although she felt a little silly walking as slowly as she did and ducking behind trees and bushes when she thought he might notice her.

Almost an hour into the hike, Draqa suddenly veered off the path. Krystal froze, sure she was finally caught. Then, a faint hum began pulsing through the air. Krystal hurried after the new sound, coming upon what looked like an old mine. A white glow shone through the half-blocked entrance.

Krystal squeezed past the barricade. A wall of light nearly blinded her on the other side. She shielded her eyes from it until they adjusted, and then her mouth fell open at the sight. The Gate shimmered from within a stone archway set into the rocky wall of the mine. It stood as tall as the ceiling and a foreign alphabet floated inside the glowing space below the intrados. Krystal glanced around, half expecting there to be some kind of hidden contraption as the cause. She took a curious step closer and reached a hand into the light. Cool air washed over her fingertips, making them tingle. She felt for the wall behind the Gate but met empty space instead. She yanked her hand back and observed it.

"No way," she muttered, wondering if all she had to do was step through the arch. But it couldn't have been that easy, right? Or what if it was a trick after all, and she jumped through only to find herself inside a cleverly hidden room? Before she could decide what to do, the shimmering space within the Gate shuddered. A wind picked up around her. With a panicked gasp, she realized the Gate was about to close. Holding her breath, she hurled herself at it. Immediately her senses became enveloped in darkness. The floor beneath her feet disappeared and her stomach dropped as a cold rush of air whipped around her. She tried to scream, but her throat constricted around her voice. Fear overtook her.

Suddenly, her back slammed against the ground, the wind knocked out of her. Coughing, she opened her eyes and the sky above her fell into focus. The first rays of the sun reached up from the horizon. A pounding vibrated through her skull. Something crumbled behind her. Slowly, rubbing her aching head, she sat up. Her surroundings were drastically different from the forest and old mine she followed Draqa into. Burned buildings and cracked stone made up this new place. A twin stone archway sat destroyed to her right. Just past it, the land dropped off into an ocean.

"Why did you follow me? I told you, you can't be here!" Draqa growled from behind Krystal. She turned, squinting up at his silhouetted figure. He towered over her with barely contained rage.

The reply she had in mind disappeared when she noticed he was shaking and struggled to hold himself upright. A stream of blood ran from his nose.

"Do you have any idea what will happen if—" Draqa staggered. He bent over and threw up at his feet.

9

Disyr, if he could find the strength, Draqa was going to strangle her. He sent a glare at Krystal before more bile made its way up his throat and he fell to his hands and knees, unable to hold himself upright as he threw up again. Opening the Gate took its toll on him. The amount of magic and energy required to get himself alone across the realms had already pushed his limit. To have to keep the Gate open at the last minute for an unwanted hitchhiker? He was astonished he wasn't dead.

He wiped his face with his sleeve and weakly looked around. Behind Krystal his precious Gate laid there nothing more than a pile of rubble, just like the ruins that surrounded it. Krystal *broke* the Gate. Draqa groaned, his one escape from reality gone. All because this—this woman, this infuriating woman just had to come see Arai for herself. He couldn't believe he didn't see her coming. Oh, and he'd been a fool. Sius Mavell Evi was right, Draqa had let himself be distracted by Krystal and her stories. He should have left Taevalear when he had the chance.

If the High Council received word that he brought an outsider into Arai, he would face charges of treason. The least that would happen was banishment to the uninhabited wastelands in the North. If the Council decided this was a crime worthy of death, then he would face the firing squad. He nearly threw up again at the thought.

He had to remove the evidence. He had to get rid of her, now, before anyone found out. Once she was gone, all the problems she had the potential to bring would disappear. He stood carefully and looked down at her. It would be so easy, and there were hundreds of ways he could do it. Throwing her off the cliff would be the easiest. Draqa glanced over the side, where the crashes of ocean waves roared below. Jagged spires jutted from the rocky bottom. Certain death would surely meet the poor soul who was unfortunate enough to lose her footing at the edge of the cliff.

Another wave of dizziness distracted Draqa from his dangerous idea. He staggered and put his hands on his knees. He focused his breathing to keep from passing out.

"Are you okay?" Krystal foolishly crawled next to him.

"You nearly killed me," he wheezed.

Krystal bit her lip. "Do you need a doctor?" she asked.

"I'll be fine. . . I just need to rest a moment," Draqa murmured. He lowered himself back to the ground and laid back. He closed his eyes.

"I'm so sorry. You said you couldn't bring me because you weren't strong enough. I didn't think it was actually this serious," Krystal said.

Draqa didn't acknowledge her. Maybe all of this was just one horrible nightmare that his mind concocted for him. Maybe he didn't even leave for Arai yet and he was still asleep in that wonderfully comfy bed at the motel. He felt Krystal nudge his arm.

"Seriously, are you okay? You aren't gonna die, are you?" she asked.

Draqa sighed, "Because of you, we both might. But I *do* appreciate the concern."

"What do you mean?"

"Did you forget that the only ones allowed to cross between realms are the Gatekeepers?"

"Uh, not exactly, but. . . coming here can't be *that* bad, can it?" Krystal asked.

Oh, she had no idea.

"Once I explain why I had to come here," she continued, "I'm sure they'll understand. It's not like I'm some random human who followed you, right?"

Draqa let out a dry laugh.

"Wh—I'm just saying they might be reasonable if they knew why this happened," Krystal snapped.

"The most reasonable anyone would be is charging me with treason."

Krystal hesitated, mouth partly open. She closed it and then her eyes shot wide. "You're not a Gatekeeper."

Draqa heaved himself into a sitting position. "No, I'm not."

Krystal moved back from him. "Why didn't you tell me?"

"You weren't supposed to know! I wasn't expecting you to follow me here!"

Krystal averted her eyes. She folded her arms and remained silent for a few minutes.

"I guess, are you able to take me back, then?" she asked finally.

Oh, Draqa wanted to scream. He gestured to the remains of the Gate.

"Are there other Gates around?"

Draqa massaged his temples. "This was the only one I could find that wasn't being watched or regulated. Even then, if you think I'm going to take you through another Gate after the shit you just pulled. . ." he said.

"Then what do we do?

Draqa drew in a sharp inhale. "I don't know, *Monarain*, did you not plan this far ahead?" he spat.

"I didn't think it was going to turn out like this. . ." Krystal muttered.

"Well, it did. Now let me think."

No. Draqa couldn't kill her, no matter how tempting it was. But what to do?

"I really don't have time for this," he muttered.

"Could you show me to the nearest town or something? I could probably find my way around from there," Krystal suggested.

That was a horrible idea. Krystal would be caught immediately. Then, she would be interrogated and lead the authorities back to Draqa. What Draqa needed, was to get her off his hands before anyone had a chance to realize what he did. He could do that. There was also the issue of Sius Mavell Evi, however. He would never let Draqa go off on his own once he got back. Unless Sius Mavell Evi never found out that he had returned.

Draqa turned to Krystal, who rocked on her toes—with anticipation or nervousness he couldn't tell. "All right. . . I'll take you to Averil."

"Wait—Really?"

"Yes, but I'm going to set down some rules. Do not, under any circumstances, talk to anyone. People don't speak your English here. Pretend that you're mute, or deaf, or both if you have to. I don't care what, as long as you don't interact with anyone. Otherwise, people will know right away that you aren't from here. Understand?" Draqa said, hoping it was clear that he was the authority here.

Krystal nodded.

"Good." Draqa looked Krystal over. "We need to find you less conspicuous attire."

Krystal looked from her clothing to Draqa's. An oversized pale green sweater and a pair of jeans screamed that she was an outsider.

"You'll wear this until I can find you something better," Draqa said. He stood and took off his coat. Krystal hesitantly took it, staring at him.

"What?" he huffed.

"What do you do, exactly, if you're not a Gatekeeper?" Krystal asked.

Draqa looked at himself and rolled his eyes. With his pistols holstered under his arms and a couple of knives on his belt, he must have seemed quite intimidating, but this was nothing compared to what he usually carried.

"That's not important. Just put the damn coat on."

He tapped his foot impatiently as Krystal buttoned down his

coat. With Draqa at nearly six feet tall, his coat fell just below Krystal's knees. It still wasn't enough to fully hide her pants, or her ridiculously colorful, flat-bottomed shoes. Draqa wondered for a moment if he was willing to let his toes nearly fall off by giving his boots to Krystal as well, then decided her current appearance would have to do for now. This unfortunately also meant that he was going to have to find Krystal new clothes before they got to Talnoq-Vyn.

Krystal stooped to pick up her leather bag from the ground. A phone and a couple of black tubes had rolled out. Draqa frowned. He didn't notice those before. Krystal messed with the phone and frowned.

"Well this is toast," she said.

She showed Draqa the shattered screen on the phone. Draqa scoffed. It served her right. She stuck the phone and the tubes back into the bag, then pulled out the camera she'd used to trick him. She looked it over carefully and sighed.

"Thank goodness."

"Why did you bring that?" Draqa asked.

"I bring it everywhere. Don't worry, I won't let anyone see it," Krystal said, returning the camera to the bag and buckling it. She tucked the bag under his coat.

Draqa folded his arms. The last thing he needed was a camera of all things to give him away. "If I see you take that thing out even once, I'll break it," he said.

Krystal gave him an offended look, but he ignored it and started for home.

Draqa made sure Krystal followed closely behind him as they walked through Sius Mavell Evi's manor. Despite being drained of almost all his energy, he moved as quickly as he could, and encouraged Krystal to do the same. The sooner they were out of Sius Mavell Evi's domain, the better. Draqa took Krystal up to his room where he started rummaging through his drawers and tossing anything that might fit the woman onto the bed.

"These are huge," Krystal said, holding up a pair of pants.

"Just try them on."

Krystal didn't appear happy about it, but she had Draqa turn around and tried on the pants. She had to hold them up to keep them from falling.

"Please don't make me wear this," she said.

Draqa groaned, "All right. Don't leave the room."

He hurried back down the stairs and to the room where the servants' laundry was kept. There had to be something around that would fit. Draqa scrunched his nose at the scent of sweat as he passed the dirty laundry laying in a heap. Preferably something that fit *and* was clean. He checked the chest in the corner that sometimes held spare clothing. He procured a blue tunic with white lining and stitches, and some straight-legged cloth pants. Both were made of thin material and were more suited for the summer months, but Krystal could probably wear one of Draqa's coats or cloaks over the top of them.

Draqa's hand was already on the doorknob when he heard a pair of voices. He held his breath.

"—and what of the Minister? Does he suspect anything?" Sius Mavell Evi asked.

An unfamiliar, grating voice answered, "He's none the wiser, dear Governor. Without proof, the ambassador's claims mean nothing to him. Lhorsan Phar trusts you too much to listen to the words of that *nal*."

Draqa frowned at the stranger's use of the derogatory term. He pressed his ear to the door to hear better as they walked past.

Sius Mavell Evi grunted. "What else did the ambassador say?"

"He was able to track our movements to Adonis. Phar plans to confront Vasiir about this the next time the High Council meets. I have already taken the liberty to notify her."

"We'll all need to be more careful. The drād clans were meant to distract them, not lead them right to us. As for the ambassador. . . I'll make sure he won't be sticking his nose any further into where it doesn't belong."

As Sius Mavell Evi's voice faded, Draqa peered out of the room, hoping to glimpse this stranger whom Sius Mavell Evi was meeting with. He moved just in time to see a shriveled face change into one Draqa recognized as belonging to a member of Erothel's Board. His blood ran cold. He knew Sius Mavell Evi dealt with shady people, but just what business did he have with a shapeshifter? Draqa ducked around the corner before he could be seen and hurried back to his room. He knew what was coming next, and he wanted no part of it.

He knocked on his door a bit frantically. "*Vara* Monarain? Are you decent?"

"Yeah."

Draqa opened the door.

"There you are, Draqa," Sius Mavell Evi said from behind him.

Draqa threw the clothes into the room and slammed the door shut. He whipped around, standing at attention.

"Sir."

Sius Mavell Evi gave him a once over. "I don't know what has me more surprised, the fact you are back so soon, or that I thought I saw a woman in your bed."

Draqa cleared his throat. "She's from a brothel in the Vyn," he choked out.

"Really? I last recall you saying you had no interest in sexual pursuits. Ah, but I suppose things can change," Sius Mavell Evi said rather disinterestedly. "If you're spending your time like this, you must be feeling well enough to get back to work." As though he hadn't actively been using his magic to reign Draqa in the last two days.

Draqa held back the annoyance in his voice. "Of course, sir."

"Perfect. You have a choice this time, but both jobs are imperative that they are done right away."

"As always, sir. Who do you need taken care of?" Draqa asked.

Sius Mavell Evi shifted his weight onto his cane. "You remember Tolas Ruv Aen, don't you?"

Draqa nodded. There was no way he could forget that… traitor. Tolas Ruv Aen, or "Tally" as Draqa had known him best, was an elf who had worked alongside Draqa for Governor Sius Mavell Evi. Two years ago—almost three now—he turned out to be a spy for the Ard'a and had run town as soon as he was discovered. Sius Mavell Evi had Draqa going after Tolas Ruv Aen ever since, but he always managed to give them the slip.

"He was spotted again. He went into the mountains a few

days ago, and my sources say he will be meeting with the camps of hulvoqn in Worsun Pass."

Draqa's expression dropped. This lunatic wanted him to deal with the hulvoqn? The full moon wasn't for another three weeks, but. . .

"What's the other job?" Draqa asked.

"The other I think you will enjoy. There is an ambassador who has been sticking his nose into my business lately," Sius Mavell Evi explained. He pulled a square piece of paper from his pocket and handed it to Draqa. On it was a washed-out picture of a man wearing ovular glasses. Draqa would have recognized the blue eyes and curly head of hair anywhere.

Never in a hundred years would Draqa have actually thought that Ambassador Zevos would end up on the wrong side of Sius Mavell Evi. He was almost a no-name and never got involved in internal politics. As far as Draqa was aware, Zevos didn't spend much time in Erothel. In all Zevos' career as ambassador, Draqa hadn't even seen him on the picturecast apart from the day he was appointed. Draqa couldn't imagine what Zevos could have possibly done to upset Sius Mavell Evi. Not that he particularly cared, but between facing an unpredictable traitor and his abandoned past, he'd rather face the traitor.

"I'm sure you remember who this is," Sius Mavell Evi said.

"I do. You'll have to send someone else after him," Draqa decided, "I'll go after Tolas Ruv Aen again. I'm getting tired of his frequent escapes."

Sius Mavell Evi raised his eyebrows. Danger lurked in his beady eyes, and Draqa realized the Governor actually wanted him to go after Zevos. He readied himself for the accusations that were sure to come, when suddenly Sius Mavell Evi's whole demeanor changed. He tilted his head, looking past Draqa with an uncharacteristically shocked expression. Draqa looked back to see Monarain's head peeking out of the doorway. Draqa went to shove her back in, but Sius Mavell Evi gripped his arm.

"Now, there's no need for that, Draqa. Why don't you introduce me to your friend?"

Draqa kept his hand by Krystal, still ready to close the door on her. "She's no one," he said, "I was actually about to take her back to the Vyn—"

"Ah, but everybody is someone," Sius Mavell Evi said. He motioned for Krystal to come forward.

She stepped out of Draqa's room. The clothes he brought her mostly fit, although the tunic was clearly for someone with a wider frame, and it slid down one shoulder. She was completely barefoot. Sius Mavell Evi took her hand and kissed it. Her face flushed bright red.

"What's your name, my dear?" Sius Mavell Evi asked. "Wait, no, I think I can guess. Something with Avi, perhaps?"

Krystal glanced at Draqa, her eyes as round as saucers.

"She's mute," Draqa blurted, disturbed by the Governor's behavior. He could only image how uncomfortable Krystal must have been, being unable to understand Sius Mavell Evi.

Sius Mavell Evi released Krystal's hand. He raised an eyebrow at Draqa. "Is that so?"

Draqa nodded.

"Well, that is. . . very unfortunate. Perhaps I could give you a voice, then," Sius Mavell Evi said. He raised a hand towards Krystal's face.

Draqa stepped between them. "You would only be wasting your time, sir. She has nothing for you to heal, and anyway, I should be getting her back before people start to wonder where she is."

All four of Sius Mavell Evi's eyes locked with Draqa's. Draqa could suddenly feel the rest of his strength leaving him, but he couldn't look away. His knees grew weak as he felt something prodding in the back of his mind. He forced his eyes closed and was struck by a splitting pain throughout his skull. He winced and held his forehead. Sius Mavell Evi stepped away.

"Very well. While you're at it, you may as well leave straight from the Vyn to go after Tolas Ruv Aen. I expect regular updates," he said. He looked past Draqa to Krystal and gave her a dangerous smile. "I will just have to come visit you myself, *Krystal Monarain*."

Draqa stared after Sius Mavell Evi, a sick feeling in his gut, as he walked away down the hall. Only once he was out of earshot did Krystal voice what Draqa was thinking.

"Was. . . was that your boss?"

Draqa slowly nodded. "Governor Sius Mavell Evi."

"How did he know my name?" Krystal whispered.

Draqa closed his eyes, his head still aching from that most recent violation. "I don't know," he lied.

"What were you talking about before I came out? What do you do for him?"

"Too much," is what Draqa wished he could say. Instead, his words betrayed him, as usual. "I told you, it's not important. Are you ready to go yet?"

Krystal's eyes lingered in the direction Sius Mavell Evi left before she shook her head. She went back into Draqa's room.

"I still need shoes. And a coat or something," she said.

"Just wear your shoes. I'm sure one of my cloaks will hide them well enough for now."

While Krystal put on her shoes and a cloak, Draqa armed himself further. More teeth, more ammunition, and more skill was always needed when dealing with Tolas Ruv Aen. Draqa felt a rush of anxiety. There was too much going on. Sure, it wasn't likely that Averil had moved from his old dwellings in Kerevel Tul, but how was he going to get Krystal to Averil when he had to come up with a plan to catch Tolas Ruv Aen? He certainly couldn't leave Krystal behind somewhere until the bastard was caught, but bringing her along had the potential to end just as badly, or worse.

Then there was Sius Mavell Evi. Draqa dreaded the inevitable punishment that would be waiting for him as soon as the Governor caught him alone. Sius Mavell Evi knew he had lied about Krystal, but how much of Draqa's other lies did he learn? Draqa suppressed a shudder and turned back to Krystal, hoping her name was the only thing Sius Mavell Evi searched for.

10

A GUST OF WIND THREATENED to blow away the oversized cloak that Krystal was wearing when she stepped out onto the front steps of the manor. She shivered and clung tightly to the fabric. Draqa appeared to be completely unphased by the sudden chill in the air. He pulled out a brassy, leaf-shaped object attached to a chain on his coat. He slid his thumb across the surface, and it flowered open, revealing a soft, green glow. A holographic projection appeared above it. Krystal stared as Draqa interacted with it.

"What is that?" she asked.

"An aspectacaster," Draqa said. He was somehow typing onto the projection as though it were a screen. "I'm summoning a carriage."

Krystal mouthed her disbelief. "How does that work?" She reached to touch the device, but Draqa snatched it away, stuffing it back into his pocket.

"That's not in my realm of knowledge. Our driver will be here in twenty minutes," he said.

Krystal nodded, glad they wouldn't be spending any more time in this place. Something about the Governor still unnerved her, and not just because he knew her name. The way he made Draqa almost cower before him. . . was disturbing. It reminded Krystal of when she soul-traveled, and heard that angry voice behind the door, as well as Draqa's distinct cry of pain. Were beatings a frequent occurrence? Or, more likely, was something else at play entirely? Either way, the further away from Sius Mavell Evi, the less likely Krystal would have to find out what it was.

An odd, shimmering object approached from the road. Krystal squinted to make out the shape. As it grew closer, she realized it was some sort of oblong vehicle, floating a few feet off the ground. It looked like a stagecoach, only the driver was seated on a covered platform in the back, elevated so they could see above the cab.

The vehicle stopped in front of the manor steps. The driver stepped down and pulled down on a lever, causing the long window on the front of the cab to open to the inside. Draqa said something to the driver in what Krystal presumed to be Yrlun and handed him some money.

"*Komm, de nou irfurda,*" Draqa said, motioning Krystal over. He helped her into the cab and got in after her. The windows closed.

A squeal of excitement escaped Krystal's mouth. She leaned out of her seat to peer out the window as the vehicle started moving.

"This is amazing!" she gasped.

In the seat beside her, Draqa leaned his head back and sighed heavily. Krystal glanced back at him, noticing just how tired he looked. A weight in her chest formed as she remembered that she was the cause of it. She wanted to apologize, even though Draqa technically brought this situation upon himself, but he ignored Krystal for the entire ride. This did nothing to quell her wandering thoughts or the newfound worries she had about the kind of person she traveled with.

Upon arriving in the Vyn, Draqa brought Krystal from the vehicle. The sprawling port city before her left her in awe. With its glittering rooftops and stained-glass windows, it was as though the city had been taken straight out of a storybook. For every vehicle, there were even more people on tall bicycles and rickshaws. There was even an occasional person on horseback. Krystal recognized many of the same sorts of people as she saw in her "dreams."

Draqa grabbed her arm and pulled her close. "Remember what I said before. Don't talk to anyone, and stay close to me," he whispered. Krystal nodded. "Good. Now follow me. We are going to go buy some supplies."

"For what?" Krystal asked.

"I will explain to you somewhere private. Now come." Draqa said nothing more and made no notion of wanting to speak to Krystal at all while they were around others.

Draqa led Krystal to a variety of stores. More than once, she noticed people staring at the pair of them. More than a few store clerks conducted themselves nervously around Draqa, apologizing for things as trivial as not counting change fast enough, and then again when their rush made them clumsily drop coins on the floor. One very short-statured old man with the same bat-like ears as the butler in the manor was left stumbling over himself in his attempt to make way as he saw Draqa and Krystal approach the store he was leaving. Draqa ushered Krystal into the store when she stopped to help the old man to his feet.

The pair finished their shopping after Draqa purchased a coat and better shoes for Krystal. He disposed of her old ones off the side of the dock at the end of an alleyway. He brought her then to a quaint little place. The homey interior, with white shiplap walls and dark, wooden tables, and a wall garden surrounding a fireplace with dying embers made the place feel sleepy. The only visible person inside ate alone in the corner. Just when Krystal was about to wonder why they were there, Draqa finally turned his attention to her.

"Are you hungry?" he asked.

The thought of food made Krystal's empty stomach growl. She would have asked if they could get food earlier, but she'd been afraid she would be heard.

"Very. What is this place?" she asked.

Draqa paused and then uttered, "I don't know the word. *Huum* is what we call it. People pay to sleep and eat here," he said.

"Oh, we would still call this a hotel or an inn."

Draqa nodded. He walked Krystal up to the vacant counter and rang the little bell sitting there. A moment later, a woman came out from a room in the back. A thick, hair-tufted tail followed suit. Krystal's eyes widened. The woman walked up to the counter, arms wide, and a sharp-toothed grin on her face. Although more of a silver, her face had the same sort of shimmer that Draqa's did.

"Ah, Draqa!" She pulled Draqa forward as she leaned over the counter and kissed his cheeks. Draqa barely returned the gesture.

"*En dokva hachus dursin?*" the woman asked, gesturing her

thumb at the stairs. She looked at Krystal, her eyes shifting colors in the light like an opal, and gave Draqa a smirk. "*Ud en bur wonsus?*"

Draqa scoffed and gazed up at a wooden sign hanging behind the counter. "*Noon. Esh wonsda.*" He pointed to a couple of items scrawled on the sign. "*Naganda cherak. . . ofasmyl jodn uonvlas.*"

He reached into the small leather pouch tied to his belt and handed the woman a few dull coins. The woman grinned. She winked at Draqa and went into the kitchen behind her.

Draqa rolled his eyes and beckoned for Krystal to follow him to a table near the fireplace.

Krystal sat, her eyes still wide. She leaned across the table.

"She has a tail!" she whispered.

"She's a naol," Draqa said, "She's the owner here."

Krystal leaned over to look him up and down. From his appearance, she would never have guessed.

"What? Did you expect her to look more human?" Draqa asked.

Krystal shrugged. "I guess so. Is she your girlfriend or was that. . .?"

"That was just a way of greeting that some naols grow up with," Draqa said, his lip curling. He rubbed his cheeks with the back of his hand.

The disgusted look vanished from his face as the two of them were briefly interrupted by the naolen woman as she brought a pair of mugs filled with a thick, dark liquid. Steam rose off the tops. Draqa muttered a thanks and sent her away.

Krystal tentatively sipped the drink, expecting something like a coffee, but was surprised to find it tasted nothing like it. It was sickeningly sweet. The closest flavors she could think of were tamarind and black licorice. She gagged and pushed her mug to the side. Amusement danced in Draqa's eyes. Krystal cleared her throat.

"So," she said, "you said you would tell me where we're going."

"Right. I have an errand to run at the Governor's request. It's in the mountains."

Krystal frowned. "What about my brother?"

"We'll get to that, but this takes priority," Draqa paused. He tilted his head. "You aren't afraid of wolves, are you?" he asked.

"Wolves?"

Draqa nodded. "Camps of hulvoqn live out where we will be going. Chances are, we're going to have to deal with them."

Nervousness settled over Krystal. "What are—are they dangerous?" she asked, unable to keep the quiver from her voice.

"Not inherently. . . but people can act unpredictably after they become wolf-cursed. The ones who live in the canyon don't like Sius Mavell Evi much, and by extension, me." Draqa explained.

Krystal stared down at the table as "wolf-cursed" brought to mind gruesome images of men transforming into the werewolves of film and folklore. If these hulvoqn were anything that, she wasn't sure she wanted to go with Draqa to the mountains. Besides. . . was she even able to trust Draqa with something like this? He committed treason. He was a criminal. Not to mention, Krystal didn't like the vibes that the Governor gave off. If she went along on this errand that Draqa was doing for him, she was afraid she was going to be led right into harm's way.

"Maybe I should stay here," she said, "People can do that, right?"

Draqa raised his eyebrows. "And have me pay for you to stay here, just for you to be caught? Are you stupid? You don't know any of our languages here. The moment you try to communicate, you will be recognized as an outsider."

"I'm just not comfortable going somewhere dangerous with you. I can figure out my way around without anyone knowing where I'm from until you get back." Krystal said, hoping to reason with the man.

Draqa, however, looked ready to explode. He covered his mouth with his fist. "You should have thought of that before you came here," he growled through his teeth. "I will not risk my own life by letting you stay and do as you please when you clearly can't be trusted to follow even the simple request of staying in your own goddamn realm! I don't want you to come with me any more than you do, but that is how it's going to have to be. I would appreciate if you didn't make this any harder."

Krystal moved back from him, unnerved by his near outburst. "How can I trust you?" she asked.

Draqa countered, "How did you trust me before?"

11

Javis observed the entry to the pub for the eleventh time. He was right on schedule for his meeting with his contractor, but he couldn't actually encourage himself to go inside. All confidence he'd had before disappeared after he was told of Sius Mavell Evi's threat towards him. While Javis was certain that the Governor couldn't know who he was, and his contractor certainly didn't yet, Javis wasn't sure how long that would last now that the Governor was on the lookout.

Talara had wanted to go with Javis today to ensure he was safe, but he couldn't justify her getting involved. He had agreed instead to see her after to tell her how things went. Now he second guessed that decision just a little bit. If things went horribly wrong, Talara was always better in a fight than he was. But it was too late turn around and get her now. Javis just hoped that the glamor he wore over his usual one would work the way he intended and make him forgettable to those who didn't know him.

He gathered his courage and stepped inside. The pub was a large and cozy place, warmed by a fire glowing on the hearth. Javis sat at the bar.

"There's a familiar face!" the bartender said, leaning on the counter. "It's been a while. What can I get you?"

Javis gave him a curt nod. "I'm here on business today, maybe later," he said, looking around at the other patrons.

A sylfan and a satyr sat close and whispered passionately in each other's ears. A couple of elves grouped together at the bar on Javis' left. A human-looking fellow sat by himself at a table near the back.

"You meeting someone?" the bartender asked.

Javis nodded, his eye falling on the blond elf sitting at the table in the corner. His lower eyes were wrapped in bandages. He made eye-contact with Javis and straightened in his chair.

"I believe I found him," Javis said.

He made his way over to his contractor and sat in front of him. The elf looked him over and scowled.

"You?" he said disbelievingly.

"Were you hoping for someone else?" Javis asked.

"I didn't think I risked my life for some *nal* ambassador," the elf said.

Javis bit his tongue before replying. It wouldn't do him any good to get offended. He looked over the elf's bandages, also done around one of his hands where two fingers should have been. They were new and tightly wrapped.

"Could nothing be done?" he asked.

The elf simply scoffed.

"Then you have my deepest apologies," he said, "and my gratitude. I know from experience how painful it is." For just a moment he revealed the damage to his right eye.

The scowl on his contractor's face deepened. "I want double."

His request didn't come as a surprise, and Javis was relieved he came prepared. This situation may have been new to him, but those motivated by coin were generally predictable.

"As you should after what you have been through," Javis said. He glanced about the pub as he placed a large sack on the table. The elf reached for it, but Javis held it firm. "But first, I want to know what you found."

The elf kept his hand by the coin but pulled out a marble-sized glass device that could have been mistaken for a cabochon from a distance.

"Here. I was able to record most of Sius Mavell Evi's meeting before I was caught."

"Play it for me," Javis said.

The elf retrieved an aspectacaster from his pocket and pressed the Glass into a divot on the back of the rhombic device.

Sius Mavell Evi's voice crackled from the speakers of the aspectacaster. He spoke with someone, but the other voice was too quiet, and the audio too muffled for Javis to discern who it was. They spoke of a plan, and the Minister, and a hulvoq, and Councilwoman Ilriel Vasiir. They were discontent.

Javis listened intently, hoping the Governor would give away just what exactly it was that he was planning, but then he called for someone called "Draqa." Javis could only assume this was the man whom his contractor had the misfortune of fighting. He didn't recognize the man as anyone significant, but he knew the name from another folktale in the clans. He couldn't think why anyone would name their child after such an ill-fated character.

The audio ended. It wouldn't be enough.

"Who was he meeting with? Did you see?" Javis asked.

"I didn't get to wait around to find out," the elf said.

Javis muttered and ran his hand through his hair, frizzing his curls slightly. He couldn't ask the elf to go out and get more information for him, but he couldn't give the Glass to Phar or the Board with so little context.

"If you don't need anything else, I'd like to leave," the elf said.

Javis started to slide over the coin then stopped. "Wait. Tell me about the man who did that to you—Draqa. Was he a drād?"

The elf huffed impatiently. "No, he was a nal like you—" Tilting his head, the elf suddenly looked very interested in Javis. He leaned across the table. "Just like you, actually. I didn't think it before cause he has this nasty scar across his face."

Javis leaned back, uneasy. "You mean part naol?" he asked.

The elf shook his head. "I mean he looks just like you. Same eyes, same hair. You even look the same height." He laughed. "It seems you have an imposter on your hands ambassador."

It didn't seem possible. He rarely had contact with any yilura, and even then, he would know if one had gotten ahold of his blood in order to become him. Still, there was only one way to know for sure.

"What, ah, kind of scar did he have?" Javis asked.

The elf thought a moment. His answer was even more impossible. "I don't know for sure. He looked like he got a face full of firework."

Pocketing the Glass, Javis thanked the elf and gave him his money. The elf went on his way. Javis leaned back in his chair, his mind reeling. A man who looked like him, who worked for Sius Mavell Evi. A man who looked like him and had a *burn* scar. Javis refused to believe it. It was impossible. It was a coincidence.

Javis flagged down the bartender. "I think I need that drink now."

Talara came for Javis an hour later. She stood above him, her arms crossed. Javis pried his face from his hands to look up at her. Her lips twisted in a rather unbecoming scowl and her eyes narrowed. It took Javis a moment to realize what would have her so upset, then he quickly sat up and rubbed his eyes.

"I'm so sorry, I must have lost track of time," he muttered.

"Did you even *meet* with him?" Talara's voice bit, and he cringed.

"I did," Javis said.

"And?"

Javis laughed bitterly. "And it was useless. The Board will never listen to something so sparse. Not from me, anyway."

Talara grabbed Javis' empty mug away from him. "So, you wallow in drinks and feel sorry for yourself?"

"Well—" Javis started.

"You promised me that you would stop! Disyr, Javis, I thought something happened to you!"

Javis massaged his temples. "Please, not so loud. Someone may hear you." Although, any patrons in this place were sure to already suspect he had a problem.

Talara grabbed his arm and yanked him to his feet. He stumbled into her. She paid the bartender for him and dragged him outside, then she silently escorted him back to his home. He could feel her fuming next to him the entire walk. He stuffed his hands in his pockets and kept his head down.

When they reached his home, Talara sat him down with a large cup of water.

"You promised," she repeated.

"I know, I know," Javis sighed.

"Do you? Or do I need to remind you of what happened to your father?" Talara said.

"I'm *not*—" Javis stopped himself before he yelled. He tried again, calmer. "I'm not my father."

Talara looked at him, her eyebrows knit. Javis ignored her and drank his water. Talara grabbed a chair from the kitchen to sit next to him.

"Tell me what happened today," she said.

Javis was almost too annoyed to tell her. But then he finally asked, "Have you heard of someone called Draqa?"

Talara hesitated. "I've not seen him myself, but his name is well known in Talnoq-Vyn," she said.

"What do people say about him?"

"Not good things. There's a reason they call him Draqa. I do not know how many rumors I've heard of him killing someone on behalf of the Governor," Talara muttered. "Did something happen with him?"

Javis explained what his contractor had told him in the pub

about Draqa's appearance. The news of a yilura pretending to be someone else would have been concerning to most, regardless of how infrequently it actually happened. But Javis and Talara both knew that he wasn't upset because a yilura was pretending to be *him*.

"How could anyone have taken your brother's blood? You said he died years ago," Talara said when Javis' explanation was finished.

"I don't know," Javis said. He had been thinking about it all day now, but he couldn't make any sense of it. He had seen the body, he had watched it get buried. There hadn't been a moment where Javis had taken his eye off it. Yet, Draqa's existence said otherwise.

"I think I'm going to look into him," he said. "At the very least, I may be able to use him as the rest of the proof I need to make the Board listen to me about Sius Mavell Evi."

Talara shook her head. "You shouldn't. The elf you hired is proof of that being a bad idea."

Javis took her hand in his and ran his thumb over the back of it to reassure her. "You know I'm not the kind of person to back out of things halfway."

Talara sighed and pulled her hand away. "I wish you were. You are going to hurt yourself one day." She stood and returned her chair to the kitchen. Javis followed her.

"I need to get back so I can rest before I leave tomorrow," she said.

"My bed's big enough for two," Javis offered. Even in his mood, he couldn't resist a suggestive smirk.

Talara looked less than amused. "I expect to see you at the station in the morning, unless you're too hungover for it."

She left Javis to brood. He sat a while, thinking. Was Sius Mavell Evi the reason why a yilura was pretending to be his brother? Even if he wasn't, he had to know something.

There was only one person Javis could think of to ask about this. It was risky, given his close relationship to the Governor, but Javis trusted Averil Monarain like a brother.

He tapped in the numbers on the glowing screen of his aspectacaster and waited. The device remained silent for a moment, Javis feared Averil was away, then a flickering image of a black-haired man with a ponytail appeared above the aspectacaster.

"Javis. I wasn't expecting to hear from you today," Averil said. Despite his smile, he grumbled stuffily. His four green eyes were red, and heavy bags sat underneath them. His normally close-trimmed beard showed the first signs of growing out of control.

"How are you?" Javis said. The last time he had spoken with his friend was almost two months ago, when Averil contacted him with the news that his son was missing. Javis had still been in the mountains then and could only provide moral support. Looking at his current state, things had clearly not gotten better for him.

"I've . . ." Averil let out a shaky breath and dabbed his eyes with a handkerchief. "I could be better. Zalé's still missing. They haven't been able to find him. I have so little time to look for him in a day, and if I spend much more time away from work, they may fire me," he croaked.

Javis hesitated. "I apologize if I caught you at a bad time."

Averil shook his head and straightened himself up. "There's no helping it. I appreciate being able to hear from you. What can I help you with?"

"I was hoping to meet with you. I have some things I need to speak with you about."

"We can't talk now?" Averil asked.

"It would be better, I think, if we spoke in person. I promise I won't take up too much of your time."

Averil nodded slowly. "I know you wouldn't ask if it wasn't important. I'm getting back into town tomorrow by train. Meet me at the station, and we can talk then."

Javis thanked him graciously. He bid Averil a good afternoon and let him get on with his day. Averil's timing could not have been more perfect, since Javis was going to be at the station seeing Talara off that same morning.

He sat back in his chair, pondering how he might bring up the subject of Draqa to Averil. He couldn't ask him to spy on Governor Sius Mavell Evi, but it was possible Averil knew something about the Governor's relationship to Draqa. Averil could clear up this mess.

Javis closed his eyes. He could hear the bells of the Kerevel distantly ringing. The familiar sound brought him back to the days in his youth when he had attended his schooling there. Had things gone differently, he would have gone on to become a scholar of sacred texts and magics.

In his reminiscing, Javis got up and started searching through the stacks of papers on the bookshelf in his study. They were very unorganized, but he soon found what he was looking for hidden among the papers at the bottom.

The certificate was worn after sixteen years of age, but it was still intact, and the writing was mostly legible. The words were plain as day:

Name of deceased: Jair Zevos, 17

Date of death: 13, May, 1,996

Cause of death: Arson—found with severe burns, possible smoke inhalation.

Draqa was not Javis' brother. Jair was dead. Javis had seen the body with his own eyes. The thought of someone going around murdering people while pretending to be his dead brother left a sour taste in his mouth. If impersonating a dead man was convenient, why, oh why did it have to be Jair? Such a thing would only ruin his name further. But. . .a part of Javis couldn't help but entertain the impossible idea that this Draqa character really was his brother. He didn't know what scared him more.

The next morning, Javis stood at the train station expectantly waiting for Averil to arrive. Talara had already left, warning Javis to keep himself out of trouble. He'd only half-heartedly agreed and gave her a parting wink. She shook her head in disapproval, but she smiled anyway.

He shuffled his feet and breathed into his hands. Just in the days since he visited Arkaven, the air temperature had greatly decreased. Today however, seemed especially cold, enough that Javis needed to wear a heavy coat. He shivered and became impatient.

A passenger train finally pulled into the station. Folks of different kinds deboarded, including Averil. He greeted Javis with a brotherly hug.

"It really has been too long, my friend," he cheered. He seemed to be in a slightly better mood than the day before, though his exhaustion showed in the way his shimmering, sylfan wings drooped behind him.

Javis grinned. "It has. I only wish we were meeting at a better time for you."

Averil waved him off. "Thank you, but I told you there's no helping it. Now what about you? How are those drād you love visiting so much?"

"I'm very well, all things considered. It's good to finally be home after so long."

"You were there for a year, weren't you?"

"One and seven months," Javis corrected.

"Goodness, I don't know how you do it. They have such strict rules there."

"I don't mind it, and they seem to like me."

"I'm surprised at you, with how much you, well, you know. Aren't they rather prudish in the clans?"

Javis raised an eyebrow. Averil gave him a look.

"Is it not true?"

"The dragons aren't *that* bad. Don't believe everything you hear about them. They're just selective when it comes to people outside of their own. Past traumas and all that," Javis said. "That's hardly any different from the rest of the fae, you know that."

Averil smirked. "Right. Whereas you're indiscriminate as long as a person is an adult and breathing," he teased, "or has your criteria begun to include the still-warm?"

Javis cuffed Averil over the head. Averil laughed, shoving him away.

"You, my friend, are disgusting," Javis scoffed. Averil only laughed more.

"I jest, you know that," he said. His eyes were a-light with his laughter, although it only lasted for a moment. He sighed. "Anyway, what did you want to discuss?"

They walked through the city, and Javis delicately explained his recent findings on Governor Sius Mavell Evi and Draqa, who may or may not have been a yilura. Averil was silent while he spoke, and he would have thought Averil's mind had wandered off, if it weren't for the deep green eyes constantly trained on his own. Only once was his attention stolen away when they passed a light post with a poster on it. He paused to tear it down before they continued on. Still, he did not speak, even when Javis had finished.

"I hoped the rumours would not prove to be true," Averil finally said dejectedly.

Javis put a hand on his shoulder. "I understand it must be hard to accept. I know how close the two of you are."

Averil put a hand over his face. "He's helped me so much over the years. He's like a father to me," he muttered.

"I know. I'm sorry."

Averil went silent again, longer this time. Javis did not push him until he spoke again.

"I think I can help you with Draqa," he said.

Javis perked up. "Anything will help."

"I haven't met him myself, but Governor Sius Mavell Evi likes to keep him nearby. I think he lives with Sius Mavell Evi's other servants."

"So, Draqa is a servant."

Averil nodded. "Sius Mavell Evi always sends him on errands whenever I visit."

"Do you know what kind?" Javis pried further.

"Unfortunately, no. Trivial things if I wanted to guess. But if you want to find out for yourself, going to the Vyn would be your best bet," Averil hesitated. "Actually, I might be able to arrange a meeting with him for you if you think it would be worth it."

Javis reacted with surprise. "You would do that? Even though. . ."

"I won't lie and pretend I don't want him to be innocent, but I want the truth even more. If it turns out that he's guilty of what you claim, that is how it will have to be."

Javis took Averil's hand in both of his and shook it. "This means the world to me. Thank you, Averil."

Javis planned to visit Talnoq-Vyn in two weeks. Averil promised he would try to get a meeting arranged for Javis with the Governor. Hopefully light would then be shed on his actions and the man who he had working for him. All Javis would have to do was make sure Sius Mavell Evi didn't suspect anything.

Javis and Averil stopped in front of Averil's house before parting ways. Another poster was tacked to the front door. It depicted a shriveled face with white eyes. *Beware the Deceivers*, it read.

Averil grumbled and tore it down, ripping it to pieces.

"Damn propaganda," he muttered. Javis gave him a sympathetic look.

"Kerevel Tul is the only place in Erothel where yilura are safe. They don't need this shit getting shoved in their faces," Averil continued. He shook his head with a dramatic sigh. "I'll let you know if I'm able to secure the meeting."

Javis once again thanked him profusely.

"Oh, and Averil," he spoke up before his friend went inside.

"Yes?"

"Don't worry too much about Zalé. The boy's smart for his age. He'll be all right."

Averil tossed the poster shreds off his porch.

"You know his smarts aren't the reason I worry."

12

KRYSTAL FOLLOWED DRAQA back through the streets of Talnoq-Vyn, trying hard to keep up with him. He had a few more things to buy before they left, and he mentioned something about renting horses because the vehicles weren't built to go off the roads.

As the day grew busier, the streets became more crowded, at which point Draqa practically dragged Krystal along by the arm at times. "Pirates," was the only explanation he gave.

Once again, people grew wary when they saw Draqa. This time it was more than just the shopkeepers. Krystal finally questioned Draqa about this.

"You're a bit well known around here, are you? People are acting like they're afraid of you."

Draqa shrugged. "They have reason to. I work for the Governor. And I don't know if you've noticed, but I'm not exactly pleasant to look at."

"Yeah, we established that, I think. But what do you do for

him?"

"I'm just a servant."

Just a servant indeed. Krystal gave Draqa a skeptical look but didn't pry any further.

By the time Draqa bought the necessary supplies, the sun was already past its midpoint in the sky, and they still needed to get a horse. Draqa lead Krystal quickly past a gathering of people. The commotion stole her attention.

"Oon deuth jaskith! Gluq I'tseg steluq?" A burly street vendor held a boy with matted black hair by his wrist. The boy looked like he might have been nalingur, if not fully human. He tried in vain to escape.

"*Ich noon-wythe stelin*!" he yelped, "*Ich geim ijineq!*"

Krystal moved to get a better look at what was happening. The vendor grabbed something—food it looked like—from the boy's pocket and held it up for everyone to see.

"*Steluth! Oon tapetseq guru!*" he shouted at the boy. The boy cowered.

Krystal felt a tug on her sleeve. "We have to go," Draqa quietly reminded from behind her.

"What's going on over there?" she asked.

"He caught the child stealing," Draqa said.

"Shouldn't we do something?"

"Not our problem. Come."

Krystal began following Draqa again when she heard the boy shriek. She looked back to see that the vendor had pinned the boy's arm to his table and held a knife high above it. Krystal couldn't stand to watch what was about to unfold. She ran to the vendor and yanked the boy away.

"Noon!" she cried. At least, she hoped that was what she understood as the word for 'no.'

The vendor stared at her, his actions momentarily halted. He finally asked something gruffly.

"Uh—" Krystal started. The boy nodded frantically.

"Yis, yis. Kit Muma'in gur," he said.

The vendor grumbled and looked directly at Krystal. He pointed at the boy with his knife, saying something else she couldn't understand. When Krystal didn't answer, he repeated himself, looking expectant.

Krystal looked at the boy, then smiled apologetically. She shook her head and pointed to her ear, hoping the vendor would think she was deaf.

The vendor glanced at her ear and scowled. *"Oon nal guru?"*

From his expression, Krystal wasn't sure if it was a good idea to agree or not. She didn't have a chance to figure out an answer before a heavy hand landed on her shoulder. She jumped in fright.

"Ich bleetag pevish sargei grejee wonsgorin, bot Tafath Sius Mavell Evi novol me rounuv." Draqa grated out. A chill went up Krystal's spine.

The street vendor lost all confidence at Draqa's sudden appearance. He muttered something unintelligible and averted his gaze. *"Oh . . .Ve gutarum'hin gurvel?"*

"Gurgorvel," Draqa said. The warning in his voice was enough to make the other back down entirely.

Krystal felt Draqa's hand clench around the fabric of her tunic, and she and the boy were steered away from the vendor. Draqa didn't let go of either of them until they were a far distance from the crowd. Draqa stopped suddenly, tossing Krystal and the boy forward. The boy clung to Krystal fearfully.

"If you want to travel with me, you need to listen to everything I tell you. If I say not to get involved in another's affairs, I expect you to do just that!"

Krystal had to look away from his burning eyes. "I couldn't just let him get hurt. He's just a kid," she mumbled.

"He's a thief! *Sujorqr—*" Draqa gestured in a stiff cutting motion, "—is what happens to people who steal!"

Krystal stepped back, pulling the boy close. "Well, he's safe now. Nothing bad happened and the guy over there didn't suspect anything," she said.

The boy looked up at her and then at Draqa with his round, hazel eyes, confusion written all over his dirty face. *"Ivog ketivethur?"* he whispered.

Draqa sent the boy a glare that shut him up instantly. Draqa's clenched fists trembled.

"And what if he *did*? What if he did suspect something, or I wasn't able to get you out of there?" He paused and took a deep breath. "A random child is not that important."

Krystal opened her mouth to retort, but her words failed her. Would Draqa have really preferred to let the boy get hurt? Was he really that cruel? Krystal glanced back in the direction they came, the thought making her sick.

When she looked back at Draqa, her face shifted into a steely glare. "Does it matter?" she challenged. "None of that happened, so you shouldn't dwell on it. Now we should try to find his parents and get him inside somewhere. I mean, just look at him—he's freezing."

Draqa looked away and paced in front of her. He huffed, then crouched in front of the boy.

"*Ivog nim'ur?*" he asked.

The boy held on to Krystal tighter. ". . .Zalé," he whispered.

Draqa looked up at Krystal. "That was his name."

Krystal nodded in approval. "Good. Now ask him where his parents are."

Draqa relayed the question. Zalé moved from Krystal and stepped in a circle. He pointed in a random direction.

"*Ihn Pupa'in orv Kerevel Tul.*"

Draqa once again looked at Krystal. "We are not going all the way to Kerevel Tul."

Krystal waved him off. "Ask how he got here."

Zalé replied with fear in his voice. This elicited a growl of frustration from Draqa, and he explained the boy had been kidnapped.

"You see, *vara* Monarain? There's nothing we can—"

"*Nim'in Monarain,*" Zalé said.

Draqa paused. "*Ivog?*"

"*Nim'in Zalé Monarain.*"

Krystal's eyes widened.

"His name is Monarain," Draqa confirmed. The irritation in his voice disappeared in an instant. "*Iss Pupa'ur Averil?*" he asked.

Zalé nodded. Draqa went quiet for a long moment. He stood, his eyes not meeting Krystal's.

"We should. . . go back to the *huum*," he muttered.

Krystal waited outside the bathroom while Draqa helped Zalé set up his bath. She was relieved that Draqa changed his mind about the boy. He even rented a pair of rooms so Zalé could rest, but Krystal had a feeling that if Draqa hadn't found out who Zalé was, he would have insisted that the boy get left on the street. Not that they had a plan with what to do with him either way. At first, Draqa wanted to contact Averil so he could get both Zalé and Krystal off his hands.

Unfortunately, Zalé didn't know how to get ahold of Averil's aspectacaster and there was no other way to contact him. There wasn't a lot of time for Draqa to ask around to see if anyone in the Port knew Averil, either and according to Draqa, the authorities were unlikely to help them in any reasonable amount of time. It was looking like Zalé was going to have to come along with them, something Krystal had to agree wasn't the best idea.

After a few minutes, Draqa left the bathroom and leaned against the wall.

"I told him to come get me if he needs anything," he said.

"Thank you."

"I'll buy him some food after he's done, and tomorrow I will buy him warm clothes."

"So, he's coming with us?" Krystal asked.

"Yes." Draqa's head fell back, as though the idea hurt his very soul. Krystal leaned next to him.

"I'm going to guess you don't really like kids," she said.

"I despise them."

"Why?"

Draqa gestured at the bathroom door. "Children—kids—they're noisy. They're too wild, and whine about petty things. Little demons, like the vendor put it. . . and they're so mean to each other, and only get worse as they get older," he said. His gaze dropped to the floor.

Krystal tilted her head forward. "Kids aren't *that* cruel."

Draqa gave her no response, but the way he drew his arms inward was enough of an answer for her. She kept talking. "Well, I guess they can be sometimes, but the same goes for adults, wouldn't you say?"

". . .just keep the boy out of my way."

"I can do that."

The bath cleaned Zalé up well. His chin-length hair now had a silky sheen to it. Freckles sparsely dotted his face, not unlike the ones that covered Krystal's own.

Draqa went downstairs to order Zalé some food to be brought up to the room he would be sharing with Krystal. Zalé seemed content when he was finally able to eat something, and the food was finished off within minutes of it being placed before him.

His trust in Krystal and Draqa must have increased as well because he began talking excitedly to Krystal despite her being unable to understand a word he was saying. Nonetheless, it was sweet. Draqa translated just enough for Krystal to learn that Zalé was ten, and that he was very excited at the prospect of having an aunt. Krystal, too, was excited by the revelation.

She had been so focused on the idea of simply having a brother that the thought of him having a child of his own had never crossed her mind. Perhaps it was because she had the subconscious notion that Averil would somehow be like her. She herself loved kids, but the prospect of having them made her uneasy. Her mother may have been previously uninjured, but she still died giving birth to her. But of course, Averil wouldn't have a reason like that to fear having kids.

Regardless, Krystal found herself loving Zalé already. He asked many other questions, until Draqa eventually excused himself to bed. He encouraged Krystal and Zalé to do the same.

Krystal couldn't help but lie awake, her thoughts still on the boy. What bothered her was how he said he had arrived in the Port. If he really had been kidnapped, how did he escape? Were the kidnappers still looking for him? And. . . how long had he been away from home? She observed Zalé's sleeping figure in the other bed, wishing she could ask him herself and frustrated she couldn't understand him. If she was going to be in Arai for a while, she would need to learn Yrlun. . .She was going to have to make Draqa teach her whether he liked it or not.

***

A boy with a mud-caked face stared at Draqa through the pond. The child's lip was busted, blood bubbling, dribbling onto his taste buds. Wet streaks cleaned his cheeks in trails leading from his eyes. His shoulders shook with silent cries. His hands rubbed numbly at his face in an attempt to cleanse himself of the hate that the other children felt for him.

This had been going on for about two years now, off and on since Draqa's three-person family moved to Baren. Everything had gone so well at first. It was his mother's hometown. Her family was welcoming to his. The rest of the townspeople were not as friendly; Draqa's father was a human, after all. This itty-bitty fact meant that Draqa and his brother were nalingur. Nal. *Due to sour feelings of the past, humans were disliked in some places and nalingur, the disgraces that they were, were hated. This hatred, added onto Draqa's quiet and passive personality, made him the perfect target for bullying.*

Why did they do this to him? Draqa always kept to himself, he never spoke out of turn, he was kind to almost everyone. His father said they were jealous. As though a dead mother and going home with purple eyes and blue skin was something to be desired.

Kids could be cruel.

Draqa gave up cleaning his face in favour of staring into the crystalline waters of the pond. Pretty little fish circled each other, dancing an aquatic ballet. A sickly fish lost its step, falling behind. One of the bigger ones lashed out at it, the others followed suit. Without so much as a cry, or even any struggle, the fish sank to the bottom of the pond, lifeless. Was that the destiny of the weak?

"Jair?"

Draqa started at the hand that touched his shoulder. He turned with saucer-like eyes, then calmed.

"H-hey, Javis."

Although he didn't need to from the visible state that Draqa was in, Javis asked, "You all right?"

Forcing a smile, Draqa replied, "Yeah. . . I'm fine. Nothing but . . .sunshine and daisies over here." His voice came out mangled. The smile fell with a quivering lip, and he shook his head. A new rush of tears left his eyes.

"What did I do, Javis? They don't even treat you like this! Why am I the one they pick on?"

Javis sat down next to him. "I don't know. I really don't know. People are just stupid like that."

Draqa looked back into the pond, remembering the fish and their brutality towards the weak one. Was that his destiny? He didn't want to live his life being the target of others.

"I want to die." The words came out without him realising.

"What? What are you talking about?" Javis asked, horrified.

"What's the point in living if I'm just going to be pushed down by others? If I'm just going to keep falling back? Everyone hates me and all I ever seem to do is get in the way."

Javis grew angry, taking Draqa by the shoulders. "Don't you talk like that! Don't ever talk like that! You are worth more than those bullies could ever know, got it? If you—if you killed yourself or something—that would be wasting your life!" He let go.

Draqa ceased his crying, shocked by Javis' outburst. Javis bit his lip. He brought up a hand to Draqa's face and wiped away a tear.

"Besides, I'd miss you. Who else is a better pranking partner than you? I bet, without you, even uncle Alarach would get lonely."

The two brothers sat by the pond until dusk, then Draqa was lead home, where their father was waiting for them with a warm meal. It was a pleasant surprise; Father rarely cooked anymore.

Draqa kicked off his shoes and dropped his jacket on top of them. Javis followed behind and hung it up. Father greeted them both with a hug, pausing at the mud smeared across Draqa's face.

"What happened? You're filthy," he said.

Draqa rubbed his nose. "I tripped, sir."

Father raised an eyebrow. He smoothed the hair atop Draqa's head. "Hurry and clean up, then. You don't want your dinner to get cold."

Father gave Draqa a warm smile that was all too scarce anymore. Draqa forced himself to give one in return and rushed off to the bathroom.

The fish were not forgotten, nor was the bullying, only temporarily pushed behind other, happier, thoughts.

13

THE HEAT BLOWING DOWN from the vents burned the right side of Draqa's face as he stepped back inside the *huum* from the cold. He had gone out early that morning to buy Zalé some warm clothes. He didn't want to have to waste any time leaving Talnoq-Vyn once Krystal and Zalé were awake. It was bad enough that Draqa was already a day behind. The longer he took, the less likely he would be able to catch up with Tolas Ruv Aen, and the more likely he would have to face Sius Mavell Evi's wrath. Neither outcome was very favorable to him.

He dragged the bag of clothing up to the Monarains' shared room and pounded on the door. To his surprise, the door opened mid-knock.

"Good morning," Krystal beamed up at him. She was already fully dressed and ready to go. Draqa peered into the room to see that Zalé was as well. The boy looked up at Draqa and gave him a tiny smile.

"Right. . . Morning. I wasn't expecting either of you to be awake," Draqa said.

Krystal shrugged and let him into the room. "I woke up during the night and couldn't get back to sleep. I figured I'd get Zalé up so we wouldn't have to rush to leave," she said.

Draqa stood silently for a moment, unsure how to react to this gesture.

"I see. Perfect. I have some clothes for *vei* Monarain," he said. He held out the bag of clothing.

Zalé jumped up and ran over. He peeked inside it and clapped his hands. He pulled out the coat Draqa bought for him, and then the winter shirts and pants. A smile stretched from one cheek to the other.

"Thank you!" His eyes twinkled. He took the clothes back to his bed. "Can you turn around?" he asked.

Draqa faced the wall, motioning for Krystal to do the same. He could feel her eyes on him.

"Hey Draqa?" she asked.

"What is it?"

"I'd like to learn your language," she said.

Draqa wasn't sure he heard correctly. "You—I'm sorry, you want to what?"

"Learn your language. Can you teach me?" Krystal earnestly asked.

Draqa wavered. "I. . . know a lot of languages."

Krystal put a hand on her hip. "Oh, you know what I mean. The one you've been speaking with everyone—Yrlun, or whatever you called it."

Draqa considered that. He hated the idea. "I'm not a teacher," he said, "I wouldn't know where to begin."

"That's okay. But I think if I'm gonna be here a while, I need to at least learn *something*. Like, how did you learn English?"

"I had to listen. I've also been visiting the Other Realm for at least eleven years. And there is still a lot I don't know. I'm still learning."

"But that's exactly why you should teach me. I would learn way faster that way, and then I could teach you whatever you don't know," Krystal proposed.

Zalé hopped up between them, interrupting their conversation.

"I'm ready now. Can I have breakfast?" he asked.

Draqa gave Zalé a nod and returned his look to Krystal. She was right; it would be beneficial for the both of them if she learned Yrlun, if Draqa was able to figure out how to teach her.

"I'll think about it."

Instead of more pestering like he expected, Krystal only smiled at him.

"Thanks," she said.

A set of pursed lips was all Draqa was able to muster in return. He brought Krystal and Zalé downstairs to eat. He resisted the urge to rush them; he felt patient now. The three of them were out of the *huum* before the day even started to warm up. They didn't have to wait long for the stables to open, either. Draqa brought out three horses, introducing them as Virsh, Feriosh, and a pack horse named Eldoc. Feriosh and Eldoc were property of Sius Mavell Evi, but Virsh was his own. Once Draqa gave Krystal a brief riding lesson, they were finally off.

The trio rode throughout the day. Draqa, atop Virsh, led Eldoc, never too far ahead of Krystal and Zalé. He wanted to ensure that Krystal managed all right after such a short riding lesson. He understood there was no real need for horses in the Other Realm, what with "cars" and "ATVs" and other modes of transportation, but he still couldn't believe that Krystal had never even been close to a horse before. Zalé, on the other hand, was a natural.

When it came to be evening, Draqa stopped them in a small clearing bedded with broad, yellow and orange leaves. They had entered the beginning of the forest. The trees were still short here, but as they continued the trees would eventually grow taller and denser, until the canopy blocked out the sky.

Draqa gave Krystal the task of gathering wood and starting a fire while he secured the horses and started setting up the tent. He watched her struggle with the flames from his safe distance away. The evening wind was dead set on blowing out each and every match Krystal tried to light. Zalé laughed at her.

"I think the fire hates you," he said.

Draqa's lips upturned. He, too, found Krystal's efforts to be amusing.

Zalé soon left Krystal to her struggles, unrolling a blanket and dragging it inside the tent once Draqa finished setting it up a few feet from where the fire was meant to be built. Draqa returned to the horses to feed them while he waited for Krystal to complete her own task. Of course, Draqa could use magic to start the fire quickly, but truth be told he preferred to avoid that method if he could. Luckily, Krystal built a blazing pyre that steadily consumed tinder before nightfall. She looked around with a frown, her brow furrowed. She stood and turned about more frantically.

Draqa stepped from his hiding place behind the horses, causing the woman to jump.

"I'm right here," he said smoothly. "You actually started a fire. I will admit, I didn't think you knew how to do it." He sat against a tree some distance behind Krystal. She faced him, sitting back down slowly.

"Of course I do. I've been camping before," she said. The awful frown on her face deepened.

Draqa rested his head against the tree trunk. "You're more useful than I thought, then—"

"I thought you left us," Krystal interrupted.

Left? Draqa cocked his head. "Why. . . would you think I would do something like that?"

"I didn't see you. And you don't want me here anyway, or Zalé," Krystal said. She barley spoke above a whisper.

A snicker left Draqa's mouth before he could stop it. "And leave Sius Mavell Evi's horses? And all of our supplies?" He meant this as a joke, but it only served to make Krystal look even more upset. Draqa strained to offer her a reassuring smile.

"All right, all right. I might say things out of my. . . anger, but I would never actually do something that cruel." Even as he said this, he had to wonder if it was true, recalling how he very nearly threw Krystal over the cliff. Then again, those weren't *his* desires. . . only the influenced ones.

"Promise?" Krystal asked.

"Promises are a dangerous thing to make here. But if you trust me, that's one thing you'll never have to worry about from me," Draqa said. Internally, he did promise. He wouldn't abandon Krystal, at least, not before he had her in a safe place.

The last light of day quickly vanished, thousands upon thousands of twinkling stars appearing in the sky. Krystal stared up at them, breathing out a sigh of awe. The night air grew colder. Draqa wrapped his coat more tightly around himself and huffed. He was tempted to join Zalé in the tent. He felt a twinge of envy towards Krystal, now laying directly in front of the fire, obviously unaffected by the cold or her proximity to the flames.

Draqa suppressed a shiver and stood.

"You can come over here, if you want," Krystal said. She patted next to her. "There's still room."

Draqa eyed the fire. "Thank you but no. The tent will be warm enough."

"Are you sure? You look really cold."

"I'm sure."

Careful to avoid stepping on Zalé, Draqa entered the tent and lay just so he could keep an eye on Krystal and the fire through the opening. Krystal stifled a huge yawn and continued to gaze up at the stars. Draqa closed his eyes.

Just when he was beginning to fall asleep, he heard Krystal ask, "Did you have any siblings?"

Draqa grumbled to himself. What did she need to know that for?

"I was just wondering because you seem like you might've," Krystal continued, "and I was wondering what growing up with Averil could have been like."

The crackling of the fire filled the silence between them. Krystal didn't really need to know about Draqa's personal life, did she? There was nothing wonderful to say about the remaining member of his family. All those memories were better left in the past. Even thinking about them for a moment made his chest ache.

"Hm. I guess you're asleep," Krystal whispered. Draqa heard her stand and enter the tent. She brushed against him as she laid in the spot between him and Zalé.

Draqa peeked an eye open to watch her as she shifted around to make herself comfortable. Eventually, she turned right to face him. He closed his eye again and huffed.

"I have a brother. We don't get along, and he may as well be dead to me. You're lucky you didn't grow up with a sibling," he said.

Krystal remarked with a hum. "Do you have similar names by any chance?"

Draqa almost didn't realize what she meant at first, and then his heart skipped a beat. How could she have known? No. That was a ridiculous question. He knew exactly how Krystal knew, and he should have expected it.

"Go to sleep, Monarain," he said. He squeezed his eyes tighter, willing himself to fall asleep as well. It was no use. His thoughts were now too focused on the past.

14

"So, what exactly is a hulvoq?" Krystal asked the following morning while Draqa made breakfast.

"Someone who's wolf-cursed," Draqa replied without looking up.

"Yes, but what does that mean? Are they actually, I mean, do they *really* become werewolves?"

"*Where* wolves?" Draqa repeated. He glanced at Krystal a couple of times.

Krystal explained, "Werewolves. They're people in folklore who become wolves during the full moon."

Draqa's jaw dropped a touch. "Ah. The Hulvoqn are very similar." He finished cooking and handed out the food to Krystal and Zalé. He sat back with his own.

After a few quiet bites, he continued, "Hulvoqn came about when a man from the Other Realm tried to trick a wolf who offered aid to him. The wolf turned out to be a sorceress, or a goddess depending on who you ask, and she cursed him. For a night every month, he had no choice but turn into a horrible monster and spread his curse. At least, that's what our books say is what most likely happened. The incident was hundreds of years ago, so no one knows for sure."

As she thought about it, Krystal realized she knew the story. She recognized it from a tune she and a few other kids would sing while playing jump-rope in elementary school. She hummed quietly, trying to think of the tune, but it had been too long since she had last heard it. She recited the first verse,

"Two young brothers, long ago, farmed the land where apples grow."

Draqa tilted his head. "What was that?"

"Oh, nothing really. I just know a similar story," Krystal said.

"Do you?"

Krystal nodded. "I can't remember exactly how it goes, but it's about a young farmer who tried to trick a witch who had offered to help his failing crops. She cursed him and his brother, turning them both into wolves."

To her surprise, Draqa smiled. "I never thought our realms would still have the same stories to share. But hulvoqn don't become anything like ordinary wolves."

"What do they become?" Krystal asked. She wasn't expecting Draqa to grimace.

"With any luck, you won't have to find out," he said.

Krystal suppressed a shudder as her imagination got the better of her. She again couldn't help but wonder why they had to go to where the hulvoqn were in the first place.

"What does Sius want that's so important?"

Instead of answering, Draqa stood and patted the dirt off the back of his pants. He looked around.

"We should leave soon. I want us to get as far as we can today. Hurry and finish your food," he said.

Krystal began to protest, but her companion was already off to take down the tent. Krystal huffed and shoveled down the rest of her food. Once Zalé was finished as well, she cleaned up and helped pack. Soon after, the trio was off once again.

They road for quite some time. The clip-clopping of the horses' hooves lulled Krystal, but the chill in the air kept her awake. Zalé, on the other hand, seemed to have dozed off and was leaned back against her. On the horse beside them, Draqa remained silent. He seemed to be a quiet man in general, but Krystal couldn't help but worry that he was avoiding conversation with her because of her question about his brother the night before. She had tested her luck, asking about his family after Draqa had reacted so badly to the first time she had a dream about him.

It wasn't as though she could control it. It wasn't as though she *wanted* to dream about Draqa's past, either. She didn't have so much as a guess as to what was causing them. Though it made her wonder, were the dreams she would occasionally have about other people also real? She never paid the thought any mind until now. Perhaps, if she tried hard enough, she would be able to control the dreams before they got too out of hand.

The relative silence in the group continued on as they travelled throughout the week. Conversation was attempted by both Zalé and

Krystal on multiple occasions, but it always devolved into simple games with each other, as Draqa was an unwilling translator and cut short any talk they tried to make with him. Krystal's favorite game quickly became one where she would point at objects and say their names in English, and Zalé would repeat back the names in Yrlun. Maybe it was a bit inaccurate, but Krystal learned plenty. She learned that horse was "*gerat*" and snow was "*eena,*" and many other things. Nothing she learned could actually aid her in having a coherent conversation with anyone, though.

During the nights, Draqa would sometimes break his silence. He didn't often say more than simple instructions. If he did, he spoke mostly to Zalé. But there were still a few other times that Krystal would be surprised.

"Did you like working at the bookstore?" he once asked.

Krystal did but told Draqa about how she wanted to travel and document her experiences. She seemed to be able to hold his interest, and he asked about which places she would want to go to first.

"I haven't decided," she replied. "I like Slavic folklore, so maybe somewhere like Russia or the Czech Republic."

Another time, Krystal expressed a mild interest in how Erothel's government functioned. This sent Draqa into a long-winded explanation of the country's politics, and an even longer history lesson on Erothel and its relations with its neighboring countries and the High Council. He became unexpectedly heated when he reached the topic of why the Council was formed, voicing an anger not towards the humans of the past who sent parties into Arai to kill the fae, but towards how the Council had conducted itself around humans ever since. According to him, humans and nalingur weren't the only ones there was a widely held hatred towards; hulvoqn and the shapeshifting yilura were also treated poorly.

"And what do we all have in common? Humans!" Draqa said, throwing up his arms. "We are all related to humans! You and I, Monarain? Nalingur. We're half human. Hulvoqn? The first hulvoq *was* a human. They have a human curse. And yilura? They were *created* by a human.

"The Council might claim their regulations on us are for the good of the people, but we know better. They're afraid, so they stir up hate." Draqa went on to list off a number of ridiculous regulations, from being required to give a baby who's nalingur a human name, and hulvoqn being forced to live outside the cities, to yilura being arrested if they're caught changing into another race without the papers giving them permission to.

"How did humans create the yilura?" Krystal asked.

Draqa went silent in thought, leaving her to listen to the horses before he explained, "A magician was doing experiments on those of the fae who could transform. Drād, caelkin. As I understand, he was trying to create what I think you call a homunculus. Where he failed to create that, he made the yilura instead."

Krystal squirmed in her saddle. "So, what? The rest of the fae or the Council see them as abominations?"

Draqa scoffed. "Monarain, they see all of us as abominations."

Zalé nodded gravely. Draqa was a passionate man, Krystal realized. As long as the topic wasn't himself, she could get him to talk.

After Draqa and Zalé would go to sleep, Krystal would stay up to try to practice gaining control of the dreams she had. She tried meditating and focusing her intents and thoughts, but no matter how hard she tried, she couldn't figure out what to do. Not once did she dream about Draqa again, and she also had no idea whether what she was doing was working or not. She decided the matter couldn't be helped. If she dreamt about Draqa again, she would just have to keep it to herself.

The monotony of travel ended one afternoon at the start of the next week when Draqa slowed his horse to a stop and signaled for Krystal to do the same. They had made it far into the mountains at this point, the forest around them never ending. But now, the sea of trees appeared to disperse abruptly up ahead.

Draqa steered Virsh back around to Krystal.

"Why are we stopping? Is everything okay?" Krystal asked.

Draqa nodded, whispering, "The canyon is ahead. We're here."

Krystal's eyes went wide. "We are? But I don't see anyone."

"The hulvọqn live down below, in the canyon. There are often many patrols up here, however. One should find us soon," Draqa said.

Krystal's voice rose in pitch. "You mean, they already know we're here?"

"It isn't anything to worry about. They won't hurt us. Probably. Now come on."

Draqa began leading Krystal and Zalé east along the tree line onto a set path that followed the direction of the canyon. Krystal found herself trembling, spooking at the smallest of sounds despite being assured they were safe. Hulvoqn were people. Hulvoqn were people. Repeating this to herself helped little. Images of lycanthropes from media filled her head. She never did have the chance to tell Draqa when he asked, but she was *very* afraid of wolves.

"Stop."

Krystal snapped her focus to Draqa. "Huh?" Feriosh was behaving oddly, as were Virsh and Eldoc.

"Gerat'ur anon ress!" Draqa hissed. He leaned over and started to pull on Feriosh's reins, but Zalé was already slowing him down.

Krystal's heartrate quickened. "What's going on?"

Draqa silently directed their attention directly ahead on the path. It was then that Krystal noticed the smell. It was putrid and burned her nostrils. She had the misfortune of leaving meat to rot in her fridge once, but this didn't even compare. Further ahead, there was a red patch of snow and. . . Krystal covered her mouth. Zalé gasped. The dead were scattered across the ground, the earth beneath them dark.

Draqa hopped down from Virsh and took her and Feriosh's reins in hand. He allowed Eldoc to continue behind. He stroked Feriosh's neck and guided the three horses forward. Feriosh shook his head, trying to back up as he grew more restless. Krystal held her breath, sure that the horse would bolt any moment, but Draqa clicked and spoke softly, drawing Feriosh's attention away from the bodies as they passed. Eldoc and Virsh remained relatively calm.

Krystal would have been impressed with Draqa's control over the horses, but her attention was stolen away by the sight of all the bodies they passed. She counted five in total. Most were elves, and one had the distinctive tail of a naol. Their bodies were ripped open, their organs exposed.

Not soon enough, Draqa lead them away from the carnage. Once the horses had relaxed, he stopped and mounted Virsh.

". . . Did a patrol do all of that?" Krystal asked, glancing back.

"It isn't likely to have been anyone else. Many mercenaries and bounty hunter types try to kill hulvoqn. As you can see, they don't typically succeed," Draqa explained. He appeared unbothered.

The path drew closer and closer to the edge of the canyon the further the trio went. Far below was a meandering, thin blue line and small shapes that might have been structures. A nervous laugh escaped Krystal's lips. They were. . . very high. The airy feeling only worsened as they reached a series of switchbacks cut into the side of the canyon, steeply leading down. Here, they dismounted their horses to lead them by hand. Krystal tried to keep up with Draqa despite the shakiness in her legs. Though, if it weren't for her horse and Zalé' s hand clasped tightly around hers, she might have frozen up.

They finally reached the bottom where the path turned back to follow the frozen river upstream. The shapes from before were indeed structures, built over and around the river and up onto the canyon walls. Ladders and rope bridges led from hut to stilted hut. Before they had a chance to enter the village, however, Draqa signaled for Krystal and Zalé to stop. Krystal peered past him and Virsh. Exiting the village was a group of three, headed directly for them.

The newcomers held no visible weapons, but they wore a kind of leather-like armor. Krystal recognized two of them as naols.

Scars traced their faces, but the gray-skinned woman with green scales on her cheekbones was scarred the worst of the three. She stepped right up to Draqa, her lips stretched in a deep scowl. She stood tall, much, much taller than Draqa—at least three heads above his. A pair of horns curled around the sides of her head like a ram's. Draqa looked up at her. He began to speak when the woman punched him in the face.

15

DRAQA BARELY HEARD Krystal's gasp as he stumbled back and grabbed his mouth in pain. He swore.

"We told you what would happen the next time you came here uninvited, Draqa," the drenen hulvoq woman sneered. Her accent grated across her tongue, uninviting like her words.

Draqa sneered and spit blood at the ground. "I'm not even *here* yet," he muttered. He straightened, massaging his jaw. "But if I had known this was how I was going to be greeted, I would have snuck in the back."

"Why are you here? And who are your companions?" the woman demanded.

Draqa glanced back at Krystal, who held Zalé close.

"I'm guiding this woman and her young nephew home," he said.

"So, you take them through the mountains on a pair of horses, far from any village or city?"

Draqa held up his hands, the lies sliding off his tongue. "They're being hunted. Their pursuers are expecting for them to take a common route back to their home. So, I do take them through the mountains."

The drenen woman clearly pondered this. Her iron gaze swept over Zalé and Krystal. "Where are you taking them?"

"I'm afraid it might compromise their safety if I told you," Draqa said.

"If you fear for their safety, why would you bring them here?"

"They need to rest, and they need sanctuary. We've been traveling for days and have had hardly any time to stop. No one would expect to find them here. Besides, the full moon is still days away and I don't believe you would hurt them just for the fun of it," Draqa mused, "That is, assuming you will let us stay a night or two."

He held his breath, hoping he and the others would be allowed in. If they weren't, he didn't have a backup plan. The last thing he wanted was to resort to a violent entry, but he would if he had no other choice.

"Your companions' situation is very unfortunate, but we don't let just anyone stay here. For our *own* safety. Escort them back." The woman directed her two companions at her sides forward.

One came at Draqa and pushed him back. "You heard her. Off you go." He made to push Draqa again, but Draqa hit his arm away.

"Wait a moment, don't be hasty. I can—" Draqa started.

"Duuzran? This one's a yilura." The other naol had pulled Zalé away from Krystal and gripped him by the arm.

Draqa tilted his head, not sure he heard right. "You must be mistaken. We have no yilura with us." Even as he said this, Zalé's wide eyes met his own. The boy had been caught.

"I can smell him. It's faint, but it's there. He's probably only half."

The drenen woman approached Zalé, who cowered.

"Is this true?" she asked.

Zalé shook his head frantically. "No. I'm not a yilura. I'm not."

Duuzran crouched to his level. "You don't have to hide it from us. You're safe here."

Zalé didn't look convinced. Duuzran gave him a pitying look. "Is your father also a yilura? Or your mother?"

". . .mother," Zalé whispered.

"Will you show me? It's safe here."

Zalé took a few deep breaths, then before Draqa's eyes, he changed. His eyes turned white, and his ears grew more pointed. When he opened his mouth to speak, it revealed rows of serrated teeth. Draqa was admittedly relieved; for a moment he thought Zalé might have been a random yilura disguised as the Monarain child.

"Is this okay?" Zalé asked, turning back.

Duuzran smiled. "Yes. It's okay." She stood and turned to Draqa. "You may stay here, but only because of the boy."

Draqa dipped his head in thanks. "We really do appreciate this."

"I'm sure. Know that we'll be keeping an eye on you, Draqa. You had better watch yourself."

Draqa and his group were led into the village. Duuzran sent the others off with the horses once they were taken to a small hut elevated high above the river by a rope bridge that led to the ground.

Before leaving them alone, Duuzran pulled some blankets from a chest and laid them on a cot in the corner. "I will send someone in soon to show you around. Until then, it's best you stay inside. The others won't be happy to see you before they're prepared."

Krystal hounded Draqa almost immediately after the door closed behind Duuzran.

"Did I get that right? Zalé's a yilura?" she demanded.

Draqa immediately clamped his hand over Krystal's mouth and shot a fearful look at the door. *Disyr*, what was the woman thinking? Oh, but Draqa never warned her. Hulvoqn had hearing too keen for him to be comfortable even whispering in her language with her. She let out a muffled huff under his grip, but he didn't release her until he was sure no one heard her. She made a disgusted scrunch of her nose and rubbed her mouth with the back of her hand when he released. Draqa held a finger to his lips.

"Sorry," Krystal muttered, then gestured expectantly at Zalé.

Draqa nodded in confirmation. He eyed Zalé as the boy picked up a blanket and wrapped himself in it, nuzzling his face into the fabric. He sat on the cot. If it weren't for him, Draqa wouldn't have been able to get them inside so easily. He almost thanked him, but he wasn't entirely sure that would have been appropriate.

Krystal seemed to have another question at the edge of her tongue, but Draqa ignored it and sat heavily next to Zalé. He nursed his busted lip with the edge of his sleeve.

Krystal's eyebrows raised and she crouched in front of him.

He inhaled and let out a long sigh. He'd had worse.

Krystal's lips twisted to the side. She hovered her hand near Draqa's, as though asking for permission. He lowered his hand. Krystal's fingers barely pressed into his skin as she observed his mouth. She pulled down on his bottom lip slightly, making him wince.

To Draqa's further alarm, she whispered, "It doesn't look like any teeth got broken," and then, "I'll grab some snow from outside to help with the swelling."

Krystal was out the door and back before Draqa had time to stop her. She held out a tightly packed ball of snow. With some hesitation, Draqa took it from her and held it to his mouth. He held back another wince and tried to relax.

Krystal pulled up a stool from the side of the room and sat across from him. She hummed. Before she could continue to jeopardize their safety with her obnoxious whispering, Draqa hunched to rummage through his bag until he found a pen. He handed it and the back of the photo of Ambassador Zevos to use.

Krystal wrote in her lap. *How are you able to handle it?* She passed the picture back to Draqa.

Draqa's reply to her was slow—he wasn't as practiced with writing in English as he was with reading and speaking it, and his old injuries on his hands made it difficult to be precise with his letters. *Handle what?*

Krystal seemed to be able to read his nearly-illegible writing well enough and passed back the picture with her explanation. *Getting hurt like this. You brushed it off so easily.*

Draqa wasn't sure what to say, certain he had already answered this before. And what else could he say? He had experience and knew how to hide it. Sius Mavell Evi made sure of that.

Still, he wrote, *If you show weakness to the wrong people, they'll take advantage of that weakness. I learned when I need to hide my weakness, and when I can show it.*

A tiny smile flashed over Krystal's lips when she read his words. *I see. Did someone teach you how?*

They ran out of room on the back of the picture. Draqa turned it over, nearly writing right on the Ambassador's face, but then deciding instead to answer in the bottom corner of the photo. *Tolas Ruv Aen. The man we're here to see.* Draqa paused. He loathed to read those words for himself. Yes. That aggravatingly quick, no-good traitor was his mentor. Draqa resented that fact every day. But now that he was here to finish the man off, he had no reason to hide it from Krystal. *The Governor wants me to kill him.*

Reading that, Krystal scrunched her face and said aloud, "*Oh.*"

Draqa gave her a warning look. She ducked her head and returned to using the photo.

It's just, is it really a good idea to go after him? Do you even want to?

Draqa tossed the melting ball of snow to the side and wiped the damp from his hand before he took the pen back. *I don't have a choice. And while I'm at it, you and Zalé need to stay out of my way. I don't need one of you getting hurt because you were stupid enough to get involved.* He stuffed the pen and picture back into his bag.

Krystal bit her lip. Perhaps Draqa could have used a different choice of words.

A faun entered the hut about thirty minutes later. They introduced themself as Maer and took Draqa and his companions on a small tour of the village. Maer didn't ask any questions, getting straight to the point: where the dining area was, the kitchens, the communal toilets, etcetera. Draqa paid close attention to the areas they passed, keeping an eye out for Tolas Ruv Aen and areas he might have been hiding.

Unlike in Talnoq-Vyn, the people here weren't afraid to show their dislike of Draqa, many glaring at him or loudly voicing their disgust. Draqa didn't blame them. They hated Sius Mavell Evi almost as much as Minister Lhorsan Phar, albeit for different reasons, and the last time Draqa paid them a visit it went very badly. Although, he couldn't quite remember why. . .

". . .And this hut belongs to Duuzran," Maer pointed to the large, elevated hut they had stopped in front of. "She's the leader here and the one who allowed you to come in," Maer said, "if you need anything, talk to me first, unless it's of dire importance. Dinner is this evening at sunset. If you want food, don't be late."

The faun brought Draqa, Krystal and Zalé back to their hut and left. Krystal tapped Draqa's arm, looking very confused. Draqa sighed and went inside so he could again translate for her in private. He had to admit, translating all the time was getting to be impractical. Once he had taken care of Tolas Ruv Aen, he would take the time to teach Krystal Yrlun.

Dinner that evening was uncomfortable. If it wasn't against the rules, Draqa would have had himself and the others eat in their hut. Apparently, huts were often damaged and destroyed if food was left inside too close to the full moon. They left Draqa's group alone for the most part. A few younger hulvoqn did dare to approach them to speak with Zalé, which Draqa was fine with, but he quickly shut them down when they attempted the same with Krystal.

"She can't speak and can't understand you. Don't even bother."

They muttered that Draqa was rude and sent him dirty looks, but ultimately left. He would rather be rude than dead.

Nearing the end of dinner, Draqa ushered his group back to the guest hut. He grew tense. His hands trembled. He would find Tolas Ruv Aen soon, he could feel it. He waited for Krystal and Zalé to fall asleep, and then waited even longer just to be sure most of the village was as well. When the coast was clear, he tip-toed out of the hut and muttered a spell to muffle his sounds. Once again, he summoned the spell-wolf to help him search.

As he sent the spell-wolf to check each hut, he mentally prepared himself to face Tolas Ruv Aen. He could remember all the elf's tricks, all his moves. The elf was quick, and there was no way Draqa would be able to kill him if Draqa didn't have the element of surprise. Logic told him to attack the elf in his sleep, but pride wanted otherwise.

With every hut he searched, the spell-wolf grew more and more excited, until it bolted for Duuzran's hut. Draqa tore after it, stopping just short of the door. Candlelight shone faintly from underneath. Draqa could hear whispers inside. He wordlessly banished the spell-wolf and worked his way around the hut to the window. It was open. He crouched next to it and listened.

"I've told you, our answer is no," Duuzran said. A growl rumbled in her throat.

A heavy sigh drifted through the window and Tolas Ruv Aen's smooth drawl followed. "I know you want this curse broken but joining with Vasiir's crowd isn't the answer. You can't believe these people are going to help you."

"It isn't just about the curse being broken. It is about gaining respect. Ilriel Vasiir wants the same."

Draqa's breath caught. The president of Adonis and the hulvoqn? Despite himself, Draqa moved directly below the window to listen better.

"Enlighten me, then," Tolas Ruv Aen said.

"She's like us. She wants respect for her people. For our people," Duuzran said.

Tolas Ruv Aen let out a disbelieving laugh. "And you think that retrieving some old man from Taevalear is really going to solve it? Don't you *know* who Orias is?"

"He's our father. When his curse is broken, ours will be as well."

"Assuming he's even alive, and if he is, why would he want to break—What's the matter?"

Duuzran approached the window. Draqa held his breath and pressed against the wall. The woman took a deep sniff.

"We're being listened to," she said.

Shit.

Tolas Ruv Aen stepped up to the window as well and leaned out of it. His long bunch of loosely braided hair hung over his shoulder and the cologne and wet gunpowder scent that always clung to him wafted down to Draqa. Draqa made to reach for a weapon, but the elf only closed the shutters. Draqa held a hand over his heart.

The hut was silent for a few minutes before Tolas Ruv Aen

spoke again. "I'm gonna get some fresh air. Have a good night."

Tolas Ruv Aen's heavy footsteps thumped down the wood ladder from Duuzran's hut. Draqa peered down at him as he strode in the direction of the little stable. He wore his usual wide-brimmed, high-crowned hat, and a heavy leather coat that swept his knees. He didn't have his sword. Draqa hurried to follow, making sure he didn't get close enough to be seen. Tolas Ruv Aen stopped in front of the four horses in the stable and started untying one before he paused. He observed Draqa's horse before approaching it. The sleepy horse nuzzled his hand. Draqa's gut twisted.

"Virsh?" Tolas Ruv Aen whispered.

Draqa drew his gun, flicking off the safety. It was now or never. He raised his arms. Tolas Ruv Aen spun around, sending a knife flying at him before he could even properly aim the damn thing. It caught the back of his hand, and he dropped his gun, hissing. Tolas Ruv Aen leapt in front of him instantly, causing him to stumble back. The elf nudged the gun behind himself with his foot.

"Hello, Jair. A wonder to see you, as always."

16

Javis waited for Averil at the airstop, tapping his foot. He huffed, his breath condensing in the air; his friend was late. Today they were supposed to meet with Governor Sius Mavell Evi, that is, assuming Averil ever arrived. He was late to everything, but this was ridiculous. The gloomy sky draped everything in light gray, snow fell lightly from the clouds, melting before it hit the ground. No matter how many weeks off the solstice holiday was, winter had already come.

Javis stuffed his hands into his coat pockets, balling them up inside his gloves, not that it did him any good; the cold had already seeped its way into his bones. Dammit! Where the hell was Averil? Not only was Javis freezing his ass off, but if Averil didn't hurry soon, they were going to miss their flight!

Feet plodded on the cobble behind Javis. He turned to see Averil half running, half flying towards him, a hand on his flatcap, long ponytail bouncing and his scarf flowing behind him.

Javis stared at him quizzically as he apologized for his lateness. His eyes looked red and heavy.

"You look like you were up all night. How do you expect to find Zalé if you're going to be falling asleep on your feet?" Javis chided. "Also, you're late. What exactly were you doing? Did you forget what today was?"

Averil held up a hand, breathing heavily. "He's—He's been sighted! A week ago, in Talnoq-Vyn!" he exclaimed breathlessly.

"Then it's a good thing we are going there ourselves. Come on, before our flight leaves without us!" Javis said, hearing the final boarding call.

With the speed of an airship, the trip to Talnoq-Vyn only lasted a couple hours. A carriage ride later and they stood at the entrance of Sius Mavell Evi's manor. The driver left them there, informing them to contact him when they were done. Javis knocked on the massive double doors. A middle-aged dwerin greeted them. Like many dwerinians, he wore a wide-brimmed hat behind his large ears. Dwerinians may have had generally poor eyesight, but their incredible hearing made up for it, and the aid of their hats increased it ten-fold.

Javis began to introduce himself when Averil cut him off.

"Hello, Ramnik. Is the Governor in?"

Ramnik nodded, guiding them inside. "Wait here," he said, and wandered off.

Javis observed the ornate patterns on the walls and the sheer open space in the building. A grand staircase led up to the second floor, walkways outlining the room. Boastful and extravagant. Javis whistled and muttered, "He sure knows how to use his money."

Ramnik returned with an older elf at his side. The Governor held a cane, but he didn't look like he used it for anything but show as he stood with perfect posture and no sign of a limp in his gait.

"Sir." Averil stepped forward and shook Sius Mavell Evi's hand.

"Averil, my boy, how are you? You didn't sound well when we spoke last." Sius Mavell Evi took no notice of Javis.

Averil waved him off. "I'm fine. I was having a frustrating day is all. And you?"

"Quite well, quite well. And this is—" Sius Mavell Evi finally turned to Javis.

"Javis Zevos," he replied, bowing.

"Ah, that's right, *Zevos*. How could I forget." Sius Mavell Evi leaned on his cane, smiling. It didn't reach his eyes. "How can I help you, Ambassador?"

"If you don't mind, sir, I would like to get some information," Javis said.

"Information?"

Javis gave a stiff nod. "Yes, pertaining to the rumors—"

"You must be incredibly hungry," Sius Mavell Evi interrupted.

Javis sputtered. Was he hungry? What was this?

"I took the liberty of having my kitchen staff prepare us a lunch. Why don't you join me in the dining room?" Sius Mavell Evi was already walking away.

Javis exchanged glances with Averil, who nodded for him to follow. He quickly fell into step with Sius Mavell Evi.

"I greatly appreciate this, Governor, but we have a schedule to keep to, and. . ." Javis slowed as he reached the dining room. There had to be room enough for at least twenty guests at the lengthy dining table that reached from one end of the room to the other. An assortment of food—breads, grilled fish smelling of lemon and nuts, and granat berry salads—was already set at three places at the end of the table nearest to the fireplace. The fire burned low.

Averil patted Javis on the back and urged him forward. "Go with it," he mouthed.

Sius Mavell Evi sat, motioning for Averil and Javis to do the same. They sat on either side of him.

"Help yourselves. There's plenty," Sius Mavell Evi said.

The food did look tempting. Almost too tempting. Across from Javis, Averil already filled his plate. Javis mimicked him to not seem rude, but he only poked at the fish now on his plate.

"Is it not to your liking?" Sius Mavell Evi inquired. His beady gaze scrutinized Javis' every move.

"Not at all—I mean, it's perfectly fine. Sorry, I'm careful around other people's cooking. My stomach is sensitive." Javis hoped his excuse would suffice.

Sius Mavell Evi pursed his lips. "I understand. Perhaps some wine?" He picked up the bottle, offering to pour it in Javis' glass. That was even more tempting. Javis nodded slowly, Averil giving him a look that said he was being rude. Sius Mavell Evi poured his glass, then sat back and poured his own. He took a sip, his eyes remaining on Javis.

Javis took a hesitant sip, trying to hide his face. Again, what the hell was all this? At least the wine was good.

"Tell me, Ambassador. You just arrived back from the clans in the south, correct?" Sius Mavell Evi asked.

Javis startled, spilling wine down the corner of his mouth. "The clans. . .?" He wiped his face. "Er, yes. I did."

"How did it go?"

"It. . . went well. They're upset that their territory was reduced again. I have suggested many times that Erothel would have better relations with them if we returned their land, but the Minister is a busy man," Javis said.

Sius Mavell Evi chuckled. "That he is. It would seem he's a trouble to us all."

Javis hesitated. "A trouble, sir?"

"Indeed. When has he ever done what the people want?"

That was rich, considering how much Sius Mavell Evi was disliked. Javis did his best to remain cordial. "The Minister tries his best with the time he has. He has a lot on his hands."

"Perhaps," Sius Mavell Evi stopped to eat a forkful of salad. "But, I think Averil would agree with me."

Averil licked his lips and exchanged another glance with Javis. He whispered, "I'm sure the Minister does try his best. However, he has done things I can't agree with. Jailing yilura for shapeshifting without a permit, then making permits too expensive for most people? He must know how dangerous it is for yilura to travel undisguised."

Sius Mavell Evi snapped his fingers. "My point exactly. Your son is half yiluran, isn't he? And your late partner. Why, if it weren't for the Minister's ridiculous laws, she would still be alive."

Averil only nodded. Javis tried to stop his leg from bouncing. The room seemed a little too warm. He wasn't sure he liked where this conversation was heading.

Sius Mavell Evi continued, "You shouldn't forget about the laws against people like the two of you, either."

Javis frowned. They couldn't blame Phar for that. "Those laws have been around longer than the Minister. The High Council—"

"Minister Lhorsan Phar has voted against every single reform proposed and he has the most influence out of all the Council's members. Half of the twelve are in his pocket," Sius Mavell Evi said.

"They may not be fair, but the laws the Council puts forth are for the safety of the fae in Arai," Javis grated, his voice losing its even tone. Was Sius Mavell Evi deliberately trying to antagonize him?

Sius Mavell Evi leaned over, smirking. "*Ambassador.* Oh, Ambassador, tell me. Is there safety in you not being able to legally take a faerish name?"

Silence fell over the table when Javis' words failed him. Sius Mavell Evi leaned back, chuckling again. Javis could feel his face burning. The Governor was right of course. Even Averil, who had the luck of looking more faerish than human, had to deal with the Council's ridiculous laws.

"What's your point in saying all of this?" he asked.

"I think you're clever enough to figure that out on your own."

Suddenly, the wine seemed unappetizing, too.

Lunch continued to draw on forever, Sius Mavell Evi and Averil chatting about pointless things. Javis could no longer stop his leg from bouncing. He began tapping his fingers on the table. He wasn't here for petty conversation about politicians. He couldn't take it anymore. He pushed his plate and mostly untouched wine away, clearing his throat.

"Governor, I hate to be rude, but if we could cut to the matter at hand."

Sius Mavell Evi's expression melted away, his eyes losing their humor.

"Very well." He stood and called for a pretty faun to clear the plates. "Come to my study. I assume you will want to speak in private."

He led Javis to his study. It was a cozy place with wood flooring and a red-brown rug. Sius Mavell Evi sat behind the carved oak desk and clasped his lower hands, leaning on them. His other two lit a pipe.

Javis took a breath to steady himself.

"Sir, I'm here because—"

"I know why you're here. Averil already informed me. So, what would you like to know?"

Javis pulled up a chair. "You are aware of the things people say about you?" he asked.

"That I am." Sius Mavell Evi looked bored. This threw Javis off.

He adjusted his glasses and carefully explained, "Someone has been trying to turn the southern clans against Erothel. I've been investigating, and while most of the airships have gone from there to Adonis and back, a few have traced back here, to Talnoq-Vyn. Since you have a tight hold in this province, I thought you would be the best person to ask. Have you seen anything suspicious?"

Sius Mavell Evi took a long draw from his pipe. "You believe it was me."

Javis floundered, taken aback by the older man's bluntness. He hadn't even planned to suggest it.

"I. . . Given your history, it does look suspicious, sir."

"I hate to disappoint you, Ambassador, but I haven't been near any of the clans in years," Sius Mavell Evi said, pulling out his aspectacaster. He rummaged through some drawers, pulling out a folder, and slid it with the device over to Javis.

"Both of these contain records of all of my affairs in the last year. They're the same."

Javis opened the folder. He flipped through the papers carefully, checking each and every one. Sius Mavell Evi must have been paranoid, having paper copies of his travel records and meetings made. It was almost as if he knew people would be keeping an eye on him. Javis checked the aspectacaster next, but as Sius Mavell Evi said, the information was the same. Not one showed any evidence of him meeting with someone from Adonis.

"Well?" Sius Mavell Evi's eyes glittered, smiling in triumph.

Javis slid the documents and aspectacaster back across the desk.

"Nothing," he muttered.

"There you have it," said Sius Mavell Evi, "if you want to take the time contacting every person I've met with to confirm, be my guest, but I can assure you, you won't find what you're looking for."

The way the Governor looked at him then, Javis knew: Sius Mavell Evi had been aware of what Javis was doing long before he came here. Javis felt himself sweating. He clenched his teeth. Sius Mavell Evi returned the documents to the drawer and went to stand.

"If that is all, then I have a lot of work to do—"

"No," Javis said. He stood, looking down at the Governor. "There's just one more thing. I want to know about Draqa." Javis took pride in the surprise that passed over Sius Mavell Evi's features, even though it only lasted a second.

Sius Mavell Evi took another draw from his pipe and blew a smoke ring in Javis' face. Javis waved it away, coughing.

"Draqa?"

"The man who works for you, whatever he does. Who is he?"

Sius Mavell Evi traced a pale finger along the edge of his desk. The sardonic grin on his face was infuriating. He hummed.

"Chasing ghosts, are we? You need to be careful with that nose of yours. One day it's going to lead you where you don't belong."

Javis swallowed. "Are you threatening me?"

Sius Mavell Evi stood and approached him. He stood his ground.

"Let's call it an observation," Sius Mavell Evi said.

A shiver ran down Javis' spine. He returned to Averil, and Ramnik saw the two of them back to the front entrance. Javis wanted to get as far away from the Governor as he possibly could. They were about to leave when Sius Mavell Evi spoke up from behind them.

"Perhaps both of you would rather stay the night. You won't get far in this weather." Unfortunately, he was right; outside of the window, a wall of white covered the sky. Wind blew snow and ice harshly in one direction, before changing its mind, whipping it in another. Traveling in this weather would be difficult and dangerous. The joys of being on the coast.

Javis and Averil were given two rooms next to each other on

the upper level. The guest rooms were as extravagant as the rest of the manor. If Javis hadn't been so worked up, he might have taken note of the luxury, and would have usually enjoyed such a thing. He loved to be surrounded by wealth. Not now. Instead, he paced the room. Sius Mavell Evi's words echoed in his mind. A chill had taken hold of him despite the warmth of the room and his sweater.

Was he in danger?

Obviously, Sius Mavell Evi was lying about where he had been. Even if he weren't, he could have been sending someone else to the clans in his place. He could have sent Draqa in his place. Javis fingered the aspectacaster in his pocket. He'd recorded the conversations with Sius Mavell Evi both at dinner and alone, but even after all that, Javis still had no proof of what it was the Governor was doing.

His pacing quickened. What to do? He activated his aspectacaster, wondering if this was worth contacting anyone. Not Lhorsan Phar—that man wouldn't listen. Talara? No. . .she would only chastise Javis for his actions, which he was beginning to regret.

Chasing ghosts, are we? Was that an affirmation of who Draqa was? A mockery of Javis, surely. Sius Mavell Evi couldn't have known who Javis thought Draqa was. He ran a hand through his hair. He pulled off his glasses and rubbed his eyes. Sitting on the bed, he pulled a flask from his bag. The liquor burned his throat as he downed the entire thing. It calmed him. Things were going to be fine.

Javis laid back on the pillow-y bed. His drunken mind drifted to other times. To safer, less confusing times. He began to doze. . .

He awoke suddenly in the dead of night. The storm was still raging outside. Surely, it was the wind that disturbed him. He lay still, listening. The room light was off. Had he really slept that long? He reached for the table lamp, turning it on. A tray of cold food sat underneath.

Carefully, Javis left the bed and exited his room. His first instinct was to check that Averil was all right. Hearing silence in his friend's room, he peered in. Averil was gone. Javis looked along the dark hallways, anxiety creeping into his heart. He could see the faint outline of the stairs and took them, his hand hovering above the rail. The stairs creaked. He held his breath in horror. Once again, he listened, and again he heard nothing. Everyone was asleep, he assured himself. He continued on, treading lighter this time.

He tiptoed along, finding himself retracing his steps to Sius Mavell Evi's study. Turning a corner, he froze, voices floating through the corridor. Ahead of him were the shadowy outlines of two people: Sius Mavell Evi and Averil. Javis couldn't understand what they were saying, but Sius Mavell Evi did most of the talking; he appeared to be comforting Averil. The tone of his voice remained cool, seductive, and in the dark, frightening. Javis crept towards them.

"Did you ever finish it, by the way?" Sius Mavell Evi asked. He seemed to have changed the subject.

"I have, despite the. . .*complications* in trying to improve the formula," Averil replied.

"If it's ready for use, why don't you—"

Javis didn't catch the rest of what the Governor said: a hand grasped his wrist, yanking him back around the corner. His heart skipped a beat and he bit back the yell that jumped into his throat. Looking around, he saw the outline of a short, brawny figure.

"It is impolite to eavesdrop," Ramnik whispered.

Javis let out his breath. "I wasn't intentionally," he lied, "I was looking for the toilet."

The dwerinian man held his gaze and shook his head. "Sneaking around. It never does visitors well, you especially."

Javis glanced towards Sius Mavell Evi and Averil. The latter was gone and Sius Mavell Evi stood at the far end of the hallway. He stared in Javis' direction, his eyes appearing to glow amber. The faint light faded, but the man still watched him. Javis backed away. Ignoring the dwerin, he returned to his room and stayed there.

17

Elves were a pain to deal with. They had an advantage over other races in almost everything. Speed, multitasking, flexibility, fighting. Tolas Ruv Aen was even more skilled than most, so Draqa honestly wasn't surprised that there was now a knife being held to his neck.

"I can't say it's ever been a wonder to see *you*. And my name is Draqa," he growled. Tolas Ruv Aen had been the only one to still call him Jair after he abandoned the name. But that was before the betrayal.

Tolas Ruv Aen pouted, tracing a mock tear down his cheek. Draqa reached into his coat for his other gun, already fed up with this man. Tolas Ruv Aen pressed his dagger harder against his throat, waggling a finger. Draqa lowered his hand. The dagger broke skin.

"What are you doing here, *Draqa*?" Tolas Ruv Aen asked. He was serious now.

Draqa gritted his teeth. "Sius Mavell Evi hasn't forgotten what you did." He once more tried to make a grab for his gun. Tolas Ruv Aen grabbed both of Draqa's hands, stretching his arms apart.

"I should'a guessed. At least you both make my life more entertaining. Now, Duuzran mentioned there were *three* people staying in the guest hut. Who're the two you brought with you?"

"No one. They don't have anything to do with this," Draqa said. He took in the elf's form, looking for an opening.

"More likely they work for Sius Mavell Evi, too, isn't it? Ambushes aren't usually like you," Tolas Ruv Aen said.

"A lot has changed since we last saw each other. You could say I'm getting desperate," Draqa suggested.

Tolas Ruv Aen glanced around. Draqa grinned to himself. He would continue to let his opponent think that Krystal and the boy were lying in wait for him somewhere.

"I heard you talking with Duuzran. What's this about Vasiir and an old man in the Other Realm?" he asked.

Tolas Ruv Aen glanced around again. "None of yer concern. That's strictly between Duuzran and the Ard'a."

"You're going on secret missions for them now? How many others did you have to betray to secure that level of trust?"

Tolas Ruv Aen narrowed his eyes. "You know why I betrayed Sius Mavell Evi. You know what he was doing."

Draqa thought back. The memories were fuzzy. Trying any harder to remember made his head ache. He shrugged.

"I'm afraid I don't."

"That's a lie," accused the elf.

"Is it?"

Tolas Ruv Aen frowned. He observed Draqa, his brow knit tightly. "Just how much has that bastard made you forget?"

Draqa tilted his head as much as he dared. "Would I really know that?"

Yes, that's it. His opponent grew hesitant now. Tolas Ruv Aen always was a sentimental one, getting too caught up in the past. It would be his downfall. Draqa made an exaggerated glance to the side. Tolas Ruv Aen's three real eyes followed. He loosened his grip on Draqa suddenly.

"I know what yer doing—"

Draqa ripped his arms away and kicked Tolas Ruv Aen in the stomach, knocking him back. He twisted the dagger out of Tolas Ruv Aen's hand. He aimed for his face, slicing open his cheek. Tolas Ruv Aen hissed. As fast as he could, Draqa brought up the dagger to taste the blood on it. Tolas Ruv Aen was faster, tackling him to the ground.

"You do not get to use yer disgusting tricks!" He pinned Draqa's arms, squeezing his wrist until he was forced to drop the knife. Draqa struggled underneath Tolas Ruv Aen's weight.

"*Suum hulr!*" he growled.

The spell wolf barreled into Tolas Ruv Aen from the side. He rolled away from Draqa. Draqa reached for the bloody dagger, but found it in Tolas Ruv Aen's hands. Letting out a noise of frustration, Draqa reached for the gun still holstered under his arm. It was gone. So was his knife belt. That fucking elf! Draqa whipped his head around, looking for his fallen gun. There—by the stable! Draqa ran for it while the spell-wolf had Tolas Ruv Aen occupied. He grabbed it off the ground. A woman screamed.

Draqa's blood ran cold.

"Drop it, Draqa," Tolas Ruv Aen said.

Draqa turned. Tolas Ruv Aen had Krystal in his arms, Draqa's stolen gun pointed at her head. How was that possible? Krystal was asleep. . . unless she woke when Draqa left and followed him. That damned woman! She was more trouble than she was worth. She fought back against Tolas Ruv Aen hard, though, kicking and writhing to get away. She might have if she wasn't outmatched in limbs.

"I don't want to hurt her, but I will. Drop yer gun," Tolas Ruv Aen repeated.

Draqa scowled. He trained his weapon on Tolas Ruv Aen despite the threat.

"Draqa. . ." Tolas Ruv Aen warned, pushing Krystal's head sideways with the gun, making her whimper.

Draqa couldn't get a clear shot. Krystal moved too much, blocking too much of Tolas Ruv Aen. He couldn't hesitate any longer. He would have to shoot through her. It served her right for getting in the way. Any second now, she and Tolas Ruv Aen would be gone, and with them, so would Draqa's problems. His finger found the trigger and he began to squeeze. The horror on Krystal's face wrenched his heart.

What was he doing? He slowly lowered his gun. A familiar ache pulsed in his temples, and he struggled against Sius Mavell Evi's magic to lower the gun any further. But he had to. He couldn't kill Krystal. A gunshot split the air, sudden pain searing through his left shoulder, collarbone cracking. He gasped, falling to his knees. He gripped his shoulder. He looked back up in time to see Krystal stumbling to the side as Tolas Ruv Aen tossed her away. Draqa tried to lift his arm to shoot back. He couldn't move it. The last thing he saw was Tolas Ruv Aen coming for him before his head slammed into the dirt.

18

Krystal wanted to cry out for Draqa, but her voice refused to leave her throat. She could only watch as he was knocked unconscious. At least, she hoped he was only unconscious. The four-armed man, Tolas Ruv. . . Tolas stood from Draqa's side, brushing himself off. He wiped blood from the cut on his face. He walked around, gathering a few weapons that were strewn through the dirt and snow, adding them to his person. He stooped back over Draqa and turned him over. Krystal covered her mouth. Draqa's forehead was bloodied.

This was her fault. This was all her fault. She saw Draqa on her way back from the bathroom and decided to follow him. She didn't mean to get in the way. She didn't think she'd be seen.

She must have gagged, or sobbed, because Tolas looked up at her. He left Draqa and started walking towards her. She crawled backwards to get away. Tolas raised his arm. Oh God, he was going to kill her next! Krystal squeezed her eyes shut. Nothing happened.

Krystal peeked an eye open. Tolas' hand was simply held out to her in offering. She stared at it, wide-eyed and confused. When she didn't take the elf's hand, he crouched in front of her. She flinched. He said something she couldn't understand, gesturing to her hands. Looking at them now, Krystal saw they were bleeding. She must have scraped them when Tolas dropped her. Now that she was aware, they stung like hell.

Tolas spoke to her again. She didn't dare reply. Tolas frowned and repeated himself in a different language this time. Krystal remained at a loss. Tolas sighed and stood up. Around them, people were beginning to leave their huts, murmuring, likely wondering what the commotion was. Tolas returned to Draqa and lifted him up over his shoulder.

Duuzran came running. She shouted all kinds of things, a growl in her voice. Tolas was calm, mildly gesturing to Krystal and Draqa and the horses. Duuzran jabbed a finger at Draqa's limp form and pointed above the canyon. Tolas nodded. He walked back to Krystal and bent, grabbing her wrist, and helping her to her feet. He asked her another question. Krystal managed to shrug this time. Tolas scratched his black goatee, then mimed the shape of a hut and pointed at Krystal.

Where was she staying? That must have been the question, as Tolas followed Krystal when she led him back to the guest hut. Inside, Zalé still slept soundly. Krystal was about to wake him when Tolas held her back. With his free hands, he switched Draqa and Zalé's places on the cot and laid Zalé with a blanket on the floor. He muttered something else and left.

Krystal kept her eyes on the door for a moment before rushing to Draqa's side. She felt his chest. Thankfully, he was breathing, but how long would that last? His shoulder bled profusely. Krystal pulled back Draqa's coat. She needed to stop the bleeding somehow.

The door opened again and Tolas re-entered the hut, carrying a bag. Krystal moved out of the way as he knelt in front of Draqa. He emptied the bag of its contents—bandages, gauze, and other first aid equipment. He leaned over Draqa with a knife, cutting his turtleneck down the middle and peeling it away. Krystal gawked. The scar on Draqa's face continued down his neck and spread across his torso. Where the scarring was worse, his skin was rough and sinewy.

Tolas startled Krystal by holding out some kind of device to her face while he worked on Draqa. Krystal took it tentatively, turning it over in her hands. It was an odd, flat thing, curved like a crescent moon with short, metal leaves stemming from the edges. What was it? Tolas turned his head. He wore the same device behind his ear. Krystal fumbled to put it on. Once in place, it grew hot, and Krystal felt a prickling sensation. She tried to take it off again, but it felt as though it had fused to her head.

"You should be able to understand me now," Tolas said.

Krystal's eyes widened. It was like when she had soul-traveled, how she didn't know the language Draqa had been speaking, yet somehow understood it.

"How?" she asked.

Despite not looking up from his work on Draqa, Tolas smiled. *"It's a translator the Ard'a uses. As long as we both have one, we can talk to and understand each other."*

Did this mean Krystal could understand anyone now? That

she could finally stop relying on Draqa to translate for her? She opened her mouth to thank Tolas before stopping herself. Could she trust this man?

Tolas wrapped Draqa's shoulder now. *"I'm sorry for scaring you before. It was a life-or-death situation. I'm sure you understand."*

"No, I don't. Who are you and why was Draqa after you?" Krystal asked.

"My name's Tolas Ruv Aen. Draqa and I are old friends, or we were. But I've known him since. . . gosh, he must'a been seventeen or so when I met him," Tolas said.

"As for why he's after me, I don't know how much he's told you, but I used to work for Governor Sius Mavell Evi, too, and for a lot longer than Draqa has. But it didn't sit right when I learned what Sius Mavell Evi was doing, and I knew had to leave. I joined the Ard'a and sold them information. Maybe I'm just unlucky, but Sius Mavell Evi found out it was me and ever since then I've had a target on my back."

Krystal was unsure she'd heard Draqa mention that name before. "What's the Ard'a?" she asked.

Finishing the bandages, Tolas Ruv Aen tied Draqa's arm in a makeshift sling. He tended to Draqa's forehead next.

"The Ard'ahlen. We're an organization. Think of us almost as—ah—a syndicate of sorts," he said. He wrapped Draqa's head in bandages as well and let him rest.

Tolas' actions didn't make a lot of sense to Krystal. Wouldn't it have been easier for him to let Draqa die?

"Why did you help him?"

Tolas Ruv Aen turned to face her and took her hands. Cleaning them off, he dabbed ointment on them. He spoke thoughtfully.

"Deep down in him somewhere I know he's still a friend. Sius Mavell Evi is just in the way. While we're on the topic, how do you know Draqa?"

Krystal bit her lip. She didn't want to cause more trouble for Draqa than she already had.

Tolas Ruv Aen continued, *"I'm just asking, cause if I remember right, that language yer speaking is English, which means yer from Taevalear. Am I right?"*

Krystal shut her mouth. Of course, the translator went both ways. She was stupid to have let her guard down.

"S'all right. I'm not one to snitch, but if yer in trouble, I'd like to help you."

Krystal frantically shook her head. "I'm not. I didn't listen and followed Draqa here even though he told me to stay behind. That's not his fault."

Tolas Ruv Aen raised his brow. *"Hold on, hold on. Are you saying Draqa was meeting you in the Other Realm? For how long?"*

"Not long. I accidentally soul-traveled here, and then he showed up at my work a few days later. He said I was part fae and he told me so many wonderful things about this place. I just couldn't hear about all of it and not get to see it for myself. I didn't mean for him to get caught like this," Krystal said. "Please don't tell anyone. I'll do anything."

Tolas Ruv Aen simply chuckled. *"I told you, I'm no snitch, Miss. . ."*

"It's Krystal. . . Monarain."

The way Tolas Ruv Aen' spider eyes widened was almost comical. He leaned closer to her.

"Not as in Sal Monarain?"

"Draqa seems to think so."

Tolas Ruv Aen held his head. His brain must have ceased functioning, because he sat in that position for a long minute, not even blinking.

"Krystal Monarain," he croaked finally, *"I think I'm going to need you to explain from the very beginning."*

So, Krystal did, hesitantly at first, worried about what she might have just gotten herself into. She mentioned the strange circumstances of her birth and explained in further detail how she met Draqa. How she had assumed he was a Gatekeeper and only learned he was breaking the law after the fact, and how the two of them met Zalé before leaving Talnoq-Vyn. The only thing Krystal didn't bring up were her dreams about Draqa's past. Tolas Ruv Aen didn't know what to say about any of it. In fact, he seemed almost as confused as Krystal was.

"Are you going to have Draqa arrested?" Krystal asked.

Tolas Ruv Aen shook his head. *"I don't think that would be a good idea."* He stood, sighing.

"Look, I have to go before Draqa wakes up. You need to get him to a doctor as soon as he does. He'll be all right, but his shoulder is definitely broken. Wouldn't be surprised if I terribly concussed him, too."

"Is there one here?"

"None qualified, but there is in a town about a day and a half's ride from here. It would better for you to leave anyway. Duuzran and the others aren't too happy with Draqa."

Krystal nodded. The last thing she wanted was to toy with Duuzran's hospitality further. She felt behind her ear again.

"Do you want this back?"

"The translator? Nah. Keep it, you'll find it useful. Just don't let Draqa see ya with it. And ah, don't tell him we talked." With a foot out the door, Tolas Ruv Aen added, *"I'll be in touch."* And then he left.

Krystal rested her elbows on the cot and watched Draqa, praying he would wake soon. The queasiness she felt had only worsened when she talked to Tolas Ruv Aen. She hated not knowing who to trust—as if she could ever trust Draqa in the first place. She tiredly dropped her head into her arms, closing her eyes. Hopefully, she hadn't made a big mistake in telling Tolas Ruv Aen everything she did.

***

Draqa's entire body screamed. He was being torn apart. His skin peeled from his bones. It burned. Draqa begged for someone—anyone—to put him out of his misery. Was this what hell felt like?

His eyes flew open. The white lights of the room assaulted him, and he squinted. Hunched over him, an elder elf dabbed a cloth to his chest. It stung, making him groan. The elf didn't spare him a glance. Instincts told him to get away, but the moment he tried, the pain flared up and he cried out.

"Kill me!" His voice cracked. Even his throat burned.

The elf chuckled, "It is clear someone was trying to. I found you lying in a heap outside of. . ."

Draqa couldn't focus on what the elf said. He couldn't remember what happened. He couldn't think. He just wanted the pain to end. He wanted to die. He should have died.

"Please," he choked, "pl-ease!"

The elf shook his head. "It's painful, isn't it? Luckily for you, I need to put you back under for surgery."

He administered something to Draqa with a needle and he fell back into a nightmarish sleep.

When Draqa woke next, he found himself in a different room. A dim room. A faint light streamed through heavy curtains. Draqa's body ached as he forced himself to sit up. He could only just make out the shapes of a dresser, and an armchair placed by the window. Bandages wrapped around his torso and limbs and even half his face, but he couldn't feel them touching his skin. In fact, he could barely feel much at all.

He turned, noticing a table lamp, and struggled to find the switch. His heartrate quickened. His fingers were worse. He couldn't feel anything, no matter how hard he pressed them to the lamp's surface. He tried his other hand. He couldn't feel it, either. He sobbed. Was he even moving his fingers? He couldn't breathe. His eyes blurred, stinging with tears.

The lamp turned on. Draqa gasped, looking up. An elf, much younger than the one from before and dressed in a sheer, lichen-colored shirt, stood by Draqa's bed.

"S'all right, I'm not going to hurt you." He sat on the edge of the bed. One of his eyes was a lighter green than the rest and didn't move quite the right way.

"I—I can't feel my hands," Draqa said, "I can't feel anything."

The elf nodded. "You were in bad shape. I wasn't thinking you were going to make it."

"Are you. . . are you the one who saved me?" Draqa asked.

The elf shook his head. "Nah. That was Sius Mavell Evi. He did a lot to keep you alive the other night."

Sius Mavell Evi. . . He was one of Draqa's father's old political opponents. Wasn't he a governor now? Draqa could vaguely recall the man bent over him in a bright room. It was like a dream. But why would Sius Mavell Evi of all people save him?

"Who are you then?" he asked uneasily.

"Me? Oh, I'm Tolas Ruv Aen. I just work for Sius Mavell Evi and offered to keep an eye on you while yer healing."

Draqa sniffed. "Where is this?"

"Sius Mavell Evi's home, just a mile past the Vyn," Tolas replied. "You were asleep for about three days. Sius Mavell Evi mentioned you woke up when he was getting ready to operate on you. That must'a been a fright."

Draqa closed his eyes, ignoring the man. Did his family know where he was? Did they care? Did they even know what had happened? Draqa held back a quiver in his lip.

"Are you thirsty? I can have the kitchen bring you something if you'd like," Tolas Ruv Aen said.

Draqa nodded. He didn't want this stranger to see him cry.

"I'll. . . I'll just have water," he whispered so faintly he wasn't sure he said it out loud.

Tolas Ruv Aen nodded but he didn't leave. He offered Draqa a sympathetic smile. "I know this must be a lot to take in, but yer in good hands. Sius Mavell Evi and I are going to do everything we can for you. If you need anything from me, anything at all, just ask."

Something about him struck Draqa as genuine. He couldn't remember the last time anyone had even asked if he was okay and truly meant it. The tears he held back began to fall freely. Tolas Ruv Aen didn't call attention to them. He didn't berate or mock Draqa. Yet, Draqa still felt the need to push him away.

"Please leave. Leave me alone."

Tolas Ruv Aen obliged and left him to cry in silence.

***

Krystal felt Draqa shudder beside her. She opened her eyes, sitting up. She must have fallen asleep. She peered over Draqa to check on him. He groaned, reaching for his head. His eyes were twisted shut. Tear stains ran down his face, and when he finally did open his eyes, they were red. He squinted at Krystal.

"Monarain. . .are you crying?"

Krystal rubbed her cheek. So she was.

19

JAVIS WAS STILL ON EDGE when he and Averil left the manor in the early morning. Thoughts from the night before swirled in his mind. He felt any moment now something would happen, and he was unable to sit still on the ride back to the Vyn. When questioned, he brushed it off as the cold. Averil appeared oblivious to Javis' predicament, and Javis wanted it to stay that way.

The carriage arrived within the city and came to a halt. Javis paid the driver and watched her continue on down the street. Perhaps it was the gray skies and chill in the air, but the energy of the day was off somehow. Perhaps Javis was just paranoid. Averil took him by the shoulder and pulled him to the side.

"Now that we're here, I need to look for Zalé. What will you do?" Averil asked.

Javis regarded the snow-covered buildings around them. "I need to take care of something. I can help look when I'm done."

Averil agreed. "Then, we can talk about where to meet up

later."

They went off in their separate directions. Buttoning up his coat, Javis headed for a skinny, two-story building a few blocks down and around the corner. He came to its crooked steps and lingered, swallowing his pride. A bell rang and a pleasant aroma floated around his head as he entered the apothecary. Berries and sage.

Javis gazed about the place, taking in all the neatly organized jars and bottles and dried herbs hanging from the ceiling. A young sylfan greeted him from behind the counter.

"Good morning. How can I help you today?"

"Is Talara in?" Javis asked.

The boy bobbed his head. "She's upstairs. Shall I fetch her for you?"

"I would greatly appreciate that. Tell her Javis Zevos needs to speak with her rather urgently."

He watched the boy scamper off and turned to wander the shop as he waited. This place calmed his nerves. He picked up a glass bottle from a shelf and observed its contents. Would Talara be willing to help him after he so blatantly went against her advice? He wasn't quite sure what he was going to say to her. He wasn't even sure his fears were warranted. It was possible that Governor Sius Mavell Evi just wanted him scared, to run away with his tail between his legs.

"Javis?"

Talara's voice startled him, and the bottle slipped from his hand. It shattered on the floor, spilling powder everywhere.

"Oh dear. I'm so sorry. I don't know what's gotten into me. I've been off all morning." He fumbled through his words and bent to pick up the glass. Talara lightly smacked his hand away. She swept the powder and broken bottle into a waste bin. Javis apologized again.

Talara poked him with her hand broom. "I wasn't expecting for you to come visit. What's wrong?" she asked.

Javis nervously turned his attention back to the shelves. "I may have made a mistake," he murmured.

Talara stepped in front of him. "You need to speak up. I can't understand a word you are saying."

Javis held her gaze. He repeated, "I said, I think I may have made a mistake."

"What did you do?"

"Last night, I met with Governor Sius Mavell Evi."

Talara's eyes widened. She hurriedly clamped her hand over Javis' mouth. It smelled strongly of incense.

"How could you do that? After everything I warned you about?" she hissed. She dragged Javis to the room upstairs. There was a single bed, and a rustic kitchenette sat under a little window looking out onto the street below. Javis instantly became caught up in his memories of the last time he had been in this room. He and Talara had still been together back then. His heart gave a longing squeeze, but then Talara's voice cut through his thoughts.

"What were you *thinking*?"

Javis wrung his hands. "I'm sorry, I had to."

Talara turned away from him with her hands on her hips. She looked truly angry with him, rubbing her face and muttering under her breath.

"Tell me what happened," she said.

Javis described the events from the night before and how unnerving his meeting with Sius Mavell Evi was. Talara was most concerned hearing about Sius Mavell Evi's threat. She chided Javis.

"You're lucky he did not have you killed in your sleep."

"I'm afraid you're right." Javis pulled off his glasses to clean them. "And I have no idea what to do."

"Leave," Talara said.

Javis hesitated. "What?"

Talara elaborated, "Leave Talnoq-Vyn and hope you make it home."

"You expect me to sit and wait for him to kill me? I can't just do nothing," Javis said.

"Because nothing is all you can do, unless you believe you can kill him first. You should have listened to me, Javis."

Javis lowered his head. He didn't know what to say. He felt like a fool, but he knew Talara spoke the truth. There was nothing he could do. Worst of all, he learned nothing by talking to Sius Mavell Evi in the first place.

Talara squeezed his arm. "I'm sorry. I wish I could help you."

Javis left Talara's apothecary no better than when he went in. He fiddled with his aspectacaster in his pocket, debating whether he yet wanted to meet back with Averil. He was rather nervous to be wandering the Vyn knowing the threat of death loomed over his head. He called Averil after much deliberation, but Averil didn't answer after the first two tries and Javis decided Averil must have been busy with someone.

Steeling his nerves, he began to search for Zalé on his own. He asked around, entering a few shops here and there, speaking with nearly everyone he came across. No one had seen him, or they had already been asked by Averil. Javis even brought out an image of Zalé he had on his aspectacaster, and still he had no luck. Eventually, he made his way to the pier. It was a risky choice to ask around that side of the Vyn for anything, but its shady reputation was exactly why he needed to look.

The first many people he asked gave him the same answer as the others. He leaned against a lamp on the dock tiredly. His hands and feet were beginning to ache from the numbing cold and his nose stung. It started snowing. He wished to heat himself with a spell but his lack of skill in that area of magic would potentially drain his energy and make him even more susceptible to the cold, so he had to settle for hopelessly rubbing his limbs together. Damn humidity.

Beside him, sailors carried cargo onto their ship. Back and forth, Javis watched them, and a thought slowly occurred to him. What if Zalé had ended up on a ship? Horrified, Javis called to one of the seamen.

"Excuse me!"—the man didn't hear him— "Excuse me! How long have you been here?" he asked.

"Eh, not longer than a month, I think. Been waiting for these shipments to arrive," he said, nodding to the crate in his arms.

Javis excitedly pulled up his picture of Zalé. It took some time with his frozen fingers.

"Have you seen this boy anywhere?"

The sailor shook his head. "No. Haven't seen—"

"I have!" A younger member of the crew stopped next to them, noticing the picture. "I've seen him." The young sailor thought a moment. "He was with a group of slavers. They were boarding people onto a ship."

Slavers? Javis' stomach dropped. "They took him?" he whispered.

"No, he caused a commotion and escaped into the city somewhere. The slavers didn't bother looking."

Javis shook the young sailor's hand, thanking him, and hurried off in search of Averil, calling for Zalé along the way. He found the man exiting a *huum*.

"Averil! Good news! Zalé—" Javis stopped himself, catching the expression on his friend's face. "What happened?"

"Draqa has him."

"What . . .?"

Averil explained what the manager told him. Draqa, accompanied by a red-haired woman, stayed at the inn for a night. At first, they visited alone, and they had Zalé with them on the night they stayed. The manager overheard them mention going to Kerevel Tul. This was over a week ago. By now the three of them had already left the city.

Javis couldn't fathom why Draqa of all people would have Zalé. He and Averil both agreed that Sius Mavell Evi had nothing to do with it, but it was certainly no coincidence that Draqa took Zalé to Kerevel Tul. It couldn't have been.

"He must be delivering Zalé back to you," Javis said.

Averil didn't look convinced.

"We don't know that he truly means to go to Kerevel Tul.

Wouldn't I have had Zalé back by now if he did?" Averil did have a point. It took only hours to get to Kerevel Tul by airship, and just a matter of days by train. If Draqa was looking for Averil, he should have found him by now.

"Do you think it's possible Draqa was held up? Or took a detour? Perhaps he decided to travel slowly—by horse maybe," Javis suggested.

Averil nodded halfheartedly in agreement. "Although I don't know anyone in his right mind who would want to travel that far by horse in the winter."

"We'll have to find out, wont we? We should get back to Kerevel Tul as soon as we possibly can," Javis said. He turned in the direction of the airstop before pausing. His stomach grumbled.

"Actually, I don't suppose you would want to go inside somewhere to get food and a hot drink first?"

"I could use a drink," Averil said.

The men found themselves a table next to a fireplace in a nearby tavern. A steady stream of jumbled conversation filled the room. Considering the time of day, Javis was surprised by how busy it was.

He ordered himself a drink and a serving of sweet fish and eggs. Averil had the same. The food was good. Comforting. Javis leaned back in his chair after he finished, swirling the mulled, honey-flavored alcohol around in his mug. He watched the heavy snowflakes fall from the sky, finding solace in the fact that Draqa was not prowling somewhere in the Vyn. But then, who was to say Draqa would go after Javis even if he was still around? If Draqa really was Javis' brother. . . Javis couldn't be sure how such an encounter would go. He downed the rest of his mead.

"Are you ready to leave?" Averil asked. He had already finished eating.

Javis shook his head. "I'd like another drink before we go." At Averil's disapproving look, he said, "I'll make it quick. You might as well have another as well."

Averil chuckled airily and stood. "All right. I'll get it and I'll pay for the food while I'm at it."

Javis offered him a smile. "Thank you."

Clicking his tongue, Averil walked off. Javis observed the other characters in the tavern while he waited. Many seedier looking folks filled the place. A few were obviously crew members from the various ships docked in the city, likely getting a meal before they set sail in the afternoon.

A handsome faun with colorful strings decorating his antlers made eye contact with Javis from across the room and winked. Javis raised an eyebrow and smirked. He nearly went over to talk to the faun when someone else caught his attention—a dwerin entering the tavern. Javis frowned. Wasn't that. . .?

Ramnik climbed onto a chair next to Averil at the bar. Javis shielded his face from view. What was *he* doing there? All at once, Javis' nervousness returned. He slouched in his chair, hoping he wouldn't be seen.

"Is that man you're with just a friend?" a voice said from his right.

He gasped, nearly knocking himself out of his chair. He turned. It was only the faun. Javis let out a breath.

"From that reaction, I would guess no," the faun said, sitting down.

Javis laughed nervously. "No, sorry. You snuck up on my blind side."

The faun leaned forward. He tilted his head. "Rough. How did it happen?"

"A fight with my brother when we were young," Javis replied absently. He glanced back at Ramnik. The faun looked, too.

"I would buy you a drink, but it looks like your friend has you covered," he said.

Javis nodded, turning his attention back to the faun.

"You're that ambassador, right? The one who goes to the drād clans or wherever? Do you have an aspectacaster?" the faun asked. He pulled out his aspectacaster and held it out to Javis.

Javis considered it for a moment before pulling out his own. He held it up to the faun's and their profiles exchanged. The faun's name was Trian.

Trian smiled and left with another wink as Averil came back to the table. Averil set Javis' drink in front of him and sat.

"Who was that?"

Javis once again looked back at the bar. Ramnik was gone.

"Just a. . . I just met him. He was hoping to buy me a drink. . ." he muttered. He took his mead and sipped it.

"I'm glad he didn't. Two should be your limit."

"Right. . . Did you notice that dwerin at the bar?" Javis asked.

Averil hummed in agreement, "I did. Why?"

Javis rubbed his throat. "I'm certain he works for Sius Mavell Evi," he said. He took another sip, his mouth feeling dry.

Averil shrugged him off. "So? By the way, I was meaning to ask how your meeting with him went. You looked off this morning."

"He had proof that he wasn't near any of the clans, and he wasn't willing to tell me about Draqa." Javis rubbed his throat again and cleared it. He felt hot.

Averil furrowed his brow. "Are you all right?"

"It's only a tickle. Anyway, Sius Mavell Evi did say something strange—" Javis interrupted himself with a cough, covering his mouth. His throat was suddenly tight. He looked at his hand. It was red.

Averil stood. "Javis?"

Javis coughed harder. What was happening? His skin began to burn inside and out. He felt his airway closing. He grabbed his neck. Averil joined his side.

"What's going on? Are you choking?"

Javis shook his head. But he couldn't breathe. His eyes fell on the cup of mead, and he realized. He pushed the cup away, knocking it over, and scrambled to his feet. He swayed, his mind hazy. Averil steadied him. The small tavern suddenly seemed so long. He took a step towards the door and collapsed. His entire body shook. He couldn't stand.

Averil tried to lift him. "Someone! We need a doctor!"

Javis tried to get Averil's attention. Talara. He needed Talara.

"Tal—a—" he couldn't speak. His vision was fading.

Averil hoisted him with his shoulders. "Hold on Javis. . ."

As Javis slipped into darkness, he saw Ramnik leave the tavern.

20

Being able to understand everyone was strange, especially as no one was able to understand Krystal. It didn't take long for Duuzran to find out that Draqa was awake, and before the sun had even the time to peak into the sky, she ordered him to take Krystal and Zalé and leave. Zalé was confused, having slept through everything the night before. Draqa wasn't much better off—he could barely remember the events he was being scolded for. This only served to make Duuzran angrier. All the while, Krystal tried not to seem too interested in the conversation, afraid she might give herself away.

Duuzran informed Draqa that he would be helped out of the canyon and that was all. He wasn't trusted to stay in the village while he recovered from his concussion. He had two hours to leave. He sighed heavily when Duuzran left.

Krystal chose her words carefully. "Does she want us gone?"

Draqa nodded, closing his eyes. A pained expression crossed

his face.

"But you're hurt! She can't make you leave—how will you even ride Virsh?" This was honestly a question Krystal had been asking herself all night.

"I'll manage," Draqa said. His words were slow and muddled. He was not doing well.

"We need to find you a doctor. Do you know where we can find one?" she asked, recalling the town Tolas Ruv Aen mentioned.

"There should be one in Baren. It's. . .a day away. Two if we're slow."

Zalé sat on the cot and leaned over Draqa's head.

"Are you going to die?" he asked.

Draqa groaned, *"Never."*

Krystal bit her lip, wondering if he really would. If he did, she and Zalé would be stranded.

"Krystal?" Draqa's use of her first name surprised her.

"Yeah?"

"I'm going to need your help. . ." Draqa said, trailing off.

He rested until his time limit was up and a burly naol came to fetch the three of them. The naol lifted Draqa and carried him out of the hut despite his meager protests.

"Where are my horses?"

"They're waiting at the top of the canyon," the naol said gruffly, leading Krystal and Zalé back along the path up the canyon wall.

Sure enough, there the horses were, waiting with Duuzran and the faun from before. The naol set Draqa down. Draqa struggled to climb onto Virsh's back, nearly falling off the other side of the horse once he was on. Krystal cringed. No matter what Draqa did, she couldn't believe they were making him leave in the condition he was in.

Krystal got onto Feriosh with Zalé and slowly followed Draqa away. He didn't have Virsh moving very quickly and leaned so far forward that he looked like he might fall at any moment. But somehow, he managed to stay on his horse the entire ride, even when the jarring motion became too much for his head and he had to stop for several minutes at a time. He proved to be either incredibly strong, or incredibly stubborn. He was certainly stubborn enough that when the sun grew low in the sky and the town of Baren was nowhere in sight, Krystal had to convince him to stop.

"Draqa, we should spend the night here. You need to rest," she said as they came upon a small clearing.

"I can keep going. It's still light," Draqa said.

Krystal halted Feriosh. "No. We're stopping. You haven't even wanted to eat, and this isn't safe for you," she demanded. She surprised herself with her own boldness.

Perhaps Draqa felt surprised, too, because he stared at her before bringing Virsh to a stop.

"Thank you. I'll set up the tent and things with Zalé, so you can just rest, okay?" Krystal assured.

After much hesitance, Draqa agreed. He tied up the horses and sat against a tree. Krystal set up the tent for him so he could lay down. Zalé kept him company while Krystal lit a fire. She was faster at it now than the first time she tried it. The fire got going quickly.

"I'm gonna heat up some food," she commented as she unpacked the bags. Draqa didn't answer. He laid back with his eyes closed. The grimace etched on his face told Krystal he remained awake.

Krystal sighed and got to cooking. Other than the occasional noise from Feriosh and Virsh, it was quiet here. Peaceful, even. Krystal couldn't allow herself to feel it. She was cold, hungry, and she was conflicted. Arai was amazing, yes, and it was beautiful. It was something out of her wildest imaginations. And she did enjoy meeting Zalé and seeing all the different peoples—the gray-skinned drād, the fauns and satyrs with their hoofed feet and magnificent horns and antlers, even the naols and the spider-like elves. Krystal was sure she would see even more and was excited to see more, but. . . that excitement wasn't as strong as it had been when she first heard about Arai. She began to regret her admittedly impulsive decision to come to Arai. Or at least, she regretted essentially forcing Draqa to be her guide. His likeable qualities were few, and it became increasingly clear that ever since she followed him, Krystal's presence was only tolerated.

And then there was the matter of Draqa's profession. Servant? Bounty Hunter? Hitman? Whatever it was, Krystal wasn't safe travelling with him, and neither was Zalé. If only she had convinced Draqa to leave her and the boy behind at the *huum* where they could have continued to try to contact Averil. Yet, guilt weighed on Krystal's chest. Draqa did his best to try to keep Krystal and Zalé out of harm's way. He could have abandoned Krystal from the very beginning or killed her, like it seemed he was going to do the night before. But he didn't. Was he really that bad? Krystal couldn't decide. All of this was a lot. She didn't want to have to think about it when there was nothing she could do. Not now, at least. Once she and Zalé were with Averil, then she would let herself worry.

She nudged Draqa with a bowl of food. He opened his eyes just a sliver. He groaned, struggling to sit up. He ate slowly with the bowl in his lap.

"Draqa?" Zalé whispered.

Draqa took so long to respond, Krystal didn't think he had heard. "*Yes?*"

"*Will you still be able to take me home?*" Zalé asked.

Draqa paused, then set his bowl to the side, sighing, *"I'm going to try my best. You don't have to worry about that."*

Zalé nodded. *"Even though you're hurt?"*

"Even though I'm hurt."

Zalé must have been reassured because he smiled and went to get his own food. Draqa leaned his head back against the fabric of the tent, leaving his bowl half-full. Krystal started to take it.

"Leave it. I'm just resting for a few minutes. . ." Draqa said. His eyes wandered before settling back on Krystal.

"I must look so pathetic to you," he muttered in a language Krystal thought she had heard other naols speaking.

She held back from responding, "You're not pathetic." Instead, she asked, "What was that?"

"Nothing. I was complaining," Draqa said.

Krystal hummed. "I don't blame you. You got beat up pretty bad." She hesitated. "Sorry for getting in the way."

Draqa looked at her, his lips downturned. Krystal rubbed the back of her neck. "I'm glad you're okay," she said.

Draqa sighed heavily. He muttered, "It's not your fault."

Krystal was taken aback. Not her fault? That wasn't right at all. "But it *is*. If I went back inside instead of following you—"

"I said it's not your fault. Please, just. . . drop it. I'm trying not to be angry with you."

Krystal lowered her head. Despite Draqa's words, she was not comforted. Draqa ate his food again, saying nothing else. Krystal didn't make him.

Eventually, Draqa went to sleep, or at least he seemed to. Zalé joined Krystal at the edge of the tent and leaned against her arm. She told him a story. It was a nonsense story, one that she came up with off the top of her head. She drew in the dirt so Zalé might understand, but even if he didn't, he was still enthralled, and the story was more for herself, anyway.

The story was about a little girl who lived in a magical bookstore. Her friends were the characters in the many books she entertained herself with. Every day, the little girl would travel to a different book, a different world. She would fight pirates and search for buried treasure, fly with fairies and play tag with lost boys. She would ride on great, talking bears and attend magic schools. The little girl loved her bookstore, and she loved her books.

Krystal saw that Zalé had fallen asleep on her arm, so she laid him in the tent and wrapped him in a blanket. She returned to her place and laid on her stomach, facing the fire. She continued her story to herself as she listened to the popping of the coals. She must have stayed awake for hours. The warmth of the fire on her face encouraged her to close her eyes. One of the horses snorted in its sleep. Krystal began to dream of her story.

Something brushed her cheek. She opened her eyes. An orb of

light flitted past the corner of her vision. She looked around and sat up, but the light was already gone. What was that? If the fire weren't already out, Krystal would have thought it was an ember. She looked around the clearing one more time before turning to go in the tent.

There it was again, just inches from her face. She startled, and the orb disappeared and reappeared in the middle of the clearing. Krystal stood, taking a hesitant step towards it. It darted left and right. Krystal squinted, but she couldn't make out what it was. She was half tempted to grab her camera, but then the orb once again disappeared, then reappeared just outside the clearing. It flitted back and forth in its place. Did it want Krystal to follow? Her feet moved on their own, bringing her closer to the light. The orb grew excited.

"What are you?" Krystal whispered, stepping out of the clearing.

The orb had no reply, dancing further and further away. Krystal followed. She paid no mind to the dark around her.

"Don't go," she said.

The orb stopped up ahead, floating above the undergrowth. It didn't fly away this time when Krystal came near. It was beautiful. It looked so soft. So delicate. It was only light and yet if Krystal reached out, surely, she would be able to hold it in her hands.

Something wrapped tightly around her wrist and yanked her back. She gasped.

"Come back to the tent," Draqa said.

He had followed Krystal? But. . . she hadn't heard him. She looked past him. Where did the tent go? Krystal looked back at the orb. It still hovered above the bushes.

"I don't understand," Krystal said.

Draqa pointed. "Do you see it? In the bushes?"

Krystal stared. There was nothing there except the orb. Wait—no. There *it* was. A short, gnarled creature with lengthy arms stepped out from the bushes. If Krystal looked directly at it, it faded from view. Did it have eyes? It had a sharp-toothed smile. It shook the long stick it held in its gnarled claws. The orb bobbed. The creature reached for Krystal. She stepped back, knocking into Draqa's chest. Draqa held her close.

"Leave us. You aren't welcome here," he said. His voice felt far away, like a dream.

The creature cocked its head.

"You are not welcome here," Draqa repeated in Yrlun.

The creature cackled—or was it a hiss? And backed away, it and the orb fading into the bushes.

"What was that?" Krystal's own voice felt far away, too.

"It was a *Naren Fané*—moon thief," Draqa said. He started pulling Krystal back the way she came. "I think you call it a wisp?"

Krystal glanced back over her shoulder. "How'd I get so far from the tent? I thought I was just outside the clearing."

"It skewed your perception of reality. . . You're lucky I saw you leave. *Naren Fané* are almost always malevolent."

Krystal asked, "How did you resist it?"

"Because it's difficult to fall for the same trick twice," Draqa said.

"What happened?" Krystal asked.

Draqa's grip on her wrist tightened. ". . .It led me to a book of spells."

"A spell book doesn't sound so bad."

"No, what you find if you follow a *Naren Fané* will always be bad." As if unnerved by his own words, Draqa picked up the pace.

Krystal shuddered. "What was wrong with the book?" she asked.

She was answered with silence. They arrived back in the clearing quite some time later, the tent and campfire appearing before Krystal's eyes like a lifting fog. Draqa guided Krystal into the tent and laid down in front of the exit, blocking her in. She laid next to him. Even in the dark, she could tell how exhausted Draqa's movements were. How long did it take for him to find her?

"I'm sorry you had to come after me," she said.

"It's all right," said Draqa, "Your eyes are beginning to see the Unseen. Something like this was inevitable."

"The Unseen?" Krystal remembered him mentioning them once before, before they'd come to Arai.

"The Fae and other beings who live alongside us in an intangible realm of existence. The Good Folk, faeries, ghosts, they are all the Unseen. Fae can see them easily, but humans and nalingur, we have a much harder time perceiving them without practice," Draqa said.

"So that's why you could see me when I soul-traveled?"

"It is."

Krystal turned on her side to face Draqa. That was the first time he had saved her.

"Do you regret it?" she asked.

There was a long hesitance from Draqa. He turned his head to her. She couldn't make out his expression.

"Not at all," he said.

Krystal would have asked why. She would have questioned Draqa about the logic behind his answer when he so blatantly disliked her. But in the short time it took for Krystal to recover from her surprise, the man had fallen asleep.

Draqa didn't wake again until late the following afternoon. When he did, he immediately expressed wanting to get moving again. He seemed somewhat better than the day before, but that didn't stop Krystal from being concerned about the inevitable ride, and she tried to convince him to rest a while longer. Draqa, of course, was stubborn, and within the hour the trio was off again. He still clearly struggled to ride Virsh, but his persistence was worth it.

Gradually, the trees thinned, and the mountain sloped down into a valley. By evening, the trio came upon the lights of a town, shining through one last thicket of trees. The buildings that came into view were quaint and cottage-like. A path lit by festive pink lanterns lead into the town center where a large fountain sat empty. From the name, Krystal expected Baren to a lot more. . . barren. And oddly, she found she recognized the place.

There were few people out at this time, most of them returning to their houses. Those who weren't didn't pay the trio any mind as they made their way to a building that was quite large in comparison to the others. Lights glowed from the windows and a sign hung in front of the double doors. Draqa slid down from Virsh and tied the horses to a lamp post.

"What's this place?" Krystal asked, helping Zalé off Feriosh.

"The hospital," Draqa said. He made no moves to go inside.

He stood frozen at the entrance until Zalé tugged on his shirt.

"*What's wrong?*" Zalé asked.

Draqa looked down at him, surprise crossing his features. He shook his head and pushed open the doors. Inside was an empty waiting room designed almost just like the ones in hospitals back in the Other Realm, buts its colors, its smells, less sterile. It was warm. Welcoming. Light emanated from somewhere on the ceiling naturally, as though there was no ceiling at all.

A lone dwerin sat behind a counter at the back of the room. She looked up when the three of them approached and gave Draqa a once-over.

"*You look like you had a rough day,*" she said. She spoke Yrlun, too.

Draqa nodded with the same demeanor that he had with the hulvoqn. "*I was shot.*"

The dwerin stood, pushing some papers over to him. "*Fill this out. I'll be back with the doctor momentarily.*"

She disappeared into a room in the back. Draqa filled out the paperwork slowly, his handwriting with his right hand almost more illegible than with his left. Or maybe that was how Yrlun was supposed to look when written? When the dwerin didn't return right away, Draqa directed Krystal and Zalé to the side where he slumped down in a chair.

"Is everything okay?" Krystal asked. Maybe it was her imagination, but Draqa seemed rather tense.

"It's fine. Just. . . impatient," Draqa muttered.

He closed his eyes, turning his face to the ceiling. Zalé curled up in a seat next to him and complained that he was tired, that the lights were too bright. Draqa quietly hushed him.

The dwerin soon returned with a naol in tow. The doctor was balding, and had deep wrinkles around his eyes, but his face was kind. He motioned the trio over and took Draqa's paperwork. He read it over and raised an eyebrow.

"You didn't put down your name," he said.

"Don't have one," Draqa said.

The doctor grunted and led him and Krystal and Zalé down a hallway and into a room. It was as bright as the rest of the hospital and was full of both familiar and foreign medical equipment. The doctor had Draqa sit on a table and Draqa obliged. The doctor turned, pulling out some kind of hand-held device from a drawer. He kept looking back at Draqa as he set it up, appearing to calibrate it with a metal plate on the wall.

"So," he said distractedly, *"you wrote that you were shot in the shoulder, and your head was bashed into the ground. What kind of mess did you get yourself into?"* He had switched to speaking that same naolen language that Draqa had spoken briefly in the tent.

Draqa nodded, keeping his head turned away from the doctor. *"We got mixed up in some trouble while we were on the road."*

"When did this happen?"

"A day and a half ago, about," Draqa said.

The doctor looked from Krystal and Zalé to Draqa. *"My—you're lucky to have made it here, then aren't you?"* He returned to Draqa. *"Now, I'll just take off these bandages to take a look at you."*

He started with Draqa's head, unwrapping the bandages slowly. Draqa met eyes with Krystal. Was that nervousness? With the bandages off, the doctor once again stared at Draqa. Draqa shifted.

"*Well?*" he asked.

"*The injury on your forehead is healing well,*" the doctor said, peeling his eyes away. "*Have you had any headaches or nausea? Dizziness or disorientation perhaps?*"

"*All but the nausea,*" replied Draqa.

"*You'll need to stay in one place and rest for a few days until those symptoms go away. There's an inn here that you can stay at,*" the doctor paused, "*I'm sorry, but I know you, don't I?*"

Draqa hesitated. "*I don't think so. . .*"

"*No, no. I know I do,*" the doctor said. He leaned closer to Draqa, squinting. "*I swear, you look just like. . . Oh, but you couldn't be. . . Jair Zevos?*"

Draqa's reaction was unexpected. "*You're mistaking me for someone else. I don't know who that is—*"

"*Why are you here? After all this time? They said you died,*" the doctor gasped, backing away.

Draqa fell silent a moment, and then he sighed heavily. "*They were wrong, obviously. I'm just here to get some help for my arm.*"

The doctor had a clear moment of crises, a million different emotions crossing his features until his mouth settled into a frown and his brows scrunched heavily over his eyes.

"*You should be in prison,*" he said.

Draqa's demeanor changed. His expression darkened. His eyes were so cold they sent a shiver down Krystal's spine.

"*Really? Sixteen years, and your first instinct is to say I should go to prison?*" he spat.

The doctor stuttered, "*That's—that's where you belong.*"

Draqa scowled dangerously. "*I think it would be in your best interest if you stopped that thought right there. Keep doing your job, take care of my shoulder and keep quiet, and I'll give you some compensation for your silence.*"

"*You can't bribe me,*" the doctor started.

"*Then Baren will find out that its oldest doctor has hung himself in the tree outside the hospital,*" Draqa said.

The doctor swallowed, and so did Krystal. Draqa had no idea she could understand his threats and the doctor's accusations. The doctor slowly nodded.

"*Y-You're right. I mistook you for someone else.*"

He hurriedly unwrapped Draqa's shoulder and brought the handheld device up to it. A holographic scan appeared in front of the metal plate on the wall, just like with the aspectacasters. The doctor nervously observed it. The scan showed a messy break along Draqa's collarbone. A dot floated in the middle of Draqa's shoulder.

The doctor said he was going to have to perform surgery, both to remove the bullet and to set Draqa's collarbone in place so that it would heal right. It would take a few hours. While he left to prepare another room, Draqa explained to Krystal and Zalé what had happened, and Krystal pretended she didn't know. She asked him why the doctor looked so shocked. Draqa lied so smoothly, so convincingly, Krystal almost believed the doctor *did* insult Draqa with slurs and other derogatory words rather than hint to more of Draqa's criminal past. Zalé commented that the doctor was mean for treating Draqa that way.

The doctor returned. He sent Krystal and Zalé back to the waiting room and escorted Draqa away. Krystal preoccupied Zalé while they waited. She didn't trust the doctor after all of that. Would he inform the police, or whoever took care of that sort of thing in Arai? Or would he try to get rid of Draqa and pretend something went wrong during the surgery? It was a far-fetched thought. Not everyone in Arai was as scheming or as tricky as Draqa was. The people in Arai were normal, good people, and Krystal just happened to be caught up with someone not-so-normal. Right?

21

Javis opened his eyes to the blurred sight of a room. Someone moved around, making a ruckus, which woke him from his painful sleep. Javis reached for his glasses on the nightstand, only to find there wasn't one. He sat up in alarm. Where was he? The person rushed to him, catching him at his shoulders and lowering him back onto the bed.

"Easy, easy." Talara cooed. She gently placed Javis' glasses on his nose. He recognised the room as the one above Talara's apothecary.

"Ta—" His voice caught, knives raking at his throat. The noise that came from it was mangled and high-pitched, not even recognizable as speech. Javis grabbed his neck, his eyes shooting wide. His breathing quickened.

"The poison did a lot of damage. You shouldn't speak if you want your voice to heal any."

Javis nodded slowly. But why attack his voice? Of all things, why attack his voice? Oh, but he knew exactly why.

Talara left his side and brought him a cup of water. He accepted it gratefully and looked around. It was then he noticed Averil sitting next to him in a chair, just watching him. He looked even more miserable than usual. Javis started to speak to him but stopped as the sound came out sounding something like a dying animal. This time his whole body shuddered with a wracking cough. Averil cringed. Javis gulped down the rest of his water. He left a bit of blood behind in the glass, and he gawked at it before shakily lowering the cup.

"Get him some paper, would you?" Averil said to Talara.

Talara pulled a notebook and pen from a drawer and handed it to Javis. Javis pushed himself up against the headboard.

"How are you feeling, Javis?" asked Averil.

How did Javis feel? His throat ached like he'd swallowed fire, his body weak like he hadn't used it in years. Slowly, he wrote, *I feel sick.* He paused, not sure what else to add. *What happened after I passed out?* he amended after a moment.

Averil exchanged looks with Talara and leaned forward on his elbows.

"One of the patrons called for a doctor. Talara showed up since, you know, she deals with poisons and that sort of thing."

Javis smiled at Talara in thanks. Heavy bags hung under her eyes. She must have been up for hours.

"I tried everything, Javis. I really did," she said, "but nothing I had had any effect. The spread of the poison slowed on its own. I have never seen anything like it before. It's almost more like a curse than a poison."

Javis' smile fell. So, he wasn't cured. *What is it doing to me?* he wrote.

"I can only describe it as eating you from the inside. Without an antidote, I'm afraid. . ."

Javis didn't need Talara to finish. He lowered the pen and notebook and stared at his hands. He could have made it to over two-hundred years old, if he were healthy. There was still so much he needed to accomplish. So much he wanted to do with his life, and he'd gone and wasted it. He was such a fool.

Averil put a hand over Javis'. "I'm so sorry. I should have been watching when the bartender made your drink. This is all my fault. I'm so sorry." His voice was trembling. Covering his mouth, he sobbed.

It was strange, watching his friend cry. All Javis could feel was a numbness that had settled over his chest. He put a hand on Averil's shoulder to comfort him. Averil pulled him into a tight hug.

"We'll fix this. We'll find an antidote, I promise. I swear on my life. You'll be fine," he said.

Javis rubbed Averil's back. The poor man didn't need this added stress in his life right now. Not while he was looking for his son. Javis pulled away to write again.

This isn't your fault. I brought this upon myself.

Averil read over Javis' messy cursive and rubbed his eyes, shaking his head. "I helped you do it."

There was nothing Javis could say to change Averil's mind. He wanted to believe as well that an antidote would be found, but that didn't stop him from writing his next words: *How long do I have?*

Talara threw up her hands defeatedly. "I don't know. Anywhere from a day to a year," she said.

A day was alarming, but a year Javis could work with. He just hoped his luck would last him that long.

He stayed in Talara's care for over a week. The first couple of days, Averil stayed with him, but Javis soon convinced him to go home to Kerevel Tul and seek out Zalé there. After that, all Javis could do was rest.

For the first few days, he still had to use paper and pen to communicate. He found it a hassle, and he was sure he would drive himself mad if he had to do it for the rest of his life, however long that may have been. Thankfully, on the fourth day, he discovered he could raise his voice ever-so-slightly to a whisper. Any louder, however, and he still could make no coherent sound. His throat ached every time he tried. It became increasingly clear that no amount of treatment would allow his voice to recover further. It was permanently damaged.

Javis began to feel fine, otherwise. His strength returned to him and the sickly feeling subsided. Even his coughing fits lessened—at least for a time. Talara didn't understand it, once again stating the poison seemed more like a curse, like it had been engineered to behave unpredictably. Javis took her word for it. He knew nothing about poisons.

The only good thing that came from all of this was his time with Talara. Granted, her job as a healer was to take care of anyone who was sick. But, Javis enjoyed her company, nonetheless.

He had never had the chance to watch Talara work before

this and wished he had sooner. The way she meticulously crushed powders and mixed solutions—mesmerizing. Not that she wasn't always. Talara was one of the most beautiful people Javis had ever met, inside and out. That hadn't changed in the entirety of the five years he'd known her. Talara was rather like a warrior, with her tall stature and eyes that burned with the ferocity of fire. But she truly was a gentle soul. Javis found it difficult not to fall in love with her all over again while she tended to him.

They first met, of course, in the drād clans of Erothel. Javis had just been relocated, so many of the people there were understandably wary of him. One person in particular he noticed seemed to be keeping an extra sharp eye on him. He paid no mind to it at first, but once the behavior had continued well into his stay with the clan, naturally, Javis became curious. He decided to introduce himself properly one day. Talara didn't seem too keen on making conversation with him at the time, and he considered himself lucky to even get a name from her. Even still, he was taken with her immediately.

It took time and many stays with her clan, but Talara allowed Javis to talk with her more and more. He learned little things at first—the foods she liked, her favorite times of year. In return, Javis opened up for her. From there, their relationship progressed rather quickly. They shared things with each other that they hadn't with anyone else. Javis learned Talara had been wary of him because outsiders—a rogue band of humans—had stripped her of her wings when she was young. He learned she wanted to leave the clans, but the action would have her denounced by the Elders if she ever tried.

Just as Javis knew who had hurt her and her insecurities, Talara learned the same of him. He told her about his troubled family, how his mother was killed when he was just a boy, how he and his brother were bullied mercilessly while their father grew to love his drink more than his own sons. Talara learned of every fight Javis had with Jair, of how Javis blamed himself for his brother's fate. That after finding his father dead on the floor, surrounded by bottles so soon after what happened to Jair, it was too much for Javis. He abandoned everything he had been working towards. All his dreams.

He and Talara tried to help each other through their pain. But while Talara grew and gained confidence, regained her trust in the world, Javis remained stagnant. He stayed stuck in his past and in his shame. Even now, he still used a glamor to hide his damaged eye more days than not.

In the end, Javis knew this was the real reason why Talara rejected him. The drinking, the denial, it would be too much for anyone to deal with. Every excuse Talara gave after that was just her giving another reason why they couldn't be together anymore. Another reason why Javis needed to move on. Really, Javis was lucky Talara tried to be there for him at all anymore. And he did try. He tried to get better and tried to move on. Some of his attempts worked, most of them didn't. But staying with Talara now, he realized all that came from any of it were more regrets.

After he had stayed in Talara's care for nearly two full weeks, Javis decided he couldn't stay any longer. He didn't want to sit around, waiting for something to happen while he only got worse.

Even if he couldn't find an antidote once he left, at the very least he could take care of things back home. He wasn't sure he could stand to face Talara any longer either way.

"I'm leaving in the morning," he said after making up his mind.

Talara worked downstairs, mixing ingredients, laboring to find an antidote. She had closed the apothecary except by appointment only, so she was alone.

"Are you sure that is wise?" she asked.

"I'm not getting any better by staying here," Javis said. Talara pursed her lips. Javis added quickly, "I know you're trying your hardest, but those are the facts. Who knows, perhaps I'll finally get Lhorsan Phar's attention and he'll get some people to investigate Sius Mavell Evi."

An unreadable expression settled in Talara's eyes. She set aside her work.

"Has it ever occurred to you that you should listen to me for once? Do you have a plan?"

"Well, I—"

"Then stay. I told you not to get involved with the Governor, and you didn't listen. You still have hope, but you need to stay here. I won't be able to help you if you don't. Please, I am begging you to be patient," Talara said.

"I can't afford to be patient. You said yourself you don't know how long I have. I need to get as much done as I can before—"

Talara slapped him. He stuttered and touched his stinging cheek, shocked.

"Listen to me! I'm trying to help you!" Talara yelled. Her eyes filled with tears as she stepped away from Javis. She had taken hold of his hand. "Why are you so reckless? You have no *idea* how you hurt the people who care about you."

Javis wasn't sure what to say. He didn't mean to upset her. This isn't what he wanted. "Ara. . ." he started.

Talara wiped her eyes on her sleeve. "Do you even want to be helped?" she asked.

Still, Javis' words failed him. The sad part was, he had to wonder if what Talara said was true.

22

Sunlight stabbed through Draqa's eyelids, sending a sharp pain through his skull. He groaned, turning his head away. His shoulder throbbed. He could vaguely recall the surgery and refusing to allow the doctor to make him sleep. He'd been given an anesthetic instead, but he must have passed out during the surgery anyway, as his memories from there on were fuzzy.

He blinked his eyes open. His arm and shoulder had been wrapped in such a way that he couldn't move them, a proper sling. Otherwise, he found he lacked any clothing from the waist up. Grimacing, he pushed himself against the headboard and observed the room. It was painted green and an off-white. The drapes were wide open, along with the window, and sunlight filtered in. Draqa cursed whoever wanted him to suffer in such a way.

To his right sat a bedside table with a cup of water and a small plate of food. Normally, Draqa might have been wary of poison in a situation like this, but he was too famished to give a damn. The food turned out to only be bland and cold.

Draqa set aside the plate when he finished. Where were Krystal and Zalé? Draqa moved to the edge of the bed, about to get up, when the door opened. The naolen doctor came in. He looked briefly startled but composed himself.

"Ah—I see you're awake. That's good," he said, once again in the Naolen tongue.

Draqa grunted. The doctor stayed back from him.

"And you—you're already moving around. Wonderful! If you'll allow me to look over everything one last time, then you're free to go," he cheered.

He nervously checked over Draqa's shoulder and head, making sure they were in order.

"Where are my companions?" Draqa asked as the doctor stepped away again.

"Who—oh—the woman and the boy? I sent them to the *huum* when it looked like you would be asleep for a while. I believe they took your horses as well," the doctor replied.

Draqa frowned. "And my things?"

The doctor gestured to a chair where Draqa's coat and shirt had been neatly folded. He stood, causing the doctor to flinch, and walked over to his belongings. He rifled through the pockets of his coat and pulled out his coin bag. He dumped a handful of flats out, along with a lantern-shaped pod scarcely bigger than a marble. Its thin, vein-like membrane revealed a smaller orb inside it, and the pod itself was filled with an amber resin. Draqa returned the money to his bag and held out the pod to the doctor.

"What's this?" the doctor asked, his eyes widening.

"An Irun's Bell. For your trouble and your silence, like I said."

Draqa could see the doctor try to fight his greed. The resin-filled pod was a rare and valuable item anywhere, used in anything from potions to poisons to perfumes, and in general just looked pretty. Draqa had this one from a trade he made a few months back. Inevitably, the doctor scooped up the pod and pocketed it. A wise choice.

Draqa carefully slipped on his shirt and coat.

"You're leaving?" There was some relief in the doctor's voice.

"No need for me to stay here," Draqa said. He pushed past the doctor, muttering a thanks, and left the hospital.

The townsfolk's eyes followed him as he trudged miserably through the town. Though certain the doctor told no one who he was, he stuck out like a wart on the tip of a warlock's nose. He was something foreign to the townsfolk. Not just a nalingur, but some scarred freak as well. He was new and different and scary. Good. Hopefully, people were scared enough to stay away and leave him alone.

If Draqa remembered correctly, the *huum* was still in the same place it had always been. Nothing in Baren ever changed. Sure enough, when Draqa rounded the corner, the *huum* sat between the deli and the bakery. Sixteen years and the place hadn't even been repainted. Behind the *huum*, Feriosh, Virsh, and Eldoc were stabled with two other horses.

Draqa entered and was met with the same stares as outside. He ignored them and made his way to the manager—a younger elf who couldn't possibly recognize him as the doctor had.

The manager looked Draqa up and down, not even bothering

to hide his suspicion and disgust. "Can I help you?"

Draqa nodded. "I'm looking for my companions. A ginger-haired woman and a young boy. I was told they came here."

The manager narrowed his eyes, saying, "We have no one like that staying here."

"No, my horses are here, so they have to—" Draqa stopped, catching sight of Krystal and Zalé coming down from upstairs. The manager looked too, and Draqa smirked.

He waved Krystal and Zalé over. They looked relieved.

"You're awake!" Zalé said, trapping him in a hug.

Draqa startled at the hug, but the friendly behavior was enough for the manager to be left stuttering when Draqa said, "Are you going to tell me next that there aren't any rooms left?"

"O—of course not," the manager mumbled.

"Good. I'll need one for a week or two," Draqa said. "My companions here will also be staying that long, so I'll be paying for their rooms as well."

"Do you even have the money for that?" the manager asked as though Draqa was some kind of pauper.

Draqa simply pulled out the silver flats from his coin bag and handed them over.

"Is this enough?"

The manager nodded. "Let me just get the key to your room." He scrambled away.

Draqa let out a sigh. He looked to Krystal. She gave him a little smile, though said nothing until the manager gave Draqa the key and they went up to Draqa's room.

"Did everything go okay?" she asked.

Draqa nodded absently. He kicked off his boots and laid on top of the bedsheets. He just wanted to go back to sleep.

"Are you hungry? Zalé and I were about to have breakfast," Krystal said.

"I ate already," Draqa said.

"Oh. Okay. . ."

Draqa watched Krystal stand beside the bed awkwardly. By now it must have been a strain for her to remain this friendly with him. Was she afraid of him? It occurred to Draqa that he never even asked if she was okay, after she'd been dragged into the middle of his fight with Tolas Ruv Aen. But Draqa didn't know what he would say to her. He certainly couldn't—and wouldn't—apologize. Could he?

"You were able to get a room here on your own?" he asked finally, then worried that he sounded like he implied Krystal was incapable.

Krystal shrugged. "I had help from Zalé. And I've picked up on some words from listening to you both. I was able to get the message across easy enough."

Draqa had to smile. "I'm impressed."

Krystal returned the smile. "Well, I'm glad you're okay. We'll let you rest now."

Zalé waved at Draqa, and Krystal returned downstairs with him. Draqa's mind drifted, settling among thoughts of his fight with Tolas Ruv Aen, Krystal trapped helplessly in the elf's grip. The look of fear in her eyes when Draqa nearly pulled the trigger was still etched in his mind. Never before had he been able to resist Sius Mavell Evi's orders. Not to that extent. Draqa's mind felt clear now, not weighed down by the Governor's presence. A wave of guilt washed over him for nearly killing Krystal, but it disappeared as quickly as it came, as Draqa closed his eyes and fell asleep.

Draqa slept for several days, only waking occasionally throughout that time to eat or drink. Krystal checked in on him more than once, but he barely noticed. He slept so heavily, he even forgot he was back in his childhood town.

The pain in his head subsided. By nearly a week, he felt well enough to move around without aggravating it. Even his shoulder began to feel a tad better. As long as he did nothing strenuous, he could ignore its throbbing.

He decided he needed a bath, and after that, he washed some of his clothes. It felt good to be clean. After a time, he grew hungry, and dared to go downstairs to order himself some food. He stopped by Krystal and Zalé's room, but they were nowhere to be found. They weren't downstairs, either. Maybe they had gone into town. Hopefully, they stayed safe.

Draqa took his food over to the corner where he ate quietly. There weren't many people in the *huum* this afternoon. Only the manager, who shot him an occasional narrow-eyed glance but otherwise left him alone.

It was very strange, being back in Baren. The place really hadn't changed since he left when he was seventeen. At least, the people hadn't changed. Was his father's house still there, he wondered? Had someone finally moved into the place? Perhaps he would walk around later, see if anything he knew as a youth was still the same as well. Perhaps he would see if the jail had been rebuilt. Surely, it had to have been by now.

Draqa returned his plate of food to the front, but he waited until Krystal and Zalé had returned before he went out. He got their attentions and nodded for them to follow him back out onto the cold street.

"Are you feeling better?" Krystal asked. "Where are we going?"

"Well enough. I needed to stretch my legs and wanted you to come along," Draqa said. Truth be told, he would have been uncomfortable going by himself.

The trio walked along in silence until they'd left the center of town. Here, there were fewer people, fewer stares. Draqa relaxed a little.

He spoke up again. "How have they been treating you and Zalé at the *huum*?"

Krystal shrugged. "They're. . . Honestly, they're not very nice."

Draqa nodded. "That's how it is here. Either way, you shouldn't go off by yourselves like that again."

"Would they try to hurt us?" Krystal asked.

"I don't know, but most people here were never the most tolerant of nalingur," Draqa said. He could remember all the times the other boys his age had harassed him. They were the violent ones, parroting their parents' opinions and taking it out on Draqa. His life had been hell.

He brought Zalé and Krystal near the edge of the forest, where the little pond with the pretty fish sat frozen, covered by a thin layer of snow. A bench now sat near the water's edge, but otherwise the area had remained the same as it had always been.

Krystal looked around, smiling. “This is pretty.”

Draqa sat at the bench and observed the pond. He expected some sort of ghost or specter to be wandering above the ice, but the pond was just a pond. No one would have guessed it had been a young man’s watery grave.

Krystal sat to Draqa’s left and Zalé to his right. Zalé rubbed his hands together and tucked them under his armpits.

“Are you cold?” Draqa asked.

Zalé nodded. Draqa opened his coat and shared it with Zalé. He closed his eyes. He found it surprisingly easy to think of nothing out here.

“Draqa?” Krystal asked.

“Hm.”

“Did you live here?”

Draqa hesitated. Was it that obvious? Or had Krystal dreamt of him again?

“. . .I did,” Draqa said finally, unsure how he felt about Krystal knowing.

“I thought so. You seem really familiar with everything,” Krystal said.

She didn’t give away anything further, but Draqa had to wonder just how much she actually knew. She knew about Draqa’s father, yes, and his brother. Did she know about this pond and what happened in the forest just beyond it? Was Krystal aware of the nature of Draqa’s relationship with Sius Mavell Evi?

Draqa didn’t know why he worried so much of what Krystal thought of him. She was no one. It shouldn’t have mattered what she thought. Yet, it did, and it bothered Draqa that she gave nothing away in her actions towards him. She was friendly and cheerful, and for the most part very passive. She showed worry that Draqa was hurt, but it was no different than the worry she had shown when Zalé, at the time even more of a stranger than Draqa, nearly had his hand cut off. It was almost as though Krystal had no underlying motives or feelings at all. But that couldn't be right.

Draqa looked back out towards the pond, annoyed with himself for feeling so bothered. Krystal was nothing to him. He didn't like her, yet he couldn't find it in himself to hate her, and he was too tired to continue being angry with her. She was just another person he had to deal with in a day.

That wasn't quite true, either. Krystal *was* the first person in a long time who'd shown him any kind of care, even despite being essentially stuck with him. Draqa found he enjoyed talking with her—she listened to him. She *understood* him. Or at least, she seemed to. The only other person like that had been Tolas Ruv Aen, but whatever spark they'd had had died when Tolas Ruv Aen joined the Ard'a.

". . .back?" Krystal asked. She was looking at him now.

"What was that?" Draqa asked.

"Do you want to head back? It's cold," Krystal repeated.

Draqa looked at his companions. Zalé huddled right up against his side. Krystal shivered just a little. Draqa's own face stung from the cold. He nodded and heaved himself to his feet.

"Didn't mean for us to be out for so long," he mumbled.

He led Krystal and Zalé back to the *huum*, pushing his thoughts aside. It was better not to worry about Krystal. She would be out of

Draqa's life soon enough, and he would be back doing his regular tasks for Sius Mavell Evi. Things would be back to normal.

The following three days proved exceedingly difficult for Draqa to follow his own advice. For every reason he came up with as to why he shouldn't allow himself to care, he came up with two more as to why he should. He soon found himself repeating the same reasons over again when he ran out of new ones.

It didn't help that Krystal made herself as useful as possible. Once again, she apologized to him for getting in the way. She even apologized for following him into Arai in the first place. Disyr, she was ridiculously genuine in her remorse. If her goal was to guilt Draqa, it worked.

Draqa was forced to the conclusion that he did care about Krystal at least a little bit, after all. He accepted that he worried what she thought of him because she made him feel some semblance of, well, not quite happiness, but some semblance of something. Draqa found himself wanting to start over with her. To pretend they had only been talking in the Other Realm for a day or so and were able to get to know each other normally. At the very least, perhaps they would be able to put aside everything that had happened thus far.

Draqa did a lot of thinking about how best to approach that subject with Krystal over those three days. He tried harder to be more pleasant with her each time she popped in to check on him or spent a few hours with Zalé in his room. With Zalé too, he did his best to be friendly. Zalé seemed to notice right away and became even more comfortable with Draqa. Krystal acted no differently, which frustrated Draqa to no end.

He took another bath, hoping he might come up with an idea, only to decide he thought too hard about all of this. The next time he saw Krystal, he would just say what had been on his mind. He returned to his room and dried himself off. In fact, he would go right to Krystal and Zalé's room and get it over with. But then someone knocked on his door while he was in the middle of struggling to put his shirt on. He thought he answered for whoever it was to wait a moment, but he clearly went unheard, and the door creaked open. He stopped, shirt stuck halfway over his head, and listened.

23

"DID YOU NEED SOME HELP with that?" Krystal asked. Her voice came as a pleasant surprise after what Draqa briefly feared.

He breathed a sigh of relief. He glanced at her, offering the tiniest of smiles.

"Help? Oh, my shirt? I can handle it. . . but thank you."

Draqa hurried himself along, ignoring the aches of protest that came from his shoulder. He then turned fully to Krystal and saw she watched him closely. He unconsciously felt over the intricate lines tattooed between his shoulder blades.

"Do you. . . need something?" he asked.

Krystal shook her head. "Not really. Just checking on you again. I thought maybe you'd want to go for another walk with us since we didn't go yesterday, but your hair's wet, so maybe later."

"I think I would like that," Draqa said. And it was true. He felt even better than he had the other day, and he was getting restless again.

He hesitated, remembering what he wanted to say.

"Actually—I need to talk to you about some things. If that's all right?" he said.

Krystal looked surprised, but she nodded. She sat on the edge of Draqa's bed.

"What's up?"

She watched Draqa even more intently now. Draqa took a breath. Why was he so nervous?

"First, I wanted to thank you. For. . . helping me after I was beaten by Tolas Ruv Aen. I know I haven't shown it, but I. . . appreciate it greatly," he said.

They way Krystal's eyebrows raised, one might have thought Draqa had asked her to marry him. She didn't answer for a long moment, her mouth moving wordlessly.

"You're welcome," she finally replied. "I mean, I couldn't just leave you to struggle like that all on your own."

Draqa pulled up a chair and sat in front of her. "But you could have. I know we're stuck with each other, but you could have. You could have taken advantage of my injury, but you didn't. All you've done is help me."

Draqa continued before Krystal had the chance to deny him further. "Also, I. . . how do you say it in English? Start . . . start over? Yes. I want to start over."

"Start over? What for?" Krystal asked, tilting her head.

"I haven't treated you as well as I could be. I've treated you horribly. Like an annoyance," Draqa said. He paused to gauge Krystal's reaction. She nodded a little. She looked confused.

". . .And I don't think you're an annoyance. Not at all. I *was* angry with you when you first came here. I'm not anymore. I should have expected that you would have wanted to come here after everything I told you. I was careless, got carried away, and that's not your fault." He clasped his hands and played with his thumbs as he thought of what to say next. "The truth is, it felt good when we talked. You're the first person I—who's made me feel comfortable in a long time. For that, I want to continue getting to know you. But I also know I've done things, and you may have seen a lot about me that. . .isn't particularly good. So, I'll understand if you don't want to. But if you'll let me, I. . . want to try to be a friend to you," he finished, looking Krystal over hopefully.

Krystal bit her lip. She took even longer to answer, and Draqa felt himself getting nervous. Perhaps he was too late.

"So. . . you know I've still been dreaming?" Krystal asked.

"You've confirmed it just now, but I suspected you were," Draqa said. He surprised himself with his next words. "I'll answer any questions you might have about them." At least then he would be able to find out how much Krystal knew.

"No. I don't want to pry. The memories seem personal," Krystal said, "I don't want to dream them at all." Bless her.

Draqa sat forward. "I want to know what you know. No—I *need* to know. What do you think of me?"

Draqa somehow had Krystal's brows furrowing and raising even higher. He realized he sounded insecure.

"I—then, tell me about your scars—or no. What does Sius have to do with them?" Krystal asked, her face pink.

Draqa couldn't stop his expression from straining. He was prepared for any question except that one. He hesitantly held out his right hand. It was bare since he hadn't the chance to put his gloves back on after the bath. Krystal gently took his hand and looked it over.

"I'm sure you saw by now, but my entire body is covered by them," Draqa said. He watched Krystal run her fingers over his palm and the back of his hand.

"You can't feel this, right?" she asked.

"Not at all. . . Maybe some pressure in some areas," Draqa said.

Krystal reached forward and touched his face. "Here too?"

No. Draqa could feel a light sensation as Krystal ran her fingers from his cheek, past his eye and to the side of his head. He swallowed.

"I can feel it a little," he said, pulling Krystal's hand away.

Krystal's eyes scanned him slowly. She said, "After Tolas left, I dreamt that you were in a lot of pain. And you were in a bed, and Tolas was there. I think Sius saved you. But it was confusing, like a dream in a dream. I couldn't tell exactly what happened to you."

Draqa closed his eyes at the memory. He knew exactly when Krystal was talking about. Even sixteen years later he could remember exactly how it felt, the flames licking, melting his skin.

"I was set on fire. Or, I was the target of the fire," he said.

"Why would anyone do that? That's horrible," Krystal said. Draqa opened his eyes again to find his hand was back in hers.

". . .I killed someone," he said. "More than one person, actually. The arson was revenge." Well, there it was. Draqa waited for the disgust. It never came.

"I'm so sorry. That must have been excruciating," Krystal said, her voice a whisper, eyes glazed over. For just a moment, Draqa was sure Krystal could picture exactly how it felt.

"It was hell," he said, "and when it happened, I knew I was dying. I thought I had, too, but then I woke in Sius Mavell Evi's care. He did everything he could for me."

He thought again of the brand on his back. He didn't know why, but he had the sudden urge to open up about it, too. Krystal caught on before he had the chance to decide.

"Are you bound in servitude to him or something because he saved your life?" she asked.

Draqa nodded. But it was much more than that. So much more. He wanted to tell Krystal of Sius Mavell Evi's strange sorcery forcing him to bend to the Governor's will, of all the things he'd made Draqa forget. He wanted to tell Krystal that no matter how aware he was of Sius Mavell Evi's doings, he was never able to go against him no matter how hard he tried. At least, until Krystal came along. But just as soon as Draqa opened his mouth, fear gripped his heart. So instead, he ran a hand through his hair and said, "I've had to do many terrible things for that man."

Truly, Draqa wasn't the same person he had been before Sius Mavell Evi entered his life. His life wasn't even his own anymore. He was just a puppet, existing solely to do his master's bidding.

He didn't notice the trembling in his voice from how upset he'd made himself. Krystal regarded him delicately and spoke with a soft tone, as though he might break at any moment.

"Like with Tolas?" she asked.

"Like with Tolas Ruv Aen. Many people know me for it, too. That's why they call me Draqa."

"What does it mean?"

Draqa exhaled heavily. "It's a drenen name. It was the name of a dragon in their folklore who destroyed entire villages in his vengeance against those who wronged him. It means something akin to hellish one." It was a name that suited him perfectly, but somehow admitting that reality to Krystal now made him feel ill. He closed his eyes again, bowing his head in shame. He felt Krystal rub his arm, tentatively at first. She said nothing, and she didn't need to. Her company just then was enough.

24

SEEING A MAN LIKE DRAQA in such a vulnerable state was strange. Here Krystal was thinking Draqa hated her, that he wanted her and Zalé out of his life as soon as possible. But then, there was the truth, sitting crumpled in front of Krystal like a broken thing. Krystal didn't know how to comfort him, didn't know if she should, didn't know if he deserved to be. What had sparked this in Draqa to make him want to open up about so many personal things? What made him want to, as he put it, "start over?"

Krystal felt sorry for him. She understood now, a little. If Draqa had no control over his life and had been through so much, it made sense why he was so bitter. But Krystal now felt more conflicted than ever. Could they really start over? Krystal didn't know if she wanted to while knowing the things Draqa had done. How could they start over when she didn't know if she could trust that he wouldn't do the same to her, either for Sius Mavell Evi, or for some other selfish reason? She also remembered the strange man she had met in the Other Realm. The man sitting in the bookshop, talking of wonderful, impossible things. The one who seemed so much more at ease, so much more content. The one who ordered the same drink every time and always added an additional three sugar packets. That was the man she trusted, the man she felt comfortable with, too.

In the end, Krystal made up her mind. "I want to start over, too," she said.

Draqa's head shot up. His eyes grew wide, as though he never expected her to feel the same. "Why?" he asked.

Krystal shrugged one shoulder, although she couldn't quite meet his eyes. "I guess. . . I just miss what we could have had? I liked you when we met back home. And you're right, you have been an ass. I dunno if we can be friends, and. . . you kind of, um. . . you scare me sometimes. A lot."

At that, Draqa closed his eyes. "I know," he muttered.

Krystal wondered if he, too, was thinking about how he almost decided to shoot her. She reached to lightly touch his hand. "But. . . . if you're willing to try, I think it's worth it for me to try." Draqa still seemed so unsure and acknowledged the fact that even if they did start over, Krystal and Zalé weren't safe travelling with him. He would take them soon to the next town over, where they could board a train to Kerevel Tul and meet Averil. From there, what happened would be up to Krystal. If she wanted to stay in Arai, Draqa would find her a place to stay, get her an aspectacaster, some clothes, some money, and whatever else she would need. If Krystal wanted to go back to the Other Realm, Draqa would do everything in his power to get her home. Krystal asked him if he still worried about what would happen if they were caught. He didn't answer, so Krystal took it that he was.

Krystal stood finally to go back to her room. "You know, if I stay, you should stay, too," she suggested.

Draqa looked up at her. "What do you mean?"

"Don't go back to Sius. You can start over, and never have to see him again," she paused and smiled. "You could become my language tutor."

A quiet chuckle left Draqa's lips. "Maybe I could."

Over those next few days, Krystal noticed the tense atmosphere between herself and Draqa gradually vanish. To her great joy, Draqa did start teaching her Yrlun. He taught whenever he felt like it, whenever there was an opportunity to learn something relevant. He was right before when he said he wasn't a teacher. His method was sporadic, and he didn't always pick up where he left off from previous lessons. But he was trying his best, and that was all Krystal could hope for. He taught her how to introduce herself, phrases to ask for help, and some general words relating to the *huum* and the town. Krystal still didn't tell Draqa she wore the translator, afraid of how he might react if he saw it. Besides, it was better to learn Yrlun in case the device was ever lost.

Tolas Ruv Aen didn't show any signs of returning like he said he would. After almost two weeks since Draqa's fight with him, it seemed he either couldn't find Krystal, or had decided it wasn't worth his time to try. Krystal was rather relieved about this. While she was curious about what Tolas Ruv Aen would have to say, she didn't want to know what would happen if Draqa saw her and the elf together. Now that she and Draqa were starting out on a clean slate, it was better to do nothing that would jeopardize that.

By the end of the second week, the trio decided it was time to get moving again. The townspeople's treatment of them continued to be unsavory more often than not, and with Draqa feeling well enough, there was no point in staying any longer. So, they packed their things and gathered the horses.

Baren had a festive, giddy air that morning. Tiny, colored lights hung from buildings and lampposts in the square. A fresh snow from the night before glistened in the streets. A small market was being set up with tents draped in ornately pattered fabrics. Krystal let out a breath of awe. It was somewhat reminiscent of home, and Krystal realized people back home would be decorating for Christmas around this time as well.

"What's the occasion?" Krystal asked.

"Hm?" Draqa muttered, more preoccupied with Virsh.

"The lights," Krystal said, gesturing.

Draqa looked around as though he was only just noticing the festive decorations for the first time.

"It's for celebrating the winter season. Most smaller towns and villages decorate for it," he said indifferently.

"Not Christmas?" Krystal asked. The lights seemed to her to be very similar to the traditional Christmas colors of green and red with the occasional gold.

Draqa's expression grew thoughtful, and he stopped to observe a table being set up. "Some people may celebrate something close to it, but that's really more of a human thing. My father's practice was derived from Christianity, but even he barely acknowledged holidays."

"Do you celebrate?" Krystal asked. Draqa struck her as the kind of man who didn't follow any traditions.

"I'll acknowledge winter the same way I acknowledge the other seasons. They're just seasons to me," Draqa said as he got moving again.

Krystal hesitated, continuing to watch people set up.

"Krystal," Draqa reminded.

Krystal took Zalé's hand and pulled Feriosh to follow Draqa.

Draqa looked over her. "There will be celebrations in Kerevel Tul. The ones there are better, anyway," he said. He led Krystal and Zalé in the direction of the entrance to Baren.

Krystal took one last look at the town and the festive lights. Down the street, a group of uniformed naols exited the hospital. Dread settled in her stomach as they made their way towards the trio.

"Draqa, look. . ." she whispered.

Draqa looked back at her, and when his eyes darkened, she knew he saw the uniformed men, too.

"Just keep moving," he said.

Krystal's gaze lingered a moment longer. One of the men pointed.

"You there! Stop!"

Draqa swore and quickened their pace.

Zalé whined. *"Oh no!"*

"Who are they?" Krystal asked.

"*Diauks.* They're—" Draqa fumbled over a few words in English and swore again before saying, "They're military police."

He stopped suddenly and tried to grab Krystal and urge her onto Feriosh. She struggled to right herself, Zalé already frantically climbing into her lap.

"Go—don't stop until I say," he growled. He smacked on Feriosh's rear, and the horse took off. Krystal held tight to Zalé and the reigns. She fought the urge to close her eyes. She looked behind her just a moment to see Draqa separating Eldoc and Virsh, sending Eldoc running. He mounted Virsh and took off after her and Zalé. Krystal desperately steered Feriosh towards the town entrance. Her heart thumped rapidly in her chest as the men shouted after them in Yrlun.

"Cut them off!"

A diauk appeared in Krystal's vision. He ran in front of Feriosh and raised his arms. A transparent yellow barrier flashed in front of him. Feriosh reared and Krystal wheezed as she landed smartly on her back. Zalé landed on top of her, making her cough. He rolled away and she groaned and pushed herself up. Feriosh had bolted in the opposite direction, back towards the pursuing diauks. The diauk who made the barrier approached Krystal and Zalé. Zalé hugged Krystal's arm and glared at the diauk. The diauk moved to grab them when Draqa came riding over, stopping Virsh in front of him. Krystal expected Draqa to wait for her and Zalé to get on, and maybe he would have, but the other diauks had caught up. Draqa slid from Virsh's back, blocking Krystal and Zalé from their view. Krystal scrambled to her feet and helped Zalé up.

A middle-aged looking naolen man came forward. The tip of his tail flicked back and forth as he eyed Draqa.

"*Would you look at that,*" he said, canines bared. His were larger and sharper than Draqa's. "*Jair Zevos, truly back from the dead.*"

Draqa clenched his fist.

The diauk continued, "*I didn't believe Doctor Morozefa at first when he said you had returned. I assumed some rogue yilura, maybe, but not* really *you. I'm surprised, truly.*"

"*Vei Iolkoszehn. . .We aren't here to cause any trouble,*" Draqa said.

"*You think I believe that? You take me for a fool?*" Iolkoszehn said, scoffing. He waved his hand and the other diauks surrounded the trio, separating them from Virsh and restraining them.

"*Don't touch my horse—*" Draqa started.

Iolkoszehn sneered, "*You're about to have a lot more to worry about than your horse.*" He turned to Krystal. "*And who's this? People you kidnapped and plan to kill, or people who plan to help you kill someone else?*"

He grabbed Krystal's chin and tilted her face to the side. She narrowed her eyes and pulled against the diauk pinning her arms back. Iolkoszehn's fingers were rough on her skin.

"*Hm. Part fae but lacking so much you might as well be fully human. What a shame. What's your name, girl?*" Iolkoszehn asked.

Krystal bit her tongue.

"*Well?*"

Zalé piped up, "*Leave her alone! She doesn't understand you!*"

Iolkoszehn clicked his tongue and turned back to Draqa. "*So, what are you doing here?*" he asked.

"*I needed a doctor. This was the closest town,*" Draqa said, "*or is it illegal now for me to get help?*"

Iolkoszehn bared his teeth again. "*Your existence is illegal as far as I'm concerned. You have a lot of nerve coming back here after everything you've done."*

"I served my sentence," Draqa said.

"Served? You **escaped** *it."*

"I didn't start that fire."

Iolkoszehn's face flushed red. *"You were supposed to die in that fire!"* he shouted. There was a pause and Draqa looked briefly surprised. Iolkoszehn composed himself.

"You have no idea how much it angers me to see you still breathing instead of my son," he said.

Draqa spat, *"Your son deserved it."*

Iolkoszehn grabbed Draqa's collar, yanking him forward. Krystal tried to pull away to help him, but he held up a hand.

Iolkoszehn got in Draqa's face. *"I'm going to make sure you're put away for a long time. I don't know how you survived before, but this time you won't be so lucky."* He dropped Draqa and turned to the others.

"Arrest him," he said.

The diauk holding Krystal gripped her wrists tighter. *"What about these two?"* he asked.

Iolkoszehn looked over Krystal and Zalé. Draqa somehow managed to pull away from the diauk holding him and moved back in front of Zalé and Krystal, blocking them with his good arm.

"Let them go," he said. Two other diauks immediately dragged him away. He struggled against them.

"They were part of an escort job I took. Let them go." Once again, Draqa sounded so convincing. Iolkoszehn hesitated.

"A job for who?" he inquired.

Draqa quickly said, *"Averil Monarain. That boy there is his son."*

Iolkoszehn repeated the words quietly. *"Averil Monarain."* His eyes dragged to Krystal. *"And her?"*

Draqa nodded. *"Also a Monarain. Or does that name not mean anything to anyone anymore?"*

Iolkoszehn scowled. *"We'll need to confirm that. Take them all away,"* he said.

The diauk holding Krystal pushed her, and she stumbled as the trio was led away. She watched Draqa for his next move, but he didn't try to fight back—not that he could have, still injured as he was.

They took the trio to a flat, one-story building shoved between two slightly smaller ones. Inside, Krystal realized they were in a jail. Krystal caught her own ghostly reflection in the polished gray floor as she and Zalé were taken to a back room, and she wondered if she looked as scared as she felt. The diauks locked them behind a barred glass door and left them alone.

"Are we going to be okay?" Zalé asked. *"Why are they doing this?"*

Krystal put a hand on his shoulder, shaking her head. She had a general idea of why this happened. She just couldn't believe how quickly it did. Just a moment ago they were leaving town. Everything was looking up. How did things go wrong so quickly?

Krystal approached the door and peered through the bars. She could see Draqa in the front room, now fully restrained. He passed Krystal's door as the two diauks holding him pushed him down the hall. Draqa made eye contact with Krystal for just a moment, and he mouthed, "Don't worry."

Krystal sat on the single bed in the back of the room with Zalé at her side. Together, they waited.

Hours crept along. They had no interactions with anyone. Occasionally, a diauk walked in view of the door. Snippets of muffled conversation filled the otherwise suppressing silence. Krystal caught the words "execution" and "murderer," which did nothing to reassure her about her and her companions' situation. Despite this, she tried to remain in a state of relative calm, comforting Zalé by running her fingers through his hair.

One of the diauks finally approached their room. Krystal grew hopeful, but the diauk only turned down the hall. He reappeared a moment later, dragging Draqa back into the front room. Krystal stood. Draqa struggled this time—frantically. Iolkoszehn walked up and grabbed Draqa's injured shoulder and squeezed until Draqa's knees buckled. They escorted him from the jail.

No. What was that? Where were they taking him? Krystal ran to the door and slammed her fist against it. She yelled.

"Hey! We're still in here!"

She didn't care that none of the diauks would understand her. She didn't care if they figured out where she was from. The only thought in her mind was that she was just separated from Draqa—perhaps for good—and she couldn't do anything about it.

She pounded harder on the door. "Hey!"

No one came. She fell to her knees, gripping her hair. They were alone now. Draqa was gone. He was there and then he was gone.

"Krystal?" Zalé asked. He sounded afraid, but when Krystal turned to him, she caught her reflection in the polished floor. She looked terrified.

25

LAUGHTER RANG *through Draqa's ears. It mocked him, humiliated him as he tried to stand. Iolkosz Wacziro's foot made contact between his shoulder blades, and he fell back into the mud. He tasted pond scum in his mouth. The other three young men around him brayed. Iolkosz's foot remained planted on Draqa's back, try as he did to escape.*

"Look at him struggle! He's like a pig wallowing it its own shit!" Iolkosz crowed. He kicked Draqa in the side.

The torment ceased for a moment, and Draqa pushed himself up onto his arms. He stared into the water. He couldn't see any of the pretty fish that usually swam about.

As Draqa had gotten older, the people in Baren had become more and more blatant about their hatred for what Draqa and his brother were. The disapproving glances that were once shot in their direction had become outright refusals to serve them in shops. The gossip and whispers that floated through the air wherever they went became slurs thrown in their faces, and spit on their shoes as they walked through the street. And

Iolkosz? He had only gotten more violent. The townspeople must have realized they could get away with anything now that Isaias Zevos was too consumed by his drink to care what happening to his sons.

Javis, of course, didn't have it nearly as bad as Draqa in the end. Iolkosz and his crew had left him alone for the most part. Javis had learned early on that if he gave in, if he denied what he was and bent at the knee and kissed their shoes, he could be easily ignored. Even if that meant abandoning his brother. Now, the prodigy was off somewhere apprenticing for some kind of clerical position, learning divine magic. And Draqa was still here, his face in the mud.

Iolkosz kicked Draqa in the side again, pushing him further into the water. Draqa grimaced and tried to stand once more. He wouldn't give in. Not to them.

"You're still trying? Damn you're stubborn. I liked it better when you cried easily," Iolkosz said.

Draqa grit his teeth. "What? Are you too weak compared to me now?"

"Me? Weak? You're the weak one, Zevos. Look at yourself. You're a mess. You can't stand right. You go home every day and wallow in self-pity, and then you can't even do us all the favor of killing yourself properly."

That hit a nerve. Draqa stood fully. He got in Iolkosz's face and spat in it. Iolkosz made a face of disgust and wiped the saliva from his eyes. He cleaned his hands on his pants and scowled, showing off his canines. Draqa immediately regret his actions.

"Big mistake," Iolkosz said.

He swung at Draqa, punching him square in the nose. He heard the crack before he felt it, and he fell backwards into the pond. Time slowed. The ringing in his ears and the splitting pain in his nose were the only things he was aware of. When he opened his eyes, Iolkosz jumped on top of him. Iolkosz grabbed Draqa's face and shoved his head into the pond. Draqa didn't have the chance to hold his breath and swallowed a lungful of water. Iolkosz yanked Draqa back up. He blubbered and coughed, only now comprehending what had just happened. His lungs burned. He made eye contact with Iolkosz and was pushed under again.

Once again, he had no time to prepare before the water entered his nose and mouth. His body expelled the water on impulse and his airway screamed the longer he was held under. Again, Iolkosz pulled him out, giving him only a moment's reprieve from the torture before his head was shoved back into the pond. It lasted longer and longer each time. Yet, somehow, Draqa wasn't afraid. He accepted it.

Then, it all ended as quickly as it started. Iolkosz's weight on top of Draqa disappeared. When he was pulled from the water, Iolkosz and the others were gone. A naol in spiritual garbs stood in their place. He eased Draqa onto his hands and knees. Draqa's body heaved, the water leaving his system. It streamed from his mouth and nose. He continued to retch for minutes after. His savior's hand on his back the whole time held him steady. Draqa finally looked up at the man.

"Vei Alarach. . ." Draqa said weakly.

He knew the cleric well. Afterall, Alarach was his mother's uncle. More importantly, he was the man who convinced Javis to leave.

"Come now, up you go," Alarach muttered, gently helping Draqa to his feet. "Let's get you to Doctor Morozefa."

Draqa leaned on his granduncle the whole walk into town. He ignored the stares he received as Alarach brought him into the hospital. Alarach stayed with him long enough to be treated, which was as much as Draqa could hope for. Even Alarach, the one who had approved of the marriage between Isaias and Draqa's mother, preferred the older, more perfect twin. Still, Draqa was grateful the old cleric came to his aid, and Alarach was nowadays more present than Isaias, despite living in Kerevel Tul.

"I informed the authorities about those boys again," Alarach said, "but Vei Iolkoszehn still likely won't do anything about it since it's his son."

Draqa shook his head, then winced at the pressure it put on his now reset nose. "It's all right. Thank you. . ."

He walked home by himself. Isaias was passed out on the couch when Draqa got in. Good riddance. The drunkard didn't even wake when Draqa stomped up the stairs to his room and slammed the door.

Draqa collapsed on his bed. He just wanted to sleep, and stay asleep for a long, long time. He wouldn't mind if he never woke up again. But his face ached too badly for him to fall asleep. Groaning, he got up and pulled his book from its hiding place under his mattress. Making himself comfortable under his bedsheets and propping himself up against the headboard, he flipped through the book's yellowing pages.

He'd learned a lot in the year since he found the old thing. While he still struggled to teleport, he could perform most of the other spells and incantations fairly well. He'd realized too, that the reason for this was that many of the spells written in the book were created or altered by humans. This also meant many of the more complicated spells were what the fae considered to be an impure kind of magic, not like what Javis studied, or the natural magic of the faerish people. Draqa would be condemned and looked down upon if anyone knew he was using it, but he didn't see how it would change much, so he didn't care.

The book contained only one spell Draqa hadn't dared to try. It was a spell of the wordless variety and Draqa knew it was dangerous from the moment he first read it. The spell allowed the caster to turn any living being into their puppet. Draqa stared at the page before him. He ran his fingers over the oxblood calligraphy, caressing each stroke, each letter. He often found himself dreaming of using the spell to control his enemies, becoming their puppeteer as their bodies betrayed their minds. Draqa dreamed of watching them plead for his mercy while he made them do unspeakable things. There was only one catch for the spell to work. Draqa would need Iolkosz Wacziro's blood.

***

Iolkoszehn returned a number of hours after he had Draqa taken away. It was nighttime by then. Or maybe early morning? Krystal wasn't really sure. She'd fallen asleep with Zalé after it seemed no one would be coming back for a long time. It wasn't a good sleep. Krystal dreamed about Draqa's past again. His torment followed her when she awoke. His hatred weighed on her heart. It made her body feel heavy and she couldn't bring herself to move. A sickly, disgusting feeling churned her stomach. She didn't want to sleep and experience that again, so she was awake when Iolkoszehn opened the door to the cell. Krystal stood.

Iolkoszehn said nothing at first, only leaning on the doorframe, observing Krystal.

Finally, he said, *"I looked into it, and it would seem Zevos told the truth. Averil Monarain really has been looking for his son. Except. . ."*

He stepped inside the cell. Krystal narrowed her eyes, but Iolkoszehn didn't get more than three feet from her.

"He isn't looking for you. In fact, I was under the impression there were only two left in the Monarain family. So, who are you really?" He paused and let out an airy laugh. *"But that's right. You can't understand me."*

Krystal held back a reply. Iolkoszehn didn't seem to have realized she spoke English and she was hesitant to give it away now. At least, not yet.

"It's a shame, really. If I knew who you were, maybe I would be more inclined to let both of you out." He stepped around Krystal and reached for Zalé.

Krystal grabbed Iolkoszehn's arm. He stopped and looked at her in surprise.

"I can understand you just fine," she said, though she knew she wouldn't be understood herself. She pushed her hair back, revealing the translator.

Iolkoszehn ripped his arm away, stepping back. His eyes grew wide, his expression angry and fearful. *"You're part of the Ard'a?"* he croaked.

Krystal hesitated before remembering what Tolas Ruv Aen said about the translator being specifically used by members of the Ard'a. She nodded sharply and pointed to the front of the cell.

"Let us out," she demanded.

Iolkoszehn eyed her, a hand moving to the weapon on his belt. He gripped it tightly, before appearing to change his mind and lowering his hand again.

"Where are you from?" he inquired instead.

Ah. So, he did recognize the language Krystal was speaking as one not from Arai. Krystal shook her head and pointed again, repeating herself. Iolkoszehn's lips twisted, and he grumbled. He stepped out of the way, bowing slightly.

"My apologies. You're free to go, Vara Monarain."

Not taking her eyes off the man, Krystal moved to Zalé and shook him awake. Zalé sat up groggily, then immediately whimpered when he saw Iolkoszehn. Krystal grabbed his hand.

"Zalé, komm," she whispered, urging him forward.

They left the cell and Iolkoszehn followed them into the front room. He ducked behind the desk and pulled out their bags. Krystal hurriedly took them.

"And *gerat?*" she asked.

Iolkoszehn cringed at her poor attempt at asking for the horses.

"They're in the stable across town," he said.

Krystal nodded and ushered Zalé out the door. The sky was lightening. It wasn't until they were out of view from the jail that Krystal stopped and turned to Zalé. He hugged her tightly.

"I was so scared," he said, his voice muffled against her stomach.

Krystal returned the hug, holding the back of Zalé's head. Zalé kept his face buried in her coat for a long moment before he pulled away. Krystal smiled at him, and he rubbed his eyes and smiled back at her. He took her hand again, and Krystal walked with him to find the stables. Krystal hoped Iolkoszehn had meant the one behind the *huum*, but neither of the horses were there when they checked. By that time, people were already making their way out of their homes and the streets grew busy.

Zalé's stomach growled. Neither he nor Krystal had eaten since the morning previous. They stopped near a streetlamp so Krystal could look through their bags. There should have been some food left, but after digging around, Krystal felt nothing. She groaned. The food was gone. The diauks must have helped themselves to the rest of the food or thrown it out while Krystal and Zalé were locked in the cell. At least they still had money. . . Except, when Krystal felt around for the bag of coins, it was gone too.

Krystal cursed aloud, pushing the bags away. She bit back tears. She had to stay calm for Zalé, but she had no idea how to deal with any of this. She didn't know where Draqa was, let alone how to get there. They had no food or money for it. What were they supposed to do? Krystal ran her hands over her face. Someone stopped in front of her and took the bags from the ground.

"Well now, sweetheart, don't go swearing in front of children. That's inappropriate," he said.

Krystal's head shot up. "Tolas!"

Tolas Ruv Aen made a face, handing the bags back to her. He said, *"Tolas? Sorry, I don't know a Tolas."* Despite his serious expression, his tone was light.

Krystal frowned in confusion. "Huh?"

"My name. It's Tolas Ruv Aen, not Tolas," The elf said. He smiled with a wink. *"For future reference."*

"Oh, sorry," Krystal said, her focus more on her relief at his presence than his reprimand. She watched Tolas Ruv Aen crouch down and cheerfully introduce himself to Zalé.

"You came back," Krystal observed.

"I said I would, didn't I?" Tolas Ruv Aen' eyes landed back on her, and he furrowed his brow. *"You look exhausted. What are you doing out here by yourselves? Where's Draqa?"*

Krystal had trouble finding her words. "Draqa, um. . . the *diauks* took him. I don't know where. We spent the whole night in jail."

"*What?*" Tolas Ruv Aen stood, looking angry. "*Who was in charge? Was it Iolkoszehn?*"

Krystal nodded, surprised Tolas Ruv Aen knew him. "He has some kind of grudge against Draqa," she said.

"*Of course he does! That piece of shit is the reason Jair—*" Tolas Ruv Aen paused and pinched the bridge of his nose. He took a breath. "*Iolkoszehn tried to have him killed when he was younger,*" he said.

Of course, Krystal had already gathered that much. "Do you know where they took him?" she asked.

"*No,*" Tolas Ruv Aen said, throwing on Krystal's pack. "*But I can find out real easy. I'm guessing they took my Virsh, too?*"

"Iolkoszehn said our horses were in a stable somewhere. We were just looking for it," Krystal said.

"*I do know where that is,*" Tolas Ruv Aen said. He started off, gesturing for Krystal and Zalé to follow.

Tolas Ruv Aen went back to the jail. Krystal could almost feel the rage pulsing from him when he entered the building, but he remained composed.

"*Where's that bastard Iolkoszehn?*" he demanded.

The diauk sitting behind the desk was one of the ones who helped with the initial arrest. He looked stupidly at Tolas Ruv Aen, then at Krystal and Zalé.

"*Er. . . What do you need him for?*" he asked.

"*That's none of yer concern. Now you can go get him, or I can get him myself,*" Tolas Ruv Aen threatened.

The diauk shrank a bit in his chair. "*He just stepped out,*" he said.

"He helped arrest Draqa. Maybe he knows," Krystal said.

Tolas Ruv Aen raised an eyebrow. He leaned over the desk, putting his weight on his fists. *"Do you know where Draqa is?"*

The diauk swallowed. *"I'm not sure I'm allowed to say."*

*"Boy, I **will** force you. Where did you send Jair Zevos?"*

"He—he was moved to the prison in Keln," the diauk sputtered.

Tolas Ruv Aen clapped his hands and straightened. *"Now see, that wasn't so hard."* His anger seemed to disappear in an instant, and he whisked Krystal and Zalé back out onto the street.

Getting over her surprise, Krystal asked, "Where's Keln?"

"It's the next town over. We can get there while its light out if we leave soon," Tolas Ruv Aen said.

Before they left town, Krystal mentioned she and Zalé hadn't eaten anything for a whole day. In response, Tolas Ruv Aen promptly bought them each a hot roll from one of the street vendors. The rolls were mildly sweet and stuffed with some kind of curry-like meat and sauce—much better tasting than what Krystal and Zalé would have been eating if their bags hadn't been raided.

Tolas Ruv Aen retrieved the horses from the stable. He tied Virsh and Eldoc to follow behind his own horse and together he and Zalé and Krystal finally left Baren.

They travelled the road for much of the day, even with the pace Tolas Ruv Aen set for the horses. Krystal still had doubts about Tolas and his intentions. He was so willing to help her and Zalé, seemingly wanting nothing in return. There had to be a catch.

"Tolas Ruv Aen. . .?" Krystal asked, "When you left us before, what did you do?"

Tolas Ruv Aen glanced back at her. *"I was in Keln, actually. Reporting to my superiors,"* he explained.

"Did you tell them about Draqa and me?"

Tolas Ruv Aen nodded. "*I did.*"

Krystal bit her lip. That didn't sound promising. "What's going to happen?" she asked.

"*Honestly? Not sure yet. I just know they want me to bring both of you in.*" Tolas Ruv Aen's voice wavered.

"Are they. . . going to kill us?"

"*Oh goodness no. Not you, at least. As for Draqa, his situation is more complicated. He committed treason against the whole realm, and he's guilty of loads of other crimes aside.*" Tolas Ruv Aen cleared his throat. "*But you shouldn't worry. The Ard'a—or my superiors at least—they're impressed with him. They might not want him dead.*"

Krystal hummed in understanding. Tolas Ruv Aen's words did nothing to reassure her, or Zalé for that matter.

"*I don't want Draqa to die . . .*" he whispered to Krystal.

Tolas Ruv Aen chuckled lightly, "*He won't.*"

"So, what does the Ard'a do?" Krystal decided to ask. "Iolko-something got scared and let us go when he saw me wearing your translator and thought I was one of you guys."

"*Did he? Serves him right,*" Tolas Ruv Aen said. His lips turned into a smirk that he clearly tried to hide.

Krystal's own mouth mimicked Tolas Ruv Aen's smirk before it drooped back into a frown.

"Are you part of the High Council?"

"*Oh no, not at all. The Council is official. The Ard'a, well, we're less legal, I'll put it that way. Both us and the Council are concerned with the security of the realm, but the Council's more diplomatic about it,*" Tolas Ruv Aen said. He looked back at Krystal. "*You know, yer father's the one who founded it, that is if you really are a Monarain."*

Krystal tilted her head. "He was? But I thought he was Erothel's president or prime minister or whatever," she said.

Tolas Ruv Aen's voice dropped an octave. "*That too. See, one could say he was getting fed up with the Council, and he realized they were functionally useless. To fix that, he founded the Ard'a to do what they couldn't, or wouldn't. We do the real protecting of Arai around here. Yeah, if the Council has you arrested for treason, sure you might face the firing squad if yer crime's bad enough, but usually you'll be taken care of by the Ard'a long before the Council even knows you exist,*" he said.

Krystal shivered. She looked around, feeling as though the Ard'a could be watching them at that very moment. "Did, um, did you know my dad?"

"*I'm sorry to say I didn't. He died long before I joined,*" Tolas Ruv Aen sighed. He closed his eyes. Smiling wistfully, he said, "*That man was truly something, I'll tell ya. I remember listening to his speeches over my aspectacaster when I was just finishing my schooling. He had visions for the future, and he made them happen.*"

Meeting her father really would have been something. The more Krystal heard about him, the more she missed him.

"Wait," she realized. "Is it okay for you to tell me all this? Isn't it supposed to be a secret? Or is this one of those 'I'd tell you, but then I'd have to kill you' situations?"

Tolas Ruv Aen laughed. It was a deep and hearty laugh that shook his whole body. It made Krystal smile.

"*I haven't told you anything classified yet. Everyone knows who we are. Fewer know how to recognize us, but it makes no difference so long as the Council don't do nothing about it—which they won't,*" Tolas Ruv

Aen said.

In the end, Tolas Ruv Aen succeeded in making Krystal feel like maybe things were going to be okay after all.

Keln was much bigger than Baren. It had a distinctly European feel, with many old, stone buildings. In the town square was a train station, and a railroad divided the town in two halves. Tolas Ruv Aen had Krystal and Zalé hop down from the horses, and he brought them to a pause in front of the station as a train pulled to a stop.

"Well, here we are. Lovely Keln. The prison's at the edge of town over that way. I'd say you and Zalé might would better wait here in the plaza till I get back," he said.

Krystal looked around. No one seemed to take notice of them standing there, but Krystal remained nervous. "I'd rather go with you," she said. Zalé nodded in agreement.

Tolas Ruv Aen tapped his foot. *"Well, if you both insist. But know this will take a while."*

"That's why we should go with," Krystal said.

Tolas Ruv Aen shrugged. He pointed ahead. *"Come on, then."*

The train began disembarking passengers as they got moving. Behind them, a voice screeched, so animalistic and ungodly sounding, Krystal almost didn't catch what it said.

"Zalé!?"

26

THE SCENERY PASSED QUICKLY in front of Javis' eyes as he stared blankly out the train window. His mind thought not on the snow or trees or bushes that rushed passed. In the end, he had still decided it would be best to leave Talara's care. He couldn't get her to approve of his actions. She fought his decision right up to when he walked out the door.

He didn't know why he chose to take the train to Arkaven instead of an airship. Trains were so slow in comparison. They were often cramped, and because this was a split-second decision, he wasn't able to reserve a compartment to himself. But the thought persisted—perhaps if he went slower, so would the poison, as ridiculous as it was.

The couple across from Javis stared at him. Were they wary because of what he was? Or were they simply confused that an ambassador wasn't riding in first class? Normally, Javis would have let it be. The couple had yet to say anything to confirm their thoughts, but the stares irked him the longer they lasted.

"Did you want something?" he asked, all too irritably. His voice was still weak.

"Er. . ." the man across from him started.

Javis tore his eyes away from the window. The couple looked at each other, then at their laps.

"Aren't you Ambassador Zevos?" the woman asked.

Javis held her gaze, wondering if he should even bother to answer. He mumbled a yes, then looked back out the window. The woman said something else, but it fell on deaf ears.

Javis didn't know who he was fooling. Lhorsan Phar wasn't going to listen to him. The Minister never listened to him. Hell, there was no reason he *should*. Javis still had no proof. He stuck his nose into something he shouldn't have—something he wasn't even qualified to handle. And now he paid the price for it. But who would have done anything otherwise? Who would have stepped up, if not Javis?

Phar agreeing to meet with him was the only other reason Javis had to justify why he was going to the capitol. Because maybe this time it would be different. Maybe this time the Minister would realize he needed to focus not on Adonis, but on the people who claimed their loyalty was to Erothel. The recordings on Javis' aspectacaster weren't solid evidence, but Javis wasn't sure he had time to gather any more.

Javis sighed and rested his forehead against the window. The cold glass made his skin ache. He never was cut out for politics. It was never something he wanted to do, yet here he was. He had always counted himself lucky. His father's name had still had just enough influence to help Javis into this position after he threw away all his other opportunities. Now though? Now, he regretted it. His life was made up of one stupid decision after the next.

He closed his eyes and convinced himself to rest. There were still over nine hours ahead before the train arrived at the city near the border of Erothel's Southern Province and Adonis. There was nothing else Javis could do until he arrived. It may have been the poison causing it, but his body felt tired and heavy, and he fell asleep within seconds.

The couple across from Javis was gone when he opened his eyes again. He had sprawled across his seat. He sat up and rubbed an eye groggily. The compartment was dark, just as it was outside. Javis frowned. He stood and activated a light which dimly lit the compartment. It was quiet. Most everyone was likely asleep.

Javis stumbled out of the compartment. The train was still moving. He could feel it as he made his way to the front. Why was it still moving?

In the cab, the driver sat back in his chair. He rested his head on his hand while his other three operated the controls.

Javis came up behind him, clearing his throat. "Where are we?" he croaked. He had to repeat himself before he was heard.

The driver looked back at Javis and said something in one of the four elven languages, none of which Javis spoke. Javis realized the driver must have been one of the many who didn't or refused to learn Yrlun.

Javis cleared his throat again. "Arkaven?" he asked hopefully.

The driver frowned and nudged his assistant awake. The driver's assistant groaned and sat up, muttering words that could have only been obscenities. The driver gestured at Javis, replying something gruffly. The assistant frowned, too, and looked at Javis.

"How close are we to Arkaven?" Javis tried again.

"You missed the stop. We're two hours out," the assistant said. She looked annoyed.

Javis' gut twisted. He mouthed the words the assistant told him. Missed? He *missed* the stop? How had he slept the whole train ride? Javis covered his mouth, feeling sick.

"When. . . when is the next stop?"

The assistant huffed. "You'll want to get comfy, cause Keln's another ten hours away." She turned back around, leaning back in her seat.

The driver went to ignoring Javis as well. Javis slowly returned to his compartment in a daze. He had to use the walls for support. Even though he knew he could get on a different train back to Arkaven, a heavy feeling settled in his chest. He lost his chance, didn't he? He was too late. He wouldn't speak to the Minister in time. He'd be dead before he even reached the walls of Arkaven.

Javis arrived back at his compartment and collapsed onto his seat. He stared at his shaking hands, then burst into tears.

When the train pulled into the station in Keln, Javis was exhausted, emotionally and physically. Overhead, the driver's assistant announced that passengers could begin disembarking. Javis raised himself from his seat with a heavy sigh and cast a final look out the window. There weren't many people wandering the plaza at this time in the afternoon, but there were still enough for Javis to be uncomfortable in his current state.

Just before Javis turned to trudge out of his compartment, a group with horses caught his eye. Really, it was the flash of ginger hair that had his attention. Panic gripped him again until he saw the hair belonged to a human woman and not Sius Mavell Evi.

Javis' eyes lingered on the group. An elf, who towered over his companions, held the horses' reins. Holding the ginger-haired woman's hand was a young boy. A very familiar, half yiluran boy. Javis had never deboarded a train faster in his life.

He tripped down the train steps, pushing his way through the crowd of other passengers and called out. His voice came out as an unintelligible screech, but it was enough to make the group turn. Javis stopped in front of them, breathing hard. He had to put his hands on his knees. His lungs burned more than they should have.

"Zalé!" he choked out.

Zalé gasped. He jumped in front of Javis and squeezed him, barely giving him a chance to catch his breath.

"Javis!" Zalé laughed.

Javis put a hand on the boy's back. He might have cried again for Averil's sake if he weren't too tired for it.

"There you are you silly child. Your father has been worried sick for you. We've been looking everywhere," he whispered.

Zalé pulled away. "I was kidnapped, but now I'm safe. And I have friends now."

Javis nodded. "Are you okay? Were you hurt?"

Zalé shook his head and asked, "Is Papa here?"

"He's still looking for you. He thought you were on your way home." Javis pulled Zalé into another, shorter hug.

Zalé smiled and looked back at the two behind him. "We are," he said.

Javis finally observed Zalé's company. The ginger-haired woman, Javis realized, wasn't human at all, but nalingur. She, like himself, had only her ears as visible proof of her faerish blood. As for the elf, he had a rugged face set with sharp eyebrows and an arrogant smirk. One of his eyes had been replaced with a prosthetic. Javis held Zalé closer. Was this Draqa? He couldn't be. If he was, he wasn't at all like what was described. But it was possible. Javis wasn't sure if he should have felt relieved or disappointed.

Meanwhile, the woman was staring at him. Her face was oddly familiar, although Javis couldn't quite place it. He remembered his manners and offered a bow.

"Hello, I'm—" His voice squeaked. He grabbed his throat and looked away in embarrassment.

But the woman didn't seem to care how he sounded. She held out a hand. "Javis Zevos?" she asked. She had a strange accent.

Javis shook her hand, nodding carefully. "Who are you?"

The woman pointed to herself. "Krystal Monarain."

It was Javis' turn to stare. Monarain? But how? Averil didn't have any siblings, or any relatives other than Zalé and Sius Mavell Evi for that matter. But now that Javis looked closer, the resemblance between Krystal and Averil was all there—their eye shape, their noses, even the way they smiled. Even more unnerving was Krystal's resemblance to Sius Mavell Evi. Her face was covered in just as many freckles and her hair was just as red as the Governor's once was.

Averil was supposed to have a sibling a long time ago, but his mother died—disappeared—before she could give birth. Had they actually survived?

All Javis could manage to stutter was, "How?"

Krystal shrugged and replied in a language Javis didn't recognize. It certainly wasn't a language that was spoken in Arai. The elf beside Krystal cleared his throat.

"She said it's a long story," he said. This accent Javis knew. The elf spoke with a heavy drawl characteristic of those who spoke the lower of the elven languages.

Javis surveyed him once more. "And who are you?"

"I'm Tolas Ruv Aen. Pleasure to finally meet you, Ambassador," the elf said. He had a charming smile.

Javis frowned. "Are you not Draqa?" he asked.

Tolas Ruv Aen's eyes widened. "Draqa? Oh goodness, no!" He laughed. Then he paused and looked at Javis seriously. As if reading Javis' mind, he said, "Yer not looking for him, are you?"

Javis wavered, unsure if he could trust this man, before nodding.

"When I was helping search for Zalé in Talnoq-Vyn, we heard Draqa had him and was on his way to Kerevel Tul."

Krystal nodded excitedly. She started to speak again, before stopping and looking to Tolas Ruv Aen.

Tolas Ruv Aen took over for her. "You heard right. He was with Krystal and Zalé, but, ah, he got arrested while they were in Baren and now he's at the prison here. We were just going to get him now."

Javis immediately made up his mind. "Can I go with you?"

Tolas Ruv Aen and Krystal looked at each other. The way they did told Javis they knew what he was thinking.

"Are you sure you want to?" Tolas Ruv Aen asked. "You might not like what you see."

"Then, tell me now. Is Draqa my brother?"

"Yes."

"Then I have to see him."

Javis had many questions on the way to the prison. Most he kept to himself. He did get an explanation, though brief, of how Krystal came to meet Draqa, and subsequently Zalé. It explained why Krystal spoke a language so unlike any of the others in Arai. What Javis didn't fully understand was how Krystal could understand everyone despite that. Stranger to Javis was how his brother got to the Other Realm to retrieve Krystal in the first place. Only Gatekeepers could do that.

Oh, his brother.

Javis quickly realized as they arrived at the prison that he was not prepared to see Jair at all. No, not just unprepared. He was terrified. All these years, he lived thinking Jair was dead. All these years, blaming himself.

The prison stood high above him. In this moment it was a dam, holding within its gates every regret he ever had and mistake he ever made, threatening to unleash them with its waters at any moment.

Tolas Ruv Aen went inside alone, having Javis and the others wait outside. It was a long, anxious wait. Then, finally, the floodgates opened. Javis braced himself for impact.

27

THE CEILING WAS LEAKING. There was a steady *drip drip drip* as the water splashed onto the floor of Draqa's cell. It wasn't *really* a cell. Draqa would have a trial before he went to one of those. But it felt like a cell. It was cool, and dark and, well. . . wet.

Here and there, Draqa heard soft, echoing voices, and a shimmering specter would pass through one of the walls. Of course there would be people who had died in this place. Draqa closed his eyes and covered his ears. He hated ghosts. All of the fae could see them, but most of the time ghosts couldn't see the fae, or at least were too trapped in their own plane of existence to be able to interact with the living.

Some said to become a ghost one must go through purgatory, and one could only move on when they repented. At least, that's what the humans in Arai said. Others said ghosts were just people who chose not to move on but could at any time. Personally, Draqa believed the former, but either way, it usually took a strong magic to force a ghost to move on to the next world.

Draqa was probably going to be executed. At least, if Iolkoszehn had any say in the matter, Draqa would. In fact, it was almost a guarantee now that the man knew Draqa had survived the fire he set sixteen years ago. Not to say Draqa didn't deserve it. He knew he did. All he could hope for was a painless death when it came down to it. His real fear came from the thought of becoming one of the ghosts who were cursed to wander the realm alone for an indefinite amount of time. Draqa shuddered. He'd rather his soul ceased existence entirely than face that fate.

Sooner or later, someone would inevitably come for Draqa and determine his punishment. He grew anxious for it. He had woken up alone in his cell some hours before, after the diauks escorting him from the jail in Baren had to sedate him. He didn't know how long he had slept, but he'd had dreams of his past in that horrible town. Obviously, Krystal dreamt them, too. But then, those dreams became twisted nightmares of Draqa falling down and down and down, further into a shadowy abyss. It was filled with hate and anger and sadness and guilt. The feelings suffocated him, squeezing out all oxygen from his lungs. When Draqa hit the bottom, he'd woken up on the cell's cold floor, his shirt soaked through with sweat. He hadn't slept since.

He tried to comfort himself. At least Krystal and Zalé would get released, although Draqa didn't have much hope of that happening, either. But if they did, maybe they would find their way to Averil. Maybe, just maybe, Draqa could escape and meet them. He could take Krystal and together they could go somewhere far away, far from Sius Mavell Evi and the dangers of Draqa's past.

They could go to the Other Realm, or else to a nation like Creus or Nymn, or an island far to the east.

Draqa laughed at that last thought. When had things gotten so bad for him that he succumbed to having child-like escapist fantasies? Certainly, Krystal wouldn't want to escape with him, anyway. She had nothing to escape from. Whereas Draqa. . . it was impossible for him to truly escape from everything he'd done. Oh, but how he wanted to. Not that he knew what he would do if he did, but he could dream.

The whispers around Draqa were suddenly interrupted by an argument that erupted on the floor below his. Draqa couldn't see out of his cell, but he could easily hear as the argument continued up to his floor.

"You can't just take him—there's paperwork to fill out first! He is meant to go on trial!"

The voice that replied was one Draqa knew immediately. "I can, and I will. Damn yer paperwork."

Draqa stood, backing against the wall of his cell. What was *he* doing here? Unwanted, dangerous desires stirred and swirled inside Draqa, just when he thought Krystal had helped get rid of them. The cell opened. Tolas Ruv Aen leaned in the doorway.

"Congratulations, yer getting rescued," Tolas Ruv Aen said.

Draqa stared at him. He was certain he heard wrong. Rescued? Beside Tolas Ruv Aen, the guard had stopped making such a fuss, but continued grumbling to himself. Tolas Ruv Aen watched Draqa expectantly, a stupid grin on his face.

"What the fuck are you doing here?" Draqa growled.

"Ah, no, this is the part where you say, 'Thank you, Tally. Yer my hero, Tally. What can I ever do to repay you?'" Tolas Ruv Aen's impression of Draqa made something inside him snap.

Draqa made to punch him, but Tolas Ruv Aen caught Draqa's arm and twisted it, forcing Draqa to his knees. Draqa cringed.

"Did you miss the part where I said I was rescuing you? Disyr's name, Jair!" Tolas Ruv Aen said.

He hoisted Draqa to his feet. Draqa glared at him.

Tolas Ruv Aen clicked his tongue. "Don't make me hurt you again. I'm doing this as a favor for yer friend, Krystal."

Krystal was okay? Relief washed over Draqa.

"How did she find you?" he asked.

"I found her. It was my idea you three go to Baren in the first place. And before you ask and start jumping to conclusions the way you do, I gave Krystal a translator so she can understand me. She's not part of the Ard'a," Tolas Ruv Aen said.

Draqa looked down at his feet as the information sunk in. Somehow it didn't at all surprise him that Tolas Ruv Aen tried to spread his influence onto Krystal. If he turned her against Draqa so soon after things might be getting better for him, that would be horrible. Despite that, this rescue—if Draqa could call it that—was really happening.

"There must be a catch. There's always a catch with you," Draqa said.

"No catch." Tolas Ruv Aen grinned almost too widely.

He turned out of the cell, pausing for Draqa to follow. Draqa did, albeit with some reservation. He had no choice but to trust the elf as he led Draqa down to the main floor. There, Tolas Ruv Aen filled out some short paperwork. Draqa waited, trying not to give away how impatient he was. Tolas Ruv Aen looked at Draqa as he returned the paperwork.

"How're you feeling?" he asked. He motioned that they could leave.

Draqa held his tongue, not keen on the idea of having small talk with his old mentor. He shrugged. "I think you know the answer to that."

Tolas Ruv Aen held open the door for him. "In that case, I hope yer prepared for a family reunion."

Too late did Draqa realize what Tolas Ruv Aen meant, already stepping outside. He froze in his tracks. Krystal ran to him. She might have asked if he was all right, but he didn't hear. It was as though all of time came to an immediate halt, for looking back at Draqa from the bottom of the steps was his brother.

When time started again, Javis was the first to move. Draqa remained rigid in his spot, his eyes following Javis' slow and nervous march up the stairs until they came face to face. They stared at each other. Javis looked older. Tired. It was the same look their father had in the last few years before he died.

Draqa could feel Javis' eyes touch every inch of the scars marring his face and hands. They traveled over his body, guessing how far the scars continued. Then, they met Draqa's own eyes and Javis covered his mouth.

"Is. . . is it really you?" he asked, his voice rough and whispery.

Draqa tilted his head. There was something off with Javis. Or else he had changed so much and for the worst in only sixteen years. That was no different from Draqa, really.

Javis reached for Draqa, but Draqa found his strength again and stepped away before he could be touched. Javis followed.

"I can't believe it. You've been alive this whole time," he said. "Is it true you've been working for Sius Mavell Evi?"

Draqa nodded. A lump formed in his throat. He glanced at the others around him. They watched him. His attention was brought back to Javis when he felt the other man pull him into a hug. Draqa's past anger almost made it to the surface. He almost—almost—pulled out of the hug and pushed Javis down the stairs. He would have been happy to watch. At least, he thought he would have. But he didn't. Instead, he remained in the hug, felt Javis tighten his grip around his torso.

"You have no idea how much I—I mean—I'm so sorry, Jair. For everything. I've blamed myself this whole time. You have no idea how much I regret," Javis said.

Draqa finally found his voice. It was calm. Emotionless—or he tried to make it so. "Regret doesn't change the past."

Javis pulled away from the hug. He wiped his eye—the blind one, Draqa recalled.

"I know. I'm sure you must hate me. I promised I would always be there for you, and I ran away. I don't expect you to forgive me for that."

Draqa had to take a few minutes to sort out how he felt. He hadn't expected to see Javis again, let alone hear an apology from him. Draqa used to play this very scenario out in his head, over and over. In each one, he shunned Javis. In some he even hurt him in similar ways Draqa did to Iolkosz and his crew. If this meeting had happened years earlier, he might have. But now, Draqa wasn't sure he felt the same anymore. Honestly, he was happy to see Sius Mavell Evi hadn't gotten to Javis yet.

Draqa sighed. He looked around at the others again, then at his feet. He couldn't meet Javis' eyes. "You're right," he murmured. "I did hate you. I still do, a little."

He paused, watching Javis' shoulders droop. Javis nodded. When had he become so accepting of things that didn't go his way? The Javis who Draqa knew when they were young was stubborn and contrary. He had no sign of any of that in him now. In fact, he could have been a husk of the person he used to be. Maybe he had suffered enough.

Draqa continued, "I don't know if I can forgive you, either. But—and I hate to admit it—I missed you." That tiny sliver of vulnerability was all he was going to let Javis have.

Javis opened his mouth, then closed it. A hopeful smile inched its way onto his face. He looked like he might try to hug Draqa again, but instead, he drew his arms in on himself. He turned his gaze downward, his eyes wet and glistening.

His weak voice cracked as he said, "I missed you, too." He took a deep breath and wiped his glasses off on his shirt. He smiled wider now and let out an awkward and breathy laugh. "I'm afraid I was actually unprepared for this. There's so much I want to ask but I don't know what to say."

Hearing this, Draqa released a breath, the tension that had been building inside him releasing with it. He felt the same. He directed his attention to Krystal and Zalé, who continued to watch. Their gazes felt less scrutinizing now.

"Have you met my, ah, friends?" Draqa asked.

Javis nodded, his smile growing. "Of course! I already know Zalé—I can't believe you found him! He's been missing for months," he said excitedly. "And Krystal. She's lovely. She said you think she's a Monarain? How do you know? Oh, and Tolas Ruv Aen—"

Draqa held up a hand to cut Javis off. Well, there was some of that old, hyperactive energy at least. Javis hadn't changed *that* much.

"Tolas Ruv Aen isn't a friend," Draqa said, sending the elf a dirty look.

Javis looked rightly confused. "No?"

"No. He's a liar and a traitor. He's an eel, and he isn't here to help, is he?"

Tolas Ruv Aen held up all four hands. "Yer right. I'm sorry, I did lie. There is a catch," he said.

Draqa didn't know what he expected, but Tolas Ruv Aen's next words stabbed into his gut like a knife.

"I'm sorry, but the Ard'a wants you."

28

DRAQA STARED AT TOLAS RUV AEN for a long, agonizing moment. Krystal was sure he was finally going to unleash his anger and attack the elf as she'd been expecting. Instead, he grew nervous.

"T-The Ard'a? What would they want with me?" he stuttered.

"Not just you. I have to bring in Krystal, too," Tolas Ruv Aen said.

Draqa looked at Krystal, realization dawning on his face. It twisted, displaying a level of hurt Krystal didn't think was possible for Draqa.

He quietly switched to English. "You told him?"

Krystal's words failed her. "Draqa, I—"

"Don't go blaming her, Draqa. It was only a matter of time we found out you were going to Taevalear," Tolas said.

He put a hand on Draqa's good shoulder. Draqa pulled away from him. He ran his fingers through his hair.

"You had me released just so I could be killed by someone else."

"That's not how it is. I said nothing about them killing you," Tolas Ruv Aen said.

"But that's what will happen, isn't it? I'll be tortured for information and killed, because your people are as bad as Sius Mavell Evi."

There was no reasoning with Draqa. Tolas Ruv Aen tried once

more but gave up. Afterall, he did say he didn't know what the Ard'a had in mind for Draqa. At least Draqa's anger didn't seem to be entirely directed at Krystal. Then again, Draqa stopped talking altogether, so she couldn't be sure.

Everyone followed Tolas Ruv Aen back to the train station. He bought tickets to Kerevel Tul for himself, Krystal, Zalé and Draqa, saying he would let them bring Zalé back before he delivered Krystal and Draqa to the Ard'a. Javis bought his own ticket as well. He said he wanted to be there when Averil and Zalé were reunited. Tolas Ruv Aen paid to have the horses ride along in one of the rear cars, and then they all sat in the plaza to wait. An oppressing silence settled over them.

Javis eventually started bouncing his knee. The tapping of his foot was rather annoying.

"*So. . .*" he finally said, "*how did you two meet?*"

Tolas Ruv Aen crossed his legs and leaned back on the bench. He looked to Draqa, sitting on the bench across from him with Krystal. He smirked. Draqa rolled his eyes and looked away.

"*We worked together for Governor Sius Mavell Evi,*" Tolas Ruv Aen said. "*I'd say we were* **real** *good friends.*"

Draqa immediately rebuked him. "*We were hardly friends. He was just a mentor.*"

Tolas Ruv Aen frowned. "*Just a mentor? Sius Mavell Evi really did make you forget everything, didn't he?*"

"*What are you implying?*"

"*We had a connection, Draqa,*" Tolas Ruv Aen said. He looked genuinely hurt.

Draqa scoffed. "*I would hardly say a few long nights watching you get drunk and make a fool of yourself was a connection.*"

"*It was more than that! We were—*"

"*Yes, I know!*" Draqa snapped. "*I know what we were, and I don't care. You betrayed Sius Mavell Evi, so you betrayed* me."

Tolas Ruv Aen visibly deflated. He sighed defeatedly and stood.

"*I'm getting some food before the train gets here. You want anything?*"

Krystal nodded, as did Javis and Zalé. Draqa only huffed. Tolas Ruv Aen sighed again and walked off to the few businesses that were still open at that hour. Draqa grumbled to himself. He might not have reacted as badly as Krystal thought he would but watching him and Tolas Ruv Aen bicker was still uncomfortable. Krystal tossed Javis a sympathetic look. Javis rubbed the back of his neck and returned her look with a strained laugh. He gave Zalé a nudge.

"You know, I think now would be a good time to contact your Papa," he said.

Zalé nodded quite frantically and the two walked over to the side. Krystal watched as Javis pulled out his aspectacaster. She looked away. She didn't know why, but she wanted to wait to see what her brother looked like until she met him in person.

"Have I mentioned I hate people?" Draqa spoke up after a few minutes of continued silence.

Krystal smiled a little then bit her lip. "Am I included in that?"

Draqa hunched over and rested his head in his hand. He let out a long and exaggerated groan.

"No."

Krystal relaxed. She cast a glance in the direction Tolas Ruv Aen went off to.

"If it's all right, what did happen between you two? Other than Sius Mavell Evi, I mean." she asked.

Draqa rubbed his eyes and barked, "You don't already know?" Krystal flinched at his accusatory tone. Draqa shook his head.

"No, I'm sorry. It's not something I like thinking about. I'm stressed."

"I understand," Krystal replied. Draqa probably wouldn't admit it, but it was easy to see he was scared.

"I might as well tell you before you find out on your own," he said. Even after saying this, his words took their time leaving his mouth.

"I said he was my mentor and that was true. Everything I know is thanks to him," he finally said, "and we eventually became close enough to have shared in some. . . intimate moments. Although he would probably say it was more, still. But nothing came of it in the end. We wanted different things. Even then, we remained close. But. . ."

The frown on Draqa's face wasn't the usual scowl he wore to show his distaste in a situation. His eyes grew heavy. Misty, even.

"But you don't like to admit it?" Krystal guessed.

After a moment, Draqa nodded.

"What made you hate him?" Krystal softly asked. She understood Draqa couldn't disobey Sius Mavell Evi, but she didn't quite understand why Draqa would have such an extreme hatred for Tolas Ruv Aen because of it. Did Draqa not dislike the Governor more?

Draqa fully hid his face from Krystal. "Sius Mavell Evi," he answered, as though simply the name explained everything. "I don't want to hate Tolas Ruv Aen, but I don't have a choice."

Krystal started to comfort Draqa when Tolas Ruv Aen returned with a bag of sandwiches. Javis and Zalé came back to the benches as he handed them out. Zalé was grinning from ear to ear. Javis sat down heavily.

"I'm guessing it went well?" Krystal asked. She instinctively looked to Draqa for him to translate. Tolas Ruv Aen beat him to it.

Javis nodded. *"I've never seen Averil more relieved. He's overjoyed."* He paused to massage his throat. He did that a lot. Krystal wondered if he was sick. If he was, he must have caught whatever it was recently enough for it to still bother him.

He continued, *"I told him we would bring Zalé to his house. You three are obviously welcome. He wants to meet you. Especially you, Krystal. He's skeptical about who you are, but he's curious."*

Krystal grinned to mask the worry she felt. What if after all this, she wasn't actually related to Averil and Zalé? The only one here who seemed confident about it was Draqa. Well, and Zalé, but he was a child and easily influenced so he didn't count. What made Draqa so positive of who Krystal was? He didn't even know Averil like Javis did, unless there was still more that he hadn't told her.

A train rolled in next to the group. Its doors opened and a few people disembarked. The next stop was announced and Tolas Ruv Aen stood.

"That'd be us. Let's go now," he said.

He ushered Draqa to his feet then handed out the tickets. He pointed at Krystal's and reminded her to keep it handy in case someone thought she wasn't supposed to be on the train. Everyone got in line and were let aboard one by one. Tolas Ruv Aen led them to a compartment in the back. Javis, in front of Krystal, stepped to the side.

"After you," he said, gesturing inside.

Krystal smiled in thanks and sat by the window. The others piled in, Javis to her left, and Zalé between Draqa and Tolas Ruv Aen on the seats across from her. With a whistle, the train eased out of the station.

Krystal had never been on a train before. She might have paid more attention to the details of it or felt more excited, but she was exhausted. She leaned against the window to relax. She wasn't the only one with that idea. Zalé leaned on Draqa, making him wince as he bumped his sling. Tolas Ruv Aen kicked up his feet in the empty seat next to Javis' left and blocking entrance into the compartment. Javis made a face.

"What? We've got a long ride to Kerevel Tul," Tolas Ruv Aen said in response. *"We might as well rest."*

He flicked a switch, dimming the lights, and closed his eyes. Krystal noticed he kept his lower two half-lidded and trained on Draqa. Probably to make sure he didn't get a knife in the back, not that Draqa could have done so anyway. The compartment was peaceful and quiet for a while. The rhythmic movement of the train lulled Krystal into closing her eyes. She could have fallen asleep, when Javis spoke up.

"All right, I need to know. How did you do it?"

"Do what?" Draqa asked, whispering.

"How did you survive?"

Draqa exhaled. *"I don't want to talk about that right now."*

One of the two men clicked their tongue.

"What about Taevalear?" Javis suggested. *"How did you get there? And how did you learn, ah—what does Krystal speak?"*

"English," Draqa offered.

"Yes, that. How did you do it? Because you couldn't have become a Gatekeeper."

Draqa hummed, *"Not technically. I don't have the official title. One of the books I traded for in the Vyn's underground market showed how to do it. I learned from that and practiced at the ruins of an old Gate in the area. I taught myself English after I got to the Other Realm."*

"You taught yourself? Jair—opening a Gate is one of the most advanced magics out there, especially for us. You could have died trying to do that."

"But I didn't. I know my limits," Draqa said.

Krystal's tired mind wandered back to when she followed Draqa into Arai, reminded of how his body reacted to being pushed past that limit.

Javis muttered under his breath, *"And how long have you done it now?"*

"Eleven years."

"Incredible. And people thought I was the prodigy."

There was silence again, but it didn't last long enough for Krystal to drift back to sleep.

"I don't go by Jair anymore."

"Why not?"

"I'm not the same person you knew. Jair is still dead," Draqa said.

Krystal felt Javis brush his arm against her as he shifted. After another pause, he said, *"You'll have to forgive me for being sentimental, then, because I'm never going to call you something as horrible as Draqa."*

They arrived in Kerevel Tul early the next morning. Krystal slept surprisingly well. She didn't have any dreams about Draqa at any point during the ride. She sleepily shuffled off the train with the others and onto Kerevel Tul's snow-covered streets. Large flakes fell from the lightening gray sky. The streetlamps were still on. The city easily compared to Talnoq-Vyn in size, but it was clearly better organized. A cathedral towered over the center of the city.

Krystal gazed up at it while Tolas Ruv Aen paid to have the horses taken to a nearby stable. "Wow."

Javis joined her side. *"Like it? It's the Kerevel. If you would like, I could show you inside sometime,"* he said.

"Really? It's beautiful." Krystal smiled.

When Tolas Ruv Aen translated, Javis returned her smile, although it didn't reach his eyes. He said, *"Yes, it is. This would be after everything is settled, of course."* He checked his aspectacaster. *"I—we don't have much time."*

He took Zalé's hand and led the way. With every step Krystal took down each road and side street, the more excited she became. She was jittery. Nervous. Any moment now, she would meet her brother. Her family. She didn't know if she was ready. What if Averil didn't accept her? What if he was awful and Krystal didn't like him?

All too soon did Javis bring the group to a stop along a street with rows of skinny two-story houses. Zalé gasped and ran to a faded baby blue house in the middle. The home's color struck Krystal with a pang of nostalgia. Zalé grabbed the knocker and pounded on the door continuously, the noise echoing through the street.

Krystal and the others caught up to him as the door opened, revealing a tall, lanky man. He had his waist-length, black hair tied back with a white ribbon. His eyes were the most vivid green Krystal had ever seen, like four peridot gems set inside his head. He had only two arms, but a set of shimmering translucent wings colored most uniquely like stained glass flowed from his back.

Zalé embraced Averil roughly, knocking him off balance. Averil pulled the boy off himself and regarded his face. He promptly pulled him back into a hug. He sobbed. He rocked Zalé and planted numerous kisses on his forehead. Zalé laughed, starting to cry too, and pressed his face into his father's chest.

"I missed you," he said.

Averil held the back of his head. *"I missed you, too. Oh, thank Disyr you're all right."* He kissed Zalé's forehead again and looked at him before hugging him longer.

Not letting go of his son, Averil eventually looked up at the others.

"Thank you, Javis," he said, *"Thank you. And the rest of you. He said you helped. Thank you for bringing Zalé back to me."*

He stood and gave every one of them a hug. After hugging Krystal, he held her arms and looked her up and down. His eyes lingered on her face.

"Krystal Monarain. . ." he said.

Krystal gulped and nodded. Averil didn't let go of her. It felt like his grip got tighter.

"Javis says you're my sister."

Krystal nodded again. Draqa came up to Averil.

"We can prove it to you," he said.

Averil shook his head. *"No. I don't need proof,"* he said, grinning. *"You look like family if I ever saw it."*

Krystal laughed as the tension broke. "I do?"

If Averil was confused by the language Krystal spoke or how she understood him, he didn't show it, saying, after he received a translation, *"You do."*

Averil gave Krystal another hug then looked around at everyone. *"Please, I insist you all come inside. I'll make us breakfast."*

His home was quaint, though much larger than its exterior suggested. The group crowded around Averil's kitchen table. He had to bring out extra chairs so they all could sit. He doted on Zalé, making sure he had food and water before he got to cooking for everyone else.

Krystal didn't know why she had even bothered to worry before. She already liked Averil and he seemed to like her as well. They talked while he prepared a dish that looked an awful lot like purple hash browns. Averil had a calm energy about him as he meticulously cut the purple potato-like vegetable. He kept his primary eyes trained on Krystal the whole time she told her story. It was the same story she felt she must have repeated a hundred times by now, but this time she didn't leave out or gloss over any details. She wanted Averil to know everything, starting from the tales Mam would tell about her mother, to how she ultimately risked coming to Arai because she needed to meet Averil. When she finished, Averil stuck the potatoes in the oven and leaned back against the counter.

"That makes a lot of sense, knowing what happened to our mother and I," he said.

Krystal sat forward in her chair. "What happened?"

For the first time, Averil lowered his gaze. *"When I was sixteen or so, our father, Sal, was assassinated. It was a dangerous time. There was a lot of tension in Erothel and people didn't like that their Minister was half human."*

Krystal remembered this from what Draqa and Tolas Ruv Aen told her. It was a sad, disgusting thing that happened.

Averil gestured at Javis and Draqa. *"Governor Zevos' wife had been killed just weeks before in an attempt against him, and our father decided the three of us needed to go into hiding. He didn't make it that long, but my mother, who was pregnant at the time, and I still left.*

"Our plan was to hide in a secret location in Taevalear until it was safe to return. We met with the Gatekeeper who agreed to help us, but when they opened the Gate, we were attacked."

Averil paused and took a deep breath. His eyes watered. Krystal's chest twinged in sadness.

Averil sounded melancholy when he continued. *"I was supposed to go in first, but in the chaos, I lost track of everyone. Mother disappeared, and the Keeper was killed. I almost was, too."* He pulled down the collar of his sweater, revealing a raised scar across his neck. Krystal cringed.

Averil said, *"I always had hope that maybe Mother was still alive. I hoped that somehow, after all these years, she found a way to survive. Even though she didn't, I'm glad, so, so glad, that you made it. I finally know what happened."*

Krystal silently gave thanks that Averil made it as well, glad she didn't have all her family stolen away from her.

Draqa spoke up, his expression intense. *"How did you escape?"*

"I didn't," Averil said. *"In fact, I was sure I died. I didn't, clearly. I woke up in a bed, my wound healed.*

Krystal tilted her head. "Who saved you?" she asked.

Draqa translated this time, but he may have been voicing it as his own question.

"Our grandfather. I owe him my life," Averil replied.

Something changed in Draqa's eyes, and he sat back, turning his face away. Krystal smiled, ideas in her head of old men bearded like Santa Claus.

"Is he still alive?"

Averil smiled as well. *"He is. Oh, I should tell him about you right away. He would love to know you."*

Krystal's excitement grew. Next to her, Javis sank in his chair. Eyes twinkling, Averil went back to his cooking. He served breakfast, and from there, they talked of other things.

Averil was very curious about Krystal's life in the Other Realm, asking many questions about her job and her hobbies, and if she had established her own family. Averil himself was a sort of scientist and worked on cures for various illnesses and diseases. He enjoyed cooking and baking and was quite good at it if the strange purple hash browns and sweetened nests of whipped egg whites were anything to go by.

He and Zalé lived on their own. Averil didn't outright say what had happened to Zalé's mother but implied she may have been murdered when Zalé was a baby.

She was aware though, that the atmosphere of the room had changed either before or during breakfast. She sensed a tension coming from the other three men at the table. She wasn't sure what she was missing and took the opportunity to ask when Averil left the kitchen to check something. She assumed it was about him. She was wrong.

Draqa pursed his lips and Tolas Ruv Aen folded his arms. Even Javis looked uncomfortable. After some awkward stares, Draqa finally spoke.

"I've been keeping something from you. Sius Mavell Evi is your grandfather,"

Krystal's heart sank. In an instant, her joyful mood vanished. "What?"

"I would have told you sooner, but I was afraid to disappoint you," Draqa said, "He no doubt already knew who you were from the moment you met him the first time."

Averil returned. Krystal stared at him. She saw it now, in Averil's sharply cut face. No wonder Draqa had been so sure of who Krystal was. Averil looked like his grandfather. And with dread, Krystal realized—so did she.

29

KRYSTAL'S LOOK MADE Draqa's heart sink, but he reasoned she would have found out who Sius Mavell Evi was sooner or later. At least this way she could be prepared and know to avoid him. Although, it was unlikely that Sius Mavell Evi wanted anything to do with Krystal since he didn't stop Draqa when he met her. Draqa hoped that was the case, anyway. He looked to Averil. Family clearly didn't matter to Sius Mavell Evi. Draqa's stomach churned at the idea of Krystal, too, finding herself in a similar position to him, forced to be at Sius Mavell Evi's every beck and call.

"Did something happen?" Averil asked.

That horrible, devastated look was still on Krystal's face. "Our grandfather is Sius Mavell Evi?"

Averil sucked in his lips. "Zalé, why don't you go change into some clean clothes?"

Zalé started to protest. "But these are clean—"

"Now, please."

Zalé pouted but obeyed and hopped down from his chair. Averil massaged the back of his neck.

"Our grandfather has always been so good to Zalé and I. . . I've had a hard time coming to terms with everything that has come out about him and what he's done. Of course, you would know. I tend to forget," he said. He stared off to the side a minute then returned his eyes to Krystal.

"I didn't mean to make you uncomfortable. If it's not what you wish, Sius Mavell Evi will never know about you."

There was hesitance in Krystal's nod. "Thanks. I don't think I want to meet him yet," she said.

Draqa breathed a sigh of relief as he translated. *"Hin iganen wonsgorus."*

Averil nodded. "I understand." He turned to Draqa now. "I assume that's why you brought Zalé directly here rather than to my grandfather."

Draqa cocked his head with a frown.

Averil clarified, "Because you work for him. I assume you do since you're here alive, which means Javis was right. You're Draqa."

"I am," Draqa said, following Averil's gaze to Javis. Javis' head was downturned, an aspectacaster now in his hands.

"In that case, maybe you could help with something?" Averil asked.

Draqa crossed his legs. He knew that look. "I don't know what Sius Mavell Evi is doing if that's what you're going to ask," he said.

Javis sat up. "You must know something. From what people say, you might as well be his right-hand man."

Draqa's jaw fell open as he laughed in disbelief.

"Not at all. And do you really have the audacity to expect me to tell you his secrets if I was?"

Javis stumbled over his words. "Well—you don't seem to like him, so I was hoping you could clarify some things. I need your help."

Draqa still couldn't believe it. He leaned back in his chair, shaking his head. "You need my help," he repeated.

Javis nodded. His hand tremored as he placed his aspectacaster on the table. It flowered open.

"I learned things about the Governor. I know it's him. It all points to him. He's doing something in Adonis, meeting someone, I don't know. I just need one last piece of evidence, and the Minister and the Board will take the threat seriously. You could be that evidence." He nudged the aspectacaster towards Draqa and pushed a button. The device's lights began pulsing blue. "Please. Even a recording would do."

Draqa scowled and turned off the aspectacaster. "This is a dangerous game you're playing. I told you I don't know anything, so drop it."

"I can't," Javis said.

Draqa slammed his hand on the table. Javis flinched.

"He asked me to kill you! He wants you dead, did you know that? I don't know what you got yourself into, but you made enemies with the wrong person. You wanted evidence? There it is!"

Draqa slumped back in his chair. His heart was beating wildly in his chest. He cared too much. Javis took back the aspectacaster. He ran a thumb over its soft edges.

". . .are you going to do it?" he asked.

"Do what?"

"Kill me?"

Draqa gestured to his sling. "Right now, I couldn't kill anyone even if I wanted to."

Javis' lips twisted. He held his throat. Tolas Ruv Aen leaned in front of him.

"You said you think Sius Mavell Evi's meeting someone in Adonis?" he asked.

Javis only nodded. Tolas Ruv Aen's face grew serious.

"I know someone who will listen," he said. He stood from his chair. "Thank you much for the delightful breakfast, Averil. I think it's time we left."

"We? Are you all going?"

"I'm afraid we must," Tolas Ruv Aen said.

"Oh. Krystal, do you know when you'll be back?" Averil asked.

Krystal shook her head. Tolas Ruv Aen said, "In a day or so, I'm sure."

Averil nodded and gave Krystal another hug. "Then I look forward to when you return. You're welcome to stay here. I know Zalé would love that."

"Thanks. I'm really happy I got to meet you," Krystal said.

Averil turned to Draqa, and Draqa tensed in preparation for another hug as well, but Averil only shook his hand. "It is good to see you again, and again, thank you for bringing Zalé back to me."

He said goodbye to the other two, giving Javis a hug as well. He whispered something in Javis' ear, to which Javis nodded. Zalé returned to the kitchen about then. He was disappointed to see they were leaving so soon.

"Will I get to see you again?" he asked, looking up at Draqa.

Draqa hesitated. "I don't know."

Zalé hugged his torso. "I hope so. I'll miss you."

Draqa couldn't help but smile. Zalé was a good kid. "Be careful from now on, all right?" he said. He patted Zalé on the back.

They parted ways, Averil and Zalé watching Draqa and the others go from the doorway. Javis didn't need anything from his home, so Tolas Ruv Aen lead everyone back towards the train station. Occasionally, he would glance back at Draqa. There was a worried look in his eye that told Draqa he was still concerned Draqa might try to make a run for it, or worse. Draqa only wished he could bring himself to. Once again, his mind was clear and those unwanted desires that weren't his own had faded away. He resigned himself to the fact that there was no escaping even if he tried.

Tolas Ruv Aen brought them inside the station and to what Draqa assumed was a maintenance room. A guard stood in front of the door. Tolas Ruv Aen grinned at her.

"Afternoon. I have some cleaning up to do," he said, flashing some symbol with his hand.

The guard looked over Draqa and Krystal and Javis, then stepped aside, opening the door for them. The room beyond glowed orange from the lights within. A deep hum reverberated through the maze of piping that stuck out from the ceiling and walls.

Tolas Ruv Aen lead them through another door at the end of the room and then a series of hallways. Right, left, left, right. . . Just as Draqa began to question whether this was a maintenance room at all, Tolas Ruv Aen stopped at yet another door. He unlocked it and it swung open on its own. Draqa peered through the doorway but there was nothing beyond it other than solid darkness. Tolas Ruv Aen snapped his fingers and a blue flame flickered to life just inside the frame. It was just bright enough to reveal the start of a stairwell leading down.

"Watch yer step," Tolas Ruv Aen warned.

The stairs were steep and narrow. Draqa stumbled more than once. They continued down and down with no signs of stopping anytime soon. The only light came from the blue flames. With each step Tolas Ruv Aen took, a new flame would appear, replacing the one before it and ensuring they couldn't ever see more than a foot in front of them.

Then, just like that, the stairs ended. Protruding from the wall at the other end of the cramped landing was a simple square archway that stood from floor to ceiling. Tolas Ruv Aen snapped again, and a line of white and blue flames set the arch aglow. Runes were carved into its old wood.

"What is that?" Krystal murmured from somewhere behind Draqa.

Tolas Ruv Aen answered, but Draqa didn't need his explanation. Draqa knew a Gate when he saw one. Tolas Ruv Aen tapped at his aspectacaster. A faun appeared above its screen.

"Tolas Ruv Aen. Good to hear from you," she said.

Tolas Ruv Aen nodded. "You as well. I need a Gate open at Station Three."

"Where are you headed?"

"Home, of course."

"I'll get right on it," the faun said.

Nothing happened for a few moments after she ended the call. Suddenly, the Gate flared to life, its center growing bright and opaque. Symbols appeared as though written by an invisible hand as the Gate began to glow. Draqa moved a hand in front of his face, the light too much for his eyes in the dark room. Still, he recognized the symbols. The Gate would take them somewhere in Arai—near the Kingdom Lus Natia from the looks of it. But knowing how secretive the Ard'a was. . .

"We're going to the unclaimed Eastern territories," Draqa said aloud.

Tolas Ruv Aen clapped. "Very good! Yer better at this than I thought. Why don't you go first?"

"What—" Draqa started.

"After you." Tolas Ruv Aen put a hand on Draqa's back and pushed him.

Draqa fell through the Gate. He experienced that familiar sensation of flying though space, but unprepared as he was, he stumbled out the other side and onto his knees. He looked up. The faun stood in front of him, her eyes cold and untrusting. Draqa heard the others come through behind him.

"Tolas Ruv Aen, you didn't say you were bringing others," the faun said.

Tolas Ruv Aen hoisted Draqa to his feet. "Notify Nephas that I'm here with Draqa, Ambassador Zevos and Krystal Monarain," he said.

The faun's eyes widened, and she nodded sharply. Tolas Ruv Aen lead Draqa and the others from the room and into a long hall.

"Nephas?" Javis asked. "You can't mean Queen Nephas of Ushal?"

Tolas Ruv Aen smirked in response. "She's led the Ard'a ever since Sal Monarain died. It was only fitting. She's the only one here who knows exactly what the High Council is doing."

"Is she here now?" Draqa asked. His stomach twisted in knots.

"It's unlikely. She doesn't usually stay here," Tolas Ruv Aen said.

"Where exactly is here?" Krystal asked.

Tolas Ruv Aen gave her a toothy smile. "I *would* have to kill you if I told you that," he said, winking.

He let them into a room located at the end of the hall. "You'll stay in here for now. I'll come back when I get word from Nephas."

Draqa did his best to keep his voice level. "And then?"

"Then, I would think she'll want to talk to you and decide for herself, Draqa."

He said nothing more and closed them in the room. Draqa heard the tell-tale click of a lock. He frowned and tried the door. He closed his eyes. As he feared, he was trapped. When he opened his eyes again, he turned and observed the room. It was nothing like a cell. There were two small beds with clean, white sheets on them. A round area rug took up half the floor. The walls were painted with elegant and detailed depictions of scenery. The ceiling portrayed the night sky.

Despite himself, Draqa relaxed. It was then he noticed the tingle of magic in the room. He walked over to the forest wall and put his hand on a tree. The feeling was much stronger here. He could feel a faint warmth radiating from the wall up into his arm. Ah, so that was why. The Ard'a must have liked to keep their captives at ease. It was oddly humane of them.

Javis watched him. "It's enchanted, isn't it?"

Draqa nodded. Javis shrugged and sat on the edge of one of the beds. "I suspected as much. The room is lovely, though."

"It's still a cell," Draqa muttered, taking a spot next to Javis.

Javis sighed and rubbed his hands on his knees. Krystal sat cross-legged on the other bed, her brow furrowed. "Are you nervous?" her face seemed to ask. Draqa leaned against a bedpost. He wanted to think of nothing until Tolas Ruv Aen returned for him, or else the room's enchantment might lose its effectiveness.

Tolas Ruv Aen returned less than an hour later. Draqa had hoped he would take longer, or at least was there to say that Nephas was held up and wouldn't be there for another few hours.

"Well?" he asked.

Tolas Ruv Aen motioned him to the door. "She's waiting for you." When Draqa got up, Tolas Ruv Aen cuffed him and apologized. "She wants me to take precautions. This is nothing personal."

Draqa dug his feet into the floor. "What is she going to do?" he asked.

"She only wants to talk. You don't need to worry."

Draqa took a last look at Krystal, who gave him a hopeful smile before he was pulled from the room. Tolas Ruv Aen lead him back down the hallway. There were others about now, but none paid him any mind as he walked past. Tolas Ruv Aen brought him to a small room. Unlike the other, it was brightly lit and plain. There sat a single table with a chair on either side—one of which was occupied. Draqa had only seen Nephas a few times over the picturecast, but he still recognized her immediately. Like all caelkins, she had many fleshy tendrils not unlike those of a water salamander instead of hair. Light-colored markings striped her dark face. She wore a sleek, spotted pelt over her shoulders like a shawl. She was the picture of regality.

"Thank you, Tolas Ruv Aen," she said.

Tolas Ruv Aen dipped his head and sat Draqa in the empty chair. He attached Draqa's restraints to the table.

"Want me to wait outside?" he asked.

"No. That will be all," Nephas said.

Tolas Ruv Aen bowed his head again and left. Draqa swallowed. Queen Nephas looked him over. Her gaze was scrutinizing.

"You know, Tolas Ruv Aen has told me much about you, but I never believed you were truly one of Isaias' boys. Until now, of course," she said.

Draqa pursed his lips, getting a grip on himself. Oh *Disyr*, his hands were shaking.

"Which do you prefer, Draqa or Zevos?" Nephas asked.

Draqa took a breath before he spoke, making sure there wasn't a single hint of fear in his voice. "Zevos is dead."

"Draqa it is, then. So, Draqa, do you know why I had Tolas Ruv Aen bring you here?"

"He didn't say exactly what it was, but its either because I committed treason or because I work for Sius Mavell Evi," Draqa suggested. He wished he were back in that enchanted room, where his heart and mind were calm.

A smile graced the Queen's lips, although only for a moment.

"I won't deny you have caused us a lot of trouble in the past year, but we've never seen you yourself as a large enough threat until we were told you've been using the Gates. If we had known Sius Mavell Evi was using someone to visit Taevalear—"

"He's not," Draqa interrupted.

"Pardon?"

"I'm not visiting Taevalear for him. He doesn't know I'm able to," Draqa said. At least not yet he didn't.

Nephas raised her chin, her black eyes boring into Draqa. "Is that so? What do you for him, then?"

Draqa's instincts told him to tell the same lie he gave everyone who asked, but this was the Ard'a he was dealing with. Nephas obviously knew he wasn't just a servant.

"I do whatever he needs me to do," Draqa said finally.

"Such as threatening his adversaries and cutting their eyes out?"

"Sometimes," Draqa said.

"Does he ever have you deal with political matters?"

Draqa was careful with his words. He couldn't say anything that would betray the Governor. "It depends on what you mean. I've never attended an event for him, but I'll. . . enforce his policies and protect him from anyone who means to hurt him. Sometimes that means I have to get my hands dirty."

Nephas tapped her webbed fingers on the table. "You don't seem to be bothered by that," she observed.

"I don't have the luxury to be," said Draqa coolly.

"Hm. Why is that?"

Draqa held his tongue now. Queen Nephas leaned forward,

clasping her hands. Her eyes were intense and unblinking.

"I only ask, because Tolas Ruv Aen informed me that he believes you're being controlled by Sius Mavell Evi in some way. If that was fact, then we may be able to help you out of your situation, provided you help us," she said.

So, she knew. Draqa narrowed his eyes. He wanted to think he couldn't be tempted that easily, but he felt his resolve waver. It wasn't actually possible for them to help him, was it?

"What makes you think you can do anything to help me? I barely understand Sius Mavell Evi's magic myself."

"If you cooperate, we will figure it out together. Although it makes me wonder why you haven't bothered to kill the Governor and solve your problems yourself."

The vicious laugh erupted from Draqa before he could stop himself. "Don't you think if I could kill Sius Mavell Evi, he'd be dead by now?" he snarled. "You're asking the impossible. It's physically impossible. I can't touch him."

The two stared at each other. Draqa had to avert his eyes. Nephas leaned back now.

"Then how about this. You can spy on him for us, and report back to us what he does, and what he has you do," she said.

"He doesn't trust me that much. Even if he did, he can know my thoughts," Draqa said.

"What if you were to report to him what happens here, so he had no reason to suspect you?"

If only it was that easy. There was a reason why the Governor only trusted Draqa with so much. And yet again he had failed to kill Tolas Ruv Aen. He could only imagine the punishment he would receive for joining the Ard'a as well.

"I'll let you think about it, Draqa," Nephas said, standing. "If you join us, I can promise that we'll make sure you are once again a free man."

"What if I refuse?" Draqa asked.

Nephas considered him. "I think you know the answer to that."

She left Draqa sitting alone in that room, an impossible ultimatum weighing over him. He broke into a cold sweat. Death or the wrath of Sius Mavell Evi? Draqa wanted to live but if he betrayed the Governor, he risked losing even more of himself to that twisted man. But for the first time, he could truly imagine what freedom looked like. It was tangible and just within his grasp. He wasn't going to get it by running away.

30

THE WALL TO JAVIS' LEFT depicted a dreamy little meadow blanketed with light purple crocuses. He preferred this mural over the other three surrounding him. Spring was his favorite season, after all. Snow still fell during that time of year in Erothel, but it was never cold for long, while still being far from the heat of summer. Spring was the time Javis was out the most. He loved to sit in the woods with his sketchbook on those mild days and draw for hours.

Sometimes, he would have the luck of meeting a sprite or two. They were often a little vain and loved the attention Javis would give them. He gifted them most of the portraits he made. In return, they gave him their company. They would sing and dance and Javis would shower them in compliments. Those were the few days he truly felt at ease. He doubted he would live to do it again this year.

With every second that passed, he knew he was getting worse. His health deteriorated slowly and subtly, but he still noticed the changes. He observed his hands. The tremor he'd developed earlier that morning hadn't improved. It felt like another attack to keep him quiet—he was too afraid to test how it affected his ability to use a pen. He didn't know how noticeable the tremor actually was, but he rested his hands on his lap to try to hide it when he realized Krystal was watching him.

He had done his best to hide his affliction from everyone so far. He didn't want to be pitied and, truth be told, he felt ashamed. But now, he wasn't sure how much he would be able to hide. There was only so much that could be hidden with a glamor.

Javis cleared his throat, growing uncomfortable under Krystal's curious gaze.

"It's unfortunate I need someone to translate for me. Now would be the perfect time to get to know you," he said, plastering a charming smile onto his face.

Krystal shrugged. For a quick moment there was a twinkle in her eye as she smiled in return.

She gestured at Javis as she spoke and cupped a hand behind her ear. Javis assumed that she meant she would listen.

Javis chuckled lightly. "I would feel selfish having a one-sided conversation. Besides, I'm more interested in what you have to say. By the way, how *are* you able to understand me? You never said."

Krystal tucked her hair behind her ear and showed off a brassy device attached flat to her head. Javis recognized it, vaguely recalling that Tolas Ruv Aen wore the same one behind his ear. So, it was some kind of translator, then. It must have been a technology made specially by the Ard'a, as Javis had never seen anyone else with one. That, or else the device was the kind of thing only the people with lots of money and power had access to. That wasn't an uncommon occurrence. The same was true for the aspectacasters, which were first only available to certain government officials and military before being altered and sold to the public.

The Ard'a clearly had more power than Javis originally thought. The High Council made the Ard'a out to be no more than random terrorists and vigilantes all swept under the same rug. Assassination? The Ard'a did it. An election was lost? Clearly the Ard'ahlen was responsible. The Ard'a was a worldwide boogeyman, really. Just something to blame any random killing on rather than facing the root of a problem. Conveniently, if an assassination worked out in someone's favor, the accusations were nowhere to be heard.

Already, Javis saw that the Ard'a was so much more than anything anyone ever made it out to be. And to think it was led by a member of the High Council itself, and Queen Nephas of all members. Did the rest of the Council know? Or were they as in the dark as it seemed everyone else was?

Tolas Ruv Aen returned without Jair ages later. Javis was about to ask where his brother was, if Jair was okay, when Queen Nephas herself followed Tolas Ruv Aen into the room. Javis shot to his feet and bowed deeply. Nephas observed him. Her intense gaze sent a chill down his spine, but he did not look away.

"Your majesty—" he started.

Queen Nephas held up her hand, silencing him. "It's just Nephas here. You're Ambassador Zevos, yes?"

Javis straightened and nodded once. He tried to speak again, but the queen continued before he could.

"Tolas Ruv Aen tells me you have important information on the Governor, Sius Mavell Evi."

"I do. The Minister, the Board—they won't listen to me," Javis said, rushing over his words. He felt Nephas wasn't keen on dilly-dallying.

Nephas' nod in return was short and stern. "We've been watching Sius Mavell Evi for almost two years now, and he's been quiet. We'll take whatever information you have for us. But first," —she turned from Javis rather dismissively— "you must be Krystal Monarain."

Krystal stared from where she was still sitting cross-legged on the bed. She nodded slowly.

"Are you able to understand me?" Nephas asked with a glance at Tolas Ruv Aen.

Krystal stood now. She floundered, then gave an awkward half-bow.

The corner of Nephas' mouth quirked upward, her hard expression melting away. She shook her head with a quiet laugh. "You're all right. Come here."

Krystal approached and Queen Nephas met her halfway. She took Krystal's hands in hers. Krystal's own lips twitched up into a rather confused looking smile. Whatever she asked next, Nephas chuckled.

"No dear, you're not in trouble. You have no idea how happy I am to see you," Nephas said. "Your father was very important to us here. If anything ever happened to him, we were supposed to look after his family."

Javis watched, intrigued by this new development.

Nephas continued, "I'm sure you're aware by now, things went wrong. Unfortunately, by the time we got to Averil, he refused to be under our protection. Of course we've kept an eye on him, but he won't even speak with us. However, that is the past. Now you're here and I can finally fulfill my promise to your father. He and I were very close. He was a good friend. The rest of the Council didn't appreciate him, or his ideas and he was the only one who could be trusted. If I may, I'd like to show you something of his."

She beckoned Krystal from the room. Javis only followed when Tolas Ruv Aen urged him to go along. He was beginning to fret that Nephas was going to take him as seriously as the Minister did and had to remind himself that he hadn't been expected and therefore wasn't the Queen's priority, even though he felt his news was more important than whatever it was she had to say to Krystal. Still, he couldn't help but pace outside the door of the office Nephas brought Krystal into.

He wrung his hands. Hopefully Nephas wouldn't take long. He didn't like waiting like this. He couldn't wait like this. Not with so much on the line.

Tolas Ruv Aen cleared his throat. Javis stopped mid-step, shrinking away from Tolas Ruv Aen's deep-set frown.

"I'm sorry. Am I bothering you?" Javis asked.

"You seem tense," Tolas Ruv Aen said.

Javis resisted the urge to be sarcastic. Of course he was tense. "I don't have much time," he muttered, certain he was too quiet to hear.

Tolas Ruv Aen cocked his head with a furrowed brow. "Yer being threatened, aren't you?"

If only Javis was just being threatened. He had trouble getting the words off his tongue. "Sius Mavell Evi had me poisoned. There is no antidote yet."

"Yer not dying, are you?" Tolas Ruv Aen's voice was all too loud.

Javis cringed. He could only bring himself to nod.

"You shoulda said something before! How are you feeling now? I'll have Nephas get a doctor."

Tolas Ruv Aen reached for the doorknob. Javis grabbed it first.

"Wait. I don't want Krystal or Jair to know. The only ones who do are Averil and my—and a friend of mine who's a doctor," he said.

Tolas Ruv Aen didn't look convinced. "Is yer doctor friend helping you?"

"She is. She's good with antidotes, but even she hasn't been able to find one yet. I couldn't continue to sit and wait in hopes I would get better," Javis said. He still doubted if that was the right decision.

Tolas Ruv Aen put a firm but gentle hand on Javis' shoulder. "I understand. We'll help you. We have access to things yer friend might not."

He stood by Javis in encouragement until Nephas allowed them into her office. Krystal lingered next to her with what appeared to be a key clenched between her fingers. Nephas offered for Javis to sit in the blue armchair across from her. He politely declined when Nephas showed no signs of sitting as well.

"So, what is this information you claim to have for me?" Nephas asked, leaning against her desk, crossing her arms.

Javis had to collect his thoughts, not unintimidated by the monarch before him.

"Well, you see," he started weakly.

Nephas' face remained unimpressed and unblinking. Where was that warm and understanding expression that she had with Krystal?

"You need to speak up," she said.

Javis tugged at his collar. "My apologies. I can't."

Nephas raised an eyebrow, but Javis took her silence as a sign that he could continue.

"Sius Mavell Evi is colluding with the president of Adonis. They're trying to get the drād clans to start a war with Erothel. Some of the clans were already agreeing while I was there. I have proof of airship activity going back and forth from the clans to Adonis and Erothel."

Nephas clicked her tongue. "How do you know it's Sius Mavell Evi and not someone else?"

"I hired someone to watch him. He found proof of Sius Mavell Evi paying people off, probably to keep them quiet, even if he wasn't going to the clans himself. He met with people as well. I have audio of one of his meetings, but it doesn't tell who the Governor was meeting with," Javis said.

"Do you have the audio with you?" Nephas asked.

Javis took out his aspectacaster and ran his thumb over the Glass still attached to it. He played back the recording. Nephas appeared to listen intently, her eyes boring into the device. When it finished, she silently tapped her lips.

Nervously, Javis said, "I know it may not be much to go on. But it's all I have, other than. . ."

"Other than what?"

"I went to see him myself. It was foolish, I know. He knew I was looking into him. He threatened me. My brother just confirmed today that he wants me dead, and he already. . ." Javis paused and looked to Tolas Ruv Aen for help.

Tolas Ruv Aen leaned over and whispered in Nephas' ear. She frowned.

"I see," she said.

"Will you help?" Javis asked.

Nephas nodded and stood upright. "You're in luck, Ambassador. As it would happen, I've had my people keeping an eye on President Vasiir as well. It didn't appear that her and Sius Mavell Evi's actions were related, but you have convinced me otherwise. We will look into this right away. It's good you came to us. As for your situation, I will send for people to help you."

Relief flooded over Javis as the Queen's words sunk in. Finally, someone was listening to him. Someone who could actually do something. He bowed despite himself.

"Thank you. My friend Talara knows more about my situation than I do. She may be able to help, or at least tell you what she's learned. If there's anything I can do for you in return, I'll make myself of use in any way I can."

Nephas finally graced him with a smile. "There is, actually. If I recall correctly, you're rather new to politics compared to your colleagues," she said.

"I am," Javis said, unsure where this was going. "I apprenticed at the Kerevel before this, but I don't see how that would be useful."

"Not to me. Krystal, on the other hand, was telling me how she has been soul-traveling and dream walking with no way to control it. It would be a great benefit to us if she learned, should she accept my offer to join the Ard'a, that is. Would you happen to know someone who could teach her?"

"Dream walking," Javis repeated. Soul-travel and dream walking were rarely taught to anyone outside of healers and holy men and were highly advanced skills to learn. Even Javis, the "prodigy" who discovered how to do it early on, hadn't attempted it in years. Yet when he looked at Krystal, who smiled back at him hopefully, he found himself a little curious about the woman who'd helped Zalé and brought his brother back into his life. He doubted his old teachers in the Kerevel would consider him qualified to train her, but it wasn't as though he had forgotten his own training.

He agreed, albeit a bit apprehensively. "I suppose I could. I'll need a translator, though."

"It is done," Nephas said. She moved to the door. "If that's all, I have things to prepare and I expect Draqa should have his answer for me by now."

She left, sending Javis and Krystal back to the enchanted room to wait once again. While no less worried, Javis felt a great deal more hopeful about his situation. Maybe things would turn out all right.

31

THE SILVER KEY Nephas gave Krystal weighed heavier than it looked. It had a tarnished finish, and a fraying red ribbon tied in a loop at its little handle. It was her father's. At least, that's what Queen Nephas claimed. She said it went to a house of his, hidden in a safe location that only she knew of now. If Krystal wished, the key, the house, could all be hers. Nephas implied it was compensation for the fact that Krystal could no longer go home. That was the catch.

She was still in Arai illegally, which meant there was too much of a risk for her to travel back and forth between the two realms. She wasn't a Gatekeeper and there was no way to ensure that she wouldn't tell Arai's secrets to the world.

She would never see her friends again. She would certainly never set foot in her Mam's café again. If Krystal didn't regret her foolish decision to follow Draqa before, she certainly did now.

"Please understand," Nephas said, *"we can't have the humans in*

Taevalear learning about our existence again. They hurt us too much in the past."

She put a kind hand over Krystal's. Her skin felt clammy.

"I know it must be difficult for you, but you don't belong there, dear. You belong here with your own kind. Just look at what the humans did to you."

Krystal looked up at the tall woman. "What do you mean?"

Nephas paced a circle around Krystal. *"You're only a quarter human. You should have had arms like an elf's, or a sylphan's wings like your brother. It's very unlikely you were only born with your ears,"* she said.

Krystal thought of the scars on her back. She already suspected as much after she saw the delicate wings that flowed gracefully from Averil's back. But she understood why her own might have been removed. She would likely have had a much harder time in the Other Realm if they weren't. Who knows? She could have ended up in some government lab rather than with her Mam.

But that was the point, wasn't it? If the Other Realm was a place for her, her wings wouldn't have been removed in the first place. Still, a part of Krystal disagreed. She would miss everyone.

"Are you sure there isn't some loophole or something?" Krystal asked.

"There is not. I'm sorry," Nephas said.

Krystal fell quiet for a long time. Everyone she knew would be hurt. But it wasn't as though they were her real family. Friends, yes, but family came first, didn't it? Hopefully, Rowen would find someone to replace her at Dahlia's. And Lillie. . . she'd be strong enough to handle it. More than likely though, they both would look for her, and they would never know if she was even alive. That part hurt the most.

Nephas offered for Krystal to join the Ard'a as well. She was particularly adamant about this, emphasizing that Krystal could do what her brother couldn't, given his proximity to Sius Mavell Evi. And if Krystal learned to soul-travel at will? She would become a valuable asset to the Ard'a. They had no one who could do that.

As exciting as joining the organization founded by her father sounded, Krystal insisted that she needed to think this decision over. She may have liked adventure, but she wasn't keen on the idea of becoming involved in the same kinds of messes that Draqa found himself in. The only reason Krystal didn't decline outright was the chance to learn how to control her dream walking. Now that she knew she could learn from Javis, however, she had no reason to join the Ard'a at all.

Javis sat across from her now, listening as Tolas Ruv Aen explained how to use the translator now fused behind his ear. Krystal probably should have been listening since Tolas Ruv Aen never properly explained to her how to take it off without ripping her skin off with it, but she was lost in her own thoughts, feeling guilty about the way things had to go.

How long would it be before Rowen or Lillie realized something was wrong? They would be worried, certainly. Rowen would even notify the authorities and get people to look for her. God, Krystal was selfish.

"*This is brilliant!*" Javis exclaimed hoarsely, leaning towards Krystal. "*Say something, say something in your language.*"

Krystal forced herself to smile. "Cool, right?"

Javis clapped his hands. *"It's not at all what I was expecting. I only hear your words, but it's conveying their meaning perfectly!"*

For someone who lived around this kind of technology, Krystal was surprised Javis marveled at it. The way his eyes lit up in awe at the device was rather sweet. If only Krystal could bring herself to feel the same.

Queen Nephas took a worryingly long time with Draqa. Krystal would never forgive herself if Draqa was killed by the Ard'a. When Tolas Ruv Aen was called back to Nephas, he made it clear that whatever happened next was out of his hands.

Some other member of the Ard'a served Krystal and Javis a hot meal while they waited for the news. The flavor was bland compared to Averil's breakfast that morning. Krystal ate it without complaint. She set her bowl aside and laid back to stare at the ceiling.

"You're worried too, right?" she asked Javis. She didn't see if he nodded.

"Of course," he whispered. *"I don't want to lose him right after getting him back."* Krystal heard him sigh. *"Though I suppose he's not the same brother I knew when we were children. Not really."*

Krystal had to agree. Even in her dreams, Draqa wasn't quite the same as how she knew him in the present.

"The two of you never got along, did you?" she said.

"No. When we were very young we did, but after our mother died and we moved, everything went downhill. I'm surprised he told you," Javis said.

"He didn't. I've been dreaming about him," Krystal said, turning to face Javis. She dropped her voice to a whisper. "That's why I need you to teach me. I don't care about the Ard'a. I just need to stop dreaming about Draqa." She recalled the dark and heavy feeling that settled in her chest the most recent time she was in Draqa's memories and shuddered.

Javis' brow furrowed in thought. *"I can see why that would be undesirable for both of you. Don't worry. I'll teach you to control it."*

Finally, Tolas Ruv Aen returned. He opened the door wide, and Draqa followed behind him. Krystal gasped and ran to him. Apart from his earlier shoulder wound, there wasn't a scrape on him. His lips were pulled in a tight frown, but he was unharmed. He was alive. Krystal pulled him into a tight embrace—she couldn't help herself. Draqa tensed in her arms, but she didn't let go.

"What's all this?" he grumbled, despite making no effort to pry Krystal off.

"You're okay! I was so scared they were going to kill you," she said. She pulled away before Draqa had a chance to complain. "You are okay, right?"

Draqa nodded. "We can leave now."

Just like that? It couldn't be that simple. "Wait, wait. Did they punish you? Why are they letting you go so easily?" Krystal asked.

Draqa cast a wary glance at Tolas Ruv Aen.

"You can tell her," Tolas Ruv Aen said with a gesture at Krystal.

Draqa switched to Yrlun. *"I have to work for them."*

Was this why Nephas wanted Krystal to join? Because Draqa was? "What about Sius Mavell Evi?" she asked.

Draqa shook his head. *"I'm going back to him. But the less you know, the better. It's being taken care of, so you don't need to worry about it."* The corner of his mouth tugged upwards, but his overall demeanor remained grim. Krystal was definitely going to pry further when she had the chance to talk to him in private.

Javis rose from the bed. "*Will the Ard'a be in contact with us?*" he asked.

"*We will,*" Tolas Ruv Aen said. "*Till then, it's best you pretend you never spoke to us at all. You especially, ambassador.*"

With that, Tolas Ruv Aen returned them back through the Gate and to the train station in Kerevel Tul. He left them there, saying, "*I trust you can get to where you need to go from here. Draqa, we'll be in touch.*"

He gave Krystal a parting nod as he turned back into the maze that was the boiler room. Then, the three went their separate ways. Krystal returned to her brother's, and Draqa went with Javis to his home on the outskirts of the city. Javis said he would begin teaching Krystal in a couple of days. For now, he needed to rest after being away from home for so long. As for Draqa, he gave no hints as to whether Krystal would get to see him before he left for the Vyn.

Krystal spent most of her time with Averil and Zalé in the days following. The two were quite happy that she would be living with them for a while. Averil set up a spare room for her, and Zalé offered up some of his stuffed toys to keep her company. The toys aside, she was grateful she had her brother and nephew, otherwise knowing she could never go home would have been much harder than it already was. More than once, she found herself waking with a start in the morning, sure that she was late for work at Dahlia's, only to be disheartened as she realized that she wouldn't be able to go at all.

Communicating with Averil and Zalé took patience, especially being unable to rely on Draqa to translate for her. She eventually asked for a pen and paper so she could at least draw out what she meant when she really needed to get a point across. From there, things got easier.

Averil didn't have much time for Krystal during the day, but when he did, he tried his best to be accommodating and showed her around the areas near his home and some of the local businesses.

"I'll help you find you find work," he said once. *"Tell me what you like, and I'll make it happen."*

There were plenty of barista-like jobs in Kerevel Tul, but when Krystal mentioned she wished she could do something with photography (this one took a long time to explain and involved demonstrating with her camera), Averil said they had a type of camera in Arai, too. They were expensive, but he could get her in touch with someone who could teach her how to work the technology.

He even offered to hire tutors for Krystal so she could focus on learning about and integrating into Arai. This included someone who could properly teach her Yrlun. This was one opportunity Krystal couldn't say no to. If she was going to live in Arai, she wanted it to be worth it.

Rather than attend school, Zalé had his own private tutors as well. Averil explained that this was because he didn't want anyone to find out that Zalé was part yilura. As Krystal understood it, it was safer for Zalé that way. He wouldn't be resuming any of his lessons for another week or so, however.

"Oh good," he whispered to Krystal after learning this. *"I hate*

math. It's boring. And my tutor's mean and smells like cabbages."

Averil gently scolded him. "*She's the best I could find after you scared away your last one. You have no right to complain.*"

Zalé groaned and fell into Krystal's shoulder as though defeated. Krystal laughed. She knew her brother and nephew for such a short amount of time, yet she felt so warm in their presence, like she had always known them. Being with them wasn't all that different from how things were growing up with Mam. Safe and warm and comfortable. Averil treated her like he felt the same.

But Krystal still couldn't stop thinking about Rowen and Lillie. Rowen had acted like family to her too, hadn't he? He had always done his best to be there for her. When Krystal got the call that Mam had a stroke, Rowen was the first person to show up at her door and hold her while she sat in sobbing pieces on the floor. Rowen had been the one to be given Mam's bookshop in her will, but he still asked Krystal to co-own the place with him, because, despite declining, the bookshop held more of her memories than his.

Rowen was the one she could count on, even when she made up stories and half-truths rather than tell him how she was feeling.

And Lillie. . . she'd been the first friend Krystal ever made, staying by each other's sides since they met in middle school. There was no one Krystal got on with quite like Lillie. When Krystal would get sent to the principal's office, Lillie would find a way to follow. When Lillie had gotten fed up with her mom's boyfriend, before she and Ema moved in with their dad, Krystal would pick her up and convince Mam to let her stay the night. They always took care of each other. Wasn't that like a family?

But it was for the best. If she had stayed in the Other Realm, she would never have met Averil and Zalé. Her real family. The family she'd been taken from, who she'd been searching for since Mam died. As long as she had them, everything would be fine.

After four days spent with her brother and nephew, a light tapping on the front door roused Krystal from her spot by the fireplace where she entertained Zalé. Averil beat her to it and let Javis inside. His dark curls were disheveled, and the rims of his glasses only just hid the dark bags under his eyes. He couldn't have possibly gotten any rest like he wanted, but his cheerful grin said otherwise.

"Good afternoon! I hope I'm not here at a bad time," he said.

"It's never a bad time for you. Are you here for Krystal?" Averil asked.

"I am." Javis pulled Krystal's coat from the rack and held it out for her. *"Are you ready?"*

Krystal rushed her arms into the sleeves. "Where are we going?"

"Back to my place. I hope you don't mind a bit of a walk in the snow."

Krystal gave him a questioning look but didn't bother asking until they were out the door; Javis gave her the impression that he wouldn't wait for long from the way he danced from foot to foot. The man shook out his arms as the two of them stepped out into the nippy air.

"I just despise the cold, don't you?" he said, blowing into his hands.

Krystal shrugged. "I don't mind it. Why are we walking through the snow if you hate it so much?"

Dimples formed on Javis' face. *"The carriages have no access to my property. As for why we're going all the way to my house, well, I would prefer some privacy when I teach you."*

He explained to Krystal a bit about magic as they walked. Simply put, magic was a form of energy. In Qo'yul, a drenen language, it was called Osne. Everyone had it and had the capability to use it and manifest it physically. Except for humans, who had very little of their own, and thus had difficulty using it without first drawing it from other sources. The same went for the children of human and faerish parents.

"*You shouldn't let your blood stop you, though. I firmly believe that with enough practice you can use almost as much magic as the average person. You also have less human blood than I, so you should have an easier time regardless,*" Javis said.

Maybe Javis just liked to talk or maybe he had an affinity for teaching, but there was something endearing about the way he spoke. Unlike Draqa, he had an animated way of speaking. He showed his passion not only through his words, but with his whole body. He jumped all over the place with his thoughts and often interrupted himself to explain a point he forgot. He kept stopping to ask if he was making sense, or to remind Krystal to stop him if he was rambling.

Nevertheless, he kept Krystal entertained for most of their hour-long trek. When Krystal peeled her eyes away from him, she realized they were now in a grove—no—a whole forest of birch trees. The further they walked, the taller the trees grew ahead of them. Each one wore a glistening layer of frost on its branches. It was the most fairytale-like place Krystal had ever seen.

"*We're getting close now,*" said Javis.

They soon arrived upon the edge of a steep crater that dropped off abruptly in front of them. Javis caught Krystal's arm as she nearly stumbled over the side.

"Careful now. I should have warned you."

Krystal stared. "You *live* here?"

Wooden steps along the circumference of the crater lead down to the bottom. Though without trees, it was full of winter-burned vegetation. There were boulders with mosses, and bushes grew out from the crater walls. Krystal could only imagine what it would look like in the springtime. A pond with a thin sheet of ice took up a good quarter of the crater, and to its left, a cozy, two floor cottage sat quietly. Light smoke puffed from its little chimney.

Javis grinned proudly. *"I found this place some years ago. I repaired it and built these stairs, too,"* he said, leading Krystal down to his front door. It was funny, Krystal didn't take him for the handyman type.

Javis opened the door for her. *"After you."*

Inside the cottage was toasty, making Krystal's cold face burn. A railing separated the small step-down living room from the entry. The back of a couch faced Krystal, but she could still make out Draqa's sleeping form spread out on its cushions. His boots were on, muddy and propped up on the couch's arm.

Javis grimaced. Krystal followed his gaze to the mud tracked onto the living room carpet. Krystal quickly took off her own shoes before she accidentally took another step and dragged more mud and snow into the house than there already was.

Javis lightly huffed. *"Why don't you go up to my study to wait for me while I clean this up. Do you take honey in your tea?"*

"Oh, uh, sure," Krystal said.

Javis' study wasn't hard to find. There were only four small rooms at the top of the landing, of which the study was the largest. It's two ceiling-height bookshelves were a disaster, filled more with a random assortment of papers and trinkets than with books.

Krystal was about to sit down at Javis' desk when something shot across its surface. Whatever it was knocked over a jar being used as a pencil holder onto the floor with a startling *clack!* Krystal jumped back with a gasp. She crouched to peer under the desk, but she couldn't locate the perpetrator.

"*What happened?*" Javis arrived at her side.

"There's something in here," she said, swallowing back the waver in her voice.

Javis bent to pick up the pencil jar. "*The only others here are the brownies. You must have startled one of them.*" He chuckled and returned the jar to its rightful place.

Krystal didn't breathe a sigh of relief just yet. She didn't enjoy her last encounter with one of the Unseen ones. "A brownie? You mean like a hob?"

Javis looked impressed. "*Yes, they're household spirits. They were already here when I moved in.*"

He held his hand open near the floor. A wavering figure moved from behind the desk leg and into Javis' palm. Krystal had to squint to make out what Javis was showing her, but it was definitely a little man. He couldn't have been taller than a teacup. Hair covered him from head to foot. Javis let the brownie scamper to the top of the nearest bookshelf.

"*I'm more so their house guest than they are mine, but our relationship is mutually beneficial. Treat them kindly and with respect, and you won't have a thing to worry about."* Javis pulled up a chair tucked in the corner. *"Now have a seat and we'll get started."*

Krystal eyed the brownie watching her as she sat across from Javis. "So, what do I do?" she asked.

"Nothing interesting yet, I'm afraid. Tell me what you have experienced so far."

Krystal told him how ever since she met Draqa, she had somehow gained access to his memories. How before that, she soul-travelled to Arai almost every night. Javis fiddled with a pen the whole time she talked, making her doubt he was listening.

Then he said, *"I am by no means an expert, but I would guess you were drawn here because of Sius Mavell Evi, either because of your relation to him or your desire to find your family. Or both. As for Jair's memories, I can't say for sure what triggered it, but it isn't uncommon for beginners to unintentionally access the memories of someone they have a connection with."*

Krystal supposed she did have some kind of connection with Draqa. And she did find him interesting when they first met.

"What can I do then? His memories make me feel horrible. I thought maybe I could try meditating and some other things, but it didn't work," she said.

Javis' dimples returned. He nodded. *"You were clever to try that. There are only two ways to dream walk and soul-travel. By physically sleeping and entering a lucid state, and through deep meditation."*

"Oh. I wasn't actually any good at it, though," Krystal said. Still, it made her smile to know she'd been on the right track.

"Neither was I when I first started. That's why we're going to

practice." Javis went into detail about the different ways to achieve a meditative state, as well as methods that worked for him as a beginner. Apparently meditating wasn't about purging Krystal's mind of all thoughts, but rather to co-exist peacefully with them.

Javis repositioned his chair. *"Make yourself comfortable and close your eyes. I'll guide you through this."*

Krystal did so. She breathed in as Javis instructed and counted to one. She exhaled on two, in on three, and so on up to ten. Then she started over like Javis told her.

"You'll know you have succeeded when you feel as though your mind is suspended between the sleeping and waking worlds," he said. *"You will be aware of your surroundings, but the sensations of your inner mind will come to you freely."*

Inner mind? Did he mean her subconscious? She shook the thoughts away, remembering she needed to be counting.

"If you find your thoughts pulled away, don't start over. Pick up where you left off," Javis murmured.

Krystal inhaled. Five.

She exhaled. Six.

Inhaled. Seven.

Javis continued to speak, his voice guiding her. Krystal fought a smirk, imagining what she would tell people who asked how she learned magic. "Oh nothing," she would say, "Just a guided meditation." Krystal considered herself to be somewhat spiritual, but she never realized how much power something as simple as meditation actually held.

Javis' quiet, raspy voice drew her back into focus once again. It was close to her ear now, soft and lulling like a spell. She continued counting. Stray thoughts floated through her head, but the longer she counted, the more they settled. Javis' words faded into the background, mixing in with her remaining thoughts.

She felt pressure on the back of her chair, an arm brushing past her shoulder. She wondered vaguely if it was still Javis, or the brownie come back down from the bookshelf.

"*Very good,*" she thought Javis said.

Images and sensations started to fade into view. They were colors, mostly. Muted shades of green, warm and fuzzy pinks. White. Lots of soft, comforting white. And then it all left for Krystal to just exist. To be an entity that simply was.

Krystal found it difficult to open her eyes, like she had taken an unintentionally long nap. Javis still sat across from her. A tiny, pleased smile ornamented his face. Krystal released a final relaxed breath.

"*Very good,*" said Javis, "*that was very good.*"

"How long was that?" Krystal asked.

"*Fifteen minutes. It felt like longer, didn't it?*"

Krystal nodded.

"*With practice, you will be able to sit for hours. Fifteen minutes is a good start,*" Javis said.

Krystal liked the sound of that. This was the calmest she'd felt since even before coming to Arai.

Draqa appeared in the doorway. He knocked, causing Javis to startle forward.

"*Jair! We're a bit busy here. Did you need something?*" Javis asked.

Draqa's gaze washed over them, lingering on Krystal before snapping back to his brother. "*Are you trying to burn the house down?"*

"*The house. . .?*" Javis jumped to his feet. "*Oh! The tea!*"

Krystal hid a chuckle behind her hand. Javis really was all over the place.

"*We may as well take a break. Feel free to join us, Jair. You did take the water off, didn't you?*" Javis said.

Draqa nodded. He looked at Krystal again. "*I will just this once.*"

32

"Do you take cream in your tea?" Javis asked, preparing Draqa a cup.

"With extra honey," Draqa said.

Javis smiled. "Of course." He stirred in the milk and a few dollops of honey and handed it over.

Draqa didn't doubt that Javis somehow felt triumphant for finally getting him to sit down for tea after asking for the past two days to no avail. The only reason Draqa did so now was because of Krystal, and they both knew it. They may have been on better terms now, but that didn't mean Draqa wanted to spend every waking moment with his brother. In fact, Draqa didn't enjoy staying with Javis much at all, but it was a better alternative to spending the last of his money at a *huum*.

He learned two things about Javis during his stay so far. One, Javis was now very nosy—worse than Krystal even. It came as no surprise to Draqa that Javis got himself into trouble with Sius

Mavell Evi.

Draqa watched Javis' hand twitch toward his hip, reaching for the flask that Draqa witnessed him hide the first night. Instead, he sat with Draqa and Krystal at the island counter. Draqa narrowed his eyes. Two, Javis had taken after their father, and he was trying desperately to hide it.

Draqa quietly sipped his tea as Javis struck up conversation with Krystal. Krystal regarded the elder twin with a sort of revere, hanging on his every word. Draqa almost scoffed. Javis had that effect on everyone, even when they were young. He made people feel like they were the only ones in the world who mattered. Draqa would not allow himself to become envious that Krystal probably liked Javis better than him. He was used to it.

"Are you enjoying your stay with Averil?" Javis asked.

Krystal nodded, her grin hidden behind her teacup. "He's really kind. He's even helping me find a job here."

Draqa sat up. "You're staying in Arai?" He didn't think Krystal would make up her mind that quickly. When she last talked to him about it, she was still hesitant about making a decision.

"Oh, yeah. I meant to tell you, I'm not allowed to the Other Realm," Krystal said.

Not allowed? Draqa didn't think he heard right. "Who told you that?" he asked.

"Nephas did." Krystal ran her thumb over the rim of her cup. "She gave me the key to my father's place, so I guess I'll move in there at some point."

Draqa resisted the urge to grab Krystal by the shoulders and shake some sense into her. She didn't care when she followed him to Arai, what the hell did Nephas say to make her care about the rules now?

"If you want to go home, I told you I would take you," he said. He hoped he hid the edge in his voice well enough.

"At this point, I'm pretty sure they'd find out if I went back. Besides, it nearly killed you last time, remember?" Krystal said.

Draqa faltered. ". . .I can get stronger. Or I can find someone who would be willing to take you back." Yes, even Gatekeepers could be bribed for the right price.

Krystal shook her head. "Even if you did, I don't want to cause trouble. And anyway, I'm glad I came here."

She said that, but Draqa swore he heard her voice tremble. The worst part was, he had no idea how to comfort her. He didn't relate at all to what she was feeling. He wasn't sure she even wanted comfort from him.

"Krystal, I—" he started.

"Did you leave people behind?" asked Javis.

Krystal smiled pitifully. "Yeah. It was only a couple friends, but I still feel bad for leaving them. We were really close."

"What were they like?" Javis asked.

"They were wonderful. Rowen owns the bookstore I worked at—It was my Mam's bookstore, and she was his great-aunt, so we were friends growing up. And there's also Lillie. We met in school, and we would spend a lot of time together. She has a little sister," Krystal said. The tremble in her voice wasn't just in Draqa's imagination. Her eyes were full of tears, too.

Javis pulled her cup from her hands, and she hid her face in them.

"I'm so sorry. They must be like family to you," Javis said.

"Yeah. . . I guess so," Krystal said. "I. . . just miss them."

She'd said something like this before, but the regret in her voice now made Draqa's chest heavy.

Javis nodded. "I understand. If there's anything I can do for you, don't hesitate to ask me. We can't replace your friends, but we'll do our best to make you feel at home here," he said.

Draqa nodded in agreement. But he would do more than that. He was in the Ard'a now, wasn't he? At the very least he might be able to help her get a message sent to her friends.

Krystal looked up from her hands. Her eyes were red, but she smiled. It almost reached her eyes. Draqa opened his mouth to try again to comfort her, but it seemed Javis had already said all that needed to be said. He fell silent and took a swig of tea. Krystal turned the rest of her attention to Javis. Damn it.

Javis and Krystal returned upstairs to continue practicing. Draqa fixed himself another cup of tea and remained in the kitchen. He leaned back, kicking his feet up on the chair next to him and pretending he wasn't at all miffed that he was interrupted and one-upped.

He felt childish for letting his brother get to him, had to remind himself that they were both adults now. Javis wasn't competition anymore. Krystal wasn't a trophy to be won. He was being selfish for feeling this way while Krystal was upset. But Draqa would be lying to himself if he didn't admit that he was worried that Javis was going to steal away Draqa's chance at friendship as he had done with others in the past.

He tapped into his aspectacaster and played around absently

with its different functions. He landed on the list of connected aspectacasters and stared at its holographic screen. More specifically, the name at the top of the list.

It had been too long since he last spoke with the Governor. He knew it would be wise to contact him before going back to Talnoq-Vyn, but so far, he'd been procrastinating. Sius Mavell Evi was going to be furious with him, that much was clear. The only question was what Draqa's punishment would be. Draqa stood with a sigh. He needed to get this over with.

He stepped outside so he wouldn't be interrupted and chimed a session with Sius Mavell Evi. He held his breath, hoping the Governor wouldn't answer. Let him be in a meeting, or busy with paperwork, or somewhere his aspectacaster wouldn't connect to Draqa's—

Sius Mavell Evi's face crackled into view. Draqa mentally cursed. Sius Mavell Evi's cool voice filled his ears.

"Well, well, Draqa. I was wondering when I would hear from you."

Draqa bowed his head. "Forgive me, sir. There were. . . complications."

"Complications?"

Draqa moved his aspectacaster so that the sling around his left arm was in view. Sius Mavell Evi pursed his lips. "Did Tolas Ruv Aen do this?"

"He did." There was no need for Draqa to say anything else. His failure was clear.

"You disappoint me. I'm beginning to lose faith in you," Sius Mavell Evi said.

Draqa remained impassive. "I understand. But if you would let me explain. I wasn't able to kill Tolas Ruv Aen, but there were some unexpected events that lead to something I think you could greatly benefit from."

"You still failed me. Again, I should add. Nothing you say will get you out of this. You need to return immediately," Sius Mavell Evi said.

Draqa's stomach twisted in knots. "Yes, sir, but if you would listen. This is about the Ard'a."

Sius Mavell Evi raised his chin. Draqa was dangerously close to speaking out of turn. "Whatever it is you have to say, it can wait until you're here," Sius Mavell Evi said.

Draqa nodded. "I can be there in the next forty-eight hours."

"I should hope so." Sius Mavell Evi left the session.

Draqa ran a hand through his hair. He stood a while on the porch, the cold numbing his face. He didn't have much faith in Queen Nephas' plan to begin with, and now he could see he didn't have much of a chance at all.

He had to step lightly when he returned to the Vyn. He had to relay the news carefully, in a way that didn't make it sound like he was trying to get out of his punishment. And he knew that if there was any chance to convince the Governor, he had to convince himself that he really was going to spy on the Ard'a for Sius Mavell Evi, and not the other way around. Otherwise Sius Mavell Evi would read his mind and then Draqa would *really* be in trouble.

He remembered the last time he made a mistake as grave as this one. Perhaps "remember" was a bit of an overstatement, but he knew more about what happened than he let on.

When Tolas Ruv Aen joined the Ard'a, Draqa had been involved. How, he didn't know. But whatever Draqa had done to illicit Sius Mavell Evi's rage, what followed was excruciating. He could still recall the pain in his head, sharp and drawn out like the Governor had driven a skewer through his skull. At the time, he didn't know what Sius Mavell Evi did to him. The only thing in his mind had been pure, black hate for Tolas Ruv Aen, and strange, hazy memories of times his old lover had wronged him.

Whatever Sius Mavell Evi did to him back then wasn't at all like when he tried to hide Draqa's memory of the night that he first met Krystal. No. What Sius Mavell Evi did three years ago had been worse. And stronger. So much so that the hate still remained even now, clinging to his heart like tar. And of course, Draqa had no choice but to follow his heart.

He couldn't let that happen again.

He finally went back inside when Krystal was about to leave. Javis looked him up and down.

"What were you doing out there without your coat?" he fretted. "You'll make yourself sick!"

Draqa rolled his eyes, though Javis was right. "I wasn't out long."

Krystal put on her own coat. Her eyes seemed a little lighter.

"Are you leaving?" Draqa asked.

Krystal bobbed her head. "I'll be back the day after tomorrow," she said.

If that was the case, Draqa wouldn't see Krystal again for what could be a long time.

"Do you mind if I take you home?" he asked. He then felt like he needed a reason for this and added, "I was about to head into the city to buy something."

Javis looked like he wanted to protest, but Krystal agreed.

"I don't mind. I actually wanted to talk to you," she said. She tucked her hair out of her face and gave Javis a grin that *was* almost enough to make Draqa envious this time. "I'll see you later."

They went out into the surrounding forest and walked in silence for a while. Draqa wasn't sure about Krystal, but he was having trouble thinking of what he wanted to say and how he wanted to say it. Really, he just wanted to be in her company one last time.

Krystal broke the silence with a sigh. "I know you told me not to worry, but I am anyway."

Draqa looked down at her. She walked with her head downturned, feet dragging through the snow.

"You're not worried about me, are you?" he asked.

"Of course I am. You joined the same group Sius Mavell Evi has you going after Tolas Ruv Aen for." Krystal said.

Draqa stuffed his hands in his pockets. "Trust me, I don't want to, but it was that or be killed."

Krystal looked at him, stopping in her tracks. Her lips twisted and her eyebrows knitted together. "That doesn't explain why you're going back to Sius Mavell Evi or how you'll deal with him. I thought you wanted to start over."

Draqa did say that didn't he?

"I do want to. Believe me I do. But I can't do that while Sius Mavell Evi still owns me." Draqa hesitated. He hadn't wanted to tell Krystal the full details of what Nephas wanted him to do in fear that the wrong person would find out. But Krystal deserved to know. "As far as he's concerned, I'm going to spy on the Ard'a for him."

Krystal's eyes grew round. "What? How do you know he won't find out this time?"

Draqa's shoulders sagged. "I don't. All I can do is try not to do something to give myself away. But if this works, Sius Mavell Evi may be gone from my life forever."

He smiled, not just in hopes that he would encourage Krystal, but himself as well. He started ambling in the direction of the city again. Krystal followed at his side. The trees around them thinned. When they reached the city, Krystal stopped him again.

"When are you leaving?" she asked.

Draqa made eye contact with her. "In two days. So, this is where we say goodbye. For how long, I don't know."

Krystal nodded slowly. Again, Draqa struggled to read her, but he wasn't left guessing for long. Krystal reached for either his wrist, or his hand or arm, then stopped short and drew her hand back. She rested it on her hip.

"You better be careful," she said. "I mean it. I want—no—I expect to see you again."

Draqa was never one to make promises as they were often dangerous and hard to keep. This time however, he did. He did for the sole reason that he wanted it to be true.

He squeezed Krystal's shoulder.

"You will, I promise."

Draqa's pace back to his brother's was slow, too slow in fact. It took two hours to get back instead of one, by which time the sunlight had already turned the land gold. Draqa tried to sneak inside, but Javis was waiting for him.

He harped on Draqa a little, threatening to make him sleep outside if he didn't take his boots off and made another mess on the living room carpet. Draqa obeyed with a roll of his eyes.

Draqa offered to make dinner, but Javis refused as he had every time Draqa offered so far. It was like he was afraid Draqa might try to poison his food. Draqa mentioned this, which served only to make Javis tense.

While they ate together, Draqa noticed that the smell of alcohol on Javis was strong, unlike it had been while Krystal was there. Draqa wasn't sure if he should be disgusted or if he should pity him. He held his tongue all the same. He wanted to be wrong about his brother.

Yet again, Javis attempted conversation with Draqa. It was something inconsequential and uninteresting to Draqa, but Draqa obliged him, albeit with reluctance. Their mostly one-sided conversation ended when Draqa finished his meal and excused himself to bed.

His sleep that night was fitful. He woke up more than once, his head too full of worries to let him fall back to sleep with ease. When he finally did get any amount of decent rest, it only lasted into the wee hours of the morning.

The sound of the door opening and voices leading into the kitchen stirred him awake. The back of his eyelids lit with pale red as someone turned on a light somewhere. He covered his face with his arm, groaning.

When the kitchen door closed and the voices quieted to whispers, he might have tried to fall asleep again. In fact, when the familiar yet comforting smell of wet gun powder and cologne filled his nose, he thought he might have been dreaming. And then he heard Tolas Ruv Aen's annoying laugh and his eyes shot open.

To his misfortune, Tolas Ruv Aen was leaned forward over the back of the couch and over him. Draqa practically threw himself onto the floor. Tolas Ruv Aen chuckled again.

"Good morning. I forgot how light a sleeper you were."

Draqa swore. "What are you doing here?"

Tolas Ruv Aen made his way around the couch and sat down. Draqa noted his boots were off.

"Javis let us in," Tolas Ruv Aen said.

Us? Draqa glanced to the kitchen, remembering the voices that woke him. "More of your people?" he guessed.

"Two of them," Tolas Ruv Aen said. "The rest are—well, it don't really matter who. They're here to discuss some things with the Ambassador."

Draqa drew his eyes back to Tolas Ruv Aen. "And you?"

"Escort."

Tolas Ruv Aen laid his head back. Draqa knew better than to think he let his guard down. Just like on the train, Tolas Ruv Aen had a tenseness in his limbs. Draqa crossed over to the armchair and sat warily.

Tolas Ruv Aen sniffed. "Early mornings like this make me feel like I'm getting old," he said.

Draqa scoffed. Tolas Ruv Aen always said that when he had to wake up any time before midday.

"You're not even middle aged yet," Draqa said.

"Two hundred's still a long time," Tolas Ruv Aen said.

He sat up and faced Draqa. His face became stern, confirming Draqa's suspicion that he was there for Draqa after all.

"Do you have a plan?" he asked.

"For what?"

"For the Governor."

Draqa narrowed his eyes. "I have ideas."

Tolas Ruv Aen shook his head. "In other words, yer just gonna hope for the best. You leaving soon?"

"Tomorrow," Draqa said.

Tolas Ruv Aen clicked his tongue. He rummaged through the pockets of his leather vest. To Draqa's surprise, he pulled out a cigar and lit it. Cigars were one of those items that no one wanted to admit came from Taevalear. Technically, it was illegal to bring back anything from the Other Realm that wasn't Council approved, but people liked them, so the Gatekeepers brought them and sold them in the underground markets. The diauks usually turned a blind eye.

"When did you start smoking?" Draqa asked, raising an eyebrow.

Tolas Ruv Aen shrugged. "Two, three years ago. . . Do you remember how Sius Mavell Evi caught me?"

Draqa thought back, but nothing came to mind. That was one of the memories that was entirely lost to Sius Mavell Evi's manipulative magic. He shook his head.

"Ramnik. He got wind of what we were planning and told Sius

Mavell Evi. Then you were forced to tell him," Tolas Ruv Aen said, sighing. "You know, I—I was trying to get you outta there."

Draqa observed Tolas Ruv Aen as he smiled and took a drag from the cigar and blew the smoke off to the side. Draqa hated how the elf always tried to act so nonchalant with everything when it was obvious these things hurt him.

"Tell me, even while we sit here, do you hate me? Are you thinking of the best way to catch me off guard and kill me?" Tolas Ruv Aen asked.

Draqa said nothing. Tolas Ruv Aen looked at him, his pale green eyes scanning every inch of Draqa. Draqa looked away. Tolas Ruv Aen hummed to himself.

"I'll take that as a yes."

Hoarse coughing erupted from the kitchen, turning both of their heads before Draqa could reply. He started to stand, but Tolas Ruv Aen waved him off. Draqa frowned.

"Don't mind it," Tolas Ruv Aen said. "One of the others don't do well in the cold. His lungs are sensitive."

Draqa sat back down. He looked to the kitchen as the coughing continued. Tolas Ruv Aen spoke again.

"I s'pose my point in bringing all this up is, I want some reassurance that you'll hide it from Sius Mavell Evi better than I did. Back then, I gotta say it was downright terrifying to watch what he did to you."

Draqa didn't need Tolas Ruv Aen to remind him. It was why he'd barely slept.

"It was for me, too," he muttered.

Tolas Ruv Aen raised his brow. He moved to the edge of the

couch. "Are you scared now?"

Draqa massaged his eyes. He didn't want to admit it. "He doesn't trust me like he used to. Even if he doesn't force me to tell him, he can still read my mind if he believes he has a reason to."

"What if you brought me to him? As a way to get his trust back?" Tolas Ruv Aen asked.

Draqa paused. Tolas Ruv Aen would do that? Would that work?

"No," Draqa said. "He would know something was wrong. He already knows I failed."

Tolas Ruv Aen's expression fell. "Then. . . Disyr guide you."

The door to the kitchen creaked open and a line of people filed out. There were five of them. Two of them Draqa vaguely recognized as members of the Ard'a. Two others held cases and wore aprons bearing medical insignia under their coats. The last was a drenen woman with orange eyes and blue scales on her cheeks.

Draqa frowned at the doctors. "What is this?"

Tolas Ruv Aen stood, putting out his cigar. "Ah, *this* is my cue to leave."

Then it dawned on Draqa. He laughed quietly in disbelief. Tolas Ruv Aen was only there to keep him distracted.

"Tally, you bastard," he said.

Tolas Ruv Aen grinned. "Aw, don't be like that. I meant everything I said."

He winked at Draqa and followed the others out into the cold, dawn air.

33

IT MAY HAVE BEEN hypocritical of Draqa considering he'd made a point of dancing around the subject of his own personal life when his brother asked, but he found himself digging for information after the doctors left. Javis wouldn't give it to him and would neither confirm nor deny anything.

Javis poured himself a cup of tea and massaged his temples. The early hours of the morning were clearly unkind to him. All he said was, "It's private business, Jair."

Private or not, it sent Draqa's mind reeling. There was no hiding the doctors. They wouldn't have been there unless Javis needed their help; the coughing from before had belonged to Javis.

But Javis didn't *seem* sick. He acted perfectly fine. He sounded well enough—no. No, he didn't. His voice had sounded horrible ever since he and Draqa had met in Keln. Draqa didn't know why he failed to realize sooner. Javis didn't smoke or show any visible signs of damage to his throat, so of course he had to be sick. And whatever the sickness, he was ill enough that he didn't want Draqa to know about it.

Only, Draqa didn't understand why the Ard'a had come as well. Was it that they had doctors that were better than the rest? Had Javis bargained for their help, perhaps refusing to give up his information on Sius Mavell Evi until Nephas agreed to help him? Unless. . .

Draqa recalled how nervous Javis had been when Draqa mentioned that Sius Mavell Evi wanted him dead. Had the Governor already reached him after all? Draqa didn't think he wanted to know now that he considered it. Besides, what could Sius Mavell Evi have done to make him ill? Javis' problem had to be related to something else, something natural. Draqa was over reacting.

Javis started from the kitchen with his tea then paused at the foot of the staircase.

"Say, do you mind going to the shops for me today?" he asked abruptly. *Too* abruptly.

Draqa had a feeling Javis wanted him out of the house. "Couldn't you go yourself?"

"I have other things to take care of, or else I would. I only need more ink, emerald if they have it, and if you could buy ingredients for dinner tonight. Soup would be best," Javis said.

Draqa frowned as Javis went up to his study. He reappeared a moment later and tossed down a small coin purse. Draqa barely caught it.

"I didn't agree to," he said.

But Javis smiled in that cheerful, dismissive fashion he always did when he didn't care how much Draqa refused his wishes—he always had his way. "You can get something for yourself with that if you do," he said.

Draqa couldn't say he was tempted by the offer, but he gave in, if only because going to the city gave him the excuse to try to see Krystal again. She wasn't home when he arrived, however, and neither were Averil and Zalé. Draqa held on to a hope that he might run into them later, but Kerevel Tul, while not as sprawling as the Vyn, was still a large city.

Oh well. Draqa already said his goodbyes to Krystal, and he didn't need to draw them out longer.

Draqa bought fixings and spices for potato soup as well as a sweet cake with a salted egg inside to nibble on while walking home. The ink took him longer to find, making him wish he'd sought it out first and the groceries after. When he finally did find a store, a tiny place hidden in a square alley, luck had it that they sold their last bottle of emerald ink earlier that morning.

Draqa settled on oxblood instead, unable to decide on an ink Javis might like. It pained him to realize he didn't know his brother's favorite color anymore. Oxblood at least was a nice color. It was a rich, deep red that bordered on a shade of burgundy, and this particular ink even glittered in the light. Even if Javis didn't like it, Draqa did. He paid for the expensive ink and went on his way.

It was late afternoon by the time Draqa got back home. He remembered to kick off his boots when he entered this time, though he couldn't be bothered to set them upright. He set the groceries at the bottom of the stairs and jogged up to deliver Javis his ink. Javis wasn't in his study. His bedroom was empty as well. The kitchen, then.

Draqa set the ink on Javis' desk, where a half-written letter laid next to a much plainer bottle of black ink. Draqa resisted the temptation to read it and went to put away the groceries.

Javis sat at the island, his head resting in his hand. His other held a bottle of spirits. It was nearly empty. Well, *that* mystery was solved, then. Draqa set down the groceries on the counter hard enough to stir Javis into consciousness. He stared at Draqa's scowling features and blinked stupidly.

"I got what you asked," Draqa said, folding his arms.

Javis sat up and rubbed his face. "What did I ask?"

"Soup and ink," Draqa huffed.

"Right. . ." Javis' eyes fell on the spirits. He seemed to sober up instantly. He returned the top and walked it over to the cabinet.

Draqa leaned against the counter. "Should I even ask?"

Javis paused, like he was considering what to say, then hid the bottle. He removed his eyeglasses to clean them in the sink.

"I believe you would come to your own conclusions even if you didn't," he added. "The right ones, probably."

"So, you *are* a drunk," Draqa said.

Nervous laughter escaped Javis' lips. "Well, when you put it like that it sounds dreadful!" He wiped off his glasses and returned them to his nose.

"I'd hoped you would be gone longer," he said.

"If that's all you're worried about, I'm leaving tomorrow," said Draqa. "Do you hide it from everyone or just me?"

Javis picked at his fingers. "Do you realize how people would talk if word got out? If people thought I—that I—Of course I hide it!" he snapped.

For the first time, Draqa caught how Javis' voice went just a little too high, became a little too loud, and Javis winced and gripped his throat. Draqa narrowed his eyes. He repeated his words from that morning.

"Why were the doctors here?" It was a demand this time.

Javis sighed, his eyes flitting everywhere but Draqa's own. "I don't think you would care if I told you, or you'll mock me and say, 'I told you so,'" he said.

Draqa creased his brow. "I'm your brother. I think I'm obligated to care at least a little."

"Fine. . ." Javis said after another moment's hesitation. He looked at his hands and tucked them behind his back. "Sius Mavell Evi already sent someone."

Draqa's arms fell. He was right? He didn't want to be right. He was already forming the answer in his head when Javis continued, "He tried to poison me—But don't worry! It didn't work. Mostly. . ."

Draqa looked his brother from head to toe. Maybe it was from the alcohol, but there was an almost unnoticeable tremor in Javis' movements.

"Are you sure?" Draqa asked.

"Yes. Rather, it's under control. It's nothing serious. It's only my voice," he said.

Draqa considered this and decided he didn't believe Javis. Still, he played along. "Then the doctors were here only to fix your voice?"

Javis' eyes shifted again. "They're going to try. Until then, well, you heard."

He returned to his chair and rested his head in his arms. Draqa took the seat next to him. He leaned in to see Javis' face.

He kept his voice level and asked, "Who poisoned you?"

Javis shrugged. "A dwerin. Re—Rim—"

"Ramnik?"

"That was it," Javis confirmed.

Somehow, the news didn't come as a surprise, especially since Tally confirmed that Ramnik was the reason why Sius Mavell Evi discovered his betrayal. Ramnik always snuck about, listening and pretending. It was only fitting Sius Mavell Evi would have him be the one to try to take out Javis after Draqa refused. No one would suspect a dwerinian butler, unassuming as he was. Draqa vowed then that he would make Ramnik pay if he ever got the chance.

Javis sighed. "He followed us to a tavern and slipped the poison into my drink. I know. It's ironic."

"A little," Draqa agreed, but he couldn't find the humor in it.

He wanted to blame himself for this. If he had accepted the job to kill Javis instead of Tolas Ruv Aen, he could have faked Javis' death somehow. Maybe then he wouldn't be in this hopeless situation with the Ard'a and Sius Mavell Evi, either. A heavy, sickening feeling tightened around his chest and made it hard to breathe. Guilt.

There had to be something Draqa could do to make up for this. And Javis finally gave in and told him the truth, or what was close to the truth, hadn't he? It was only fair that Draqa do the same. At this point it didn't matter if he said anything else to betray the

Governor after what he'd already done.

"I need to tell you something," he said, making up his mind.

Javis turned his face toward Draqa. His lips parted, but if he had a question, he didn't ask it.

"You were right to think Sius Mavell Evi was working with someone in Adonis," Draqa said. "He and Vasiir are planning something, but it has nothing to do with the clans. The drād clans were a distraction."

Javis' brow furrowed, and he sat up. "A decoy? Then what. . .?"

Draqa shook his head. "I don't know. I *do* know how Sius Mavell Evi found out what you were doing. There's a sylfan who works on the Board, with pink eyes and dark, mottled feathers."

"Tavyn Marvec. Yes, I know him," Javis said.

"He isn't who he says he is. He's working with Sius Mavell Evi and Vasiir, and he's not sylfan. He's a yilura."

Javis reached for his head, his mouth falling open. His eyes grew wide and frantic.

"Are—are you certain?"

"I heard them talking. I saw them," Draqa said.

Javis muttered an oath. "I need to warn the Minister."

He started to get up. Draqa grabbed his arm.

"Don't. You shouldn't get more involved. Leave it to the Ard'a."

He didn't know what he would do if Javis was hurt again.

"Do they know?" Javis asked.

Admittedly, Draqa hadn't told the Ard'a yet. He wasn't sure how much would be safe to tell them at the time.

"They will," he assured.

Javis slowly sat back down. He nodded. Draqa squeezed his

arm and released him.

Draqa fixed them both a late lunch while he let Javis process. He was surprised Javis didn't protest this time, but he assumed it was because Javis was too worried to bother. Draqa's own thoughts were distracted with worry, and he nearly dropped the food onto the floor more than once.

Draqa slid a sandwich and a cup of water in front of Javis' face. Javis acknowledged it with a glance but focused his attention on Draqa instead.

"You said you're leaving tomorrow?"

"I am," Draqa said, pushing the plate closer to encourage Javis to eat.

Javis picked at it. "You'll be careful?" he asked.

"Of course," Draqa said.

"What will you do when you get there?"

Draqa held back from answering, thinking about what to say. He didn't want to burden Javis with even more worry.

"Whatever I need to," he said finally. "But I'll make sure Sius Mavell Evi doesn't go after you again."

Javis dipped his head and turned his attention to his food.

Draqa boarded an airship early the following morning. He wanted to see Krystal again but knew he would use her as an excuse to not return to Sius Mavell Evi, so he had Javis send her his regards instead. Javis saw him off.

The other passengers were jovial, likely caught up in the excited atmosphere of the coming holiday. They paid Draqa no mind. The airship flew into a blizzard as it neared the port city.

Draqa found himself wishing the storm would cause the engines to fail and send him and all the others spiraling to their dooms if it meant he didn't have to disembark in Talnoq-Vyn. But, two and a half hours later, he was riding a carriage to the manor.

He wanted to tell the driver to continue on past it, to take him to the ruins just beyond. To take him where his Gate was waiting for him. Only, he remembered the Gate had been destroyed.

The driver let him off. Draqa squinted up at the manor. It loomed above him, dark and ominous in the blinding snow. There was a time that he once saw it as a fortress; a sanctuary where he could hide from the world. Now he saw it for what it was—another prison. And he was returning willingly.

His legs were lead. With each step he took, they grew heavier. Every jittery nerve inside him screamed at him to run away, yet he couldn't. He had to face this. He reached the door and raised his hand above the knocker. He faltered. Before he could recover, the door opened. Whether he somehow sensed Draqa coming or saw him arrive through the window, Sius Mavell Evi was waiting for him.

Draqa fell into a bow. Sius Mavell Evi grabbed him roughly from behind and pushed him inside, slamming the door shut behind him. Draqa didn't dare speak.

"My study," Sius Mavell Evi ordered.

Draqa obeyed. Sius Mavell Evi followed close behind him. The sound of the Governor's cane sent a chill through Draqa's back with each echoing tap it made against the black marble floor.

Draqa glimpsed Minnos and another servant across the hall. They hurried out of sight in a flurry of whispers as they saw Draqa and his Governor approach.

When they reached the study, Sius Mavell Evi had Draqa enter first. The clicking lock rattled Draqa's bones. Sius Mavell Evi pointed to the armchair in front of the cold fireplace.

"Sit."

Draqa lowered himself into the chair and stared forward. The fire roared to life, becoming hot instantly. He felt Sius Mavell Evi come behind him, felt the weight of his hands on the back of the chair.

"So, you have news about the Ard'a," Sius Mavell Evi said. His voice prickled the hairs on Draqa's neck.

Draqa nodded slowly.

Sius Mavell Evi hissed in his ear, "Speak. Fast."

Draqa swallowed. His heart beat so loud against his chest he was sure the Governor could hear it.

"The Ard'a. They," he started. He had rehearsed this in his head. It kept him up all the previous night. He'd known exactly what to say and how to say it. Now, everything he wanted to say vanished from his mind. He covered up his pause with a laugh. "They wanted me to spy on you."

Sius Mavell Evi darted in front of Draqa before he could even think to regret his phrasing. Draqa blinked, and the Governor was there, striking him across the face with the brass head of his cane. Draqa's head snapped to the side. Stars danced in his vision.

"You were caught?!" Sius Mavell Evi roared. "And you dare share my secrets!"

"No!" Draqa said before he could be accused of further betrayal.

Sius Mavell Evi struck him again. Draqa made the mistake of

trying to block the cane with his hand this time. A sharp pain shot through his knuckles, and he yanked it away. The cane contacted his jaw a second time. His teeth rattled.

"Sir—Master—I haven't betrayed you!" he pleaded, disgusted with himself.

Sius Mavell Evi halted only momentarily, crazed anger gleaming in his eyes. Draqa rushed to speak as quickly as he could. "I told them I would spy, yes, but not to do anything against you! This was the opportunity I told you about—with me in the Ard'a, we finally have someone on the inside!"

Sius Mavell Evi lowered his cane and turned to the fire. Not that it mattered much; he could raise it again in an instant. This was only a short reprieve.

Draqa continued, "I can feed you information. I can keep them out of your way. That's what you want, isn't it?"

Draqa could hear Sius Mavell Evi's long fingernails clicking against the iron fire poker as he stirred the flames.

"And why do you think I trust you? You failed again to kill Tolas Ruv Aen. You've made a habit of lying to me. About my granddaughter, about letting that little mouse escape, and you pretend as though I don't notice your disdain for every word I speak," he said.

He turned back to Draqa, raising his cane again. Draqa threw himself to the Governor's feet, bowing at his knee before he could be struck for a fourth time.

"Then let me earn your trust back. Let me prove to you I can be trusted," Draqa said. There was no hiding the desperation in his voice.

He tensed, Sius Mavell Evi lifting his chin with the cane to force him to look in his eyes. This was it. Draqa braced himself for the onslaught on his mind. It never came.

"I trust that you're an eel, only doing what you think will allow you to slip your way out of trouble," he said.

"Sir?"

"But very well. What will you do for me?" Sius Mavell Evi asked.

Draqa didn't hesitate. "Anything."

Sius Mavell Evi echoed him. He paced a circle around Draqa, his cane tapping like the ticking second hand of a clock. Draqa closed his eyes, imagining there really was a clock, counting down to his fate.

Sius Mavell Evi stopped in front of him. A dry chuckle resonated from his chest. Draqa hid his confusion.

"You will have plenty of chances to prove yourself in the coming weeks. No need to. . . overdo it," Sius Mavell Evi said.

A wave of relief passed over Draqa. "Thank you," he said. "You won't be disappointed again."

"I hope not. Now, give me your arm."

Draqa looked down at his arms, unsure why or which one the Governor wanted. "My arm, sir?"

"Your right one. Or need I remind you already that you still failed me? And you had the audacity to think I would want you joining the Ard'a, even as a spy." Sius Mavell Evi held out his hand.

Draqa didn't move. "They would have killed me otherwise."

"Then you should have let them. Your arm, Draqa."

Draqa's legs wobbled as he rose to his feet. He lifted his free arm. Then he saw the white-hot fire poker sticking out of the fireplace. He pulled his arm back. He shouldn't have.

Sius Mavell Evi took Draqa's arm and yanked it forward, twisting as he did so. All at once, Draqa felt a pop, and pain shot through his arm. Sius Mavell Evi threw him down in front of the fire. Draqa's breath caught as his elbow slammed against the floor in his attempt to catch himself.

He didn't have a chance to recover. Sius Mavell Evi brought his cane down, trapping Draqa's wrist with such force that he swore it cracked. He tried to escape, but the cane only pressed into him harder. Sius Mavell Evi pulled the iron poker from the flames. Draqa's heart stopped.

The hot metal seared through his sleeve and into his forearm. He screamed. He writhed, plead for Sius Mavell Evi to stop, but the iron stabbed him again and again up the length of his arm. The smell of melting flesh stung his nostrils. The scent brought him back to his cell as Baren's jail burned to the ground around him. He shut his eyes tight.

His only relief came from Sius Mavell Evi returning the poker to heat it once more. Draqa sobbed through gritted teeth. This—if this was his only punishment, he could bear it. He had to.

Sius Mavell Evi let Draqa go when he was burned and bloodied to his shoulder. He couldn't move his elbow. His hand was numb. Tears stung his eyes.

He lay still, panting heavily until Sius Mavell Evi nudged him with his foot.

"Go to the infirmary and wait for me there. I will tend to you when I'm ready."

Draqa grunted and rolled to his feet. He left his arm hanging at his side. He bowed to the Governor and was released from the study.

Minnos waited for him, dancing nervously in front of the door. Her eyes went round in horror when she saw his bruised face and mangled arm. Draqa was in too much pain to deny her efforts to help him and let her lead him to the infirmary. All he could think was how lucky he was to still have his mind.

34

KRYSTAL HAD ANOTHER DREAM about Draqa the night after he left. This dream. . .she'd rather have not remembered. One moment, her sleep was peaceful. The next, she was trapped in a jail cell, heat and flames surrounding her. She was helpless as she watched herself—or more accurately, watched Draqa—pound against the door in a meaningless effort to escape.

The smoke had burned Draqa's lungs and stung his eyes blind. The terror within him heightened with each piece of rubble that crashed and fell around him. All he could see on the other side of the glass door was a wall of black and red. If he didn't get out, he would either be crushed, suffocate, or cooked alive in his cell.

Finally, the glass became weak from the heat, and he was able to break through the door. By then it was too late. Draqa fell and stumbled through this hell made real. His clothes set alight easily and burned to his skin. He collapsed, falling down the short steps at the jail's entrance. He didn't move again.

Krystal awoke sobbing, bloodcurdling screams and white-hot pain clawing at her whole body. Averil ran to her room in alarm. He tried to comfort her, asking what happened, reassuring it was just a dream. Krystal cried into his shoulder, shaking her head over and over. Averil didn't understand. It wasn't just a dream.

Javis arrived for Krystal every day like clockwork. His mood was ever cheerful, no matter what the weather was like outside or how he was delayed. His good spirits were the only thing to raise Krystal's own, distracting her from the stress and nightmares plaguing her thoughts, at least for the few hours they spent together each time they met.

Javis was an amazing teacher. He had shown he was the type to lose his patience easily, but for Krystal it was like a switch flipped in his head. If he at all lost his patience with Krystal, it showed no further than a quick flash over his expression and never reached his voice.

In a week, Krystal was able to meditate for nearly an hour at a time, though she couldn't yet control her dream walking. Javis assured her that this was good, but despite her progress, Krystal became impatient. She lost sleep at night, kept awake by her fears. Every time she closed her eyes, she could almost feel the fire closing in around her, lurking behind her eyelids and waiting for her to slip into the world of sleep so it could once again steal her into its burning clutches. Krystal wasn't progressing fast enough.

Javis was empathetic and understanding when Krystal expressed her frustrations.

"I know how terrifying it can be to experience someone's memories unfiltered," he said. *"If you ever need to discuss with me what you've*

seen, don't even hesitate to ask. I'll do whatever I can to help ease that burden."

He took Krystal's hands in his own when he said this. They were warm, a little dry, and had the deceiving smoothness of someone who couldn't have done hard work a day in his life. His index fingers and thumbs were stained with ink, but it didn't rub off onto Krystal's skin.

Krystal nodded, having to turn her gaze elsewhere. Her cheeks tingled with heat. She wasn't sure she was ready to recount to him all the awful things she witnessed in Draqa's memories, but she thanked him, nonetheless.

Javis insisted that they spend some of their days in the city. He wanted to show her around now that the solstice celebrations had officially started and said that Krystal would do much better at learning if she was able to relax in between.

"And apart from that, I know someone who may be able to assist you in your learning if you ever happen to need it," he added.

He started taking Krystal on detours through Kerevel Tul and its solstice markets on their way to his house each day. While Averil had shown Krystal all the main streets, Javis took her through possibly every side street and back alley in the entire city. He was an enthusiastic tour guide, showing her the most hole-in-the-wall types of places. A hidden haberdashery, a quaint stationary store tucked in a square alley, a perfumery. They were all places suited mostly to Javis' own tastes, Krystal realized, but she didn't mind. It was sweet, in a way, to see him so unashamedly open about himself— another stark difference between him and Draqa.

She began to wonder if Javis was this way with everyone, or if he perhaps saw her as special. She couldn't muster up the courage to ask him this, although she did enjoy the thought of it.

Before she knew it, another week passed, much faster than the last. Although Averil didn't yet have the time to find Krystal a tutor because he was busy catching up on the work he missed while Zalé was missing, he did buy her an aspectacaster. Krystal wished she'd had it before Draqa left so that she wasn't left waiting for news about his wellbeing. Not that she was expecting any, but it worried her all the same.

Krystal's time with Javis quickly became a constant that she looked forward to. Then, one morning he didn't show up like he said he would. Krystal lingered within hearing range of the door knocker all morning. Averil left for work, one of Zalé's tutors came, but Javis never arrived.

Krystal tried "chiming" him over her aspectacaster, but he didn't answer. She tried not to worry. Javis was probably just late. Maybe he forgot that he had plans that day? It did take a while to walk from his house to the city.

Finally, just past noon, the knocker fell thrice against the door. Krystal sprinted from her room to open it. But it wasn't Javis waiting on the other side, it was. . . Tolas Ruv Aen?

"What are you doing here?" Krystal asked, disappointed.

"*What are you looking so glum for?*" Tolas Ruv Aen asked, leaning against the doorframe.

Krystal shook her frown away. "Sorry, I was waiting for Javis. Can I help you?"

"*Actually, that's part of why I'm here,*" Tolas Ruv Aen said. "*The Ambassador's meeting with us today and forgot to tell you.*"

A weight lifted from Krystal's chest. She was still disappointed, but at least nothing bad had happened.

"Oh, okay. That's all right. Did he say when we could meet up again?" she asked.

Tolas Ruv Aen scratched his chin. *"He didn't, but he'll be busy all of today."*

Krystal nodded with a heavy sigh.

"Now for more important business, Nephas has something to show you, if yer up for it."

Krystal tilted her head. "She does?" Then Krystal remembered: Nephas said she would take Krystal to see her father's house. She perked up.

Tolas Ruv Aen smiled as though reading her mind.

"Don't forget to bring that key," he said.

Krystal ran to get ready. She snatched up her key and camera bag and waved a quick goodbye to Zalé, who was still in the middle of his lessons. Then, she left with Tolas Ruv Aen.

"Hey," she started, smoothing out her coat. "If you don't mind, I've been wondering something. Why *is* your name so long? Is it an elf thing?"

Tolas Ruv Aen chuckled. *"It's funny you think my name's long. It's actually one of the shorter ones. But yeah, you could say it's an 'elf thing.'"*

"Tolas Ruv Aen is *short*?" Krystal raised her brow, dumbfounded.

Tolas Ruv Aen's eyes twinkled, a grin stretching across his face. *"It'd be even longer if my parents went strictly by tradition and gave me their full names. You'd be havin' to call me 'Tolas Ruvora Ayanus,' and that's still short. The elves in the east're given* **four** *names."*

"Do you ever use nicknames? I mean, I thought I heard Draqa call you Tally, once. Can I?"

Tolas Ruv Aen's face flushed a dull pink. *"Now that's a personal nickname I'd rather you didn't use." He cleared his throat and laughed again. "Maybe, if I ever get to know you better. Till then I'd like it if you kept calling me Tolas Ruv Aen. Anything less ain't me, if you understand. Names are a lot more than simply a thing to call each other, they're powerful. They hold our identity. I know humans don't share that concept, but for the fae and especially for us elves. . ."*

Krystal nodded slowly. "I understand. " She fell quiet for a few minutes. "By the way, have you heard from Draqa? Do you know if it went well with Sius Mavell Evi?"

Tolas Ruv Aen rubbed the back of his head. *"Nephas has. He's okay and will be doing small jobs for us soon. Though, it sounds like the Governor took some convincing."* Despite his optimistic tone, a worried crease set in his forehead.

"Did something happen?" Krystal asked.

"Not that Nephas said, but can I be honest with you?" Tolas Ruv Aen waited for Krystal to nod. *"I think sending him to do this for us was a bad idea on Nephas' part. An' not just cause I think Draqa could betray us."* The elf hesitated and his face twisted like he wasn't sure he should continue. *"Sius Mavell Evi ain't good to Draqa. He's sensitive about the Ard'ahlen and if something goes wrong, he might take it out on Draqa worse than last time."*

Hoping to gain more insight on Draqa's situation, Krystal asked, "What does Sius Mavell Evi do to him exactly?"

Tolas Ruv Aen clicked his tongue. *"If he didn't tell you, he don't want you knowing."*

"He said Sius Mavell Evi owns him or something."

Tolas Ruv Aen hummed under his breath. The two of them made it to the entrance of the winding boiler room at the train station before he spoke again. It took a minute for Krystal to realize he was continuing their conversation.

"I suppose. I don't claim to know how Sius Mavell Evi does it, but it's better to think it more as him the puppet master and Draqa the marionette. There were no contracts or debts, only magic. Illegal magic if I were to guess. But Draqa knows how to handle himself, so I'm sure he'll be fine. He learned from the best, after all," Tolas Ruv Aen said with a wink.

He opened the door, and they went down to the Gate hidden below. Krystal expected to be taken back to the Ard'a's base, but Queen Nephas already waited for them on this side. The Gate glowed.

Her eyes swept over Krystal, and she smiled. *"Hello again, Krystal Monarain. It's good to see you."*

Krystal offered a little smile in return. "You, too."

"How has your training been going?" Nephas asked.

Krystal faltered. If she told Nephas how she felt about her training, would the Queen take back her hospitality?

"It's slow, but it's going well," Krystal said.

"Ah, I'm glad to hear. I was prepared to find you a new teacher if you needed one," Nephas said.

Krystal shook her head. "Not at all. Javis is perfect."

Nephas turned to Tolas Ruv Aen, who lingered at the foot of the stairs. *"I can take it from here. You may go now."*

Tolas Ruv Aen left, and Queen Nephas held out her arm.

When Krystal only stared at it awkwardly, Nephas chuckled. *"I'm not going to bite. Did Tolas Ruv Aen tell you where we're going?"*

"Only that you're showing me my dad's house," Krystal replied, taking in the symbols glowing within the Gate. "Is it still in Erothel?"

"No. You will see," Nephas said.

Krystal took her arm and Nephas pulled her through the Gate. The intense dizzying sensation that rushed over Krystal didn't seem to affect Nephas at all—she stepped out the other side of the Gate as gracefully as she entered. Krystal was glad she had Nephas' arm to hold on to, or else she may have fallen. She still wasn't used to the feeling of travelling like this.

Humidity still hung in the air on this side of the Gate, but the sun and light breeze made it surprisingly warm. It tasted like the sea. Krystal let go of Nephas and spun to look around. The Gate was carved out of the center of a chalky white rock formation. Similar pillars of rock rose from the ground in varying sizes, and trees with red leaves that had yet to fall grew interspersed between them.

Ahead stood a tall hill where an asymmetrical cottage perched with a quaint little tower. It looked to be built of the same white stone that surrounded it and had blue shingles.

Krystal breathed out in surprise, "Is this it?"

Nephas nodded. Considering her father had been Minister, Krystal had half expected some grand estate not unlike Sius Mavell Evi's manor. In a way, she was relieved it wasn't. She wouldn't have known what to do with such a large house.

"Is it all right to go inside?" Krystal asked, already stepping towards it.

"Of course it is," Nephas said.

Krystal grinned and ran up the uneven steps that lead to the door. She slid to a stop, her eyes landing on the vast expanse of water stretching out in front of her.

"The Doran Sea," Nephas said as she approached. *"We're in Ortrus, one of the countries here in Arai. You cannot make it out most days, but across the water there is Isles."*

Krystal squinted to see where Queen Nephas pointed, but if there was anything there, the haze on the horizon lay too thickly to tell. What Krystal *could* see from the top of the cliff was that they stood in the middle of nowhere, surrounded by the Doran on one side, and by a red and white sea of rolling hills on the other.

Whether for the purpose of peace and quiet, or for safety and to avoid the public eye, Krystal understood why her father might have wanted to live here. It was beautiful.

She fished the old key from her pocket. It wobbled loosely in the lock when she tried it. The mechanism fought against being turned, and Krystal had to pull on the door to keep the key from bending. But, the door itself eased open with a light push and Krystal stepped inside.

The smell of old flowers filled Krystal's nose. Nephas entered beside her and pulled on a beaded cord hanging next to the door, switching on the lights. The entrance opened into a large sitting room with windows on the far wall looking out to the sea. An open doorway to the left led to a small kitchen at the bottom of the tower. Across from the kitchen were stairs leading to the rest of the house.

"It looks so clean," Krystal said.

Nephas laughed with her eyes. *"Oh, you think so? I'm the only one who has been here since Sal died, but I'm afraid I've fallen behind on the upkeep of the place as of late. I hope you don't mind."*

"Not at all," said Krystal. She eyed the stairs which were already calling her name. "Can I look around?"

"Go ahead. The house is yours now, after all," Nephas said.

Krystal didn't need to be told twice and dashed up the stairs. There were two bedrooms and a bathroom. The rest of the tower housed a library; Krystal didn't waste any time going inside. She gasped at the size of it. The curved bookshelves lining the walls stood from floor to ceiling, and she had to crane her neck to view the ones near the top. A ladder sat ready to assist in reaching them. She was sure that there were at least as many books as were sold at Mam's bookstore, if not more. A cushioned reading nook was built into an east facing windowsill.

Krystal gently pulled one of the books from a shelf at her level and flipped through it. It must have been ancient, but despite its musky, yellowing pages, it was in nearly perfect condition. Krystal sniffed its pages and sighed. For a moment she was back home, surrounded by the books in the café. She could almost smell the coffee that Rowen always set to brew in the early morning.

Maybe, just maybe, Krystal could convince herself that living in Arai wouldn't be all bad, not if she had a place like this to remind her of home. It didn't matter that she couldn't read any of the books yet—she could learn in time.

She left to explore the rest of the house next. The small bedroom had only a bed and a nightstand, and though as clean as the rest of the cottage, had the cold emptiness of disuse. Krystal passed it by for the room next to it.

This larger bedroom still held warmth. Inside was a wide bed with a canopy, and table lamps and a dresser. Paintings and photos hung on the walls. A watercolor of the Doran, another of the rock formations out front. There was also a portrait painting of a youth whom Krystal recognized as Averil. He didn't look much different, only this one's hair was cut short and had not a trace of the neatly trimmed beard he wore now.

A three-person family grinned at Krystal from the washed-out colors of the smallest photograph. She lifted it from the dresser. An even younger Averil stood with his arms crossed between two adults. On his left stood a man draped in flowing pink and white robes. His wings peeked out from behind them. The yellow ombre feathers framing his face grew into a shock of hair that stood up on his head like he'd been struck by lightning. His hand rested on Averil's shoulder. He laughed.

On Averil's right was a woman who stood the same height as Sal Monarain. She appeared exactly how Mam had always described, and more. Her hair reached her waist, blue strings and ribbons braided in. Even with the faded colors of the photo, her eyes *were* a vivid peridot. Her tan skin suggested days spent in the sun. The woman's nimble arms rested on her hips, save for one, which she used to hide her own laugh.

Krystal sat on the bed and wiped the thin layer of dust off the frame. She smiled, her heart aching with nostalgia. They looked so happy together. If only she could have been a part of it. But she'd had her own happy upbringing and was suddenly thankful she wasn't around to see Averil's end in tragedy. She hugged the frame to her chest then tucked it into her camera bag.

She took a few photos of the rooms and the view out the library window before she went back down to Nephas, who sat on a yellow cushion at the low table in the sitting room. She drank from a cup of tea. Krystal sat across from her.

"Would you like some?" Nephas asked.

Krystal nodded and Nephas poured her a cup. "Thanks so much for bringing me here," Krystal said.

"Do you like it?"

"I do. I just can't believe it's really mine."

"But of course. As Averil is the eldest it would have gone to him, but as I told you, he refuses to accept it or our protection. It's only natural for the house to go to you," Nephas said.

"Right. . ." Krystal mumbled, her thoughts going back to all Nephas wanted from her. As lovely as owning a house—her father's house of all places—sounded, she had to tell Nephas her decision before she ended up in a situation she regretted.

Nephas tenderly touched Krystal's wrist. *"Is something wrong?"*

Krystal sighed. "I don't think I can accept the house either," she said.

"Why not?" Nephas asked.

"Because I. . . don't want to join the Ard'a. I don't want to soul-travel for you. Or dream walk. Its miserable and I hate doing it," Krystal said.

Queen Nephas' expression didn't change. She slowly nodded, withdrew her hand, and sipped her tea.

"Did you think I only offered this place to you because I thought you

were joining us?" she asked.

"Well, yeah," Krystal said. "Why else would you?"

The Queen's eyes laughed again. *"I will admit I'm disappointed, but this house is yours regardless. Sal was my friend, and it wouldn't be right to hold it over your head like some bargaining chip."*

"Oh."

Nephas looked out to the sea, disregarding Krystal's surprise. She rested her chin on the back of her hand. *"It is a shame to hear you don't appreciate your abilities. I think they would be worth your while once you mastered them."*

Krystal tilted her head. "Really?" She didn't see how she could get anything positive from her abilities in her current relationship with them.

"Think of it," Nephas said, *"you wouldn't have to only rely on stories about your family. You could learn what they were truly like. How they acted, how they sounded when they spoke."*

The realization crept up on Krystal and shook her by the shoulders. "You mean, you'd let me walk in your memories?"

"I would. There's much about your father I would like you to see."

Krystal smiled, then hesitated. "There isn't a catch, is there?"

Nephas laughed for real this time. Her laugh was sharp and cold. *"There is no catch, my dear. Like this house, it's something you deserve."*

Krystal developed renewed motivation for her practice with Javis, encouraged by the ideas Nephas left her with. She was still fearful of sleep, of course, but she felt hopeful now that she would overcome it. She even found herself getting a little excited by the possibilities of what she could accomplished once she'd harnessed her abilities.

Two days later, Javis finally arrived as usual, acting as though his sudden absence had been perfectly in the ordinary. He greeted Krystal, but his usually cheerful grin was strained and didn't reach his eyes. His eyebags were heavier than the days previous.

Krystal watched him as she pulled on her cloak. There was even a tired sag in the way Javis held himself this morning.

"Are you okay?" Krystal asked.

Javis appeared startled and shook himself. He instantly livened. "*Just fine. Had a long night packing, is all.*"

Krystal stepped out the door and started walking with him.

"Packing? Are you going somewhere?"

"*Only for a day or two. After the holidays I plan to leave for Arkaven to meet with the Minister,*" Javis said.

He took her through the tents and stands set up for the ongoing holiday market. Krystal slowed to admire a table full of star-shaped chocolates and other goodies.

"Is he finally willing to listen to you?" she asked distractedly.

Javis shrugged beside her. "*You could say that. Before I forget, I want to apologize for missing the last two days. I should have notified you.*"

"It's all right. You're already doing so much more than you have to and you aren't even getting paid," Krystal said.

They started walking again.

Javis chuckled. "*You don't need to worry about payment. I enjoy teaching you.*"

They turned down a side street, veering away from the

festivities. Krystal was about to ask where they were going, until she realized Javis' trajectory led them right to the Kerevel. They stopped at the base of its steps. Krystal had to crane her neck to squint up at the blue and green stained glass decorating the building's roof.

"If I remember correctly, I promised to take you inside," Javis said.

Krystal grinned. She'd been eyeing the Kerevel for days, hoping for a chance to go inside. Every time she thought of going in on her own, she was quickly deterred by the sight of the hooded men on either side of the grand entrance. They didn't appear to let just anyone in, occasionally turning someone away.

Those same men tensed as Javis and Krystal approached. Javis waved his hand, and before Krystal's eyes, her clothes transformed into a set of robes, not dissimilar to the ones the guards wore. When she looked up, she saw Javis' clothes had transformed the same way. The guards relaxed and allowed them inside.

"What was that?" Krystal asked, looking back.

"A glamor. These aren't real," Javis explained. He passed a hand through his robes in demonstration.

The pair stepped into a massive hall. Krystal's mouth fell open. Columns reached high to the arched ceiling above them. Whole scenes were depicted on stained glass that filtered in green and blue light, and on mosaics along the walls.

Where Krystal expected there to be perhaps pews and a pulpit, there were instead two rows of various humanoid statues. Lining the back wall were arched niches, with statuettes of the same humanoid figures nested within each one.

The hall was busy despite the hallowed silence that hung over it. Nearly everyone wore the same colors of cloaks. Unlike the illusory gray fabric worn by Krystal and Javis, most were white, with either light green, orange, indigo, or turquoise accents.

"Is this. . . a church?" Krystal whispered.

"It's a kerevel," Javis said. He paused, his eyes flitting over a mosaic. *"I'm not sure there's anything else that compares. A kerevel is a kerevel. It's. . . sort of a temple and sort of a school. They teach complex magic here."*

"Like dream walking?" Krystal guessed.

"Only to a few. People believe that by dream walking one can directly communicate with the gods. Now, come with me. I want you to meet someone."

Javis took Krystal's hand and pulled her through the crowd of students and worshippers. They turned through an archway and up a flight of spiral stairs. They stopped in a hallway with a row of doors. Javis knocked on the one in the middle that was slightly ajar. Krystal peeked inside. It was filled with tables. A classroom?

A naol, much older than anyone Krystal had seen so far, looked up from his desk. His skin was much darker than Javis', but it had the same bronze-dust shimmer that Javis and Draqa's had. He pulled off his wire-rimmed glasses and stared.

"Hello," Javis began.

The naol rose and stepped around his desk.

"My word. . ." he uttered. *"Javis Zevos. Never in a hundred lifetimes did I think you would come back here."*

Javis held out his hand, but rather than shake it, the old naol pulled him forward and kissed both his cheeks.

"Vei *Alarach. It's good to see you,"* Javis said.

"And you, but my dear boy, whatever happened to your voice?"

The hesitance in Javis' answer was almost unnoticeable. Krystal thought she imagined it.

"I had an injury a while back. It was all my fault, unfortunately."

"Indeed. You should have come before it healed," Alarach said. He turned to Krystal. *"Is this the lovely Talara you told me about?"*

Javis stumbled over his words. *"What? No—This is vara Monarain. Krystal Monarain."*

"Monarain?" Alarach repeated. His tail flicked in what may have been curiosity.

Krystal waved, catching herself at the last second from saying hello. She was getting too used to being able to speak English whenever she pleased.

"Yes," Javis said. *"I'm teaching her."*

Alarach's eyebrows raised, and his tail flicked again, but he didn't interrupt Javis' introductions.

Javis gestured between Krystal and Alarach. *"Krystal, this is Alarach Milihl. He was my teacher here, and my great uncle."*

Krystal nodded with enthusiasm, recognizing the old man now. He had been in one of Draqa's memories.

Alarach smiled; he had the same smile as Javis, wide and dimpled and eye-creasing. *"Javis was one of the brightest here. He could have achieved much had he stayed."*

Javis let out a short laugh that sounded more like a disguised scoff. *"I'm happy where I am now. But I do have so many things to tell you."*

"I should think so," Alarach said. He leaned back with his hands against his desk, the stiff professionality in his posture relaxing

away. *"What is all this about you being a teacher?"*

Unlike his uncle, Javis' shoulders didn't relax. He spoke slowly. *"I can't go into detail, but ah, Krystal has the ability to dream walk."*

Alarach's lips pressed thin. *"You're teaching someone how to dream walk when you didn't even finish your own schooling for it?"*

Javis held up his hands defensively. *"I know you don't approve, but she needed someone to teach her. The memories she's reliving are too intense,"* he said. *"I'm only here now because I would like your help."*

Krystal looked at Javis in surprise. He had mentioned knowing someone who might be willing to assist in teaching her, but the way he said it now made it sound like he was having trouble doing so on his own.

Alarach scratched his eyebrow and sighed. He closed the door to the classroom and then returned to his place leaning against his desk.

"Please? You know so much more than I do. Would you help teach her?" Javis asked with a hopeful smile.

Alarach shook his head. *"I'm busy, Javis. I don't have time anymore to individually train every apprentice sent my way."*

"Then do it as a favor, as my family." There should have been no reason for them to, but Javis' words almost sounded desperate.

Alarach sighed again. He took his glasses and cleaned them on the folds of his robes. The action must have been more out of habit than anything else, as he then let them fall back against his chest to hang from their thin chain. He turned his apologetic eyes to Krystal.

"If you need the training, I can help you apply for an apprenticeship here," he said, returning to his desk. He sat and began to rummage

through a drawer.

Javis clearly didn't like this answer. He approached Alarach's desk, pressing his hands to the surface and leaned in close.

"I need it to be you. I can only trust you."

Alarach opened his mouth, but before any words left it, Javis suddenly reeled back. Krystal stepped out of his way just in time for him to begin coughing into his hand. He turned away from both of them.

Alarach stood. The hoarse, wet coughing wracked Javis' entire body. He collided with the nearest student table and used it for support. Krystal reached for him—he looked like he could barely stand. He waved her off.

After a moment he pulled out a black cloth from his coat and wiped his mouth, and then his hand. When he turned back to Krystal and Alarach, his face had lost some of its color. He tucked his hand and the cloth behind his back.

"I'm so sorry. I. . . don't know what came over me," he said.

But Krystal wasn't listening to how his voice was even weaker than usual when he apologized. No, she was watching his hand. She definitely didn't imagine the smear of red at the edge of Javis' palm as he moved to hide it.

35

VEI ALARACH KNIT HIS BROW tightly, worsening the wrinkles that were already deep-set in his forehead.

"My boy, are you ill?"

Javis stayed silent, thinking of some excuse he could give for the coughing fit that had just attacked him. He felt Krystal's eyes on him, and he buried his hand and the cloth in his pocket.

"I must be. I've had some late nights recently," he said, coming up with nothing. Hopefully Alarach believed him. Of all people, his uncle was the least Javis could bear to give the news that he might die soon. It was already bad enough that Jair knew as much as he did. Javis needed to try harder to keep his ailment a secret.

Alarach put a hand on Javis' back and guided him to his office at the back of the classroom. He sat Javis down in a cushioned chair, giving him a hard look when he tried to wave off his fussing. Krystal followed them in and stayed near the wall. From the looks she gave Javis, she was clearly itching to question him.

"You need to take better care of yourself," Alarach scolded. "You're young, and the only one in your family left. You're the only family *I* have left."

Javis suppressed a groan, covering his face with his clean hand. "I know, Uncle."

He didn't want to be made to feel worse than he already did. He had no right to pay Alarach this impromptu visit, asking for help, not when he had wasted all Alarach's kindness and kept their contact to a minimum after he threw away his apprenticeship. The last thing Javis wanted to do was hurt him more.

But while most of Alarach's family was gone, he wasn't lonely like Javis was. His relationship with his family had been good. He'd already had a fulfilled life. Alarach was only the kind of lonely that came naturally with old age, the kind that made people eager for what the afterlife had in store for them.

Javis wasn't lonely like that. His loneliness was the kind that came from years of regret and self-loathing. His loneliness was the kind you felt while you were the center of attention in a room full of friends, while knowing none of them actually *knew* you.

Still, Javis felt some consolation knowing that Alarach's words were no longer entirely true.

"Jair's alive," he said.

Alarach frowned. "What are you talking about?"

"Jair is alive. He didn't die. He was even staying with me until recently," Javis said.

His uncle's concern shifted away from Javis' poor health, letting him breathe a sigh of relief.

"That can't be," said Alarach. "We held a funeral. We buried him."

"I know, but the body must have been fake, or. . . we only thought he was dead," Javis said. It was one of the many questions he had that Jair refused to answer.

"No. Whoever you met couldn't have been him. A yilura trying to con you, maybe, but not Jair," Alarach said.

"I thought the same thing, but it's him. He knows things only he could know, and a yilura wouldn't have been able to get his blood back then. I know for a fact that no one has gotten mine, either."

"Then why did he never come back?"

Javis could only shrug. Again, a question that Jair wouldn't answer for him. Although Javis did have a guess for this one; Jair had felt betrayed by his family. He couldn't blame Alarach for his skepticism though. This was a lot of information to drop on him at once.

When the news had reached Alarach that his other nephew had died, he'd been furious. Most of that rage had been directed at Isaias Zevos for being an oblivious and incompetent father. If Isaias had paid more attention to what was happening to Jair, then he might not have turned to corrupted magic and murdered Iolkosz Wacziro and his two friends.

Alarach had then turned his anger at Jair, calling him a disappointment and an abomination, saying he would disown Jair if he could. But Javis knew there was a part of Alarach's anger that they shared: they both blamed themselves, too. They both had ignored Jair's plight. That Jair let them think he was dead all this time was no surprise.

Krystal nudged Javis' shoulder, making him jump. She whispered in his ear. He blinked slowly at her words, then thanked her and looked back at Alarach.

"You helped Jair once, didn't you? When you were visiting Baren, you stepped in when you saw Iolkosz Wacziro harassing him," he said.

Alarach looked surprised. "How did you. . .?"

Javis pointed to Krystal. "Jair is who she connected to. You know some of what he went through. I hope that's proof enough."

Alarach nodded slowly, his skepticism morphing into a hesitant joy. "Where is he?" he asked.

"In Talnoq-Vyn. He. . . works there."

"I want to see him," Alarach said.

Javis nodded. "I'll bring him next time he's in the city."

He made one more attempt to convince Alarach to teach Krystal. As much Javis hated asking, he knew that if he died, his uncle would be the best replacement there could be.

"Do you see now why I want you to be the one to help her? I don't want just anyone knowing what happened to Jair," he said. "You would know how to handle it delicately."

Alarach sighed and looked at the ceiling. He gave in, offering to provide occasional assistance to Krystal should she ever need the help. Javis said a silent prayer in thanks that he could still be convincing when he needed to be.

Krystal, on the other hand, was not so convinced when he tried to assure her that he was fine after they left the Kerevel. She seemed concerned for him. Sweet as it was, Javis wasn't ready for her to know the truth yet, either. He resorted to redirecting her questions, then ignoring them altogether. Krystal let the matter go by the time they reached Javis' house, though he doubted she would for long.

He gave Krystal her lesson for the day. Although she couldn't see it for herself, she was a fast learner and showed visible improvement each time they met. Javis decided it was time to take her lessons a step further.

"When I return from Arkaven, I want to show you how to enter my mind. I think you're ready," he said before he walked her home.

Krystal's eyes went round as saucers. *"Are you sure? What if. . ."* She trailed off, biting her lip.

"I don't have nearly as many bad memories as Jair does," Javis said, "and I'll be able to stop you if you come across something either of us don't want you to see."

He relived his own bad memories enough in his sleep that he wasn't concerned about seeing them again for himself. Krystal, however, did not need to be put through the experience. Javis had not had to block anyone from seeing his memories since before he left his apprenticeship at the Kerevel, but he would have plenty of time to prepare after he left Arkaven.

He wasn't planning to go to Arkaven at first, not after Jair advised against it. But the more he thought about it, the more he knew that he had to speak with Minister Phar. He didn't know when the Ard'a would make good on their word, and by then it could be too late.

After some thought, Javis decided he was going to resign, as well. He was meant to return to the drād clans soon, and he knew that he couldn't do it. He grew weaker every day; the amount of energy he used to just walk from his house to the city was more than he cared to admit. He didn't know how long it would be before he was too weak to move at all.

In the last few days, his veins had turned black like tar, the poison's spread visible as it spiderwebbed in all directions across his skin. He used a glamor to disguise them, now, but how long would it be before even that became too difficult for him?

Queen Nephas had found some of the best doctors that she could find, and even Talara was involved. But it was as Ara said: the poison behaved like some form of curse. Making an antidote turned out to be a slow process that required many tests. So far, none had been effective.

Javis poured himself a glass of almond liqueur and sat in his study after he arrived home later that afternoon. He stared at the unfinished letter laying on his desk. It wasn't addressed to anyone in particular and he procrastinated finishing it. Doing so would feel like an admittance that he was afraid.

Despite it looming closer every day, Javis wasn't prepared for death. He wasn't particularly religious anymore, like many of the humans, or spiritual as most of the fae were. He had nothing to comfort him. There was no god or goddess he felt he could turn to, and going back to Disyr, mother and creator of the fae, now would feel disingenuous.

This letter was all Javis had. He lifted his pen from its stand and dipped it into the ink Jair bought for him. He was disappointed by it at first, but he had to admit Jair had good taste.

Javis closed his eyes in thought. He knew who to write to. He crumpled the letter and put it aside to be burned later and took out a new sheet of paper. He pressed the nib to the paper and wrote.

Javis arrived by airship in Arkaven early the following afternoon. He felt no more confident about speaking with the Minister than before; Minister Phar had no idea Javis was here for him, as he wouldn't be available for an official meeting for another two weeks. He certainly wasn't going to take kindly Javis barging in on him in the middle of his work. Javis would have to push through it. He would make the Minister listen to him no matter what he had to do.

He marched into the capitol building and straight past the Board's meeting hall. After asking around, he realized he was in luck; the Minister was in his office and would be getting out of a meeting at any moment. But when Javis reached Phar's office on the top floor, the guards that were usually posted outside the door were nowhere to be seen.

Javis steeled his nerves and rapped loudly on the door, hoping he hadn't missed the Minister after all. Once, twice, and then he let himself in.

"Minister, I—"

There was no one there. Javis let out an unintentional sigh of relief. He looked around.

Usually, the Minister would be sitting at his carved ebony desk in front of the ceiling height window that overlooked the homes in Arkaven. If not there, he would be in the connected room that served as a less-formal meeting room. Although Javis had never been inside, he heard rumors that the Minister liked board games, and that the room reflected his tastes.

Javis approached the thick emerald curtain that divided it and the office.

"Minister?" he asked, drawing back the curtain.

Lhorsan Phar stepped out in an instant, yanking it back shut. Javis startled.

"What are you doing in here?" the Minister spat.

Lost for words, Javis stepped back. "I—" He noticed that Phar wasn't wearing his usual red cloak.

"Well?" Phar probed. "You're not allowed in here."

Before Javis could respond, the Minister was already pointing for him to leave. Javis held his ground.

"Minister, you said the Board could only act against Governor Sius Mavell Evi if presented with solid evidence with what he was doing," he said.

Phar looked uninterested. He didn't seem to notice or care about Javis' voice, either. "Did I?"

"You did. And I have plenty of evidence now. It may not be proof of what he's doing, but it's enough that you shouldn't be standing by while he does it," Javis said. He presented his aspectacaster. "I now have the audio from the man I hired, as well as from a personal meeting I had with Sius Mavell Evi. I also spoke directly with a man who works for him. He confirmed everything."

Phar crossed his arms. "Fine. Let's hear it," he said. He reached for Javis' aspectacaster, but Javis held it from him.

"Are we safe to listen here?"

Phar huffed loudly. "Why wouldn't we be? Hurry and play it,

I don't have all day."

Javis nodded. He played back the first recording. It was a conversation between Sius Mavell Evi and who Javis now suspected was the spy impersonating Tavyn Marvec.

"—what was that?" A rasping voice crackled through the speaker.

"A servant, probably. Do you have news?" Sius Mavell Evi said.

Not-Tavyn replied, "I wouldn't be here if I didn't. Ilriel's progress with him is going smoothly, although he is hesitant now that he knows his sister is involved."

There was the faint sound of Sius Mavell Evi tapping his fingers. "Will this be a problem?'

Not-Tavyn harrumphed. "You should be more faithful in the mistress. Ilriel has a plan, she always does."

"It's not her I do not have faith in. That hulvoq on the other hand, he's too distrustful of the fae. We've come too far and planned for too long for everything to fall apart because he refuses to work with us," Sius Mavell Evi said.

"If he does, Mistress has a plan for that, too. It will be slow, but we can progress without him."

"Good," said Sius Mavell Evi. There was a silence, and then he said, "After twenty-four years, I'm ready for this to be over with. I have had enough of the Minister and his influence. He's undone everything Sal worked to achieve with the High Council."

Again, there was a silence, and then light footsteps and a door creaking open.

"Draqa, come here," Sius Mavell Evi ordered.

The following response was too quiet to make out.

Sius Mavell Evi continued. "It would seem a little mouse is poking its whiskers where they don't belong. Get rid of it."

There was a series of whispered curses and shuffling in the foreground of the recording before it abruptly shut off.

Javis looked to the Minister to gauge his reaction. The Minister's face was a ghostly white. Javis pushed down the feeling of satisfaction that almost made its way into a smile.

"Is that proof enough for you?"

Phar glanced around. He tightened his arms. "It won't be me you'll have to convince. You said you have other evidence for them—us?"

"I do."

Javis played back the other recording—the one of him speaking privately with the Governor. He watched the Minister as they listened. By the end of it, Phar's shoulders drew up to his ears with tension.

"Has he made true on his threat?" he asked.

Javis nodded. "He poisoned me."

Phar licked his lips. "You're dying?"

"I am. Either way, you should know I want to resign. I can't do this anymore."

Phar stared at Javis. Javis expected the Minister at the very least to send him to fill out the customary resignation documents. Instead, he said shortly, "Of course. I'm sorry to hear that."

He put a hand on Javis' shoulder and tried to usher him to the door. "Thank you for this information, Ambassador. If you'll excuse me, I need to decide how to handle this delicately with the Board."

Javis planted his feet down. He wasn't done yet. "There's one last thing, sir. You shouldn't trust Marvec," he said.

The Minister froze. "Tavyn Marvec?"

"Yes, he's—"

There was a knock at the door and a feminine voice called for the Minister.

"One moment," Phar replied.

"But sir—"

"I said one moment!"

A satyr peaked their head into the room. "Sir, it's urgent."

Phar huffed impatiently. "Wait here," he said to Javis as he left his office. Javis could hear his irritated voice float away from the door.

The weight on his shoulders lifted as he realized that all he went through wasn't entirely for nothing. The Board had no choice but to at least consider the Minister. Javis felt a little pride, too, knowing that he protected Phar by telling him about Marvec. So, he waited.

When Phar was gone longer than a few minutes, Javis started pacing the room. He could no longer hear Phar outside the door, so he must have been dragged away to whatever urgent matter was occurring. As long as Phar returned, Javis could wait a little longer.

The longer he waited, however, the more a heaviness began to settle in the room. He almost brushed off the nearly suffocating feeling as a result of the poison, but he felt no worse physically than he had that morning. Unease prickled at the tips of his fingers. He paced faster. He glanced at the door. Phar shouldn't have been as tense as he was. He never lost his composure, even in the direst situations he was presented with during his time so far in office.

A cool draft from the other room made the green curtain flutter, catching Javis' eye. He went over and pulled it open. He didn't know why he hadn't noticed the breeze earlier; the sunless window in the room was wide open. He shivered.

A square table sat in the center of the room. One of the chairs that should have been tucked underneath was knocked backwards. A game board sat crooked on the table's surface, little white and red game pieces strewn about and on the floor. Javis turned on the light and bent to pick them up. He froze.

Shoes. A pair of bare feet stuck out from behind the table next to them. Rising, Javis peered apprehensively over the table. He only needed one look before he jumped back, a gasp caught in his throat. Minister Lhorsan Phar was lying dead on the floor in a pool of his own fabrics and blood.

Javis covered his mouth. He gagged, backing away. He needed to get out of here. He had to get out before Marvec realized he knew. He reached the curtain. A hand landed heavily on his shoulder and spun him around.

"Ambassador, I thought I told you to wait," Phar said. Only he didn't look quite like how the Minister was supposed to look anymore. His eyes were white.

Javis couldn't speak. He glanced back into the meeting room. The imposter followed his gaze and smirked. The razor-sharp teeth they revealed didn't match the Minister's face.

"I wouldn't mind that if I were you," the imposter said.

Javis couldn't move. "You. . ." he croaked.

". . .had an altercation with someone who broke in," said

the imposter, his eyes and teeth melting back into the ones that belonged to the Minister. "I think it's in both our interests that the incident stays between us."

Javis attempted to pull free of the imposter's grip, but their fingers tightened, keeping him in place. The imposter brought attention to their hip, revealing a long knife in a sheath. The handle was stained blue.

"Do you agree?"

Javis nodded frantically, his eyes plastered wide. The imposter let him go, shoving him towards the door. He stumbled and looked back. The imposter was right behind him.

Javis finally found his voice, quiet as it was. "How could you do this?" he asked. He was no fan of the Minister and knew plenty of others who weren't either, but he could never imagine anyone wanting him dead.

"Progress, Ambassador. Something you seem to have a hard time grasping," the imposter said.

Javis thought of Sius Mavell Evi's criticisms of the High Council and its unjust laws. But how was scheming and murder good for anyone?

"I—I admit the laws aren't fair, but. . ." Javis trailed off.

The imposter shook their head. "You'll see one day." They paused, looking at the ceiling. "Or maybe you won't. Politics never seemed to be a strength of yours. I don't see you lasting much longer, even without the poison."

Javis forced down the lump forming in his throat. The imposter steered him closer to the door. He could hear conversation just outside. A last shred of hope flickered in his chest. The imposter opened the door and pushed him through. Javis eyed a pair of officials as they passed, and he opened his mouth. The imposter's fingers latched onto Javis' arm again. He leaned in Javis' ear, his whisper sending ice through him.

"Unless you want tomorrow's picture-cast to be about some *nal* Ambassador who killed the Minister, you'll shut your mouth."

Javis obeyed. He looked back again, and the imposter let him go, shooing him forward. He started walking away, every one of his limbs stiff. Someone greeted him. He greeted them in return with a robotic nod and a vague smile. He didn't look to see who it was. He risked a glance behind him. The imposter still watched from within the doorway of the Minister's office. Javis picked up his pace.

When he reached the steps outside, he was almost running. He didn't stop, either. Not until he reached the airstop, out of breath and his lungs burning. He couldn't catch his breath, couldn't think to regret running the whole way instead of calling for a carriage. He collapsed on a bench and gasped for air. He sobbed. He was a coward.

The flight home was a blur. Javis couldn't remember getting on the airship. The flight took as long as it always did, but the next thing he knew, he was wandering the streets of Kerevel Tul. He didn't know how long he was out, but his limbs weakened. The shadows grew long, and he let out a white cloud with every breath he took. He coughed.

He stumbled up to a skinny blue house in the middle of a row and knocked, nearly falling into the door as he did so. A black-haired man answered. The black-haired man's eyebrows pulled tight.

"Javis? What are—oh my—come inside!"

Javis tripped as he entered, falling against the doorframe. He barely noticed the pain that shot through his shoulder. The black-haired man steadied him and lowered him onto a couch. He leaned back and stared at the ceiling. Out of the corner of his eye, the black-haired man sent a little boy to go fetch something.

The black-haired man urged Javis to sit up. Javis coughed. Someone gasped. Javis looked over at the ginger-haired woman who made the sound. She rushed to him. Her words were garbled. Javis coughed again. The woman took his hand and held it in front of him. Thick, black spiderwebs covered the back of it.

The couch was very soft on Javis' face.

36

RETURNING TO SIUS MAVELL EVI was a mistake. At least, that's what Draqa kept telling himself every time he had to interact with the Governor. He counted himself lucky that all Sius Mavell Evi did was dislocate and burn his arm—the latter injury had yet to fully heal despite going on three weeks since the Governor inflicted it. Regardless of his luck, Draqa had to tiptoe around the Governor all the while trying to make himself useful until he was able to remove his sling in another week or two. Draqa was in a never-ending state of stress.

His contact with the Ard'a remained consistent, although he never had any updates for them; just as he thought, Sius Mavell Evi was unlikely to trust him with any important information any time soon. He relayed as much to Queen Nephas, suggesting that he would first need to give the Governor reliable information on the Ard'a before he made any progress. Nephas said she would look into it. Draqa wasn't sure she would.

Life in the manor was otherwise somewhat back to normal. Draqa ignored the other servants, and they whispered about him in turn. Their most recent gossip surrounded the Governor's anger with Draqa, and they seemed to suggest Draqa was going soft. So what if he was? He was tired of being Draqa. He was tired of being feared. A few of the servants seemed to realize this. Minnos especially had started behaving as though Draqa was no different than her or any of the others. He appreciated that.

There was one person, however, who he wanted to fear him. One who never had.

Draqa had waited outside the kitchens a few days after his punishment, listening as Ramnik chatted with Minnos while she prepared the Governor's evening tea. Draqa had sworn he would make Ramnik pay, and he planned to see it through as best he could.

Ramnik left the kitchens with a tea tray in hand. Draqa ducked behind the door before he could be seen, then trailed quietly behind him. Draqa wasn't silent enough for his footfalls to go unnoticed by the dwerin's powerful ears, but Draqa gained on him just in time to pass an empty room. Draqa wrapped his arm over Ramnik's shoulders and pulled him inside.

Ramnik blubbered in shock, but to his credit, he didn't spill a single drop of tea. He quickly regained composure.

"What do you want, Draqa?" His question sounded more annoyed than anything else.

Draqa leaned against the door, trapping Ramnik inside. "I want to talk," he said. He was already planning scenarios in his head for how he might make Ramnik squirm.

"Can't this wait? Governor Sius Mavell Evi doesn't like his tea cold," Ramnik said.

"No, it can't," Draqa said. "Tell me about Ambassador Zevos."

Ramnik shifted his weight to one side and narrowed his eyes incredulously. "What of him?"

"Did Sius Mavell Evi tell you to poison him?"

Ramnik's fingers tightened on the tray. "No wonder he beats you. Show more respect for your master."

Draqa's lips flattened to a thin line. "You were there when the Ambassador was poisoned. I know it was you. Were you acting alone or on Sius Mavell Evi's orders?"

Despite his short stature, Ramnik appeared unphased.

"I'm flattered if you thought the Governor would pick me for such an important job. But no. Nor did I take things into my own hands."

Draqa didn't buy it. "Do you really expect me to believe you were, what, there by pure coincidence?"

Rather than nod, Ramnik cocked his head dismissively. "I think the more apt question is why you care so much. Even better, why are you speaking to the Governor's enemies? We might start to question your loyalties," he said.

"You don't know a thing about my loyalties," Draqa spat in reply.

"I know the Ambassador's your brother. I think that's enough."

Ramnik had then tried to move around Draqa. Draqa grabbed him by the collar and pushed him against the wall. His hat slipped off his head.

"I'm not done with you," Draqa growled.

“No? What will you do, take revenge? Kill me? Cut out my tongue and a finger or two? You can try, but the Governor won’t be pleased,” Ramnik said. Not the tiniest sliver of fear showed on his face. The tea tray remained perfectly still in his hands.

Draqa considered killing him right then and cutting out his tongue was a fine idea, but he was right. Sius Mavell Evi didn’t tolerate fighting among his servants—Draqa was certainly no exception.

“If you didn’t poison Javis, you’re going to tell me who did.”

Ramnik sighed, rolling his eyes. “I don’t keep track of everyone the governor hires, and there were a lot of people in the bar that day. Now if you would, the tea is getting cold.”

Draqa looked over the butler hoping he could glean whether or not he was lying. Ramnik’s face remained as still as the tray. Draqa tightened his jaw and let Ramnik go. Ramnik had puffed out his chest, picked up his hat and turned to leave.

In a last wave of frustration, Draqa had lashed out, hitting the tray from Ramnik’s hands. Neither the tray nor the teapot nor the cups had spilled or clattered to the floor, caught midair at the last moment by a wordless kinesis spell. Ramnik had rearranged the tray and lifted it from the air.

“Are you finished?” he huffed.

Draqa’s face burned. He raised a fist but had held back and let Ramnik leave. He still didn’t believe a word Ramnik said, but he couldn’t rationalize hurting him when he was so convincing. Draqa expected to hear afterwards that Ramnik had complained to Sius Mavell Evi about their encounter, but it seemed he could be trusted to stay quiet about some things, at least.

It wasn't until much later in Draqa's stay that he realized that Ramnik had told the truth.

The day started out much the same as the previous days. Draqa wandered out of his room early for breakfast. He ate it out in the courtyard so he wouldn't be disturbed. He let his mind wander since he had nothing better to do—mostly he worried about his situation and the Ard'a. And then he wandered back inside.

He thought about asking Sius Mavell Evi to let him visit the Vyn. Maybe he could use Minnos as an excuse, say that she asked him to accompany her. As Draqa rehearsed what to say on his way to find Sius, he heard the heavy knocker fall against the door and echo through the manor. He turned the corner and slowed, watching Ramnik let the guest inside.

Tavyn Marvec shook a light dusting of snow off himself. "Thank you. Where's the Governor? I need to speak with him."

Too late, Draqa caught himself staring. Tavyn met eyes with him and walked over.

"Well? Take me to him," Tavyn urged.

Draqa rushed out a nod. "He's usually in his study this time of day," Draqa said, leading the way.

Tavyn brushed ahead of him, making him feel like he was the one being led. He looked over the sylfan-disguised yilura. A sylfan's hair was naturally wild, but Tavyn's was more so. It didn't even look like it had been brushed that morning. Even his clothes were ragged, contrasting colors and fabrics thrown together under a brown cloak. His manner too, was wild.

They reached Sius Mavell Evi's study. Draqa pushed back memories of the last time he was inside. Tavyn didn't wait for

Draqa to announce him, instead throwing the door open and barging in.

Sius Mavell Evi was the rare picture of surprise, his eyebrows raised and wrinkling his forehead, a pipe midway to his open mouth. He looked between Draqa and Tavyn. Draqa stepped back.

"What is all this?" Sius Mavell Evi asked.

Tavyn threw himself down in the chair across from him. "We have a problem."

Sius' eyes hardened, an unspoken exchange passing between them that Draqa failed to understand. Draqa saw himself out before he could be asked and closed the door behind him.

He almost left to go sulk in annoyance at Tavyn interrupting his chance to leave the manor for the day. But then he remembered his duty to the Ard'a, and Tavyn said something that was alarming indeed.

"Why isn't the ambassador dead yet? You said the poison worked fast."

Draqa stilled. He shallowed his breathing and listened. The fact Javis had lied wasn't a surprise to him. He'd already suspected it.

"I said it worked effectively, not that it was fast," Sius Mavell Evi replied. His voice was tired, bored. "He will be dead soon."

Tavyn's laughter rang with hysteria. "He should have been dead before he walked in on me and the Minister four days ago."

Was Tavyn the one who poisoned Javis? It was possible. He could have been there too, disguised as someone else. Draqa leaned his ear in closer.

"Four days? You have no reason to be upset then. If you really saw this as a problem you would have killed him on the spot," Sius Mavell Evi said.

Tavyn huffed in a way that reminded Draqa of a petulant child. "It's hard enough trying to hide one body, let alone two. It was the middle of the day. What else was I supposed to do?"

The Minister was dead. Not only that, but it had already been four days and the nation didn't seem to know. Which meant Tavyn—or someone—had replaced him. Draqa had to consider the irony of it. The High Council did their best of convincing the people that "deceivers" walked among them when there was an imposter right under their own noses. Regardless, Queen Nephas would need to know before the imposter had a chance to attend a meeting with the High Council.

Sius Mavell Evi spoke again. "I suppose I can send someone to finish the job."

"Draqa?" Tavyn asked.

Draqa tensed.

"No, someone a bit more reliable. Draqa has been. . . indisposed as of late," Sius Mavell Evi said. The way he said it reminded Draqa that he still wasn't off the hook where the Governor was concerned.

Tavyn scoffed. "Why do you keep him? Nal are useless."

The air stilled. Then Draqa could hear Sius Mavell Evi's fingernails clicking against his cane. "Not useless. Although I could ask your mistress the same of you when you don't share our views."

More silence. Tavyn muttered, "When will you send someone?"

"Soon," was all Sius Mavell Evi replied.

The first thing Draqa did was hole himself in his room and

chime Javis. He tried over and over, hoping to see his brother's face above the screen. He never did.

He tried someone else. He didn't know how else he could warn Javis. Not when Sius Mavell Evi wasn't letting him leave the manor without a good reason.

Tolas Ruv Aen appeared above Draqa's aspectacaster screen and Draqa sighed in relief. Tolas Ruv Aen was taken off guard.

"This is a surprise," he said. He didn't look at all upset to be hearing from Draqa, of course. He never did. "It must be my lucky day."

Draqa cut to the chase. "Javis is in trouble, and the Minister's dead."

"*Dead?*"

Both of them cringed at how loud Tolas Ruv Aen said it, and Draqa glanced behind himself nervously.

"What do you mean he's dead?" Tolas Ruv Aen whispered. "Where'd you hear that?"

Draqa went over what he overheard Sius Mavell Evi and Tavyn discussing.

". . .and Javis saw it happen, or he knows about it at least. Sius Mavell Evi is planning to send someone to kill him," he finished. "You need to send him somewhere safe."

Tolas Ruv Aen shook his head, a solemn look coming onto his face. It left Draqa unsettled.

"Yer brother's been bedridden for a week. We have doctors on him every hour, but. . ." Tolas Ruv Aen didn't need to continue for Draqa to understand.

It may well turn out that Sius Mavell Evi wouldn't need to

send someone after all.

Draqa left the next moment he had the chance, listening for when Sius Mavell Evi might plan to send the assassin. After a few days of convincing, dropping hints when he could and claiming the Ard'a had summoned him, the Governor let him go, under the pretense that, although Draqa didn't yet know what they wanted, he would try to bring back information.

Sius Mavell Evi was rightfully suspicious. However, Draqa had been on his best behavior, so his master agreed to let off the reigns a little; Draqa had to be back in five days, max. If he didn't return, the Governor would retrieve Draqa himself.

Javis' house, when Draqa arrived, smelled strongly of a sweet incense, in the way that places often did when someone was trying to cover up a much less appealing smell. With a quick look around, there was one visible guard who could protect Javis if someone came to do him in. Draqa silently thanked Tolas Ruv Aen for providing at least that much.

The doctor who let Draqa in was one of the same from the morning before he left. He directed Draqa upstairs. Draqa hesitated on the steps, preparing himself. He didn't want to see the state Javis was in. Tolas Ruv Aen had contacted Draqa again and told him that the doctors found something that would help Javis. It wasn't a full antidote yet, but it was the closest they had so far.

A drenen woman ducked out from Javis' bedroom as Draqa reached it. She was here the last time, too. Draqa stepped out of her way.

"You're his brother?" she asked.

"Yes. . . Is he awake?"

The woman nodded. Draqa went in.

In here, whatever sour smell the incense tried to conceal assaulted Draqa's nose, and he instinctively covered it. A weak, raspy laugh responded.

Javis was partly sitting up, propped against the headboard by a few pillows. His laugh devolved into hoarse coughing that wracked his whole body. He closed his eyes and leaned his head back. His face was ashen, his bronze shimmer gone entirely. Stark black lines ran along nearly every inch of his skin.

Draqa sat in the chair already pulled close to Javis' bed. Javis peered at him and offered him a feeble smile.

"I know. It's awful in here." He nodded to a bucket sitting by his bed. Draqa made a point not to look too closely at what was inside.

He didn't know what to say. He tried, but everything he thought of sounded to him insincere or uncaring. When he finally did think of something, Javis beat him to it.

"I suppose I ought to apologize."

"For what?"

"Keeping this a secret. For lying about it. I was. . . I didn't—"

Draqa shook his head. "I knew. You're not very good at lying."

"Oh." Javis' gaze wandered away from Draqa. It seemed that he, too, had lost his words.

They didn't speak for a least a few minutes. Draqa picked at his thumbs. Javis readjusted his pillow more than once. For the first time, Draqa found himself resenting that he and his brother's relationship had deteriorated so much. They never used to dance around each other in awkward silence when they had something to say.

"Tolas Ruv Aen said you're getting better," Draqa finally said.

Javis shrugged. "Well, I can sit up now and walk to the toilet, so the doctors must be doing something right." He said it cheerfully, like he tried to make light of his situation, but he immediately sighed, running a hand across his eyes. "I can't keep anything down. Not even water or. . . The doctors said that's how it will be until the poison is out of my system or they find a better antidote."

Draqa nodded, imagining Javis may have been experiencing withdrawals on top of all his other problems as well.

"Do you think in a few days you would be able to leave the house?" he asked. "If you had assistance?"

Javis looked at him strangely. "I. . . don't know. Why?"

Draqa held his breath before he told him. "Sius Mavell Evi knows what happened with you and Marvec."

Javis did not look at all surprised. Draqa was glad to know the poison didn't rid him of his small amount of common sense. Javis closed his eyes again. With an exhale, his body looked even more frail and tired.

"Am I not dying fast enough for him?" he asked.

"I think you need to go somewhere safe, where he can't find you. Stay with the Ard'a a while," Draqa urged.

Javis said nothing, the corners of his mouth dipping into a frown. Draqa put a hand on his arm.

"I don't know if I can. It's already been several days since I saw Marvec. . . If Sius Mavell Evi really wants me dead. . ."

"I won't let him do anything else to you."

"Is that really why you came?"

"I told you, I care."

Javis' frown deepened. His eyes grew wet, and he blinked his oncoming tears away with a nod. He opened his mouth, but instead of speaking, he froze, threw his head over the bucket, and retched.

Thick, black sludge passed his lips. He half missed the bucket and the pungent smell wafted under Draqa's nose, fully undisguised. Draqa cringed, covering his nose again.

Javis sat back, groaning, and wiped his mouth with a cloth.

"Averil and Zalé were here," he said, his voice weaker than before. At Draqa's questioning look, he added, "and Krystal." He took a long, shuddering breath, "They have visited almost every day. Go to my study, would you? Bring me the envelope on my desk."

This time Draqa didn't push back against Javis' wishes. The envelope was a pretty emerald green, not unlike the ink Javis had wanted him to get. Draqa delivered it gently into Javis' hands.

Javis turned it over. It wasn't yet sealed, and he pulled out the letter inside. Draqa let him quietly—privately—read it, until he returned it to the envelope. He held it out for Draqa with a trembling arm. Draqa started to take it, unaware that his caution showed on his face.

"It's for you," said Javis.

"Me?" Draqa ran his thumb over the envelope. Although he couldn't feel them, it had the deckled edges and imperfections of handmade paper.

A letter for him. . . His chest twisted in pain. He saw what Javis expected—whether it be from the poison or by the hand of an assassin sent by Sius Mavell Evi didn't matter.

Draqa tried to shove the letter back into Javis' hands. Javis wouldn't take it.

"I don't want it," Draqa emphasized.

That might have been the wrong thing to say. Something in Javis' eyes died, and he started to nod. Draqa pulled the envelope back. He corrected himself. "Whatever you wrote, tell me when you're healed. I want to hear it." *So, keep it in mind and don't die,* he silently added. He tucked the letter into his coat pocket.

This elicited a strained smile from his brother.

"Always so stubborn. Come here."

Javis held out his hand. Draqa stared at it, but in the end, he took it. With a surprising, perhaps renewed amount of strength, Javis pulled him into a tight embrace. Draqa ignored the putrid scent of vomit, ignored the ice in Javis' fingers, and hugged him back.

He felt Javis' chin on his shoulder and a whispering breath pleading in his ear.

"Read it anyway."

37

"WHEN I RETURN FROM ARKAVEN, *I want to show you how to enter my mind,"* Javis had said.

After Javis did return from Arkaven and arrived at Averil's house, delirious, Krystal didn't think he would be able to follow through on his word.

She had known something was off that day at the Kerevel. She should have pried more. She should have convinced Javis to stay home instead of going off when he knew he was ill.

She understood now why he had been so adamant that his uncle help train her. Only, Alarach wouldn't just be helping, he would be taking over entirely.

Averil had known the whole time that there was something wrong with Javis. When Javis showed up, Krystal thought that he might have had a stroke or something. She didn't know if that would have been better or worse than the real problem: that Javis had been poisoned at the will of her grandfather.

For a few days, Javis' doctors hadn't been sure he was going to make it. They didn't know why his condition had suddenly gotten worse, but they believed it was because he had exerted himself, and his exhaustion left him vulnerable. That was one theory, at least.

One of the doctors, a drenen woman named Talara, had eventually found an antidote. It wouldn't be an instantaneous cure, but it would work by encouraging Javis' body to reject the poison on its own. It wasn't a pretty sight. And yet, despite days in bed, his body weakened by the poison and its solution, he was still able to contact Krystal early one morning in the middle of the week.

A soft dinging and pulsing glow from her aspectacaster stirred her awake. Neither were very obnoxious but sleeping as poorly as she had been, it wasn't hard to wake her. She turned over and fumbled to answer it on the nightstand. She heard Javis' voice before she saw his face.

"Oh dear, I'm sorry. I didn't mean to wake you."

Krystal rubbed the sleep from her eyes. "No, it's okay. Call me whenever. How are you feeling?"

"Ah . . . better than yesterday," Javis said. Krystal could see the shape of his bed behind him. *"But that isn't important. Were you visiting again today? I know Averil won't be able to."* Javis had been like this the whole time, downplaying the severity of his situation even though it was known by now what was at stake. But was it for Krystal's sake or his own?

Krystal answered through a stifled yawn, "I'll come."

"Good. Be early. I want you to continue your lessons," Javis said.

Krystal sat up. "What? Are you sure you're up for that?"

Javis waved her off. *"I'll be all right. It isn't as though teaching is physical. I can sit and instruct you."*

"I don't know . . . Did you at least check with Talara that this would be okay?"

"Trust me. Let me do this for you."

Krystal wanted to say that she couldn't trust him when he'd already made a habit of pretending nothing was wrong. Instead, she said, "We'll see when I get there. You shouldn't do this if you're feeling bad."

Krystal knocked when she arrived. A familiar voice that couldn't have been Javis' called her inside. Javis sat in his armchair, a blanket warming his legs over his nightclothes. He didn't look much better. Draqa set a teacup in his hands. Draqa's eyes lingered distractedly on Krystal. There was not a doctor in sight.

"Where is everyone?" Krystal asked.

"They will be here later," Javis said. He looked at her expectantly. *"Well?"*

His bucket wasn't near his chair. The awful sick smell lingered in the house, but it wasn't as bad as the day before. Though, this might have just been a result of thorough cleaning.

"He won't take no for an answer," Draqa said.

Hearing him speak English with his usual accent caught Krystal off guard. She'd become accustomed to relying entirely on the translator. She removed her shoes and joined Draqa's side.

"When did you get here?"

Javis answered for Draqa. *"Yesterday. He's going to stay for a few days. He's already quite helpful."*

Krystal looked over Draqa. She was glad to see him again, but for a moment she had other concerns.

"You're not going to help today, are you?"

Draqa shook his head. "I'll stay out of your way."

Javis still watched Krystal expectantly. He sat forward. Krystal sighed, giving in. She did want to continue learning. "Okay."

Draqa disappeared into another room, and Javis had her sit on the couch across from him.

"Do you remember how to start?" he asked.

Krystal closed her eyes, nodding. This was the easy part, now.

"What do I do differently?" she asked.

"Remember when we practiced determining your intent? This time I want you to focus on me. Try to picture your memories bridging to mine," Javis said. His voice was still soothing. *"I'm going to meet you halfway across that bridge to make it easier for you."*

"What if I do find something distressing?"

"I'll guide you away from it. Whenever you're ready."

Krystal began. She counted, and gradually the colors and warm sensations returned. In the back of her mind, she thought of Javis, of what his own mind might be like, and found herself listening to his breathing. Each breath was long and measured. Stone by stone, memory by memory, Krystal built a bridge. She didn't know which direction to go but trusted it would lead her to Javis.

The last block was placed, and suddenly the bridge stretched out before Krystal. The half of the bridge in front of her was different than her own. Instead of stone it was made of glass and mirrors. As Krystal moved across, the colors changed from greens and pinks to cool blues and muddied white. A smiling warmth joined her side, and she could imagine Javis linking arms with her and leading her across his side of the bridge. Then they stepped off, and Krystal found herself standing alone at the edge of a forest, her body now an eight-year-old boy's.

***

Two days ago, Alarehn Ianda, Javis' mother, was murdered. He understood what had happened—that part was obvious. He knew why a scream and the shattering of pottery had woken him and his brother in the middle of the night.

Javis understood too, that Mother liked to stay up late reading, that she had been in the kitchen, getting a snack or another cup of tea. He understood that there was a fight, and that the murderer ran after pushing the display case down on top of her, even though she was already wounded. He understood because he had seen it. He saw it unfold before him, right up until the crash had woken him. The first time he had ever soul-traveled, he had watched his mother die.

The only thing Javis didn't understand, was why it had to happen. His mother had been a good, kind woman. He couldn't imagine anyone hating her. But his father had sat him and his brother down that morning before their mother's body was given to the trees and explained that people hadn't hated her. She was killed to try to make their father hurt, because people hated their father, and people hated his children.

Jair hadn't taken that well. Father was out now, looking for him. Javis waited just inside the edge of the forest, because father had told him to stay inside. The forest's edge was as far as he was willing to disobey.

Krystal already wanted to move on to the next memory, the child's emotions so painful and complex that they made her heart ache. But then, Isaias Zevos came trudging out of the woods, Jair held firm in his arms. Javis ran to them both and Father set Jair on the ground. Javis hugged his brother as tightly as he could. For a moment as he had waited, he had been afraid Jair would go away too.

The boys' father crouched down in front of them, his mossy eyes dark with worry.

"Things are going to be hard for a while. So, I need you both to promise me that you'll be there for each other, no matter what happens."

Javis nodded furiously and held on to his brother even tighter. Jair was less enthusiastic and remained limp in his arms.

"Yes, Father," Jair whispered.

Their father smiled sadly at them and pulled them into his arms.

Krystal felt a tug at her being, encouraging her to move on, and so she urged herself from this memory and into the next.

When Javis pulled out of the hug, Jair and his father were no longer before him. Instead, a wingless, Clydesdale-sized dragon with curved horns and blue scales transformed into a woman before him. The sight in Javis' right eye was gone; with the smallest bit of probing Krystal knew the injury was old.

Javis' heart leapt as he gazed up at Talara. His eye drank in each of her scales and trailed over her slender proportions as she transformed. He bit his lip.

"I've missed you," *he said in her language.*

Talara graced him with a warm smile and sat on her knees in front of him.

"I'm sorry I was away for so long," *she said.* "I found work in

Talnoq-Vyn."

Javis clapped his hands together. "That's wonderful! With whom?"

"Myself. I started an apothecary," *Talara said.*

Javis paused as her words sunk in. "You're settling down?" *he asked.*

Talara nodded with pride. Javis could feel it radiating from her. He grinned and embraced her again. Talara had wanted this for a long time. To find a place where she finally felt at home. Javis couldn't be happier for her.

The pair settled into the grass together and laid back to watch the clouds drift across the sky. Talara held Javis' hand, delicately tracing her fingers over his palm.

"Javis?" *she asked.*

Javis turned his head to look at her. She kept her eyes to the sky.

"When you return home again," *she continued,* "I would like for you to come live with me."

Javis' eyes widened and he had to stop himself from agreeing too quickly. His already present smile grew too large for his face. He couldn't count how many times he had fantasized about this, the two of them moving together somewhere near the city, that they would go together for long walks and explore the streets. He thought they could have a small garden with flowers, or perhaps now a garden of herbs. And he had never thought much of anything like children, but now he wondered if Talara had. It was easy enough to adopt—oh, but he was getting ahead of himself. They hadn't even discussed yet if they even wanted to marry.

Javis squeezed Talara's hand. One step at a time. "My dear, I would love nothing more in the world than to live with you."

They never did.

Krystal wasn't sure why she did it, but she followed Javis' overwhelming regret out of the memory. The feeling was unexpected, and she ignored the pulls of protest as she entered the next memory. Javis sat on a hospital bed and the entire right side of his head throbbed. His eye didn't bleed, but the sharp pain behind it every time it moved made him feel like he was being stabbed. Doctor Morozefa hunched over, examining it.

"Do you know how he did this to you?" he asked.

Javis shook his head (an immediate mistake) and said, "I don't remember."

That was a lie. Javis knew exactly how Jair had stolen his sight. They had fought. Javis had learned what Jair had done: that he had murdered someone. Javis hadn't taken the time to consider who or why and had approached Jair with accusations and insults flying from his tongue. Even then, he hadn't realized how far past his breaking point Jair already was. And then he had told Jair that he had already notified the authorities.

Javis' stomach churned the more he thought about it, and he braced himself on Morozefa's shoulder. Jair had seemed to panic right after the spell hit Javis, but in the moment Javis had felt the pure hatred charged behind it. And now Jair was locked away, waiting to be taken to the prison in Keln.

Morozefa steadied Javis. "Easy there." He let Javis recover for a moment before he continued tending him. He gave Javis a tonic for the pain and put a patch over his eye. Then he sighed. "I'm sorry. That's all I can do. The pain should subside in a few days. If not, come see me again."

Javis' shoulders sagged. He thanked the doctor and carefully walked himself back to his home in the middle of town. He snuck inside and found his father sitting at the round table in their little kitchen. His father's head rested on one hand and his other clutched a bottle. Three others sat empty next to him.

Javis sat heavily across from him. "Morozefa can't do anything," he said.

His father continued to stare at the table. He took another drink.

Javis frowned. "Isaias."

His father didn't even blink.

"Father," he tried again, reaching for the bottle in his hand. His father moved it away before Javis could take it. He closed his eyes.

"S'all my fault," he slurred.

"It's not your fault," Javis said. His words caught in his throat, and he had to pause to breathe. "This was the path Jair chose. He did this to himself."

His father looked at him now with red eyes. "I failed him. Failed both of you."

Javis knew he was kidding himself, but he felt the need to reassure him. "No, no. You did your best. Jair has. . . he. . ." He, what? He wasn't right since their mother died? That could have been said for all three of them, and there was more to it than that.

Javis lowered his head, once again feeling the pang of nausea. His father took a long drink and finished off the bottle. He tried to set it down but knocked over the other bottles in the process. One rolled off the table and shattered on the floor. He went to pick it up, but Javis beat him to it. He tried not to feel too disappointed in his father as he did so. His father leaned back in his chair and stared at the ceiling. He said nothing while Javis cleaned. Javis thought he must have fallen asleep, but then he said, "Iolkosz and the others bullied him."

Javis hesitated. "... They did."

His father sniffed. "He came to me about it once, after you left. I didn't take him seriously."

Javis didn't sleep that night. His hurt, his anger, his guilt, it was all too much. He tossed and turned late into the night when most by then should have been asleep.

He smelled the smoke before he heard the screams. He leapt from his bed and ran to the window. The far end town was lit by an orange glow so bright it could have been a hellish sunrise. Javis ran to his father's room and shook him awake.

"There's a fire!" he yelled.

His right shoulder slammed into the doorframe as he ran out to where people were fleeing from the direction of the flames. So many houses were already ablaze. Javis fearfully drew closer, barely avoiding a collision with a mother and her child.

It was hot. Smoke choked the air and made Javis' eye water. He squinted through the chaos. His heart suddenly went cold. At the center of it all was the jail, engulfed in flames. And then Krystal was ripped from the memory.

***

Her eyes shot open. Javis was out of his armchair, standing right in front of her with his palm pressed flat to her forehead. He stepped back. They stared at each other. Javis swayed and lowered himself onto the cushion next to Krystal. Krystal continued to stare.

"*Sorry,*" Javis said, his voice back to its horse, present day whisper. *"I was trying to keep you from seeing that one."*

He wouldn't meet Krystal's eyes. She realized this was at least a partial lie, but she couldn't bring herself to be upset with him. She knew why he wanted to train her today. It took her awhile to find the right words.

"Thank you for showing me."

Maybe it was just luck, but Javis' rate of recovery improved over the next two days. The doctors were able to find a better antidote, and the change in Javis was almost immediate. He didn't entirely stop vomiting, but his skin began to return to a healthy color. His veins lightened. Even his attitude started improving, his smiles becoming less forced and a twinkle returning to his eyes. The collective breath everyone had been holding was finally released.

Most importantly of all, Javis felt well enough to leave. Krystal learned on the second day of his recovery that Tolas Ruv Aen was going to take him to stay in a guarded location that the Ard'a had set up for him. Sius Mavell Evi was unlikely to rest until he knew for sure that Javis was dead.

So, Krystal and Averil and Zalé paid him a visit the following morning. He was leaving that afternoon. He was again resting in his armchair when they got there. He had a sketchbook in his lap and a pen in his hand. He was dressed in a fine powder blue vest.

"Oh, you made it!" He started to get up, but Averil met him where he was.

Averil smiled and grasped Javis' hand. *"You're looking so much better."* The last time he was here with Krystal, Javis was still bedridden.

Javis' smile was tired. *"Not quite back to normal yet, but better than I have been."*

Zalé pushed his way past Averil and threw himself into a hug. Javis coughed.

"Careful—"

Zalé pulled away with his little brows furrowed. *"Sorry."*

Javis patted his back. *"You're all right,"* he said.

Krystal glanced up the stairs. "Do you need any help packing?" she asked. She didn't see any of his bags.

Javis shook his head. He eased himself to his feet. *"Jair is taking care of it for me. Although, I was going to make some lunch. Would you care to help with that?"*

The trio followed Javis into the kitchen. Draqa stayed upstairs and told them to let him know when the food was ready. Javis instructed Krystal on where the pots and ingredients for a soup were and hovered over her while she prepared it. He tried to direct every detail. *"Ah, that's a lot of salt, don't you think? Make it sweeter,"* and *"No, you need to chop those finer, you don't want to chew a soup."*

Krystal dragged him to the island and forced him to sit before he could work himself up. "You're in the wrong job," she laughed. "You should be a king instead!"

Javis protested. *"I'm just particular. Is that such a bad thing?"*

Averil, who seemed to pick up on the context from Javis' reply, chuckled from his end of the counter. *"He was like this when we were young, too. Everything had to go his way. He's bossy."*

Javis' jaw dropped, and he stretched his eyebrows comedically high. "*I am* not." The corners of his frown twitched.

Krystal snorted. Zalé giggled into his hands. Javis turned to him.

"Zalé, am I bossy?" he asked, contorting his face.

Zalé frantically shook his head, but even as he did, his laughter couldn't be contained. He did it in that real but slightly exaggerated way that kids often did to keep the attention on themselves for a little longer. He accidentally knocked himself backwards off his chair. There was a beat of silence, and then all four of them laughed hard.

Javis braced himself on the counter, his fingers brushing Krystal's. *"All right, all right,"* he said, breathing heavily. *"Is that soup done?"*

Still in a fit of giggles, Krystal wiped her eyes and tried to steady herself long enough to taste it.

"I think so," she said.

Averil lifted Zalé—the only one laughing now—from the floor. *"Time to go wash up."*

Krystal met eyes with Javis as the other two went up to the bathroom. He smiled at her.

"Are you okay?" Krystal asked.

Javis still seemed a bit breathless, but he nodded and stood to take out some bowls. *"It feels good to laugh."*

Krystal leaned against the counter and observed him. He wasn't exactly a reserved person, but Krystal had never seen him act so carefree. Even the way he held himself was lighter.

"You seem more you when Averil's around. More real," Krystal said.

Javis leaned next to her. *"He's been with me through everything. When my mother died, and then my father. And of course, when Jair. . . I wish I could have been there for him more than I have, but I don't think I'm as close with anyone else, except for maybe Talara,"* he sighed.

Krystal couldn't hold her tongue. "Do you still love her?"

Javis looked surprised. *"I forgot you saw."* He stared off ahead for a moment. *"I do. But our relationship, as I think you picked up on, is complicated."*

Their eyes found each other again. Krystal tore her own away and started ladling some soup into one of the bowls. Javis drew closer and eased the ladle from her fingers.

"I think I can take care of at least this much. Could you get Jair?"

Krystal lingered before hurrying up to fetch him. She almost ran into Averil on his way down and she ducked around him with a distracted apology.

Draqa brought a tan suitcase to the door of Javis' bedroom.

"You four sounded like you were having fun," he said. "I'm almost sorry I wasn't a part of it."

"Next time you should be. You didn't have to do this by yourself. The food's done now," Krystal said.

"Averil told me," Draqa said, making her feel silly for telling him.

He winced as he set down the suitcase. He'd been favoring his right arm since he got back, but with so much focus on Javis the last few days, Krystal had felt it would have been wrong for her to ask what happened. She moved to grab the case for him.

"Just leave it there," he said.

"I heard Sius Mavell Evi didn't take things very well," Krystal said.

Draqa looked at his arm. "It wasn't anything I couldn't handle.

Don't worry about it."

That only made her want to worry anyway. The more she heard about her grandfather, the more she feared for Draqa.

"Did he hurt you?" she asked.

After a moment, Draqa nodded. He didn't explain further. Zalé left the bathroom, playfully shaking water off his hands at them. Draqa shot him a look.

Zalé snickered. *"Hurry up! You don't want cold soup!"*

Krystal rolled her eyes, grinning. "Okay, we're coming!" She started to follow him down. Draqa grabbed her wrist.

"Wait. I wanted to ask you something." He lowered his voice, capturing her attention. "How willing are you to dream walk again?"

This took Krystal by surprise. "I thought you didn't like me in your memories."

"I don't. I need to find out something from Sius Mavell Evi, and I was hoping you could—"

An earsplitting shriek tore through their conversation. They froze, and a thud and the sound of shattering clay had them running to the kitchen. Zalé was backing away from the entrance. Javis laid slumped against the counter, his hand gripping a knife in his chest. A bowl had broken next to him. Averil was calm.

Draqa acted quicker than Krystal. He pushed past her and ripped Averil away from Javis.

"What have you done?!"

Averil remained impassive. *"What I had to."*

Krystal stared. She looked from her brother, to Javis, to her brother—Javis sputtered.

Krystal snapped out of her panic and hurried to his side. He'd pulled the knife out and was gasping for air. His powder blue vest rapidly stained red. Krystal pressed her hands to his wound and looked around helplessly.

"Draqa!"

Draqa swore and released Averil. He kneeled next to them. He removed his coat and replaced it over the wound. Javis' breath cut off mid-gasp. He stilled.

Draqa yelled. Krystal was deaf to it. Her eyes shifted to her hands, wet with blood. She looked back at Averil. He stood over them, nothing on his face at all. His voice was soft as he spoke to Zalé.

"I'm sorry you had to see this," he said.

Draqa pulled out his gun and shot him.

38

"PAPA!" ZALÉ TRIED TO RUN forward, but Draqa grabbed him and thrust him into Krystal's arms.

He ignored Zalé's sobs as he crouched over Averil. Averil was gripping his thigh where the bullet hit him. Draqa hadn't been aiming there, but he was a terrible shot with his right. Averil let out a strained laugh through clenched teeth.

"You shouldn't be so surprised," he said.

He was right. Draqa should have realized it was Averil from the moment the man had said that Sius Mavell Evi had saved his life. Averil's situation was so like Draqa's own and yet it never crossed his mind even once that Averil would kill his own best friend, let alone that Sius Mavell Evi would do what he did to Draqa to his own family. At least, that was what he assumed. Even then, the desire to kill Averil gripped him. He wanted to turn Averil's own knife against him and drag it limb from limb. It took all of his strength not to.

"Krystal, find me some bandages and a rope," he said.

Krystal didn't hesitate. She took Zalé's hand and hurried with him out of the kitchen. Averil tipped his head back. He wore a grimace that looked a bit too much like a smile. Draqa scowled.

"How could you? And in front of your own son," he spat.

Averil didn't look at him, but his eyes were dull. "Don't school me. Javis was getting better, he was going to leave. We were out of time."

"He *trusted* you."

"I had no other choice. He was in our way," Averil said.

Krystal returned without Zalé and knelt next to Draqa. She held out the bandages, keeping her eyes down. Her blood-stained hands trembled. Averil gave her a pitying look.

"I know you liked him," he said.

"Shut up," Draqa threatened.

He tightly wrapped the bandages around Averil's thigh. Krystal wasn't able to find any rope, so Draqa used the remaining bandages to tie Averil's arms behind his back. It wasn't much, but it was enough to subdue him and keep him from trying to escape while Draqa contacted Tolas Ruv Aen to inform him of the news.

Krystal went back out to comfort Zalé. It was for the best. Draqa wouldn't know how, and he doubted the boy would want to speak with him after what he'd just witnessed. He honestly didn't know how he would comfort Krystal, either. He barely knew how to handle the situation for himself.

Had Javis been one of his own kills for Sius Mavell Evi, that would have been the end of it. At most, he would have hidden the body where it wouldn't be found for a day or two, and he would have gone on his way. But this? This was his brother. Other than his mother, no one close to him had ever died before. This wasn't a situation he could handle professionally.

He left the body lying where it was and paced the length of the hallway to the kitchen until Tolas Ruv Aen arrived. Two others were with him. Draqa couldn't have been happier to see him, but the words he had were lost before they could reach his lips, so he silently led Tolas Ruv Aen and the others into the kitchen.

To his credit, Tolas Ruv Aen didn't make any comments or try to console Draqa. He simply asked, "What do you want us to do?"

Draqa clumsily gestured at Averil while he retrieved his blood-wet coat from the body. "Take him away."

Tolas Ruv Aen nodded. His company lifted Averil on either side and dragged him to the front room. Draqa heard Zalé begin sobbing again.

"Why?" he asked.

Draqa thought the question was in reference to his father being taken away, but it was Averil who answered.

"I'm sorry. One day you'll understand that I did this for your sake."

Tolas Ruv Aen remained behind.

"I can get someone here to take care of his body," he said.

"Yes. Do that," Draqa muttered. "I need to. . . Sius Mavell Evi needs to know what happened before he starts wondering why I'm not on my way back."

He went up to Javis' bedroom and locked himself in. He looked at the ceiling and let out a breath. Would he be allowed to stay?

He chimed Sius Mavell Evi. The Governor answered almost

right away. He appeared to be eating lunch.

"What's the matter with you, Draqa? You look like someone died."

Draqa cleared his throat. "I have news."

Sius Mavell Evi sat up keenly. "Yes?"

Draqa took another deep breath. "I think you'll be glad to hear that the ambassador is no longer a threat. Your grandson made sure of that today." The words made him feel ill, and he didn't bother trying to hide it this time.

"Ambassador Zevos is dead?"

"Yes. However, Averil was caught by the Ard'a."

Sius Mavell Evi's expression fell. "I see. And you know this how?" he asked.

"I was. . . there when they brought Averil in. Do you want me to see if I can have him released?" Draqa loathed to even suggest it.

Sius Mavell Evi sat back, considering this. He drew out his pipe and lit it. Draqa waited patiently for his answer.

"I'm sure they'll try to use him to get to me, but I want you to leave him for now. Watch him and I'll tell you what to do when we're ready," Sius Mavell Evi said.

Draqa nodded. "Yes, sir."

He opened his mouth to ask if he could stay but found he couldn't. Sius Mavell Evi would surely say no. He didn't realize he'd bowed his head until the Governor said, "You are the Ambassador's only surviving family."

Draqa forced himself to meet his gaze. "No, there's one other."

Sius Mavell Evi gave him a smile that made his stomach roil with unease. "This is an opportunity for us then. I want you to take charge of his funeral, and when the public asks, you'll tell them that he killed himself. That should be believable enough."

Revulsion struck him. "Why can't we just say he was assassinated by someone who disagreed with him?"

Sius Mavell Evi shook his head. "People won't care the extent we need them to if someone else killed him."

"*Care*?" Draqa shouted, then covered his mouth in restraint. "People don't care about nalingur," he said.

"Then you should trust me. I always have a plan," Sius Mavell Evi said.

What kind of plan involved lying about Javis' death? Draqa wanted to throw the Governor's face at the wall. "When do you want me back?" he asked.

"Another week should be long enough. If you must have any longer to mourn, you can do it here. That is what I assume you wanted to ask?"

"A week is fine," Draqa said.

He stared at his feet after the session ended, unable to bring himself back downstairs. He wandered Javis' room, thinking on Sius Mavell Evi's words. The curtains on both windows were drawn but it was the wrong time of day for the sun to shine through. The room was dim and quiet. It was strange how barely lived in it looked without Javis inside, as though he'd never been there in the first place. If Draqa left now, it would almost be too easy to forget, and move on with his life.

There was movement in the corner of his vision, and he turned. It was a brownie, watching him with wide eyes. Javis had said he shared his home with brownies, but they had avoided Draqa's sight until now.

The brownie turned his head in the direction of the kitchen. *What will you do with him?* Draqa heard the brownie's voice in his head rather than aloud.

He shrugged. He didn't know if he could do what Sius Mavell Evi tasked of him. The brownie sat at the edge of the nightstand. He swung his little hairy legs, his eyes still trained on the kitchen.

There is room in the garden for a tree. Plant one there, and forever he'll be.

Draqa approached the window and peered out at the clearing. The ground was carpeted with fresh snow from the night before. There were boulders, frost-dressed bushes, but all the trees stood high above the crater. There was an open spot by the edge of the pond that looked like it might have been large enough.

Draqa turned back to the brownie. He nodded at Draqa and hopped to the floor. He disappeared behind the nightstand, probably into some hidden room in the wall.

Draqa returned downstairs.

"Well?" Tolas Ruv Aen asked. "What did he say?"

He sat with Krystal and Zalé on the couch. His hand was on Krystal's back. Zalé was on Krystal's lap, his face pressed into her shoulder.

Again, Draqa's words were lost. He almost sat in Javis' chair, but then corrected himself and leaned over the back of it instead. The others watched him expectantly.

"Sius Mavell Evi wants me to tell everyone that Javis ended his own life," he finally said.

Krystal gasped, "You wouldn't!"

Draqa hung his head. “It’s not my decision.”

Tolas Ruv Aen frowned, but he nodded. “I understand. You need to keep up your act with the Governor.”

The mortician arrived what seemed like an eternity later. She was shocked to learn who had died. Javis had apparently been well known and well-liked by those in Kerevel Tul.

“Who did this to him?” she asked as she prepared the body to be moved. She cast Draqa a suspicious glance.

Draqa almost didn’t say. He didn’t see what difference it would make no matter what answer he gave. But Tolas Ruv Aen was right, he had to do this. He crouched by the body and took the knife delicately in hand.

“We were too late to stop him,” he said.

A service was held for Javis within the halls of the Kerevel two days later. Ideally, Javis would have been buried right away, as it was traditionally considered disrespectful or bad luck to wait, but Javis had been one of Erothel’s ambassadors, and traditions of the government trumped all others. Once word got out, Draqa didn’t have much of a hand in the planning of things apart from where and when the funeral would take place. Sius Mavell Evi directed everything else. Specific people had to be invited, people Draqa was certain were only meant to attend out of political obligation. At the end of the service, Tavyn Marvec as the Minister would stand before everyone and make a speech. It would even be on the picturecast.

Family was invited too, of course, but given there were only two surviving members and Draqa was instructed to stay out of the way and not draw attention to himself, there weren't many genuine attendees at all. In fact, if it weren't for Krystal and Zalé, Talara and Alarach, and a few citizens from Kerevel Tul who found the time to attend, the entirety of the procession would have been for show.

Draqa looked around as everyone settled into the space that was given to them for the service; one of the Kerevel's great halls. There were many *sonnes* that would have looked beautiful on any other day, as colored light would have filtered through to the polished floors. But it seemed even the sky was in mourning.

Draqa lingered at the back of the hall while the procession took place. Krystal and the others stood among the crowd. He didn't feel like joining them. He only half listened while his uncle, and others who claimed to care about Javis, spoke. He was more concerned about what Marvec would have to say about Javis while wearing the Minister's face.

When the Minister stood in front of everyone, his voice was regal as it echoed through the hall and people's aspectacasters.

"It is my deepest sorrow that we must say goodbye to our ambassador. For those who are unaware, he committed suicide in his home two days ago, not long before he would have been returning to the drād clans in the mountains."

A murmur spread through the crowd. The Minister waited for everyone to settle—none of those before the Minister had dared to say it out loud and this was still the first that many were hearing of it.

"The Ambassador was true and dedicated to his work. He has well maintained Erothel's good relationship with the clans. He was beloved by many in parliament, and without him, we would not have achieved as much as we have. We feel this loss deeply."

Draqa didn't know whether to laugh or feel slighted on Javis' behalf. He was sickened further by how easily the crowd seemed convinced by the charlatan's words. How many of them were aware of how Javis had really been treated by them?

"But this loss could have been prevented," the Minister said.

Draqa made eye contact with Krystal, who made a confused face at him. He shrugged.

"It was no secret that the Ambassador was nalingur. I'm sure many of you recall his father as well, a human who had succeeded in becoming the governor of our Southern province for many years before his family was attacked and his wife murdered by those who believed a human shouldn't have been in such a position of power. I believe you all can see the problem here. Had, perhaps, the treatment of nalingur and humans in our country been better, then Zevos would not have felt the need to end his life."

Another wave of murmurs surged through the crowd. Draqa's mouth fell open in disbelief. The real Minister had never cared about the treatment of nalingur and from his conversation with Sius Mavell Evi, it didn't sound as though Marvec did either. Draqa wished now that the Governor had had enough faith in him to confide in him the details of his plan.

Someone who had more nerve than Draqa spoke up.

"What exactly are you getting at?" They didn't sound pleased by the Minister's insinuation, and Draqa looked for their face as people shushed them.

The Minister cleared his throat. "I'll admit that in the time since my predecessor's assassination, I haven't done my duty to quell the hatred that exists here. It is time for that to change. Starting today, I will do what is necessary for the safety and prosperity of all in Erothel, not just those who the Council has deemed most worthy."

The crowd erupted, pushing out the last of what had remained of the silence and solemnity that the procession should have kept. Krystal left her spot and made her way over to Draqa. Her eyes were red, and her cheeks were wet.

"I don't understand. Why would they lie about his death for this?" she asked.

Draqa barely heard her. He watched the Minister as he stepped back from the lectern. Had Draqa been as unaware as everyone else in the hall, he might have been caught up in the excitement. Surely, with the Minister's change of heart, good things were on the horizon. But this wasn't the Minister, and there was no way Draqa could convince himself that this was being done with a better future in mind.

"I wish I knew," he said.

Javis was given to the trees in the dark, early hours of the following morning. It was a long, ritualistic ceremony. Draqa had sought out Alarach to lead it. He seemed shocked to finally see Draqa, but the time for reunions would come later; with Alarach now designated as speaker it would have been disrespectful for Draqa to utter a single word.

Everyone who cared to be there, Draqa, Zalé, Krystal and Talara, and Alarach, gathered at the pond in front of Javis' home by lamplight. With the only shovel in hand, Alarach said a blessing, then cut into the snow packed earth. Then, with the exception of Draqa because of his shoulder, everyone wordlessly took their turns with the shovel until the hole was at the right depth. It was a shallow hole, but it was an agonizingly slow process, made worse the longer they stood out in the frozen air. Draqa ignored the thought that this would have gone much faster if Averil had been there. But even if he had, he would never have been allowed to partake.

They lowered Javis' body into the hole unclothed; clothing was unnecessary, although sometimes a personal belongings were buried with the deceased. They would have buried Javis' sketchbook, but in an act of selfishness, Draqa had hidden it for himself.

Before they began the task of returning the soil to its place, Alarach gave Draqa a seed. It was a small thing, dwarfed by the palm of his hand. A willow's seed. All his family had been buried with the same tree, or so he'd been told.

He knelt at the edge of the hole and pushed the seed into the wound on Javis' chest. He bowed his head a moment then stepped away, letting the others take over again. A knot formed in his chest while he watched them. He just wanted this to be over with.

Finally, Alarach raised his hands over the newly turned earth. He whispered a final prayer and directed his magic into the ground. As he spoke, the dirt crumbled aside, and a sapling pushed its way to the surface. Alarach kept it growing until it was at least a foot in height. The light of dawn was just beginning to break the sky.

"It is done," Alarach said.

They all lingered around the sapling for a few minutes out of respect. Then, Alarach went inside with Zalé, and Talara followed soon after. Krystal shivered beside Draqa. He felt her tug on his hand.

"We should go inside," she whispered. There was a quiver in her voice.

Draqa drew his hand away from her. "Go on. I. . . need a few more minutes."

Krystal nodded, shivered again, and went inside too.

The little willow sapling didn't have any leaves. Winter was such a dreary time to plant a tree. If it hadn't just sprouted from the earth at Alarach's hand, the tree could have been mistaken for one that had been long dead. It would survive, though. Trees like this always did.

The knot in Draqa's chest still wouldn't ease. A part of Javis' spirit might go on living in the tree, but it did nothing to undo or fix what had already been done. He hadn't deserved to be used; he hadn't deserved to die. He had just been trying to do what was right, which was far more than Draqa could say for himself.

Damn Sius Mavell Evi. Damn Averil and Marvec. Draqa's eyes started to burn. He rubbed them before he could begin to cry. He stuffed his hand into his pocket. His fingers brushed against a sheet of paper, startling him. He slowly pulled out the envelope, briefly wondering what it could be. The knot in his chest tightened further. Javis' letter. Draqa still hadn't read it. The edges of the envelope were a bit crumpled now from how long it was in his pocket. A corner was stained red. Draqa was suddenly relieved he hadn't had the time to do any major washing of his coat, or else he may have lost the letter entirely.

He opened the envelope against his leg and unfolded the paper inside. Javis' handwriting was a shaky scrawl of oxblood ink. Draqa squinted to read it. "Jair, brother," it was addressed. Draqa laughed pitifully. Javis never once called him Draqa. He continued to read.

Jair, brother, or whoever you find yourself to be—

Our father made us promise to be there for each other always, and I broke that promise more times than you ever deserved. I have never truly been happy because of it, and I never dreamed that I would see you again in this life or the next. I wish we could have met again under better circumstances, but regardless, to say I was overjoyed to hear your voice and see your face at the top of those steps would be an understatement. You said you don't know if you can forgive me, but the fact you've given me a second chance, that you were still willing to call me your brother and even care about my situation when you have no obligation to do anything about it at all, makes me hope that maybe one day things can be different between us.

Hopeful as I might be, however, I need to acknowledge that the chances of that happening are slim. I wouldn't be surprised if you've realized by now that I lied about the extent to which I was poisoned, so here it is plain for you—I'm growing weaker by the day, and death is imminent. I'm scared. Even with so many good people around trying to help me, I feel more alone than I ever have.

I don't know if I'll give this to you, or if you'll read it if I do, but if you do and I'm dead, then I need you to know how much I care about you. I don't know if you believe in such things after all you've been through, but I love you. I wish I knew it when we were young, and I believe I'll regret forever not doing anything to prove it to you back then. Despite that, I'm glad for the recent days we've had together. No matter what happens, I'll cherish them.

As for you, I sincerely hope that you can have your own second chance if you want it. You deserve a life of happiness. I hope you find one.

Javis

Draqa didn't realize he'd stopped breathing until he reached the end of the letter. He forced himself to take in the crisp morning air. It was the first deep breath he'd taken in years, and it pushed him to his knees. He read the letter again. His next breath was deeper. The knot in his chest finally released. Javis' letter fell to rest in front of the sapling as Jair Zevos curled before it and wept.

38.5

A MAN STUMBLED barefooted and naked through the mountainous ponderosa forest surrounding him. The dried needles on the icy forest floor bit at his feet and the freezing morning air stung his skin.

The wailing police and ambulance sirens reached him from the road and echoed in his ears. They instilled fear and a fury within him.

Damn that bitch.

He continued the opposite way. He had to keep moving. He didn't stop until he reached his tiny, private cabin buried deep in the woods. He climbed its short steps and collapsed onto the creaky wood floor inside. He wrapped his arms around himself. He took a deep breath. The harsh warmth in his lungs promptly made him wheeze after being exposed to the cold for so long.

He looked at his hands. They still trembled from a few hours before. Dark blood caked underneath his claw-like fingernails. It stained his fingertips. He could taste it smeared around his lips as well.

He moved to scratch the blood off his face, but he winced, his jaw still aching. Not all of his teeth had gone back to normal yet. Some of his extra molars remained, and all his canines were still sharp and painfully large for his mouth.

He ran his tongue along them. Bits of flesh were caught between the largest; further confirmation that the night hadn't gone well.

The man let his head fall. He laid on the floor a few minutes longer, recovering. He closed his gray eyes.

It was all *her* fault. Everything was ruined because of her. Because of her, he would once again have to leave. He once again would have to go into hiding. Probably have to change his name again, too.

He thought of the high school girl whose father he'd been staying with these last few months, and the chunks of flesh in his teeth suddenly tasted sour. He threw up in his mouth—he didn't let it go past his lips, afraid of what his stomach contents might reveal.

Finally, he pushed himself to stand, his shrinking joints screaming in protest. It was then that he smelled it. A scent that didn't belong in his home yet was still familiar to him. It was a smell he had come to hate in recent weeks.

The scent changed every time he encountered it like it was wearing a mask, but underneath that mask, it always smelled the same. Faerish.

The man cast his gaze to the chair—his favorite chair—in his small living room where the smell took the shape of a brunette, leaning back with her legs crossed like she owned the place. The man resolved to burn his chair; the smell would never go away.

"Rough night?" The woman asked. If the twinkle in her eye was anything to go by, she wasn't bothered by the man's undressed state, but amused.

A vein on the man's forehead pulsed. "Don't pretend you have no idea. You know exactly how my night was," he slurred. His German accent always got thicker when he was angry, and with his teeth taking up too much space in his mouth, he was sure he was nearly impossible to understand.

The woman smiled. "You're blaming me for this?"

"Of course I am! You—You—"

"If I did anything, I reminded you that you'll never be accepted here. You're the one who let your guard down, Orias."

The man lunged at the woman, what remained of the feral instincts from the night before taking over for a split second.

He stopped himself, his clawed hand mere inches from her face.

"Don't call me that! Don't ever call me that!"

The woman didn't even flinch. She stood and patted the man on the shoulder.

"Then what do I call you? What is your name? Do you even remember who you are?"

The man faltered. It had been a long, long time since he had used his true name. Although, he could still clearly remember the day it was taken from him. At the woman's expectant look, his shoulders sagged.

"You know what I currently go by," he muttered.

The woman sneered. "Oh yes. 'Little wolf.' That is a bit, how would you say. . . on the nose, don't you think?"

The man turned away from her. He didn't want to deal with her right now. Not after last night. He needed rest, and he needed to pack.

"After eight hundred lifetimes worth of names, you stop paying attention to what they mean," he said.

The woman moved around to his front, blocking his path. She put a hand on his chest and stroked it. He stiffened.

"We both know that's not true. I think it's your way of embracing what you are. Admit it," she whispered. "You like it."

The man would've scoffed if it weren't for the fact the woman read him like a book. She was entirely right; he just didn't want to admit it. There were days he thoroughly enjoyed the benefits of being what he was. But other days, like now, he only saw himself as the monster he truly was.

He started to push past her, but she guided him backward. He was too exhausted to deny her.

"Come sit. I lit a fire for you," she said, gesturing to the wood-burning stove in the corner. She sat him down in the chair in front of it. It was his least comfortable and least favorite chair. She started massaging his shoulders.

The man rested his face in his hands. His teeth shrank now, and the aching was less intense. It was tempting to relax in front of the fire's warmth, and he desperately needed to sleep, but he knew better than to do it while she was here.

Again, his mind went to his landlord's daughter.

"Is Accalia—do you know if she. . .?"

The woman paused her massaging fingers at the nape of his neck. "She's dead."

So that was it. Bile rose in the man's throat. He swallowed down the bits of flesh as they dislodged from his teeth, and he shuddered. But he was thankful. If he had only wounded the girl, she inevitably would have become like him. Better dead than cursed.

The woman continued massaging him. "Where will you go now?" she asked.

The man shrugged halfheartedly. His present location had been the perfect place. Plenty of forest to hide in, far enough from people that he shouldn't have had to worry about anyone getting hurt. And if someone did, it should have been enough to claim that an escaped wolf or wolf-dog from a nearby sanctuary was the culprit. But as he saw last night, it wasn't enough. It would never be enough.

The authorities would come for him. As soon as they put the pieces together, they would come. They would probably be too stupid and closed-minded to realize what he was, but they would know it was him. And it was all *her* fault.

"Further west, probably. There's still a lot of land here. Otherwise, I'll go someplace like Washington or some other forested state," he said.

"Or," the woman said, "you could finally take me up on my proposal."

The man did scoff now. "I'm not going to Arai. From what you've told me, I'll be even less welcome there."

The woman leaned over his shoulder, her face close to his own. "Not for long. Remember, I said I have a plan. You've been long expected there, and with your help, Arai will become a place where all of us are welcome."

The man looked up at her. He'd been refusing her for weeks. First, because he wanted nothing else to do with the fae. Second, because his younger sister was involved. He should have had a better reason to refuse the woman again. She was why he had just killed someone dear to him.

Instead, he pitifully said, "I can't leave. . . This is my home."

The woman pinched his cheek. "You have no home, Orias. You've lived on the road your whole life. You'll get used to it."

The man clenched his teeth in response, then immediately regretted it, one of his extra molars coming loose. Growling, he ripped it from his mouth and threw it to the side.

"Why should I go with you? You keep asking all these things from me, but you still haven't told me who *you* are."

The woman stepped back from him. "Will you come if I tell you?"

The man hesitated. This woman had backed him into a corner. He didn't have many options anymore. At the very least, if he went to Arai, he may not have to run anymore. Not in the same way he had to here, at least. And the woman's words certainly were tempting. He would love to be welcome somewhere again. He might even find a way to break his curse in Arai.

"I will," he said.

The woman grinned widely, revealing two rows of serrated teeth. Before him, she changed. Her ears lengthened and pointed outward. Her hair fell away, leaving behind an ornately tattooed head. Her skin tightened on her face and her nose flattened. Her eyes turned white.

"My name is Ilriel Vasiir, president of Adonis, and you're going to help me change the world."

Acknowledgments

The process of writing The Dreamer and the Marked has been an incredible (and incredibly long) journey, from the day the idea for this story first popped into my head, to when I finally finished my final round of edits. I can't express how relieved I feel for it to finally be finished and in the hands of readers, and I want to thank everyone who has supported me along the way. I am so fortunate to have had family, friends, and teachers who encouraged me to pursue not only the completion of this book, but also my passion for writing every step of the way. I've learned so much as a writer and it would have been so much harder without you. Thank you!

About The Author

Airic Fenn is a child of the Rocky Mountains and spends more of their time in their own vivid imaginings than perhaps is proper (but who really cares about proper?). When they aren't writing, you can find them making art or dabbling in one of their many hobbies, from leathercraft and bookbinding to exploring the outdoors and attending renfaires. The Dreamer and the Marked is their debut novel.

To find out more, you can visit www.airicfenn.com

If you enjoyed this book, please consider leaving a review on Goodreads.

www.ingramcontent.com/pod-product-compliance
Lightning Source LLC
Chambersburg PA
CBHW020931310726
48980CB00007B/715/J

* 9 7 8 0 5 7 8 3 1 4 1 2 9 *